THE FIRST ETHEREAL

E. L. WILLIAMS

To Shelagh,
with all
best wishes
Emma :)

Bramble Leaf
BOOKS

First edition

ISBN: 978-1-8382726-1-6

Cover art by Eclipse Studios

PRAISE FOR E. L. WILLIAMS

Reader Reviews

"Like nothing I've ever read before. I can't recommend this book more highly. I absolutely loved it. An intelligent, generous and ambitious novel.'

— Z. ARDEN

"'A powerful and beautiful story of a passionate fight for the greater good and the earnest hope for a better future. I can't wait for the sequel!'

— M. WISH

'Eerily predictive following current world events! Not only an exciting read but thought provoking and magical at the same time.'

— S. ANGEL

PRAISE FOR E. L. WILLIAMS

'An amazing story filled with love! I could not put it down! I fell in love with the story, and oh my, the plot twist!'

— K. ARBUCKLE

'Beautifully written story with engaging and relatable characters that'll keep you turning the pages till the very end. Timeless in its message but particularly relevant to society today, but also fun and easy to read.'

— DAVID

'Wow...what an imagination....I just loved this book. It keeps you guessing right up to the end.'

— J.KINNAIRD

To my parents, Ronnie & Joy

* * *

'The world is full of magic things, patiently waiting for our senses to grow sharper.'

— W.B. YEATS

CHAPTER 1

$\mathcal{L}$illy woke with a start, her heart hammering. As if stumbling out of thick fog, it took her mind a few seconds to realise that she was at home in her bed. She reached out her hand and found the wall against which her single bed was pressed in the tiny bedsit flat. Had someone called her name?

'Lil,' whispered a familiar voice from the darkness, his voice hoarse.

Lilly's heart slowed. She pushed herself up and groped for the bedside light, the chill air giving her instant goosebumps.

She squinted, her eyes struggling to adjust to the brightness and then her mind to comprehend what she was seeing. After a moment she said, 'Jack. What the hell? Who are you meant to be this time?'

He was dressed as a 1970s rock star, complete with skinny black jeans, cowboy boots and a tight shirt. His usually short-cropped fair hair had been replaced with a thick mop of unruly dark waves that stretched past his shoulders. To complete the look, he was holding a microphone stand and posing as if the photographer from NME was standing behind her. She laughed in spite of herself.

'Steven Tyler?' she asked while trying and failing to suppress a yawn.

Jack rolled his eyes. 'Not even close. Ian Gillan. Smoke on the Water. Get it?'

It took her a minute to make the connection. 'Oh no, really? Again?'

'Afraid so,' he said with a grimace and then instantly transformed back to his usual uniform of white T-shirt and jeans before slumping down into the flat's single armchair. 'I was just trying to cheer you up in advance.'

She smiled at him, grateful for the gesture but already bone weary at the thought of another night on a camp bed in the community centre. 'How long do you think?'

'About fifteen minutes before the sirens go off, give or take. I gatecrashed the emergency services meeting and they're mobilising the pumps and boats again. If you ask me, this one will be worse than the last few – the river looks like it's bloody possessed.'

Lilly sighed and scanned the tiny basement flat, which was one square room with a chunk taken out of the far corner to squeeze in a bathroom. It had been her haven once. Even at sixteen and desperate to find anywhere to live that wasn't her parents' farm, she'd been impressed by the crisp whitewashed exterior of the old Georgian house, the window boxes stuffed full of cheerful pink geraniums and the modern Scandi interior that convinced her to trade square footage for style. Three years had passed without incident, but in the last twelve months she'd been evacuated seven times as the river surged to levels no one had thought possible. So far, her flat had only been flooded once, but something told her that it was only a matter of time before the damage would necessitate more than a few weeks of drying time and a new carpet.

Reluctantly, Lilly flung off the thick duvet and padded over to the suitcase that served as her wardrobe. 'Did you let them see you?' she asked Jack as he filled the kettle and spooned coffee into her travel mug.

'Nah,' Jack said. 'Everyone was so stressed out I thought it best to keep a low profile. I will though when we go to the community centre, unless of course you want to get a reputation for talking to yourself,' he added with a smile.

Lilly had been able to see Jack for as long as she could remember. They grew up together, although he always looked to be a few years older than her. When Lilly had a scooter, Jack had a bike. When she had a bike with stabilisers, Jack had one he could do wheelies on. The older she got, the older Jack appeared. The perpetual big brother.

Her parents had tolerated what they dismissed as her 'imaginary friend' when she was very small, but their patience had quickly run out as it did with most things. There was no place for magic or mystery at the farm, even for a child. Arguing the point proved futile, so she had just stopped talking about him to avoid the consequences, but he remained as real and as corporeal to her as any living person. She knew that if he allowed it, other people could see him too – they just couldn't remember him for longer than a few seconds.

Lilly was well aware that Jack wasn't human in the sense that other people were. When she was little, she once asked him if he was a ghost. He'd just laughed and said he was her friend. She only ever broached the subject once after that and he said there were rules about how much he was allowed to tell her. Having always hated arguments, she decided it was as good an explanation as any. He was her only friend, after all, so she wasn't going to push her luck.

Lilly reluctantly pulled off the T-shirt she was wearing once she'd found a long-sleeved top, sweater and jeans to put on, then pulled her long auburn hair into a bun.

'You've lost more weight, Lil,' Jack said flatly. Lilly could almost feel his eyes on her bare back, inspecting her. She shrugged and ignored the comment. She wasn't in the mood for that particular debate tonight. Thankfully, he let it drop.

By the time the flood siren sounded twenty minutes later, Lilly had everything she considered essential stuffed into her backpack. Jack had spent the time putting anything that they couldn't take with them hopefully out of reach of any flood-water. Lilly's drawing board he'd balanced on top of the shower unit. Her printer, lamps and kettle had been given refuge on top of the kitchen cabinets.

Picking up her art portfolio and her rucksack she scanned the room. The routine was horribly familiar now.

'Ready?' Jack asked, relieving her of the rucksack and then handing her the travel mug of coffee.

Lilly nodded sadly.

'You've shielded yourself? There's going to be some seri-ously high-octane emotions out there tonight,' he said, putting his hand on her shoulder and studying her face.

It had been Jack who had taught her how to control her 'gift'. As gifts went, she thought it was probably about the worst sort you could get. A kind of super-empathy that meant she felt the emotions of any living soul within about a ten-mile radius. Worse, she seemed to be tuned to the lower vibrations of pain and misery because she could never recall feeling anyone's joy or elation. It wasn't just an awful gift – it was a defective one to boot.

Had it not been for Jack teaching her how to protect herself and switch off all but the emotions that were hers, she guessed she'd be living in a cave, half mad – or worse.

'Yep,' she said, 'hatches all well and truly battened down.'

He looked worried so she tried to smile reassuringly, but the truth was that she felt sick to her stomach at the thought of having to spend a night crammed into a hall with half of the town. Shielding herself was one thing, but short of making herself invisible like Jack, she still had to cope with being in a crowd of people for hours on end. Sucking in a deep breath, she grabbed her coat and keys and they headed out of the door.

CHAPTER 2

*T*he wail of the siren sounded indecently loud in the darkness as they stepped out of the house. Street lights had been routinely turned off after midnight since the power shortages had begun and while they were usually turned back on during emergencies, whoever had responsibility for flicking the switch had clearly not yet received the memo.

Lilly handed Jack her travel cup so that she could find the torch she kept in her coat pocket. As she did, a strong gust of wind caught the side of her portfolio case and almost dragged her off her feet. Instinctively, Jack threw his free arm around her.

'Thanks,' she said, feeling suddenly close to tears.

'Always said a strong gust of wind could have you over,' Jack said, only half joking. 'Come on, you'll feel better once we're back in the warm. If we hurry, we might get a spot at the back again.'

Perched on the Welsh-English border, Pont Nefoedd was a hilltop market town built high above the banks of the river

Wye. Three steep hills connected the Old Road at the base of the town, where Lilly lived, to the New Road at the top which was bounded by the start of the forested mountains. The town, which could trace its history back to Roman times, had never flooded before. It was a fact the news-readers liked to trot out when reporting on the unprece-dented nature of the country-wide flooding. The implication was that if even Pont Nefoedd could flood, then nowhere was really safe.

Lilly and Jack were halfway up the hill, the wind and rain blessedly at their backs and the glow of the community centre just a few hundred yards ahead of them, when Lilly felt her vision blur. 'No,' she muttered, but it was too late. As her heart slammed into high gear, she felt her breath hitch high in her chest as her back slicked with sweat and her legs turned to jelly.

When she opened her eyes, she was leaning against a wall. Jack was holding her arms and staring at her in the glow from the now working street lights, his brow knitted together. At least she was still on her feet, she thought.

'Did you have another one?' he asked, scanning her face, although for what, Lilly wasn't sure.

The question confused her for a second until, like frag-ments of a torn photograph, the pieces of her memory rearranged themselves. Her stomach reacted first, lurching as if she was about to vomit. Swallowing hard, she took a deep breath as the picture in her mind settled into coherence.

Realising she'd not answered his question she said, 'I saw someone,' then faltered as her eyes swam with tears. 'I saw someone I loved very much being,' the last word was a choked whisper, 'beheaded.'

Jack pulled her into a tight hug and planted a kiss on top of her head. She held on tightly, anchoring herself as if without him she really would blow away on the next gust of wind. She breathed in the scent of him, wild honeysuckle and summer meadows, and tried to forget the smell of blood and sawdust that had so recently overwhelmed her.

'It was so real, Jack,' she said quietly. 'I felt the rough wood under my hand as I climbed the steps up to the execution platform, the weakness in my knees, the nausea. I could even smell the sawdust, the sweat of the guard behind me and the blood. There was so much blood.' When she lifted her eyes to meet his she saw that he was on the verge of tears too.

'Drink this,' Jack said, pressing her travel mug into her hand.

After fumbling with the lid, she took a swig of her coffee. It was still close to scalding and she winced, but the pain helped to ground her. She hadn't wanted to kick off another argument, especially now she was facing who knew how long in the evacuation centre again, but neither could she go on like this. The nightmares were bad enough, but now it no longer seemed to matter whether she was asleep or awake for these horrors to attack her. Only the day before she'd had to abandon her shopping basket in the market after a particularly brutal episode had sparked a full panic attack that her bent double and gasping for breath.

'I need to know, Jack,' she said, holding his gaze. 'Please, I can't go on being hijacked like this. I feel like I'm losing my mind.'

Jack looked away quickly, but Lilly reached up with her free hand and gently turned his face to look at her. 'Please.'

She held his gaze and after a moment he nodded slowly. 'But you have to be sure,' he said.

'I am sure,' Lilly replied, hoping that he could read the absolute conviction in her eyes, but not her fear.

'Okay, but not here eh? Let's get in the warm first and then I'll tell you,' he said. 'I promise.'

'Okay,' Lilly said and pushed herself away from the wall. Her legs felt weak, but there was no way she'd admit as much to Jack. After months of nagging and pleading he was actually going to tell her what was happening to her and she wanted nothing to get in the way.

CHAPTER 3

$\mathcal{B}$y the time they reached the community centre there were already a dozen families settling themselves onto the camp beds that would be their temporary home for the night, but possibly longer. Lilly remembered the first time they'd been evacuated. The children had been wide-eyed with the adventure of it all, racing around excitedly despite the best efforts of their anxious-looking parents to contain them. There was no such excitement in the air tonight, just the howls of over-tired toddlers and the loud sobs of one little boy who had forgotten his favourite teddy in the rush. Even the pets seemed fed up with the repeat performance. A Siamese cat yowled loudly from its carrier, while an old chocolate Labrador turned in circles trying to get comfortable on a makeshift bed of thin blankets and what looked to be its owner's padded coat.

'Lilly isn't it?' asked a stocky man wearing a bright orange tabard with 'volunteer' stamped back and front. 'You'll have to remind me of your last name,' he said, smiling, although Lilly could see the tiredness on his face.

'Jones,' Lilly said quietly, 'And this is my friend Jack Smith.'

He gave Jack a nod of acknowledgement and Lilly watched as he added her name to the list on his clipboard. He frowned, his pen hovering over the paper as if he had lost his train of thought, then said quickly, 'Great. Well Lilly, you know the routine by now unfortunately. Grab yourself a spot. There's tea and coffee in the kitchen next door so just help yourself.'

As the volunteer strode away, Lilly turned to Jack. 'That never gets old, you know.'

'What, people forgetting me the instant they've met me?' Jack said.

'Yep. You're like a wizard,' she said, yawning. 'I wish I could do it.'

After finding two beds together in the corner, they dumped Lilly's things and went into the kitchen. Lilly longed to sleep. What she had come to think of as her waking nightmares always left her feeling physically and emotionally drained, but now that Jack had at last promised to explain things to her, she had to stay awake.

After helping themselves to coffee they were drawn to the small crowd of people standing around the large wall-mounted TV watching the news. The banner at the bottom of the screen read, 'live from Venice'. The reporter, a polished thirty-something in a suspiciously new-looking rain jacket, was standing in a boat next to an elderly man wrapped in a foil blanket. As the camera pulled back, the old man heaved back a sob before being comforted by a younger woman, herself in tears.

'So, there you have it,' said the reporter, his voice wobbling slightly. Making a visible effort to contain himself he said, 'The Adriatic has finally claimed this unique, magnificent city. A UNESCO World Heritage Site, beloved by honeymooners and tourists the world over, but now lost to us all under the waves. Feeling that loss, of course, most acutely, are the people who called this beautiful city their home. Here on this boat and the handful of others in this final flotilla of evacuees are the last of the Venetians.'

The last sentence comes out in a hurry as if he too is holding back a tide that might any second overtake him. The camera panned to take in a half-dozen small boats before the shot switched to images of the inundated and now forcibly abandoned city.

'Not just us being washed out of our homes then,' said an elderly man standing next to them. 'Poor buggers,' he added, shaking his head before, with shoulders drooped, he left the room.

Lilly lingered, hoping that the next item might be news of the UK-wide flooding, but instead it was a report on the nationwide state of emergency in Australia prompted by record-breaking bush fires. Images of charred koalas, sheep and kangaroos filled the screen before being replaced by aerial shots of log-jammed highways and still smouldering towns that look like something out of Mad Max.

The newsreader said, 'As the scale of this latest disaster escalates, the focus is now on evacuation. Both New Zealand and Indonesia have said that they will review the Australian government's request for emergency refugee status for its citizens over the coming months, but that no change in their initial decisions to refuse the application would be forthcoming in the short term. Humanitarian aid in the form of medical supplies, food and water would, though, continue.'

Lilly became aware of Jack's hand on her arm, then realised that her breathing was coming in short hiccupping gulps. As the newsreader began reading out the daily death toll from the sepsis crisis, Jack gently steered her out of the kitchen. 'How's that shielding holding up?' he asked quietly.

Lilly forced herself to take a deep breath, centring herself and checking that everything she was currently feeling belonged to her and nobody else. 'All mine,' she said breathily, 'the misery, despair and anger is one hundred percent coming from me,' looking up at Jack and seeing what she considered to be similar emotions mirrored in his own face.

'How one species can quite so spectacularly fuck up an entire planet in so short a space of time is kind of beyond me,' he said, almost spitting out the words.

Lilly didn't have the words to reply. They had talked about this so many times but always seemed to circle back to the same point of hopelessness. Lilly felt hot tears fill her eyes and a split second later, Jack pulled her into a hug.

'At least the troubles haven't spread here yet,' Jack said, referring to the frequent riots that had been blighting most of the big towns and cities for months. If he'd intended to point out a bright side, Lilly thought, he'd majorly missed the mark.

'Come on, why don't you get an hour's sleep at least,' Jack said, tucking an escaped strand of her hair back behind Lilly's ear. 'And no, I'm not trying to get out of telling you about the dream stuff – I promise. But you look done in.'

Lilly nodded her agreement and led the way back into the main hall. Although her back still ached at the memory of the last night she'd had to spend on the emergency camp beds, she decided that she was probably tired enough to sleep on the floor if she had to. She sat on the bed, pulled off her boots and laid down. The last thing she saw before sleep overwhelmed her was Jack pulling a blanket over her shoulders.

When she woke a few hours later, the first feeble rays of watery winter sun were filtering in through the gaps in the mismatched curtains. Her eyes felt puffy and with a sinking heart she recalled snatches of the latest dream.

'Hello, sleepyhead,' Jack said quietly from where he sat on the bed next to hers, 'that was another rough one. The nuns, right?'

Levering herself up, she nodded, caught off balance for a second that Jack knew exactly what she'd just been dreaming about. This time she had been sitting in the street, fat cold cobblestones beneath her and crippled with pain all over her body. She had been freezing and soaked to the skin. Two figures had hurried towards her, lanterns swinging in the darkness. They had started to lift her with strong but gentle hands, their kind words as comforting as their touch, but when her hood slipped back and they had seen her disfigured face caught in the swinging lamplight, they called her a whore and let her fall back onto the cobblestones. The physical pain was blinding but had been eclipsed by her sense of heart shattering despair.

Before she could ask him, he said, 'I don't see all of the dreams, just the ones where I was ...' he hesitated slightly then added, 'close by.'

Swinging her thin legs off the bed so that she could sit facing him, Lilly held her head in her hands and rubbed at her temples, trying to kick her brain into gear and process what Jack had just said to her while still struggling to banish the image of the pinched, pious-faced nuns from her mind.

Failing, she said, 'I don't understand. How did you know?'

Jack hesitated for a beat but then said, 'What you're going through, it's called the Remembering.' He paused as if waiting for some kind of recognition. She racked her brain, but she'd never even heard the term before. Pressing on, he said, 'So you see, Lil, they're not just nightmares or panic attacks ...' He paused again and Lilly felt a mixture of irritation and apprehension rising in her chest. If he's hoping to avoid having to spell it out, she thought, then he's bang out of luck.

'What do you mean?' she asked, lifting her head so that she could look at him. She probably knew Jack's face better than her own. She studied it, trying to figure out the expression in his gold-flecked green eyes.

'What I mean is that what you're seeing, feeling, they're …' He hesitated and Lilly cursed herself for not being sharp enough to fill in the blanks for him. 'They're memories,' he said at last; the last two words were almost a whisper directed at the floor. She let the silence stretch, unsure about what to say. He raised his head, lifting his eyes hesitantly to meet hers.

The realisation dawned slowly. 'Memories?' she asked. Her mind wrestling with the idea of what he might be trying to tell her. Jack nodded slowly and Lilly took a few deep, deliberate breaths, conscious that her heartbeat had broken into a trot and may at any point bolt into an all-out gallop. Willing her voice to stay level, she added, 'As in past lives?'

'Yes, Lil, you're remembering your past lives,' he said, sounding relieved to finally say the words aloud.

Lilly exhaled as if she'd been winded. She scanned the hall, feeling suddenly trapped by the thirty or so people dotted around the cavernous space. Some were still sleeping, others were huddled over their phones and talking quietly in small groups at the front of the hall. Quelling the compulsion to bolt from the room, after a few fumbled starts she said in a whisper, 'So, just to be clear, you're telling me that all these horrific, terrible, murderous dreams that make the worst horror films feel like a trip to Disneyland are real?' She shivered, but when Jack reached out to take her hands she snatched them away. He had known this. For the past nine months, he'd known this, but he hadn't told her.

'Well, yes and no. Yes, they happened, but no, they're not

real. They can't hurt you – they belong to a life that's long past,' Jack said in an urgent whisper. Taking her face tentatively in his hands he said, 'Please don't be mad at me, Lil. I couldn't tell you until you were ready. There are rules, you know that.'

Lilly felt her eyes brim with tears and she pulled away, turning her head away from him and wiping her face on her sleeve. Then, all at once, as if she was watching a hundred horror films on fast forward, a barrage of terrible scenes flashed before her eyes at lightning speed. The sensation made her giddy and she held her head in her hands to steady it.

Jack sat down next to her and put his arm around her shoulders. 'That's just the data coming in – it's nothing to worry about. It's normal,' he said. He was doing his best to sound calm, but she could hear the tension in his voice, feel it in his fingers as he gently rubbed her back with hands that were trembling.

Lilly had no idea why she was so upset. It wasn't like she didn't already believe in past lives. When your best friend is invisible to everyone but you, reincarnation is not much of a stretch. As she considered it, she supposed that it was knowing that her current life wasn't an anomaly. Just another miserable existence in a long and seemingly endless line. Granted, it was a million times better than it was growing up on the farm – that was hell on Earth – but she was far from happy. She couldn't even claim to be content. Apart from Jack, she had no one. The world was dying around them and she sometimes felt like she was the only one who felt it – this impending, unquestionable sense of everything ending. They had already lost most of world's wildlife; entire ecosystems were collapsing almost overnight, yet everyone else just seemed to want to carry on as normal, like toddlers *la-la-la*-ing with their fingers in their ears.

There were so many days when she didn't even leave the flat. Daren't turn on the radio or TV. Instead, she would sit and draw new worlds for herself on paper, so she supposed she was no better than the rest of them. Weren't they all pretending the truth wasn't real?

'So, these flashbacks, will they stop now that I know?' she asked, pulling herself back to the present.

Jack made a face halfway between a grimace and a wince but shook his head. 'Sorry, Lil, no. If anything, you may have more than you've been getting.'

Lilly's stomach lurched in complaint. The hope that this milestone would bring some relief withered as quickly as it came to bud.

'But why now?' she asked. He stopped rubbing her back and she heard him catch his breath and hold it for a long moment.

'Now that's the question I was hoping you wouldn't ask me. Not yet anyway,' he said quietly. She didn't need to be an empath to spot sadness in his voice. Preoccupied with a thread on the knee of his jeans, without looking at her he said, 'But now that you've asked, I have to tell you. The thing is, Lil, I'm pretty sure you're going to like this answer even less than you liked the last one.'

CHAPTER 4

*L*illy closed her eyes trying to simultaneously process what she'd just been told and prepare herself for whatever might be coming next. Feeling her anxiety levels rise, she imagined herself in what she thought of as her forest. It was the place in her mind that she'd always retreated to when real life proved too much. She pictured herself there, sitting under the great oak, Snow the lamb curled in her lap like he used to. At the thought of Snow, Lilly felt hot familiar tears pool behind her lids.

When Lilly was only seven, her father's attempt to toughen up his only child had landed her in hospital. In an uncharacteristic fit of generosity, he had given her an orphaned lamb to raise. She'd named him Snow because he'd been found half frozen in a drift trying to suckle from his dead mother. She had loved him the minute she set eyes on him and, ignoring Jack's warnings, had forged a deep bond with the funny little ram.

For nearly a year, Lilly and Snow were inseparable. He followed her everywhere, sharing in her adventures as she roamed the fields and woods as far from the farmhouse as she dared. At night when her parents were asleep, she'd sneak down to the kitchen to snuggle beside him in the old dog bed by the Aga where she'd tell him stories while stroking the soft velvet of his nose. Then one day in school she'd heard him – as clear in her mind as if he was standing beside her. He was screaming for her. She knew what happened to every animal on the farm, how every soul was just a lump of meat and a number on a spreadsheet to her parents, but her father had given Snow to her. He was hers to keep – and keep safe. She had climbed over the school gates and bolted for home, calling to him, telling him to hang on, that she was coming for him. That it was all just a terrible mistake. That it would be okay. His terrified cries filled her head and their shared terror pumped through her veins as she ran. But then there had been only silence.

The headteacher found her collapsed in the road almost a full mile from the school. Lilly's parents had rushed to the hospital but when they discovered that she was physically unhurt, her father had asked her crossly what on earth had made her run off like that. She would never forget the horror on his face when she uttered the last word she would speak to anyone for more than six months – and the last word she'd voluntarily offer her father for the next nine years. She had looked him straight in the eye and said, 'Snow.'

In the months that followed, Lilly had retreated into herself. She had spent hours in her forest where she would play with Jack and Snow, paddle in the stream and climb the trees. She felt more than safe there, she felt at peace.

Lilly opened her eyes, comprehension dawning. To her the forest had been her idea of heaven – the peace to come when this existence was finally over and done with. But now she knew the truth. There was no heaven. There was no peace, just life after miserable life. The truth of it felt like a punch and her mouth seemed to make the decision while her brain was still trying to process all of the finer details.

'I don't want to know,' she blurted. 'I mean I do. But I don't. I need some time to get my head around all of this first.'

A look of sheer relief flooded over Jack's face. 'It's entirely your call. You tell me when you're ready,' he said, taking her hand in his and squeezing gently.

Suddenly exhausted, Lilly slumped sideways and as Jack wrapped his arm around her, she closed her eyes and tried to imagine when she'd ever feel ready to know something that by all accounts could be worse than this.

The all clear was announced shortly after ten a.m. The capricious river it seemed had spared Lilly's flat this time, although homes just a few hundred yards down the road hadn't been so lucky. There had been a steady exodus of evacuees from the community centre since first light. Lilly had been one of them the first time it happened, craning her neck at the cordon, desperate to see for herself what might have befallen her home, giddy with relief when she saw that the flood water hadn't reached her flat. Then the fourth time it happened she'd arrived only to see the fire brigade pumping sludge-coloured water out of her precious flat. She'd had to stay in a grotty B&B for three weeks. It had been packed to the gills with displaced local families and, friendly as they all seemed, Lilly had struggled with their proximity. After a lifetime spent trying not to feel the emotions of every Tom, Dick and Harry in her vicinity, she'd learned to avoid people as much as possible. Being suddenly stuffed cheek-by-jowl into the B&B with shared bathrooms and a communal dining room had felt like hell. It wasn't that Lilly didn't like people per se, she just didn't know how to be around them.

'Want to head off then?' Jack asked after the volunteer had finished his list of updates, which included news of a landslide that had blocked part of New Road and a new nighttime curfew in Bristol and Cardiff which would mean anyone planning on travelling to friends and relatives would need to do so before nightfall.

Lilly's eyes were on the couple with the old Labrador. The woman held a handful of crumpled tissues to her face, her eyes red rimmed and puffy, her husband, who was deep in conversation with a man in a fluorescent jacket and mud spattered waders, rubbed her back as he spoke.

'Let's get out of here,' Lilly said.

CHAPTER 5

*I*n the days following the latest evacuation, Lilly tried hard to concentrate on her work. She was working on a new commission for a series of children's books about Brian the Wonder Mouse. It was about a mouse who wanted to be a lion. He meets a witch; his wish is granted and then he realises everything he loved about being a mouse. Art had been Lilly's escape ever since she was a child. When it came to a career, there had never been anything else she had wanted to do.

Sitting back in her chair to stretch her aching shoulders she realised that the room had darkened around her, the lamp on her desk making her into an island in the otherwise shadowy room. She glanced up at an early but rejected little watercolour of the mouse that she'd pinned to the board above her desk. 'What do you think little fella, time for coffee?'

'Now talking to animals is one thing but talking to drawings of animals is something else entirely.' Jack's voice from the darkness made her start, even though she should be used to it by now. Lilly smiled.

'There's a lot I could say about people who skulk around in dark corners too,' she retorted, aiming for tartness but without turning around so that he couldn't see her smiling.

'Technically, I wasn't in a corner and if you want to get really precise, I'm not sure *people* is entirely accurate either, even overlooking the use of the collective as opposed to the singular,' Jack said smugly. 'Shoulders hurting again?' he asked, changing tack. She didn't hear him cross the room, but his warm hands on her shoulders weren't unexpected; unknotting her knots was just one of the things Jack excelled at.

When Lilly was younger, he always managed to show up as her tension levels edged towards boiling point. Arguments with her parents were an almost daily occurrence, but he'd be there too when she was studying for exams or, as happened almost as much as the arguments at home, having trouble with kids at school. He always seemed to know just what to say or not say. Sometimes he would just sit there letting her rant and rave until the anger gave way to tears and then grim resignation. She'd lost count of the times she'd cried herself to sleep with Jack stroking her hair. Sometimes distraction was his tactic of choice and within minutes they'd be laughing at something, her troubles forgotten. He'd been her best friend her entire life and yet, she realised, she knew next to nothing about him.

The tension in her muscles dissipated under the gentle pressure of his hands. Like butter in a hot pan, she felt it melt away within seconds. Although the pain had gone, there was something enormously comforting about the touch. Touch was important. She had read a story in a magazine at the dentists about an elderly lady who cried when she had a manicure because it was the first time anyone had held her hand in more than five years. The article made Lilly cry so much that she was still blubbing when her name was called.

Feeling suitably unknotted, she put her hand on Jack's to let him know it was alright to stop. 'Thank you. As usual you've worked your magic,' she said, moving to push back her chair to get up, but Jack remained where he was, his hands still on her shoulders, and for a moment she thought he'd not heard her. There was something in the air she couldn't put a name to. She was about to say it again when he abruptly let go and stepped back.

'So how's Brian coming along?' he asked quickly.

'Getting there. Although I wasn't able to talk the client out of the baseball cap and high tops. Brian is looking more like an eighties throwback by the day poor little soul, but it's what she wants,' Lilly said with a shrug.

'Bloody stupid name for a mouse anyway,' Jack said. They both laughed. 'Want me to make you some dinner?'

Lilly bristled, but as she was in no mood for an argument, headed over to the kitchen and rummaged through the cupboard.

'I'm good, thanks. It might have been a rough few days, but I think I can still throw together a pasta,' she said, even though eating was the last thing she felt like doing. She knew he worried about her. Hell, there were days she worried about herself, so she pushed aside her irritation and smiled.

'You okay, Lil?' he asked.

She nodded. 'I will be. I just need time to get my head around it all.'

Jack had been right about the dreams increasing since the night of the evacuation. To her relief, most had been in the form of dreams; she'd not had a flashback in waking hours since. She was hugely relieved that not every dream had been as horrific as the early ones. A few had been quite beautiful. Holding a newborn baby in her arms and being over-whelmed with love; having her picture taken at graduation and seeing the delight on her parents' faces. In one she was standing on top of a snow-capped mountain, every inch of her body screaming with pain and fatigue but with such joy in her heart that she felt like flying. The nightmares outnumbered the nice dreams by about three to one, but she hoped that ratio might change.

'I suppose I should leave you to it then,' Jack said, making for the door. 'Maybe take it easy this evening. Call if you need me, okay? Promise?'

She had no idea why he went through the charade of doors. For someone who appeared and disappeared at will, making the effort to leave by walking out of a door seemed a little pointless, but she supposed he had his reasons.

'Okay. I promise,' she said, meaning it.

With his hand on the door handle, he said, 'And Lil, don't forget to make that pasta. You're wasting away.'

She opened her mouth to protest but it was too late – the door was already closing. She had no idea how much she weighed – had never been interested in such things – but she knew she must have lost weight as she had had to give in and buy new jeans last week from the charity shop. There hadn't been much to choose from in a size six, but she was just grateful to wear something that at least fit her.

Her stomach chose that moment to remind her that she'd not eaten anything since a breakfast and she scowled, imagining it siding with Jack. Pulling the hair band from her wrist, she tipped her head forward and let her long dark auburn hair fall to the floor. She remembered her grandmother chasing her around the kitchen table with the kitchen scissors when she was a child. She had been convinced that Lilly's long luxuriant hair was sapping her strength and was the reason for what the doctors had called her failure to thrive. Her mother had come into the kitchen just in time. Lilly sighed at the memory and wrestled her hair into a top-knot.

Although she thought of herself as pale, freakishly freckled and scrawny-looking, she at least liked her hair. Her eyes too but only because they were green like Jack's.

Lacking the energy to make the pasta from scratch, she opted instead for a packet mix that she could microwave. As she leant against the counter listening to it hum, she thought of her Brian the Mouse client, Charlotte. They'd only ever spoken on the phone, but from what she'd said about her now grown-up children, Lilly guessed that she was her fifties.

Try as she might, Lilly couldn't imagine being that old. While she reasoned that she must have reached her fifties during one of her previous lives, she just couldn't picture for herself. It felt like an impossibly long road stretched out ahead of her. Mile after mile of arid, dusty nothingness where someone could drive for days in a straight line and barely see or be seen by another living soul.

Her train of thought was broken by the sound of an envelope being slipped under the front door. It took exactly three steps to retrieve it from its resting place on the grey carpet tiles. She read the four paragraphs twice, but the first few lines told her all she needed to know. Due to the persistent and increasing risk of flooding, she and the other residents were all being served notice.

It wasn't a shock. She had heard it muttered about in the community centre and the local news reports had been speculating for months about how long the local authorities could try and hold back the relentless forces of nature. She guessed that the insurers had long since refused to cover the building. She was sad, but, she realised, not as devastated as she might have been before the floods. Home after all was the place you felt safe.

Conscious that the microwave had fallen silent, Lilly pulled out the bowl and dumped the pasta onto a plate. Hopping up to sit on the counter, she managed half a dozen mouthfuls before tipping the evidence of her abandoned meal down the toilet.

CHAPTER 6

*T*he sun is hot on my face. I'm lying on a thick carpet of wildflowers and soft meadow grasses that feel as comfortable as any feather bed. I can hear bees buzzing and, in the distance, the birds are singing sweetly in the trees. The smell of the meadow, the delicate perfume of the flowers mixed with the warm scent of the earth is so comforting, so exquisite, I can't bring myself to open my eyes.

I feel a jolt in my belly and gasp in surprise. Then I hear a deep, throaty chuckle.

'This one is determined to make his presence known then.'

I open my eyes and my stomach does another flip, but this time it isn't the baby kicking, it's the same feeling I get every single time I lay eyes on my husband. His bright green eyes dusted with a blessing of gold crease up at the corners as he grins at me. His face is golden brown after so long outdoors and his hair is long and the colour of August wheat. He puts his hand on my bump and bends down to kiss it. Then he kisses me, and I'm lost.

We hear the horses before we see them, a rhythmic pounding of hooves on the hard dirt track above the meadow. The power of it races through the earth to me like a frantic messenger trying to *outrun a storm. I try to keep my thoughts here in the moment, where we're safe, but it's too late. I know. We know.*

We stay where we are, neither of us wanting to move before we have to. I screw my eyes shut so that he might not be able to see the fear in them or the tears that will make leaving slice his heart with an even more bitter blade. We hear one of the guards dismount, the scuff of stones underfoot as he crosses the dirt track, and then the quiet whispers of the grasses as he makes his way through the meadow.

'My lord, please forgive me but the border has been breached, the king has recalled us to the fight.' I open my eyes to see Johan nod silently and the guard turn and make his way back to his waiting horse and men.

'I had hoped ...' he says, his hand again on my swollen belly. I feel the baby writhe and kick as if adding its own feeble protest to the scene. He loses his words and turns his head away so that I don't see the tears in his own eyes.

'You'll be home in time,' I say, reaching up to take his face in my hands and trying to sear the memory of it into my mind as if doing so would protect me from the widow's forgetting. It's a lie and we both know it.

LILLY WOKE CONFUSED that instead of the soft meadow, she could feel only the probing springs of a tired old mattress. She felt leaden – pinned down like a butterfly in a collector's case and resigned to her fate. She struggled to find the word that might sum up this new feeling; desolate came close, but not nearly close enough to describe the sheer weight of the thing.

She felt like her soul had been cleaved in two and it was so clear to her in that moment that there would never be any joy in her world ever again. She reached unthinkingly for her belly but found just drum-taut skin and protruding hip bones and a wave of grief hit her so forcibly that for a moment, she couldn't even breathe.

Without the energy to sit up or even to cry, she lay there, staring at the brown watermark on the ceiling. Hearing what sounded like a drip, she peered harder at the stain, wondering if the pipe from the upstairs flat may be leaking again.

Hearing the noise again, she turned her head to the source of the noise only to see Jack sitting in the lone armchair, his head in his hands at the temples and a book open in his lap. Another drip confirmed what she was struggling at first to process – there were tears falling from his eyes onto the page in front of him. It was only then that Lilly realised that she'd never before seen Jack cry.

CHAPTER 7

*J*ack had gone by the time Lilly found the energy to get out of bed. Seeing him cry like that had torn her in two. She had wanted to ask him about it, but she had no idea where to begin. It rocked her a little, seeing him so vulnerable and, if she was completely honest, her own reaction had shamed her a little too. All her life Jack had been there to support her, guide her, help her. It was always him helping her and never, she realised now, her helping him.

After worrying about it all day, when Jack arrived later that evening, Lilly was at a loss as to how to start the conversation. She told him instead about needing to find somewhere new to live and they chatted through the options, such that they were on her meagre budget. When the conversation turned to the latest news on the flooding more generally, Lilly was relieved, but surprising her, Jack all but blurted, 'So, you had another dream last night? Do you want a coffee?' the sentences tumbling into one another as he yanked off the lid of the kettle.

She closed her eyes as the memory of the meadow dream washed over her – the warm sunshine on her face and her heart and belly so filled with love that she could almost believe that she was back there. She nodded, not trusting her voice.

'See anyone you know? I mean, sometimes the dreams can be helpful that way.' His voice was tight and, as she opened her eyes, she saw him thrust the kettle under the tap. He pushed the lever too far and swore as the cold water missed the hole, hit the sides of the kettle and soaked the front of his T-shirt. In other circumstances she would have laughed, but the air was suddenly heavy around them.

Jack stared at her, his T-shirt dripping.

She shook her head. 'No. I wish you'd been close by in that one – it was the worst one yet, Jack. I was—' she began to say, but he cut her off.

'Have you eaten today?' he asked accusingly, opening the fridge and peering inside. 'I thought you were having that fresh soup for lunch?' Feeling her hackles rise at the mention of Jack's favourite and her least favourite subject, Lilly took a deep breath in the hope that they could get back on topic.

'No, I've not eaten the soup, but I have eaten,' she said, trying to keep her voice calm and even.

Pulling the bin out from under the sink he yanked off the lid. 'Well there's nothing in here that wasn't there yesterday morning,' he said, his tone ratcheting up on the accusatory scale and sounding every bit like the disappointed grown-up.

'Why do you do this?' she asked, her temper rising.

'Do what?' Jack snapped. 'Give a shit?'

'Is that what you call it? Acting like a cross between my father and the food police? Poking around in my fridge. In my bloody bin? What the hell is wrong with you lately?' she snapped as she grabbed the bin out of his hands and thumped it back into the cupboard.

They stood glaring at each other in the tiny space, hemmed in by kitchen units on two sides and a sink on the other. The tap dripped steadily, marking the time, and Lilly steeled herself not to reach over and turn it off. It was bugging her almost as much as Jack, but moving would imply defeat so she stood her ground.

'Humans eat, Lilly. That's the way it works, or did you miss that part in school?'

When in doubt, be sarcastic might well be Jack's life motto. In fact, she wouldn't be surprised to see it tattooed somewhere.

'Thanks for enlightening me, Jack,' she spat out his name as if it left a nasty taste in her mouth, 'but I'm well aware of that and even though it's absolutely none of your bloody business, I eat plenty.'

'Well that's where your enlightenment on the subject ends, Lilly,' he said, matching her in tone. 'You are very much my business, which means I'm allowed to give a shit when you deliberately neglect yourself,' he said, his voice rising to just under a shout.

'Neglect myself? Neglect myself?' she yelled, incredulous now. 'I'm not some doddery old granny forgetting to take her pills. I have work to do, clients to pander to and bills to pay in case you hadn't noticed. And I need to find somewhere else to call home sweet fucking home, so cooking up a storm is hardly high on my priority list right now!' Her mother used to tell her that her eyes flashed when she was angry, and she could almost feel them flaming now as she held Jack's equally defiant stare.

'None of which you'll be able to do if you're ill,' he said, and she saw him soften ever so slightly. 'I just want what's right for you.' He let out a long breath as he raked his hands through his thick dark hair. He turned away from her and all at once there was such sadness in the air that it seemed to push out all of the oxygen in the small space. Lilly took a huge gasping breath and grabbed for the worktop to steady herself.

'What the hell?' she said, her voice almost a shout.

'It's nothing, Lil, just drop it,' Jack said, walking back to the bedroom end of the bedsit.

Over the years Jack had tried and failed to convince her that her empathy was a gift that made her special, but Lilly had only ever seen it as a curse. At school the teachers labelled her 'sensitive', but it didn't even come close to describing how it would feel to walk into a room and feel like she'd just been hit in the face with the granite of other people's fear, grief and anxiety. Living on a livestock farm was overwhelming, hence her frequent and infamous escapes that invariably ended with her being hauled back to her parents like an errant sheepdog by a busybody neighbour or the local police.

It took her years to learn how to live in the world without being crushed by it, and she had Jack to thank for that. He taught her to recognise which emotions belonged to her and which belonged to another and, most importantly, how to turn down the volume on the empathy even when she couldn't manage to shield herself completely.

'That wasn't nothing. What's going on?' she asked gently, her anger completely forgotten. Crossing the room, she put her hand on his back. 'What are you so sad about?'

Turning, Jack tried to smile but it didn't reach his eyes. 'It's nothing, really. I'm sorry I was being an arse. I just worry about you, Lil.' The sadness she felt was gone now, tucked back behind Jack's own mental shield which has always been so much stronger than her own. Taking her head in his hands, he planted a kiss so light and insubstantial on her forehead it might have been a butterfly's kiss. Before she could say anything more, he whispered, 'See you soon,' and then he was gone. No pretence of doors this time. She could still feel the impression of his lips on her skin.

CHAPTER 8

*T*he long hand of the old wall clock juddered as if the effort of moving was playing havoc with its cogs. Click. Five fifty-eight and counting. Storm had been watching it from behind the long polished oak counter in Cordelia's bookshop and café, willing it to speed up for the past hour. She could have closed up whenever she wanted, of course – as the owner it was her prerogative – but it just didn't feel right to say one thing and then do something else. Trade had been slow that afternoon though, the result of the cold wet front that seemed to be dithering on the Welsh border combined with a vicious north-easterly wind that made it feel more like February than April.

There had been the usual lunchtime rush in the café end of the shop, two hours of organised chaos split between take-away soups and sandwiches and table service for a mix of loyal locals and the few early tourists brave enough to do battle with the ever-more erratic weather. Takings-wise the bookshop had done okay, but only because Meg from the art gallery at the top of the high street had come in to order a pile of books for her husband's birthday. Without that, sales for the day would amount to just two OS maps and a fancy notebook.

Storm's eyes wandered back to the clock. It had been Nick, her late husband, who had talked her into buying it. They'd been in Glastonbury, supposedly to pick up some retailing tips for their new venture but, Storm remembered with a smile, they had spent most of their time either in bed or pub hopping.

Nick had spotted the clock through the window of a crystal shop on one of their strolls around the town. Unlike the comforting cheek-by-jowl Aladdin's caves of curiosities that had enthralled them in the other shops in town, this one had very little stock. What remained was scattered confetti-like across shelves designed to carry ten times the merchandise. The air inside was frigid and so dank not even the incense sticks burnt to ash on the counter could mask the smell of defeat.

It was a sad little place and Storm had wanted to leave the moment they had walked in, but their arrival had been announced by the jangling of an overly loud bell above the door. Before they could make good their escape, a middle-aged woman wearing a thick black corduroy coat and fingerless red woollen gloves had huffed into the shop and reluctantly taken to her station behind the counter.

Her irritation at being summoned into the chilly little shop had evaporated the moment she'd laid eyes on Nick. It was a reaction Storm had become used to over the years. Grown women old enough to be his mother, some old enough to be his grandmother, would take one look at those chiselled cheekbones and sooty blue eyes and become instantly lost. The dark blond hair, rough cut to just below his collar, completed the rock-star look. That Nick himself always seemed so genuinely oblivious to the faltering glances, flushed cheeks and rapidly dilating pupils only served to make him even more endearing.

The clock, it transpired, wasn't for sale, but after Nick and 'you can call me Janice, darling' had chatted for a while, it seemed she was more than happy to negotiate. Twenty minutes later they were heading back to the B&B with the clock tucked under Nick's arm.

'There you go, our first investment,' Nick had said, wrapping his free arm tightly around Storm's shoulders.

'Investment?' She'd laughed, incredulous. 'It's not some Swiss timepiece, my love, it was probably knocked up in Taiwan.'

'Oh really? Well, Miss Smarty Pants, fancy a little wager on that?' Nick had stopped and, grinning, pulled her into kissing distance by the ends of her long woolly scarf.

'Fiver says it'll be kaput by Christmas,' she'd said, landing a kiss on his lips.

'Rubbish! Fiver says it'll last till we're old and grey,' he had countered, pulling her back in for a longer kiss.

She had lost the bet, of course, as she knew she would. Nick's mother used to tell her that he was charmed as well as charming. There was a time when she had believed it too.

It was hard to believe now that she'd not wanted the clock. Its slow, steady tick had marked out twelve years in Cordelia's, nine of them the happiest of her entire life. But since Nick's death there hadn't been a single day that she'd not wished for the power to turn back those hands and take that time – their time – back.

'Kitchen's all tucked up for the night,' Veronica said, startling Storm back to the present. 'You were miles away, love, you okay?'

Storm mustered a tired smile and nodded while suppressing a yawn. Veronica, as always, looked like she'd just stepped out of the hairdressers. Her soft silver-blonde curls bounced obediently around her shoulders, not a hair out of place, despite the fact that she'd been running the café side of the business since eight o'clock that morning. Storm had no idea how she always managed to look so effortlessly together. Despite being close to a size sixteen, Vee moved with the grace of a dancer and could light up a room just by smiling. That was probably the reason she had to have three parties for her fiftieth birthday last year, just to make sure that everyone who wanted to celebrate with her got the opportunity.

'Want to hear something funny?' Vee asked but ploughed on before Storm could reply. 'Old Ted only asked Jerry yesterday if he had any leftover bones for his dog, Milo. He's been eating here how many years?' She giggled, her eyes twinkling.

Storm laughed. 'Only since we opened. I thought the "purely plants" sub-head on the sign was clear enough, but bless him, I think we should take it as a compliment if he's not noticed. What did Jerry say to him?'

'His story got interrupted by an order, so he didn't get chance to tell me, but Ted and Milo were in as usual this morning, so whatever it was it didn't put them off,' Veronica said, giggling again.

'Thanks, Vee,' Storm said and wished, not for the first time, that she could bottle her best friend's sunny disposition. 'What would I do without you?'

'Knowing you, probably turn the whole place into a bloody cat rescue and go bankrupt in a fortnight,' she said, laughing as she leaned over to give her friend a quick hug and enveloping Storm in a warm wave of delicate and, knowing her, very expensive artisan perfume in the process.

'True enough. Remind me again why you waste your considerable talents on us?' Storm asked, teasing.

'As I've told you before, darling heart, because selling

frocks was tedious and if I stayed home playing the dutiful wife I'd lose my mind, my husband, or most likely both in no time at all – and that's despite my other responsibilities,' she said, winking theatrically and tapping the side of her nose with a neatly manicured finger. 'Far better to hang around here feeding people – literally and metaphorically.' She nodded towards the rows of books that occupied half the ground floor.

'Have you spoken to Michael yet about the apprenticeship?' Storm asked, deliberately lowering her voice even though they were alone.

Veronica shook her head. 'I want to do it in person, so I'll wait until he gets home from uni. I can't think of anyone I'd rather pass the library on to, but it's not something to take on lightly. It's a lifelong commitment and, as we know, it's not without its risks.'

They were both silent for a moment, lost in their thoughts. Then Veronica said, 'I'll be in early in the morning. My niece is bringing in some new cakes for us to try so no dinner tonight, you'll need cake storage capacity.' She fished in her huge handbag for her car keys as she made her way to the front door. The lights on a white Tesla parked outside the window flashed obediently. She was still giggling at her own joke as she went out, only to duck her head back in the door a second later to add, 'Oh, and remember the book club tomorrow evening, won't you.'

'Yep, all sorted,' Storm fibbed, kicking herself for forgetting yet again.

Veronica raised an eyebrow. 'Love ya,' she said with a knowing grin as she pulled the door behind her. Storm didn't mind hosting the local book club. It was good for business, filled an otherwise lonely evening and she got to talk about books with people she liked. The only downside was that as the host, responsibility for leading the group discussion had somehow fallen to her and, try as she might, there was something about having to read a book that made her rebel like a stroppy teenager.

She rummaged under the counter for the book they'd be discussing. A train ticket poked out of the top of the paperback proudly announcing that she'd made it all the way to page seventeen on her last sitting – which had also been her first sitting. She sighed, locked up and, with paperback in hand, headed for the back stairs, her legs already feeling the weight of every step; it was going to be a long night.

CHAPTER 9

The book club had been great fun as usual, despite the midnight oil Storm had burned speed-reading. There were twelve of them in all, ranging in age from seventeen to eighty-two. They'd read everything from Austen to Dan Brown and it was their willingness to give anything a go that Storm loved. Their monthly meet-ups always lifted her spirits.

Aside from the book club, Cordelia's also hosted about a dozen other regular gatherings from gardening groups to 'bitch and stitch' knitting clubs. She'd known Pont Nefoedd to be a special place the day she and Nick stumbled upon it, lost in their bid to take the pretty way to the Brecon Beacons. She'd felt it the moment she'd stepped out of the car and when they'd seen the For Sale sign on the building it had felt like fate. Here they could have a business and a home all in one. They'd fallen in love with the forest-covered mountains that surrounded the town and the plucky little high street of independent shops, but had soon come to realise it was the people who made the place so wonderful.

While the lower reaches of the town hadn't been spared

from flooding, by some miracle, Pont Nefoedd had escaped the violence that had been sweeping through the country. Close to six months on and the news was still dominated by reports of the bitter street protests that quickly turned into pitch battles between police and a mob that seemed incapable of settling around any single grievance. Some said it was the flooding, others blamed the food shortages and the currency troubles, while others pointed the finger at the sepsis crisis that was fast putting medicine back a few hundred years. Whatever it was, it felt like anger itself had taken form. The bigger cities were most seriously affected, with almost every major city in the country under night-time curfew orders and the army drafted in to support a police force stretched beyond breaking point.

Storm was proud of her community. In the face of such widespread unrest and division, they'd come together and redoubled efforts to help each other. There were still tourists, even more so now that the pound was so weak, and the cities weren't as attractive as destination spots. Few travellers wanted a postcard from a picket line or a selfie in front of barbed wire. There were still taxes to pay and laundry to do. On a good day you could almost ignore the gnawing sense that something was very, very wrong.

Storm lay in bed, listening to the radio. The weather report warned that the UK should brace itself for the tail end of a hurricane by the evening but, even as the presenter spoke, she could hear a volley of rain hurl itself against the bedroom window. She wondered whether predicting the weather had always been so difficult. It was a standing joke in Britain of course, but they had had a blizzard last September and it had been a balmy twenty-six degrees at Halloween, which hadn't felt funny at all.

She switched off the radio, not wanting to hear the headlines again and the daily tally of sepsis-related deaths.

It seemed that they were losing the battle against bacteria too.

She prised herself reluctantly out of bed, earning herself a disgruntled look from Anchor, her cat, who was curled up on the pillow next to her. She tickled his ear, but he merely scowled and curled one of his huge ginger paws over his nose before rolling over and winding himself into an even smaller ball – he had never been one for mornings. Hope, on the other hand, springer by breed and nature, greeted her with her usual wag-a-thon then grabbed Storm's slipper and bounced around the bedroom with it. She accepted her ear tickle with unveiled delight and Storm marvelled, not for the first time, at the capacity of dogs for unbridled joy at the smallest of things.

It was still dark outside and Storm's head felt leaden through lack of sleep. She hadn't dreamed properly since Nick had died, which was coming up for three years now, but for the past few weeks she'd been aware of dreaming almost every night. They were fractious, disturbing dreams that brought her to wakefulness multiple times a night and the broken sleep was catching up with her. She'd wake just in time to feel the image of whatever it was scurry away from her into the shadows again, then slip back into the dream only for the process to repeat itself. It was as exhausting as it was frustrating.

Storm grabbed her dressing gown and headed to the kitchen to make coffee and give Hope her breakfast. The noise of a window banging in the wind caught her attention. There were only sash windows on the ground floor and in Storm's flat, which meant that it had to be coming from the attic. Resigned, she took her coffee out onto the landing but, as she closed the flat door, she heard a muffled meow. Anchor, never one to miss out on a trip to the attic, was sitting just inside the door when she opened it again, his huge orange eyes slow blinking into hers. He treated her to one of his funny little chirrups so she held the door for him and together they ambled down the corridor before climbing the steep attic stairs.

Anchor beat her to the top and stretched up the door to bat the tassel on the old key that was poking out of the lock. If Storm didn't know any better, she'd swear he had a spare hidden somewhere because even when the door was locked, as it was now, he had an uncanny habit of finding his way into the attic flat. He had always loved it because it had served as Nick's art studio and Storm's room for mediumship readings. It had been such a happy, creative space – maybe that's why he was so drawn to it. Some of Nick's paintings still hung on the walls and, despite the decorating, if you knew where to look you could still see bright specks of acrylic paint on the polished honey-coloured floorboards.

Storm had so loved giving readings. That people would wait eighteen months for an appointment with her felt ridiculous to her now. She remembered how clients would practically race up the attic stairs, eager to hear from whoever it was they had lost. Some chatted non-stop, excited and anxious and no doubt hoping against hope that the past eighteen months hadn't been in vain. Nearly all were oblivious to the fact that the people they so longed to hear from had walked unseen in the door with them, climbed the stairs at their side and stood with them through the whole thing. Sometimes spirits arrived days in advance of a reading, so eager to be seen and heard that they followed her around, although nearly always at a polite distance. God, how she missed them. Seeing the look on clients' faces when a spirit shared something so meaningful that all doubt melted away, the joy and love replacing the grief and the pain in their expressions – it was work like no other she could imagine. There were usually tears, hers and theirs, but laughter too and hugs and the unshakeable knowledge that she was of service to spirit and the world. And then, just like that, spirit had abandoned her and her magic had left her.

Standing in the flat now, the space felt so forlorn. She felt a lump rise in her throat and quick tears pricked at her eyes. The memories of happier times, of what she'd lost, seemed more potent up here somehow. She checked the bathroom and bedroom windows, but just like the kitchen and living space, they were all secured. She was about to head back, eager to disentangle herself from the memories and distract herself with something, anything else, when Anchor hopped onto the living room windowsill and another memory hit her: Nick sitting up here in the easy chair, his back to the window, staring at a blank canvas in the pre-dawn dark. He used to love to watch the sunrise because he believed that the first rays of the day provided the best light for his painting. To most people it would have looked like he was simply staring at the canvas, planning his painting, but Nick had an altogether more romantic explanation. 'I'm waiting for the sun to stir the shadows on the canvas and let me know what it wants me to paint,' he'd say with a smile that would put sunbeams to shame.

Crossing to the window, Storm looked out into the darkness, then slumped down in the easy chair, swiftly joined by Anchor who perched on the arm, his feet all buttoned up into a neat base and his eyes trained on the window. 'So, Anc, why are we in the attic, eh?' she asked, swallowing the lump in her throat while tickling him under the chin and igniting the purr machine. He turned his head to look at her, gently head-bopped her chin a few times and then turned his attention back to the window and the soon-to-be-waking world.

With Anchor purring contentedly beside her, Storm closed her eyes as a brief break in the clouds allowed the first rays of pale morning light to touch her tired face. She stayed like that for a few minutes, remembering something of the joy this place had brought them over the years. How much love had flooded into this room from spirit, all those happy tears, the laughter and the alchemy of feeling sadness transmuted into comfort, pain into love, separation into connection. She thought too of how much beautiful art had been created here, the creatures that Nick had coaxed into being from a blank canvas with nothing more than sunlight and paint. And while her magic had always been simple, it was here that she had come to meditate and practise her craft. These walls held so much love, so much power, and yet here they stood, empty save for a visiting feline.

'You're a clever cat,' she said, smiling into his slow-blinking amber eyes. 'Maybe it's time this place worked its magic again. It needs someone to love it.' She smiled, scooped him gently into her arms and feeling the thrum of his purr against her chest, headed back downstairs.

The rain was torrential when Storm and Hope stepped out for their early morning walk and a bitter north-easterly was rattling just about anything not already tied down. When Hope pulled for home after a lacklustre trot around the park, Storm relented; it was her walk after all. Making a mental note to do some training with her instead during her break, they jogged all the way back home.

After a quick shower and a bowl of porridge, Storm went down to the café kitchen. It was Jerry's day off, which meant that she was playing chef. While the soups, chillies and stews would be already prepped and waiting for her in the fridge, with much of their menu being freshly made, there would still be an awful lot to do – that was if the weather didn't keep everyone indoors.

A love of cooking had come later in life for Storm. Nick had always been the foodie, Storm, for so long, just the grateful recipient of his culinary passion. When he died and

Storm found herself cut off from all she had ever known, cooking had been one of the things that had grounded her. Jerry had given her lessons and in cooking she found that she could come as close to alchemy as she was now ever going to get. In making food for others she had found comfort, even if it still so often tasted of ash in her own mouth.

Storm tipped back her head and gathered up her hair into a ponytail. Tying it up was always a mission. She had cut it short when Nick died, shearing it herself with the kitchen scissors one night when, had it not been for the ever-watchful eyes of Anchor and Hope, she might have done much worse to herself. It had grown, of course, and was now back to its long, thick, unruly dark lengths. Winding it into a tight bun at the back of her neck, she wrapped it securely and donned a hairnet. After washing her hands, she said a quick blessing for the meal she was about to prepare, thanked all those who had played a part in creating it, and then she began.

CHAPTER 10

*S*torm had just surfaced from the kitchen to lend a hand front-of-house, when she saw Veronica arrive to open the bookshop. Stowing her bag behind the counter, Veronica strode over to the cafe to help clear away the breakfast things.

'Morning, gorgeous one,' Veronica said after picking up an empty cake stand in each hand and following Storm back to the kitchen. 'Been skiving again, I see?'

Storm laughed and wiped a strand of hair from her forehead that had strayed out of her hairnet. 'Hell, yes, and I've done *The Times* crossword and three Sudokus,' she said grinning. 'Seriously, Vee, I do not know how Jerry does this every day. It's bloody exhausting – and I've still got lunch to do yet.'

'Well, grab a cuppa and some breakfast now while it's quiet,' Veronica said, shooing Storm out of the kitchen door ahead of her.

Helping herself to a black coffee and an almond croissant she'd saved for herself, Storm followed Veronica over to the bookshop and flopped into one of the armchairs. They chatted while Veronica opened a delivery and scanned the new arrivals into stock, Storm keeping one eye on the café in case she was needed.

She had just finished her coffee when a smartly dressed elderly lady came into the shop accompanied by a weaselly man with thinning fair hair in a zip-up fawn jacket. There was something familiar about the woman, Storm thought. She was leaning heavily on a stick and looked to be in her eighties. She was trying without much success to persuade the younger man that she was not in need of his arm. 'But Mother, if you fell and broke your other hip,' he said, exasperated.

'What?' she demanded, cutting him off, her voice high and light but still commanding. 'You'd feel compelled to look after me? To hell with that, Jeremy. I'd make my own arrangements, thank you, so you needn't fear. Now please stop fussing and go and find us a table, will you? I'll have an oat milk hot chocolate and a muffin of some sort, please. Chocolate chip preferably. And don't give me that look – at my age I'm allowed treats.' Storm suppressed a smile as he huffed off into the café, leaving his mother to shuffle her way to the bookshelves.

'Good morning,' Veronica said brightly once he'd gone. 'Do shout if you're after anything in particular, won't you. And if you'd rather take a pew, I'm happy to bring books to you if you tell me what you'd like.'

'That's incredibly sweet of you, dear, but I'm meant to walk on it – new hip and all. Besides, I'd have no idea what to ask for – I've not heard one singing to me yet.'

Storm snapped to attention and studied the woman in more detail. She couldn't be sure, especially side on, but, 'Doreen?' she asked, getting up and walking over to her.

'Stormy?' The older woman beamed with delight, her eyes wide with surprise as she peered at Storm. 'You're all grown up,' she said, 'I didn't recognise you.'

'Nor I, you, but so few people talk about singing books that I—' Storm stopped abruptly, her smile fading fast as Doreen's quick, bright eyes searched her face then filled to the brim with tears.

The older woman wobbled slightly, and both Storm and Veronica rushed to steady her. 'Stormy, my darling, what happened? Where's your magic?' Doreen asked in a choked whisper, reaching her free hand to hold Storm's, still searching her face as if her magic were hiding in there somewhere, waiting to be rescued.

Storm's own eyes swam. Unable to speak, she just shook her head and shrugged, the gesture of the young girl she had been when her mentor, Margot, had first taken her to meet Doreen, who, after Margot herself, was one of the most learned and powerful witches she had ever met. That and a chemical engineer to boot, which had impressed the young Storm nearly as much as the witchcraft. Doreen had tutored Storm for more than a year when she was around sixteen, sharing with her the techniques of the high magic that had so accelerated her learning and abilities.

'But, you ...' Doreen looked around, as if afraid to say what she wanted to aloud. She shook her head. 'It's not possible, Stormy, things like this don't just happen – not to people like you. You know that, I taught you that.' Her eyes filled again but seeing her son gesturing to her from the café to hurry up, blinked them away determinedly. She pulled her mobile out of her pocket and handed it to Storm. 'Pop your number in there for me then call it so that you have mine too, will you, please.' As Storm obliged, she said, 'I've never told him,' nodding in the direction of her son, 'and if I do now he'll have me committed, sure as eggs is eggs, but,' she broke off, upset again and clearly trying to wrestle down her emotions, 'this isn't right, Stormy, not right at all. You call me, okay? Please, whenever you feel you can talk about it, but promise me you will. This is so important.' Storm nodded, hugged her and then watched as Doreen went to join her impatient son.

'One of the first things Doreen taught me was how to light candles with magic,' Storm said quietly to Veronica, her eyes still resting on her old friend's back, but seeing instead the dining room of her neat little semi-detached house in Enfield that had doubled as her classroom. 'The first time I managed it, I set her lampshade on fire.' She laughed at the memory of Doreen calmly blasting the thing with a small fire extinguisher that had been stowed under the table just in case. 'She was so good to me, so kind, but she pushed me to … to do things I would never in a million years even have thought possible, let alone possible by me.' She swallowed hard and wiped her eyes with the heel of her hand.

'Maybe—' Veronica began, but Storm held up her hands and shook her head.

'No, Vee, I can't hear it again.' Her voice was just a whisper even though they were alone in the shop. 'My magic, just like my connection to spirit is gone. It's over. Whatever gift I had has been revoked and I can't spend the rest of my life hoping and wishing it would come back. I've accepted it now – it's just how it has to be – and I need to learn to get on with it.' Straightening her back and taking a deep breath, she said, 'Right, I'd better get back to work, people to feed and all that.' She tried to force a smile but the look on her friend's face told her that Veronica wouldn't be so easily fooled.

CHAPTER 11

*M*argot Depworth's face was aching. By her calculations, taking into account the media interviews, the publicity shots and now the signing at Waterstones, her lips had been contorted skywards for close to six hours. She found it hard to believe that she'd once dreamed about moments like these. She'd lit up like a candle the first time someone had recognised her in Waitrose and asked for her autograph. *Her* autograph. Now it was all she could do to tolerate the simpering idiots who fawned around her at every signing, recording and stage appearance.

Her first book, *Stepping into the Light*, had been a runaway success both in the UK and, altogether more profitably, the US. A show on an American cable channel had followed hot on its heels which, after just one series, was picked up by a major station and syndicated across the country. She'd burst onto the scene just as stage mediumship had been having something of a revival.

She flicked her eyes to the clock that hung over the stairs and considered a quick spell to move it on half an hour and bring the tedium to an end. She dismissed the idea almost at once. The clock was child's play, but altering everyone's phones and smart watches would take more time than she could realistically claw back, so instead, she conjured a quick glamour so she could at least relax her face while making sure that her adoring fans saw nothing but her bright, attentive eyes and perfect smile.

'I've got all yer books,' said a large woman, beaming. She was wearing a dress Margot thought could easily double as a marquee. The woman was pink-cheeked and sweat beaded on her top lip, making the fine hairs on her overly bleached moustache glisten in the spotlight. Margot wondered why so many women let themselves balloon to such disgusting weights in middle age.

'I'm so flattered, darling,' Margot said with a practised air. 'Now, what's your name?' Her Mont Blanc pen tapped lightly on the opened book.

'Er, I'm Angie, but the book's for one of me cleaning clients, Calum. His wife just passed, only thirty-two she was. Left two kiddies an' all. Such a tragedy.' She paused, her large, cow-brown eyes filling with tears. Behind the mask of her glamour, Margot rolled her eyes.

Blinking hard and dabbing at her nose with a crumpled tissue, Angie continued, 'He's started watching yer show since it happened, and I was thinking maybe you could write something to make him feel better? Something hopeful like? Like you says to people on the show.' Her eyes, still dewy with tears, opened wide in encouragement.

'Of course,' Margot said emphatically, gritting her teeth as Angie spelt out the man's name letter by letter, then turned to survey the snaking queue.

Margot scrawled, 'To Colin, best wishes, Margot Depworth.'

'Here you go,' Margot said, handing her the closed hardback book.

'Thank you so, so much, he'll be thrilled to bits,' Angie said, but Margot was already talking to the woman behind her.

Two hours later, after politely but firmly refusing her agent's offer of dinner, Margot closed the door of her suite at the Dorchester and, with a heavy sigh, allowed the glamour to slip. They might be ridiculously simple spells to conjure, but holding them for extended periods of time was the work of an adept and even a witch of Margot's ability had only so much energy at her disposal. She kicked off her heels and threw her jacket on the sofa. Then she made herself a camomile tea before settling herself down onto an ornate chaise for her last meditation of the day and a chance to recharge her batteries.

There were many frauds in this business, but Margot prided herself on not being one of them. Not that she had a particularly strong moral code in that sense anymore – life had beaten that out of her in no uncertain terms – but because she had been brought up to focus on the things she'd been good at. As it turned out, talking to the dead had just happened to be one of them. She was also, even if she did say so herself, one of the most talented and powerful witches on the planet, but, for her own protection, that was something she didn't share with the masses. The great unwashed might be ready for stage mediums, but witches were another thing entirely.

She closed her eyes, took several long deliberate breaths, and slipped quickly into the world few got to see. Thirty minutes later her cold blue eyes snapped open. Swinging her long skinny legs off the chaise, she was on her feet in less than a second and had reached the desk in under three. She snatched her mobile from where it was charging and selected a name from the list of favourites. A male voice answered on the fourth ring.

'It's started,' she said, her mouth so tight it was an effort to form the words.

There was silence on the other end of the line, but she knew he was smiling.

'Good. Assemble the council.' He rang off without saying goodbye.

Margot had made another six calls before she allowed herself to sit down with a small whiskey in the hope that it would steady her nerves for the next call she wanted to make. She drained the glass and set it down. Taking a deep breath, she plastered on a smile and stood up. The phone went to answering machine and she smiled warmly at the soft, familiar voice, a flood of happy memories racing back to her as she listened.

'Hello, lovely caller, this is Storm, please leave a message after the beep. Have a beautiful day.' Her reverie was cut short as Storm's voice burst onto the line with a cheery, 'Hello?'

Margot hung up without saying a word.

CHAPTER 12

here was only one thing Lilly missed about the farmhouse where she grew up. On the whole, she hated pretty much everything about the place. It was a cold soulless house that her father was too mean to heat. She supposed that if you spent most of your waking hours on a freezing hillside, anything more than perishing would seem like a luxury, but despite her protests, the heating remained off on all but the most bitter of days. Waking up to find ice inside her bedroom window was a frequent occurrence and having to wear a bobble hat to bed in winter was the norm. The house did, however, have a utility room complete with two large washing machines, one industrial thing for her father's farm clothes capable of stripping away the mud and who knows what from his overalls, and a domestic version for everything else. There was even a tumble dryer, although the only time it got used was on a Friday night when her father was safely at the Lion getting hammered.

Lilly thought fondly of the farm's utility room every time she had to lug bags of washing up the hill to the laundrette. It was never much fun, but today was worse than usual thanks to the storm and the knowledge that she'd soon need to find somewhere else to live. She had regretted her decision the minute she'd set off up the hill, a heavy bag in each hand, and a vicious gust of wind had whipped the hood from her head. The rain was practically horizontal, and despite the fact that it was April and technically spring, it was bitterly cold. She had forced herself to make the effort, not just because she was almost out of clean clothes, but because once she was there, the laundrette would be a lot warmer than her flat. She'd even slipped the new secondhand paperback she'd picked up in the charity shop into her bag by way of a reward. As she trudged though, not even the thought of a new novel to lose herself in was much comfort.

Her spirits lifted when the bright neon sign of the laundrette came into view. As if sensing her optimism, the wind threw in another gust, showering her face and everything south of her jacket with a fresh wave of icy little needles that darted through her jeans to sting her already freezing legs. She reached the door of the laundrette and heaved her less than substantial weight against it. There was a momentary rush of comforting warm air before a fraction of a second later someone slammed into her.

'Oh, I'm so sorry! You okay?' the woman asked, the stress in her voice obvious. A bit taller than Lilly, she had thick, wavy dark hair that was hanging in sodden tails around her shoulders. A few long strands were stuck to her cheeks and had she not looked so impressively bedraggled she might have been beautiful. Like an artist's muse, Lilly thought, realising a fraction of a second too late that her guard was down, just before she felt the other woman's emotion hit her in the chest – fear and panic all mixed together like a bag of drowning puppies. Before waiting for an answer, the woman ploughed on, speaking at a million miles an hour, her eyes fixed on Lilly. 'It's my dog. Have you seen a springer spaniel?

Her name is Hope. I think the wind blew the back gate open and there must have been a noise or something and she has zero road sense and I just have to find her, she'll be so scared on her own, she doesn't like the wind, or the dark for that matter,' she said, looking and sounding so desperate that it almost broke Lilly's heart.

'I'm sorry, no. No, I haven't.'

Before Lilly could say any more, she mumbled, 'Okay, thanks, sorry,' and ran off back down the hill, her long skirt clinging to her legs like a cold wet blanket.

Lilly had always loved animals, but she learned the hard way not to get attached. One of her earliest memories was of seeing her father shoot a calf behind the cowshed. His mother had fought with everything she had to save him. Penned in, she had kicked and charged and bellowed in rage and despair but had earned herself nothing but a ruined eye from the butt of her father's gun. Then he had calmly dragged her beautiful newborn boy away from her. The heifer grieved for days and was so aggressive that Lilly's father ended up shooting her too. That's how life was for him – something to be bought, sold and ended on a whim. Lilly hated him for it.

Lilly dumped her bags in the back corner where she hoped they'd be safe, then went out into the rain. Continuing back up the hill, she headed for the park, which she hoped might be a familiar stomping ground for a lost dog. The wide green expanses were understandably deserted. Reasoning that a dog with any sense would probably try to find some shelter, she opted for the path into the little copse. The trees creaked ominously above her as the wind lashed at them, tearing loose twigs and some more substantial branches and hurling them to the ground. That was the other thing besides the weather that was weird at the moment, Lilly noticed. Some trees were in leaf as they should be by now, but others were bare. There should have been a carpet of bluebells under the trees, but they had bloomed in January this year and the daffodils didn't bloom at all. It felt to Lilly as if nature herself was falling apart.

After ten minutes of searching, her boots caked in mud and her feet soaked, Lilly considered giving up. She didn't know what had drawn her to the park in the first place, surely it would have been the first place her owner would have looked anyway. Another great gust sent a flurry of twigs and leaves flying in her direction. As she turned to avoid it, a movement caught her eye. Standing about ten feet away, half hidden in a rhododendron bush and peering nervously at her, was a dog. Lilly almost squealed in delight, but stopped herself just in time. She tried calling her name, but she was so cold it came out more like a shiver. Poor Hope must be freezing too. From the look of her she was soaked to the skin.

Lilly called again, her voice stronger with a little concentration, 'Hope.' After a moment's hesitation, the dog crept forward and gave a nervous little wag. Lilly crouched down slowly, moving her body and her head so that she wasn't staring at her face on, but at an angle. Out of the corner of her eye Lilly was sure she saw Hope soften ever so slightly. She called her again and cursed herself for not being the type to carry biscuits in her pockets.

A fresh howl of wind whipped through the trees, slamming another wall of rain into Lilly's back. Hope was rooted to the spot, obviously unsure of what to do. Lilly quickly ran through the options in her head. Leaving the park to try and find the woman from the laundrette was too risky, she might run off again and it would be completely dark soon. She could call the local police to see if she'd been reported missing. Then she remembered that her mobile was charging on her desk.

'Come on, sweet girl. Come on, Hope, let's get you home to your mum,' Lilly said, hoping she sounded more optimistic than she felt. Then she saw it. Lying just a few feet away was a tennis ball. It was so filthy it was almost the same colour as the mud. She picked it up slowly and watched as Hope's ears picked up. Giving is a squeeze to test it for bounce, to Hope's obvious delight it emitted a high-pitched slightly gurgling squeak. The combination of the unexpected noise and the sight of a now bouncing springer spaniel hurtling towards her unsteadied Lilly and she plopped unceremoniously onto the sodden ground. The rain wasted no time in penetrating what little dry fabric was left of her jeans, but she didn't care. Hope was bouncing around her, her eyes fixated on the ball like some crack addict spotting a free fix – and at least there was nobody around to witness her little tumble.

It took a full ten minutes of fetch in the rain for Hope to relax enough for Lilly to approach her. As long as Lilly had the ball, she had Hope's full and undivided attention, so taking a chance, Lilly slipped her hand in her collar. Lilly smiled when, far from pulling away, Hope offered her paw instead. 'You're a lovely girl, Hope,' she said gently. After taking off her belt, Lilly slipped it over Hope's head, wiggled two fingers into the gap to make sure that it wasn't too tight and wound the other end securely around her frozen hand.

'Come on, my love. Let's get you home,' she said, heading back towards the high street and hoping that her jeans didn't end up around her ankles.

As they approached the newsagents, Lilly saw the owner pulling down the shutters for the evening. He was a pleasant man, lean and fit-looking even though he must be in his sixties.

'Hope! You're found!' he said happily, crouching down to ruffle her head, apparently oblivious to the stench of soaking wet dog and not caring about the thick coating of fur clinging to his fingers. 'I was just heading out to look for her,' he said to Lilly, smiling broadly, 'where did you find her?'

'She was in the park, hiding in the trees,' Lilly said, suddenly self-conscious of what a state she must look.

'Looks like she gave you the runaround,' he said, his bushy eyebrows flicking momentarily skywards as a broad grin spread over his face.

'She did indeed. But thankfully I found a magic tennis ball. Do you know where she lives?'

'She's Storm's little one,' he said as if everyone would know who Storm was. When Lilly didn't reply he added, 'Cordelia's café – just down the hill on the left. She'll be so relieved. I saw her just five minutes ago – she was heading home to call all the local vets and the dog warden in case someone had picked her up.'

'That's great, thanks. I'll take her straight home then.'

'Top girl. I'm Ash, by the way,' he said.

'Lilly,' she said shyly, 'I'm Lilly Jones.'

Hope started to pull on her makeshift lead the moment she caught sight of Cordelia's, a smart double-fronted shop with its central door dividing café from bookshop. Lilly wondered why she'd not noticed it before, but as she never ate out and didn't have a budget that would stretch to new books, she supposed it wasn't surprising.

The shop was in darkness so after a moment's hesitation, Lilly buzzed the intercom. She heard a crackle at the other end and began to speak, but the wind was howling so hard she could barely hear her own voice as the words were whipped from her lips and carried off down the hill. She was about to buzz again when she saw the woman who had bumped into her at the laundrette hurrying through the darkened café to open the door.

Hope let out an excited whine and began jumping up at

the glass door. In seconds, the door was open and, the woman who Lilly guessed must be Storm was on her knees under a wriggling, wagging, whining bundle of wet fur that seemed obsessed with licking every inch of her delighted face.

'Oh, my baby girl! Where did you go to? Mamma was so worried about you,' she said as Hope continued her ecstatic greeting. Lilly grinned. It was beautiful and she found herself a little choked by the scene.

'Oh, I'm so sorry, come in! Please, come in,' Storm said to Lilly, who was standing in the doorway.

'It's okay, really. I should get going,' Lilly said, longing to get out of her wet clothes and not relishing the walk home, especially as she'd need to collect her still dirty laundry on the way and make the trip again tomorrow.

'Going? No, please, you're soaked to the skin. Come in and let me at least give you something dry to put on. You have no idea what you've done for me in bringing my baby home. Please, it's the absolute least I can do.' Her voice was strong, authoritative, but her tone was almost pleading. There was no way Lilly could say no now and the thought of something dry against her freezing skin was particularly appealing as her teeth were in danger of chattering.

Half an hour later Lilly was sitting on a floor cushion in front of a roaring log burner wearing a soft pair of jogging bottoms that were so big she had to tie the drawstring in a double bow to keep them around her middle.

According to the label, Storm was only a size twelve, but as Lilly was, she suspected, somewhere south of an eight, she was drowning in fabric. Not that she minded one bit. It was soft and warm and smelled of something wonderful – freesias perhaps. At Storm's insistence, she was also wearing a thick pair of pale pink woolly socks and a soft chunky white sweatshirt with the word 'Peace' in grey letters across the chest.

Hope was stretched out in front of Lilly on the rug, her feet twitching sporadically. Every now and again her lip quivered and Lilly wondered what she was dreaming about. She certainly seemed none the worse for her ordeal. While she was changing out of her wet things in the bathroom, she could hear Storm laughing as she chased the dog around the living room. 'Come here, you're soaking wet, you daft dog.' Next had come the sound of what must have been a biscuit jar being rattled and then that of a hairdryer, so Lilly assumed that the bribery had worked.

Storm appeared with a tray. On it there were two huge mugs: herbal tea for her and coffee for Lilly along with a plate of flapjacks. She had heard what she sincerely hoped was a coffee grinder a little while ago and her nose had been getting drunk on the smell of a rich roast for the last five minutes. While she had never been able to muster the energy to get excited about food, coffee was her weak spot.

Hope's head jerked up the minute the tray made contact with the coffee table. Her nose working overtime, she looked hopefully at Storm who shook her head but said nothing. Hope huffed, turned in a circle and laid back down.

'You obviously have a very strong bond,' Lilly said, watching Hope drift back into her twitchy slumber.

'That we do,' Storm said, her eyes following Lilly's to rest on the dog.

'Where did you get her?' Lilly asked, feeling, unusually for her, the need to make conversation.

Storm paused just long enough to make her wonder why the subject is a sore one before she said, 'My husband – my late husband, found her at a rescue centre. Someone had abandoned her on a dual carriageway of all places, poor baby. Nick saw her story on the website, and he said having a dog to look after would make sure I left the house on a daily basis.'

Although she was smiling the sadness in it brought a lump to Lilly's throat and her eyes pricked with tears. It felt like being pulled out to sea by a rip tide and she thought that the force of the emotion might drown her. First Jack and now Storm – Lilly wondered whether she was less adept at shielding herself than she had thought, or maybe the strength of this one had just crept in behind her defences to wallop her.

'I'd better get going,' she said, jumping up.

'But you've not had your coffee yet,' Storm said and she looked so genuinely disappointed that Lilly could kick herself. The thing was, Lilly didn't want to leave. The flat was so homely, so warm and welcoming that she felt that she could curl up next to Hope on the rug and sleep for a week.

'Oh yes,' she said, feeling suddenly silly and as she fumbled for an explanation for her behaviour. 'I don't want to impose, and you've been so kind, and I can't be too late because I'm packing and ...' she faltered and reached for a piece of flapjack because it was something to put in her mouth instead of her foot.

'Holiday?' Storm asked brightly, all but the merest trace of sadness now hidden.

Lilly shook her head; she'd never had a holiday. 'I wish,' she said. 'No, my flat is on the Old Road by the river. The letter said something about unsustainable risks due to the rising ground water or something, but it essentially means that they've condemned it.'

When she looked up, Storm was smiling at her. It was a broad, generous smile that lit up her face and made her grey eyes sparkle. Without a word she got up and walked to the desk by the window. She picked up a sheet of paper off the printer, folded it and then put it in the pocket of her cardigan. 'Do you want to see something? You might like this,' she said, walking back to the front door of the flat and out onto the long first floor landing.

Instead of heading back down to the shop, Lilly followed Storm along the corridor to another staircase at the back of the property. They climbed up a steep flight of stairs and emerged on a small landing. Opening the door Storm flicked on the light to reveal, not a dusty attic as Lilly had been expecting, but a large airy flat. The walls were painted a soft white and the floors were honey-coloured polished wood boards. The corner on the left was given over to a small but modern kitchen with handleless cupboards and a breakfast bar which served as a room divider and eating space.

There was an easy chair and footstool by the window, which, Lilly thought, would be the perfect spot for curling up with a book and a coffee. A white voile curtain was hitched back on one side of the window and when her eye travelled upwards, she noticed the row of skylights, dark now against the night, but it was easy to imagine how they would flood the place with light at daybreak.

Opposite the kitchen was an exposed brick chimney breast, with a fat-bellied white enamelled log burner in the hearth and a large, old but comfortable-looking sofa in front of it. Occupying almost the entire width of the chimney breast itself was a huge painting of a rearing grey stallion. He stood proud and fierce, front legs bent, ready to defend himself or his herd as a grey tempest swirled in the background. It was mesmerising and it took her a few seconds to realise that Storm was speaking to her.

'Pardon? Sorry, I was miles away,' she managed.

'Yes, he tends to have that effect on people.' Storm smiled. 'The bathroom is through there to the right – it's only titchy but there's a shower and a bath. And to the left is the bedroom.' Lilly followed her lead, still finding it hard to tear her eyes away from the incredible painting. She heard Storm laugh. 'So this is where you've been hiding, you little tinker!' Once in the bedroom Lilly saw a huge long-haired ginger cat stretched out on the crisp white bedspread. Lying on his back, he seemed to be taking none of Storm's remonstrative tone to heart and, as she leaned down to tickle him, he yawned in her face displaying an impressive set of needle-sharp teeth. On seeing Lilly he sprang to his paws and padded over to the edge of the bed so that he could push his head into her outstretched hand. Lilly knelt down so that she could get a better look at him.

'He's very particular about who he likes,' Storm began, then laughed out loud when the cat jumped onto Lilly's shoulder.

'I was about to say I think you've been approved, but that would be stating the bloody obvious,' Storm said, laughing. 'Good grief, Anc, you've barely been introduced! Lilly, meet Anchor, Anc, meet Lilly.'

Lilly couldn't help but laugh, but she was also delighted. He was possibly the biggest cat she had ever seen. He wasn't fat, just big. His feet were twice the size of a normal moggy's and he weighed a fair bit too. He looked almost lynx-like, with little tufts of hair on the tips of each ear. After discovering that her shoulder was barely big enough to support even one of his long legs, he eventually settled for hanging his head and front paws over her shoulder while she supported the rest of his sizeable form with her arm. She used her other hand to scratch his head and when she stopped, he butted his head gently into her chin, punctuating a near-deafening purr with little chirrups of encouragement.

'Please, don't feel you have to put up with him, he's not got it into his little butter brain that not everyone likes cats and even those that do seldom want to wear one like a pirate's parrot,' Storm said tickling his ear.

'Oh, he's absolutely fine. I can't remember ever having a cuddle this good,' Lilly said, holding him a little closer and redoubling her efforts on the head scratching. The penny dropping, she said, 'Hope and Anchor?'

Storm laughed and reached over to tickle his ears. 'My husband's favourite pub at uni and so the names he'd chosen for our future pets. Anc turned up first as a stray and was duly christened and then when he found madam downstairs …' She trailed off, her voice sad until she changed the subject. 'So, not much to say in here, bed, wardrobe, bedside table. The two windows make it lovely and bright in the mornings. I suppose not great if you like to sleep in, but nothing a blackout blind wouldn't fix.' Pulling the piece of paper out of her cardigan pocket, Storm unfolded it and held it up for Lilly to see. 'I was planning on putting this ad in the shop window tomorrow morning. To be honest, I've no idea why because I've not let the flat out before, except to our friend Jerry years ago, but I think that's just become clear to me.'

Lilly was about to say something about not being able to afford somewhere this nice when she saw that the rent was just twenty pounds more a month than what she was currently paying. She stared at the paper, unable to say a word for a moment. She must have stopped scratching Anchor because his head butting her chin snapped her out of her daze. 'I love it, but …' she said.

'Don't feel you have to say yes right away. If you want to take some time to think about it, talk it over with a significant other, then I'll not advertise it until you've made up your mind either way,' Storm said lightly. 'Sorry, I just sprung this on you – I didn't even ask if you'd already found somewhere.'

What am I doing dithering? Lilly thought. 'I don't need to

think about it. Yes, please, I'd love to live here,' she said so quickly that the words practically sprinted out of her mouth.

'Excellent,' Storm said, her eyes creasing to accompany her broad smile. 'That's settled then. It's the usual month as deposit and month in advance, but you can move in whenever you want. Do you have to give notice at your old place?'

'I don't, but I'll need a few days to sort out references and stuff,' Lilly said, hugging Anchor all the tighter at the thought that she'd soon be living in such an amazing space.

Storm laughed and, reaching over to tickle the cat under the chin, said, 'Don't worry about that, I think I have all the references I need.'

CHAPTER 13

Storm had insisted on driving Lilly and her recovered laundry home and while she told herself that it would probably be best to tell Jack her news in the morning, she'd been home just a few minutes when excitement got the better of her. She'd barely seen him over the past week. When he had made an appearance, he'd seemed distracted and full of excuses to leave again which she read as his reluctance to tell her the other thing he'd alluded to. Well, she thought, nothing could spoil her good mood tonight, so after telling him her good news, she'd make him spill the beans on whatever past life thing he hadn't yet confided.

While she could have called him in her head, she always preferred to say his name out loud.

'Jack …'

The knock at the door came a second later. Lilly yanked it open. 'Guess what?' she said even before he'd taken a step into the flat.

'Someone's happy,' Jack said, looking genuinely pleased. 'I dunno Lil, what?'

'I've found an amazing new flat. Complete coincidence

which I'll tell you about in a bit, but oh Jack, it's just perfect. It's an attic flat and halfway up the hill on the high street so no more flood alerts and there's this cat.' She stopped mid-sentence and stared at him. 'What?'

'It sounds amazing Lil. Tell me about the cat.'

She studied him closely, trying to read in his face whatever it was that she knew with absolute certainty he was hiding from her. He wouldn't meet her eye.

'Tell me,' she said, all trace of excitement extinguished.

'Tell you what?' he asked, but she knew that he was stalling for time.

Lilly felt her skin prickle with gooseflesh, her mouth was suddenly dry and her stomach had begun twisting itself into a fearful knot. Wrapping her arms around herself, she said, 'Three nights ago you tell me that I'm remembering my past lives. Then when I ask you why, you say I'm not going to like the answer and admittedly, I bottle it. Then ...' she hesitated, 'Then,' she started again, 'I wake in the small hours and you're crying and—' she stopped, because the look on his face was only one step away from horror-struck. The last thing she wanted was for him to disappear on her, so holding his arm gently, she said, 'If this has to do with what I didn't want you to tell me the other night, then I want to know. Right now. We don't do secrets, Jack. Tell me.'

Seconds ticked past and, not having any more words left, Lilly held his arm gently and hoped for the best. Just as the silence started to become uncomfortable, his shoulders dropped. Walking to the armchair, he slumped down heavily, folding himself forward and holding his head in his hands. When he looked up his eyes were full of tears. Lilly rushed over to kneel next to him. 'What is it?' she asked, fear swelling in her belly. Fat tears slid silently down his cheeks and she wondered how many times he'd cried like this. For a split second she felt the weight of his pain and anguish and knew with certainty that tears were something horribly familiar to Jack. The sensation was short-lived as his defences against her empathy kicked back in. How had she not known? How could he be holding on to so much pain without her realising? It made her feel like the most selfish person in the world.

Jack shook his head. 'Not yet – you said you weren't ready yet,' he said, sniffing and getting up to pace around the small space. Lilly stayed where she was on the floor for a moment, her own words on the night he agreed to tell her about the Remembering – *no, don't tell me, not yet* – coming back to haunt her. Despite her creeping feeling of dread, she could no longer put off hearing what he had to say.

'I'm ready now,' she said, her voice coming out far quieter than she'd intended, so she repeated herself to make sure he'd heard her.

He stopped pacing and looked at her. 'You need to be sure, Lil. Absolutely one hundred per cent certain. I'm not sure how you're going to react if I'm honest.' Jack's voice cracked on the last sentence and he had to clear his throat to regain his composure.

Her heart sped up so quickly that she was sure he could hear it pounding against her ribs. She wasn't ready for bad news, she was still revelling in her luck at finding the new flat, but she also knew that, whatever it was, she had to know.

Jack asked her three more times if she was definitely sure before sinking back down into the armchair. Lilly sat on the bed opposite, hugging her knees to her chest, waiting. She felt a bit like a naughty child who was about to hear how many nights she'd be grounded for. After a few false starts where the words seemed to get tangled around his teeth, he took a deep breath and began again.

'You know about the Remembering,' he said matter-of-factly, 'all of your past lives coming back to you in dreams.' She nodded, not wanting to interrupt the flow now that he'd got started. 'What you don't know is that the Remembering only happens once. Which I suppose stands to reason or we'd be hearing everyone going on about it, wouldn't we?' He tried for lightness, but it fell flat. She just nodded in what she hoped was an encouraging way, but in truth, she was already confused.

'Do you understand?' he asked, but she didn't so she shook her head, feeling a bit stupid. 'What I mean is ...' He got up and raked his hands through his hair as he paced. 'What I mean is that ... that ...' His next words came out like bolting horses through a barn door. 'The Remembering only happens during your very last life, Lil.'

Everything went still for a moment while the words found their way to her and slowly began to sink in.

'You're a Last. That's what we call humans on their last incarnation. It's why you can see me and it's why you're remembering all of your old lives now – it's so that you can reflect and review them all. Not everyone chooses to be an incarnate Last, some review things in the afterlife, but you – you chose to do it here.' He sat down again, his eyes on the floor as he wrung at his hands.

To her surprise she found that her overwhelming emotion was relief. She didn't know what exactly she had been expecting, but this wasn't bad at all. If her past lives were anything to go by then she hardly had the best track record. If her next life would have been anything like the others, or indeed anything like her current one, then she wouldn't be missing out; in fact, she'd be saving herself from a bucketload of pain. She smiled, but Jack didn't.

'What happens after your last life though?' she asked, and Jack snapped his head up to look at her.

'We go back to the forest,' he said, a faint smile on his lips and that unnameable look in his eyes again.

'That's real? I mean, that's the afterlife?' Lilly felt her chest swell in the knowledge that the happy place she'd retreated to in her head since she was a child was real, and the last of her apprehension drained away. If Jack thought she was going to be upset about this then he'd clearly got the whole thing wrong. It was brilliant news.

Jack nodded. 'It's the before, after and in-between-lives place,' he said, smiling, but it was a sad, wistful smile.

She got up, feeling the need to celebrate with at least a coffee. She put the kettle on and Jack watched her, saying nothing. 'Well, I'm glad I know,' she said, spooning instant coffee into her favourite mug. 'I mean, I suppose it puts life into a whole new perspective. No more hoping for the next life to be better than this one … no more putting off tomorrow what you can do today and all that.' She felt a rare bubble of excitement growing in her chest. 'I've always put things off, as you know, but I shouldn't. Now that I've got somewhere new to live, maybe we could think about a holiday. I've never had a holiday. Or now I'm better at shielding, I could look into art classes or something.' She was talking a mile a minute but coupled with the evening's events, she couldn't hide her excitement. She'd spent the last few days worrying that existence was just one miserable life after another, but she was wrong.

'Lilly!' Jack all but shouted at her, sounding like an exasperated teacher. She stared at him, startled, but he said nothing for a few seconds. 'You can't do any of that. I'm sorry, but the Remembering …' He groaned and holding his head in his hands, began to pace again.

'What about it?' she snapped as cold tendrils of fear snaked back up her spine.

'The Remembering begins a year and a day before,' he paused, 'before we go home for good.'

It took a few moments to process his words, but then she felt the energy drain out of her legs as the enormity of what he'd just said sank in. 'What? You mean, before I … die?' The last word took effort, like it was too big to fit in her mouth.

'That's a human word, Lil, and yes, technically I suppose it's true, but we get to go home, to be eternal again and live happily, peacefully in a realm without pain and death and fear and suffering and everything that makes this world so bloody hideous. It's so beautiful, Lil, you wait and see, it's—'

She cut him off because one thought was now blocking out everything else and it felt like a swarm of angry hornets screaming in her head.

'You're telling me I'm going to die in what, three months, and you're only now getting around to letting me know?' she shouted, her voice so shrill that she hardly recognised it.

'That's not fair. You said you didn't want to know. I had to wait for you to be ready. There are rules, Lil, you know that.' His voice was pleading but she was already past hearing him.

'How? How will I die?' she asked sharply, noticing with incredulity how ridiculous the sentence sounded to her own ears.

'I don't know. No one ever knows, but it would have been what you decided before you got here – how much time you wanted, when you wanted to leave. This was your decision, Lil, no one else's.'

'I'll just change my bloody mind then,' she said, shouting and slamming down her mug onto the counter with such force that the bottom shattered and sent shards of china skitting across the worktop.

'It doesn't work like that, Lil,' Jack said feebly, walking

towards her, his palms outstretched at his sides. 'Lil, I'm so …'

'No!' she said putting up her hands to stop him mid-stride. 'Not this time, Jack. I'm sorry. "Let's hug" won't cut it. You've known for nine long months that I'm living my last life, maybe even longer, who knows. Now you effectively hand me a fucking death sentence and tell me there's nothing I can do about it. Get out!' She all but growled the last two words. Then, because she knew it would hurt him, she added, 'Jack, I order you to leave.'

'What?' Jack shot her an incredulous look.

'You know the rules, Jack, you invented them,' she snapped but instantly regretted it.

'You're really ordering me to leave?' he asked, his voice shaking. 'But you've never—'

She didn't let him finish. 'There's a first time for everything,' she said glancing at him. The hurt looked to be etched onto his face and Lilly wanted to take her words and stuff them back into her mouth. But it was too late. She looked up at the ceiling, trying to quell the tears that were pooling in her eyes. When she looked back he was gone, and it was then that she collapsed onto the kitchen floor and dry-retched between sobs that felt vicious enough to kill her.

CHAPTER 14

*I*n the seventeen long years she'd been involved, Margot could count the number of face-to-face High Council meetings on one hand. The last had been three years ago when she had been elected to the position she now held as their official seer, her predecessor's tenure having come to an abrupt and, she knew, violent end. She shuddered at the thought and the choices that had brought her here.

Margot had never been a saint; she was the first to admit that. In her younger days she too had craved power, success and recognition. She knew she was special and saw nothing wrong in exploiting her talents, magical or spiritual, in the same way that others might have traded off their musical ability or athletic prowess for financial gain, but she had never thought of herself as a bad person. She'd gone a little wild after her divorce, ploughing through her very generous settlement from her ex-husband, partying hard and never stopping long enough to worry about who she might have been hurting along the way. It had all come to an abrupt halt though when, out of the blue, she'd met Storm.

Storm, the only child of possibly the most self-obsessed,

vacuous couple on the London party scene, had been twelve when Margot first met her. Margot had never seen a child look quite so lost before and it broke her heart. She hadn't particularly liked Clemmie and Harry and had only agreed to dinner as a favour to a mutual friend who had described them as 'well-connected'. As Margot quickly discovered, they were indeed well-connected, but that was because they surrounded themselves with interesting people in a vain attempt to mask the fact that they were as dull as dirt themselves. In the years that she knew them, they became infamous for their wild parties, or white-outs as they were called, thanks to the liberal amounts of illegal powder favoured by the hosts and hangers-on.

Margot tolerated the couple for years in the end because it had been Storm who had opened the door that first evening, a little witch who saw spirits and had no one else to reassure her that she wasn't losing her mind. While Margot had never seen herself as a teacher or indeed a mother, she had become both, and she couldn't have been happier.

That of course had been her weakness, and in the end they had used it against her – forced her to choose. Margot closed her eyes, shuttering the memories, as she felt the first pinpricks of tears.

'Where do you want dropping, luv?' the cabbie asked, snapping Margot back to the present.

'Here will be fine,' she said, sliding a twenty-pound note through the glass divider and exiting the moment the cab stopped. She'd walk the rest of the way just in case. Every member of the High Council was issued with some sort of high-tech signal scrambler to allow them to pass surveillance cameras unnoticed, but she only had their word that it actually worked. Preferring to trust in her own ways, she flicked on a glamour, relaxing ever so slightly as she felt the familiarity of her own magic slip around her. If anyone was watching her, they'd see a fat teenage boy in a tracksuit.

When she arrived at the building, a huge glass and steel monstrosity with all the softness of a razor blade, she released her disguise and followed the signs to the delivery bays at the back as instructed. She recognised Tara immediately, standing in front of an open service door. Of all the security detail, Margot considered Tara to be the most formidable. She looked more like an Instagram fitness model than a bodyguard, but she supposed that her looks often proved to be an effective weapon. Humans are programmed to associate beauty with kindness, but Tara was anything but kind. Margot shuddered at a memory of an incident that had given her nightmares for months. The problem with being a seer was often having to see things that no sane non-psychopath ever should. The memory of it now strained like a rabid beast on the end of a chain. Forcibly pushing it out of her mind, she nodded at Tara and was then ushered up a flight of concrete stairs by a second member of the detail.

After following the guard through a maze of bare pipe-lined corridors, she was eventually deposited in a green room attached to a small auditorium. She supposed it was where the CEO of the building did his shareholder and media briefings. Nothing so public for today's gathering, she thought wryly. The picture of Tara, hunting knife still in her hand, grinning like a kid on Christmas morning as she stood over the ruined man barged its way into her mind. Margot knew what came next and she did not want to see it again, even in memory, so she scanned the room for distraction. It arrived on cue in the form of Dennis Taylor. A vile, pompous little man, who was almost as wide as he was tall, he at least gave her something else to focus on.

Sir Dennis Taylor was the CEO of a British pharmaceutical company and probably the longest-serving member of the council, a fact that, along with his proper title, he never missed an opportunity to remind the other members of. When he wasn't riding that particular hobby horse, he was telling a version of the 'council house lad did good' story, painting himself as the Billy Elliot of business, working his fingers to the bone to better himself and build an empire dedicated to eradicating human suffering.

Conveniently missed out of his stories were the allegations of fraud, theft of intellectual property, sexual assault in the workplace and corrupt practices. Although she hadn't heard it from a living source, Margot had also been visited more than once by the spirits of unfortunate participants in his company's botched clinical trials – mostly African people from small, poor villages who signed consent forms in a language that wasn't their own and paid for their hope with their lives. How their deaths had been covered up Margot had no idea, but the memory made her blood boil every time she set eyes on the hideous little man.

The High Council was made up of eight members, though they represented an elite group of close to three thousand. She saw all but the chair, Charles Benedict-Hatman, file into the room over the next ten minutes. Though they came together like this rarely, they sometimes had to meet on a one-to-one basis. They had secure online communications and, in a world where secrecy and anonymity were paramount, they also communicated via post. In a digital world it sometimes felt like an absurdity, but it had kept the organisation's secrets for decades.

The council of eight was, unsurprisingly Margot thought scornfully, made up of six men and two women. The other woman, Cynthia Price, who was tapping away on a laptop at the back of the room, was a senior civil servant in the US government. She was as unremarkable-looking as Margot was striking. In her mid to late fifties, she was slightly overweight, wore a beige skirt suit and sensible low-heeled court shoes, her greying afro hair close cropped. There was absolutely nothing about her that caught the eye, which was probably deliberate for one of the most powerful and influential women in Washington, perhaps the world. Installed by the council thirty-five years before, Cynthia was able to exercise power in almost any area of government. From tax to agriculture to defence to healthcare, when the council asked for her intervention to pursue a particular cause, Cynthia always delivered. Margot knew better than to ask how she achieved the results.

Scanning the room Margot saw Zak Bannerman, internet billionaire and global philanthropist. He of course was a familiar face the world over thanks to the tireless efforts of an army of PR experts. The ageing teenager was lounged on one of the leather chairs, skinny white ankles gaping above his Converse. Martin Flynn-Rivers, their resident historian, and Kenneth Okorie stood politely as Zak bragged loudly about the new levels of surveillance and mapping achieved through voice activated interfaces.

'I'm not shitting you man. You tell me the name of your neighbour or your best friend, give me his address or mobile number and I'll tell you not just what he had for breakfast, but what he and his little woman talked about over their granola. I can tell you how overdrawn he is, how many hours he spends watching porn and what his latest prostate exam showed up,' Zak said smugly, his words carrying around the room. 'And that's not even the best bit.'

Martin and Kenneth spotted Margot at the same time, but Ken was quicker off the mark. He excused himself and headed in her direction.

'Ken darling,' Margot said, standing to her full height to make clear that his customary greeting of a kiss to both cheeks would not be welcome. She sometimes allowed it, just to see him stretch – he was a good three inches shorter than her – but she wasn't in the mood today.

He smiled broadly, his eyes twinkling. Despite his diminutive stature and age, he was considerably more attractive than he should have been. He had an innate charm and made everyone from the check-in clerk to the CEO feel like he was genuinely hanging on their every word. Margot guessed that it was that gift that had helped him make his fortune in the oil business – and enemies enough to make sure he could never safely return home to Angola.

'Always a delight to see you Margot,' he said, then lowering his voice, 'you arrived just in time too – I think Zak was about to tell us about his,' he mimed quote marks in the air, 'longevity studies.'

Margot shuddered. 'I'm very glad to have rescued you from that. Believe me, you don't want to know. Bloody hideous business. How's the oil business?'

Ken shrugged. 'Oh, about as popular as pestilence as usual. I am sure they'll try and blame us for the sepsis thing soon,' he chuckled, 'but we had a long-term plan and plastics is still booming, so it is not all bad news.'

Margot was about to reply when Marcus van de Meijer swept into the room. He reminded Margot of a crane, beady-eyed, always watching and ever ready to spear the unsuspecting.

'Here comes the banker,' Margot said carefully. Kenneth stifled a laugh. 'Which of course means that our esteemed leader won't be far behind him. Probably just waiting in the wings for Marcus' spit to dry on his loafers.'

Ken snorted as he tried to suppress another laugh, turning it into a hearty cough when Marcus strode in their direction. Margot allowed herself a small smile behind the glamour. Little pleasures and all that.

'Nasty cough you have, Kenneth,' Marcus said, arching his

eyebrow, 'I hope it's not a left-over from the pandemic? We nearly lost you then, did we not?'

Coming from anyone else the concern might have been welcome, but Margot knew this game of old. Oh, how she wished they'd all just pick a weapon and battle it out – she was so sick of this continual pissing competition between the other members of the council.

Kenneth flashed a smile, but his eyes were cold. 'Why Marcus, I am touched by your concern but that is very old news indeed. I could tell you many more stories about how I've outsmarted the Grim Reaper in the years since.'

Whatever Marcus was about to say in reply was lost, because at that moment, their chair, Charles Benedict-Hatman, bounced into the room. Had there been a book entitled 'How to Look Like an Advertising Man', Charles might well have written it. Despite being a little way north of fifty, he wore the creative uniform of a city adman with the gall of a twenty-year-old – the T-shirt under the expensive but too-bright-blue suit jacket, the coloured socks visible thanks to oh-so-trendy, slightly too short in the leg designer jeans and, of course, the chunky specs that told the world he was not only cool, but clever and creative to boot.

While Margot would have argued over cool – to her he always looked faintly ridiculous – there was absolutely no denying that he was clever. That man really could sell anything to anyone, she thought with disdain. The agency, gifted to him among other assets by his aristocratic father, had flourished under his leadership and had a client book that read like the Who's Who of consumer brands. Catch him after a few drinks and he'd cheerfully describe his work as 'peddling crap to stupid chavs', but in recent years he'd turned his considerable talents to influencing of a different kind. Trump and Brexit were triumphs he was smart enough not to crow about openly, especially now given the interstate war, but Margot knew the truth of the matter and it made her sick to her stomach.

He stood in the doorway, grinning widely at them and showing off his overly whitened teeth. 'Evening, chaps and chapesses,' he drawled, 'shall we?' He motioned for them to file into the auditorium, which they dutifully did.

When they'd all taken their seats in the front row, he remained on the small stage, ever the showman. 'Welcome,' he said, his plummy voice carrying around the room. 'It's been a while since we came together like this, but I took the decision to gather you all here in person because I feel that the gravity of the situation demands it.' He paused, waiting for the weight of his words to settle. 'I don't need to remind any of you of our shared purpose but indulge me a moment. The High Council exists for one reason and one reason alone – to support the natural evolution of mankind. Our predecessors discharged this sacred and vital duty for many hundreds of years before us and we owe them a huge debt of gratitude for every success that we and our esteemed members enjoy today.'

Margot worked hard to keep her face impassive and resisted the temptation to roll her eyes. Charles never missed an opportunity to deliver this little speech.

'Humanity has survived and thrived up to this point because of one thing: evolution. Darwin famously said, "It is not the strongest of the species that survives, but the one most adaptable to change." He was half right. Yes, it is about adaptability, but it is also about strength. If we are to survive as a species, if humanity is to even exist in a hundred years, we need to accept an unpalatable truth – only the strong must survive. Our population might be growing, but in many cases only because we are using medical science to overrule the natural order. We are weakened, not just by our sheer numbers, but by the quality of our gene pool.' He paused then for effect before continuing in the same practised tone. 'As leaders, we are often faced with seemingly impossible choices. We have reached a tipping point and, sadly, if we as a species are to survive at all, we must purge the world of the weak and begin again. This is the mission we all swore an oath to fulfil.' He fell silent, bowing his head for a few seconds before levelling his chin and scanning the faces in front of him, daring anyone to dissent. Dissent wasn't unheard of, but everyone knew that those who had crossed the ever-moving line had paid with their lives, often the lives of those they loved too.

'The work that our predecessors so diligently put in motion is coming to fruition and, like good stewards of the Earth, we must be ready for the harvest. To clear the fields so that new seeds can be grown.' Margot marvelled at how he'd not choked on that one given that the High Council had spent the best part of the last century plundering the Earth as thoroughly as possible to fund their plans. While the generous might have written off the first fifty years to the ignorance and hubris of their forebears, the last fifty years of destruction had been done in full knowledge of their consequences.

There had even been a meeting about it, a gathering of the eight members who in 1984 had made up the High Council. Their purpose had been to decide on the future of humanity. Even back then, the science was clearly predicting a catastrophic collapse in all life-sustaining ecosystems on their current trajectory of extraction and consumption. They were faced with a choice of either radically altering their business models or finding an alternative. They voted seven to one for the alternative, which also happened to be an extinction-level event for ninety-nine per cent of the human population. The one member to vote against had been killed in a random street mugging in San Diego three days later.

Margot looked at Charles's face now and realised that he actually probably believed it. Convenient delusion, it seemed, ate inconvenient truths for breakfast.

'Margot has confirmed that we are in the final stage, my friends. We'll run through the numbers and the projections shortly, but this is the beginning of the end and we are all truly blessed to be bearing witness to such a momentous point in human history – even if it will be from the safety of a Phoenix bunker.' He laughed as if he'd just delivered the most hilarious joke, then clapped his hands together excitedly. 'To work,' he said, his pale blue eyes almost dancing in delight.

Three hours later, their meeting concluded, Margot stood and smoothed down the front of her dress. Her eyes were still fixed on the last slide in the presentation, which was projected onto the enormous screen at the back of the stage. A digital clock, it displayed the weeks, days, hours, minutes, and seconds before the final collapse. Terrifying as that was, what had caught her eye was the graph beneath. Charles had gone to great lengths to explain to them that this was a live data reading showing the Earth's base energy frequency. It looked a little like a seismology readout, an expanding line graph building to the right of the screen as the seconds ticked by above, the trend of the line sinking incrementally lower. Since she'd been watching it, Margot had noticed that every now and again there would be a dramatic fall, the line shooting straight downwards for what could only be a second, before resuming its slow and steady descent. Being a witch had many advantages and, when she'd first noticed it, she'd automatically reached out into the ether to find the cause. It wasn't a foolproof spell, but what she hadn't been expecting was an immediate bounce back. That required powerful magic and as she was the only witch on the High Council, it meant that someone in this room had gone to the trouble of commissioning another witch to protect the data. Her sense of unease grew.

Seeing Charles cornered by Sir Dennis, she made a snap decision and scanned the room for Martin. He was leaning against the side wall of the auditorium being talked at by Cynthia, who, with the benefit of a being a step above him, was for once not craning her neck. Before Margot could think of an excuse to butt in, one of the security detail marched in, whispered in Cynthia's ear and then followed her out. The relief on Martin's pale face was almost palpable.

Margot got straight to the point. 'Martin, darling, I need to pick your considerable brains if I may please,' she said, making sure that her glamour showed a projection of herself with pupils that dilated on contact with Martin's muddy brown downturned eyes. She saw his cheeks flush and turned to the screen to save his blushes. 'These sudden lows,' she said, keeping her voice deliberately neutral as she pointed a perfectly French-manicured finger at the graph. She had considered the indirect approach, but conscious that they might be interrupted at any point, decided to put her theory out there. 'Am I right in thinking that we're eliminating high-vibration individuals to …' she paused and turned around to smile at him '… help matters along a bit?'

Martin's eyes widened; she saw him swallow and his eyes, wide and unblinking, flicked around the room.

Margot's heart was hammering but she smiled encouragingly and raised her eyebrows in a question. 'It is the logical approach,' she said casually, 'but I wanted to check because it wasn't in the briefing.'

Martin cleared his throat and, after another furtive check of the room, nodded. 'Cynthia and Charles thought it best to …' The words stuck in his throat and he coughed, tapping his fist into his chest. 'To, er, deal directly with troublesome individuals. We're too close now to worry about some do-gooder trying to raise the base frequency by organising mass prayer meetings, heal-the-world meditations or worse. It will just delay the inevitable for them all.'

'False hope is no hope at all,' said Charles calmly as he joined them. Margot watched as Martin's colour drained. 'And besides, we have a bloody schedule to keep to.'

Margot turned to look Charles squarely in the eye and asked lightly, 'And the reason I wasn't informed was?'

Charles smiled and placed his hand on her shoulder then slid it to the middle of her back, guiding her gently away. 'Margot, my dear, we omitted it from the briefing only because we knew it would raise questions for you. Eliminating magical people and those with high frequencies is just part of what we have to do. It's not ideal, of course it isn't, but none of this is. You and yours are always under our protection and while the loss of the others is hugely regrettable, there really is no other way of dealing with these sorts of threats when we discover them. You know as well as I do that if these people were to organise then they could put the whole mission in jeopardy.'

Margot intensified her glamour as she felt the colour drain from her own face. She nodded, then sighed in resignation. 'You're right. I wish you weren't, but what other choice is there?' she said, not needing to lie now because after all these years, she herself could see no other way either. 'You're being,' she searched for the right word, 'humane about it?'

Charles gave her a rubbery smile and had it not been for the glamour, he might have seen her recoil at the sight of the spittle on his fat, overly pink lower lip and the stink of stale coffee on his breath. 'My dear Margot, always worrying about the little lambs,' he said with a patronising laugh and a pat to the small of her back. 'Yes, we're making sure that they never see the knife coming, don't you worry.'

Margot felt her legs weaken and behind the glamour, she

swallowed down acid that had risen in her throat. To suspect it was one thing, but to hear him say it. To hear him so casually dismiss the murder of innocents. She should have been immune to it by now, but a heart could only harden by so much. She focused all of her energy on appearing calm. No glamour was strong enough to mask a faint or her bending double to throw up her lunch. Unless she wanted to meet the fate of the last seer, she had to remain calm and appear totally committed.

In the cab back to her hotel, Margot mentally ran through the list of friends and acquaintances who might be at risk. There were almost too many to count. Magical people were still a minority, and some were vastly more powerful than others, but globally they still counted in their tens of millions, all hiding in plain sight.

A great hiccupping sob escaped her and she might have lost it completely had it not been for the cabbie watching her, his eyes full of concern in the rear-view mirror. She was too exhausted to maintain the glamour so pretended to check her mobile while she pulled herself together. By the time they reached the hotel, she knew that there was nothing she could do. To warn them would mean exposing not just herself but Storm too, and that was a price she would never be willing to pay.

CHAPTER 15

*L*illy had heard people claim that moving house was meant to be one of the most stressful life events, but all things considered, she had bigger issues to think about.

Packing had taken her all of half an hour. The only pieces of furniture she owned were her drawing board, desk chair and lamp. The lack of a wardrobe meant that the few clothes she had were already in the suitcase they arrived in, to which she'd added towels and the few toiletries she owned. She'd had her bedding cleaned and then donated to the local homeless charity as she had a double bed in the new flat. As all the kitchen things belonged to the flat, that just left her laptop, art box, printer, a ream of copier printer, her portfolio case, a handful of novels and a small box of bits and bobs.

It looked a little forlorn, stacked neatly by the door. She had never been one for stuff. She didn't hanker after things the way other people seem to, she never had, but looking at her tiny pile of belongings, she was struck by how insubstantial it looked.

Her train of thought was broken by a knock at the door. As there were individual buzzers at the main front door, the only person who ever really knocked at her door was Jack. And he only ever did so when they'd fallen out, which was so rare she could count the occasions on one hand. It had been four days since she ordered him to leave and to her amazement he disappeared completely. On the rare occasions they'd argued in the past, he'd always shown up the next day looking sheepish and making her laugh until she had trouble remembering why she was mad at him. Then again, she'd never banished him before. And this, she reminded herself, was entirely different. She had barely slept since he told her. It wasn't every day that you discover that you were on borrowed time.

She had cried almost non-stop for days. For all the things she wouldn't get to do with her life, the places she wouldn't be able to see. When she realised that she didn't really have many plans anyway she felt even worse. She had read about the change curve before, how people, when they're given a terminal diagnosis, cycle through a whole host of emotions before eventually finding acceptance. All things considered she thought she had reached acceptance pretty quickly, but it wasn't like she had the luxury of time to linger in denial or anger. Jack had never lied to her, so she had no cause to doubt him now. As he said, this was her decision and the more she thought about that, the more she could almost feel the edges of a distant memory. As unpalatable as it was, she could sense the truth of it. She scolded herself too for being selfish. Jack was the only real family she'd ever had; he loved her like a sister, so this wouldn't be easy for him either.

When she opened the door, Jack was only just visible behind the huge bouquet of deep pink roses he was holding. 'I thought these might help on the forgiveness front,' he said, peering around them sheepishly.

Lilly stared at the flowers. Jack had never bought her flowers before. In fact, nobody had ever bought her flowers. She beamed at him. God, she'd missed him so much. A few days could feel like a lifetime when you're used to your best friend being at your side every day of your life. She flung her arms around him and hugged him. 'Thank you,' she said, noticing that he hesitated slightly before wrapping his free arm around her and hugging her back tightly.

'I'm so sorry, Lil,' he said quietly, still holding her. 'I should have told you sooner, but I just didn't know how to.'

Leaning away but keeping her arms around him, she said, 'You did what you had to, I see that now. I'm not ready, Jack, but if this is how it is then I suppose I can either spend the next three months fighting the inevitable or I can live what's left of my life as best I can.'

He leaned in and kissed the top of her head. As he did so he spotted the pile of belongings by the door. 'You're moving today? ' he asked, his eyebrows rising in surprise.

'Why wait?'

Jack sucked in a deep breath and then, after letting it out said, 'Good point.' She could hear the sadness in his voice. She guessed that they were both thinking the same thing. Why now? Why not two years ago when there was more time to enjoy it? She pushed the thought away forcibly. She couldn't think like that or it would just rob her of the happiness she was feeling in the moment.

After a moment's silence, he said, 'Right, let me go hire a van so we can get you moved.'

A couple of hours later, Lilly's meagre belongings were sitting piled in the middle of her new flat. Storm had left the keys in the bookshop for her. Lilly had blushed scarlet when Veronica had welcomed her with a hug, but had been immensely touched by the gesture. She had been disappointed not to see Storm, partly because she had wanted Jack to meet her, or see her at least.

The flat was just as amazing as she'd remembered it. If four walls could hug you these certainly seemed to. The wood burner was lit when they arrived; it might have been April but it was so cold outside it felt more like February, and the air was dancing with the gentle smell of woodsmoke and citrus, as if there was orange rind on the fire. Lilly had been right about the skylights – the whole room was flooded with light and in the summer it must be incredible. She was thrilled to see that the painting of the grey horse was still hanging in pride of place.

There were houseplants that she was sure weren't there when she first visited. A tall rubber tree in a large woven basket sat to the left of the hearth and there was a huge peace lily on the coffee table. Jack made a joke about it when we arrived, briefly morphing himself into a seventies hippy complete with tie-dyed T-shirt, flares and a headband as he made the very obvious 'peace, Lilly' joke while doing the whole V-sign thing.

Not knowing what to do first, Lilly decided to put the kettle on. On the kitchen counter under a glass dome was a large fat cake smothered in chocolate buttercream. Next to it was a pair of mugs, a cafetière and a bag of rich roast organic coffee. Propped up against the cake dome was a little card that read: 'Lilly, welcome to your new home! Relax, enjoy and make yourself comfortable. Oat milk in the fridge. If you need anything give me a knock. Storm x PS the cake is vegan.'

Lilly was a little overwhelmed. That someone, let alone a comparative stranger, would go so out of her way to make her feel so welcome brought a lump to her throat. Seeing the look on her face, Jack reached out to rub her arm, but as he did, they heard a strangled-sounding meow from the landing followed by a frantic scratching at the door.

Once Lilly had opened the door, Anchor wasted no time snaking figures of eight around her legs and purring so loudly she wondered whether the windows might rattle. She scooped him up into her arms and he rubbed his head against her chin, his huge front paws making imaginary bread in the air. 'Well, hello to you too,' she said, tickling him under the chin. 'If you're the welcoming committee then ten out of ten for effort and timing.' He chirruped his funny little purr-meow at that, right on cue.

Remembering Jack, Lilly walked back to the counter to make the introductions. 'Jack, this is Anchor and Anchor, although you can't see him …' she didn't get to finish the sentence because Anchor's purr turned into a deep-throated yowling growl, right before he made a decisive swipe for Jack.

'Woa!' Jack jumped backwards, just avoiding the claws.

'You let him see you? I thought that was a no-no,' she said, not knowing what to be more astonished by. With a good six feet between her and Jack, Anchor had resumed his happy cat routine and was once again purring.

'It is. And no, I didn't. He shouldn't be able to see me or even sense me. I don't get it,' Jack said, frowning, and, as he always did when he was thinking, pacing.

Anchor turned his head to track him and, purr extinguished, Lilly felt him vibrate with a deep growl as his tail lashed from side to side.

'I think we can safely say that he can most definitely see you and I'm sorry to say that I don't think he's too fond of you.' She shouldn't laugh but there was a part of her that was quite relieved that someone else could see Jack too. There was a time when she had wondered whether Jack wasn't just the product of some type of psychosis and, although she'd come to terms with the idea of a spirit guide over the years, it was still reassuring to know that she wasn't just soft in the head.

Given his obvious dislike of Jack, she thought Anchor would make for the door as soon as she put him on the floor, but instead he followed her around the flat like a chaperone, emitting a warning growl every time Jack got too close, which in Anchor's book was anything under six feet. Once everything was put away, she put her roses in a vase she found under the sink. 'Shall we have that coffee now?' she asked, eyeing the cake.

After carving two huge slices of cake she added them to the tray with the mugs and carried them to the coffee table. Anchor ran over to sit next to Lilly on the sofa, making it very clear from the swishing tail and hard stare that Jack needed to take the armchair if he knew what was good for him.

'I just don't get it,' Jack said after polishing off his cake in record time. 'There's no way he should be able to see me without my permission.'

Lilly knew Jack wanted to talk about it, but she couldn't answer him for a few seconds. The cake was perhaps the most amazing thing she had ever tasted, and she just couldn't bring herself to chew faster in order to answer him, even though she knew she should.

'And you definitely didn't grant permission just now? Couldn't have left your visibility button on from when you carried the things in?'

Jack snorted. 'Er, no. And it's not a button,' he said petulantly. 'It's an intention - a clear intention with a clear purpose so that I can interact in the physical world, but I most definitely did not intend to be seen by him.' He pointed at Anchor who had settled himself next to Lilly, tail twitching and his eyes still trained on Jack.

'When I was little you used to tell me that the memory of you faded like a Polaroid in people's minds,' she said quickly, just before devouring another forkful of cake.

'Yeah, well, I had to explain it somehow and you had that camera at the time. This isn't my life, is it? I'm here for you so people remembering me would just complicate things.'

Lilly nodded but she was only half listening because she was so distracted by the taste of the cake. Rich and moist, it tasted even more amazing after a mouthful of the strong, fresh coffee.

'Earth to Lilly …' Jack was staring at her a look of amusement on his face. 'Are you sure you and that cake don't need to get a room?'

Flushing slightly, her mouth full of the last bite and her mind already considering seconds, she stopped herself laughing just in time. She didn't know what would be worse, spitting food on the sofa or losing some of her precious cake. The thought made her want to laugh even more and she was forced to swallow the last of it so that she could release the giggle and answer.

'Sorry,' she said at last, 'but it's been an incredibly long time since I've had cake.'

'I have to admit, it was bloody good,' Jack agreed, rising to his feet. 'Look, I'm going to head off and see if I can get to the bottom of this feline mystery. Maybe some of the other guides know something. Have you got everything you need before I go?'

'Pretty much, although I think my backpack is still in the van with my phone in it,' she said, scanning the room. She should be on a high after the caffeine and sugar hit she'd just had, but with the afternoon sunshine streaming in through the windows and the log burner flickering happily, moving from the sofa was the last thing she felt like doing.

'You look like you're about to nod off,' Jack said. 'I'll grab it for you before I go. I need to get the van back anyway.'

'Really?' She beamed him her very best smile. 'You're an angel, thank you.'

CHAPTER 16

*L*etting herself in through the back door, Storm dropped the first two bags of groceries at the foot of the stairs before walking down the short corridor to the bookshop half of Cordelia's.

'Hello, lovely one,' she said to Veronica, who was in the process of cashing up for the day.

Looking up, Veronica said, 'Hello, sweetie pie. Good day?' Her glasses were perched on the end of her nose giving her a look of a slightly boss-eyed schoolteacher.

'Not bad, how's it been here?' Storm asked.

'Manic up until an hour ago. We've had a run on textbooks – lots of orders for specialist undergrad-type stuff. The usual walking and local sightseeing guides, and then lots of science fiction for some reason. Jerry and the girls have been run off their feet in the café all day too. I think the sunshine brought out a load of tourists who hadn't banked on it being so cold, so by four we'd pretty much sold out of everything. Oh, I nearly forgot, we had a food blogger in who just raved about how "awesome" we are. I've put his card on the kitchen noticeboard for you, but he's got our email so will send us a link when he publishes.' Veronica smiled, report delivered.

'Slow day then?' Storm laughed. 'Got time for a cuppa? I just need to get the rest of the shopping in from the car and then juice it up for the night, but I'll have the pot warming by the time you lock up.'

'Sounds perfect,' Veronica said, 'I'll be up in a jiffy.'

Taking the last of the shopping out of the car, Storm noticed a young man she guessed to be in his early twenties take a backpack out of a small van parked in the café's visitor space. He was handsome, but not in the same way as other young men his age. His mid-brown hair was cropped short and he had the sort of symmetry to his features that made modelling scouts and photographers go wild. Storm watched him as he walked ahead of her towards the back gate of Cordelia's.

He moved with the grace of someone used to using his body to its best effect. Athletic, she thought, but his movements were too fluid to be something obvious like a footballer. A runner perhaps, or even a dancer? She settled on dancer because there was a lyricism to him she'd rarely seen off the stage, but there was something else too that she couldn't put a name to. She was still lost in her musings when she realised they were about to reach the gate at the same time. He looked startled to see her, so she opted for the direct route. He may be handsome, and she guessed he must be Lilly's boyfriend, but if he was a random prowler, he'd have to use more than his looks to barge into her home.

'Hello, I'm Storm,' she said confidently, looking him straight in the eye. They were something else too – deep green from what she could see in the dimming light. If he was Lilly's boyfriend, they made an incredibly beautiful couple.

He still looked slightly taken aback but recovered quickly.

'Oh, hello, I'm Jack,' he said, flustered. 'I'm Lilly's friend.' He held out his hand, requiring Storm to put down one of the bags in order to shake it. Neither was prepared for what followed. A jolt of energy surged through Storm's hand and up into her arm. He must have felt it too because they both recoiled with a yelp. They stared at one another for a second, but then Jack said quickly, 'Static, probably off the carrier bag.' He looked down at the fabric bags at Storm's feet.

'Must have been,' Storm replied, trying to make light of it, even though her hand and arm were still smarting from the force of it. She stared at him, not quite trusting her own eyes.

'Here, let me help you,' Jack said, picking up the bags she'd set down and holding his hand out for the other one, which Storm handed over, feeling foolish and more than a little embarrassed for staring, but she still couldn't believe her eyes.

He carried the bags up the stairs making polite conversation about how beautiful the attic flat was, how Lilly was so happy to have found it and so on, but Storm barely had the concentration to do much more than murmur a few non-committal noises. When he reached the door to her flat, he set down the bags, said something about it being lovely to meet her and then headed up to the attic. Storm watched his retreating back, unable to tear her eyes away.

When Veronica let herself into the flat ten minutes later, Storm had only managed to unpack the frozen items. 'Oh, my good God, what could have happened in the last ten minutes? You're as white as a sheet. Here, sit down and I'll sort the coffee and put this lot away,' she said, taking tins out of Storm's hands.

For once, Storm did as she was told, needing more time to think before she shared what had just happened. Veronica joined her at the table with two huge mugs of coffee and a small bottle of brandy, which she held up in a question.

When Storm nodded numbly, she added a generous slug to her friend's mug.

Storm recounted the bare bones of the story – how she'd met Jack outside and how he'd carried her shopping in, but then she took a deep breath and said, 'But the weird bit, Vee, was that when I shook his hand it was like I'd been zapped with a taser.'

Veronica's eyes widened. 'Is he a bit of a joker?' she said. 'Not very funny if you ask me.'

Storm shook her head. 'Tasers don't usually hurt the one doing the tasering too. He recoiled just as much as I did. But that's not all of it.'

'Could it have been static? That can hurt quite a bit and be felt by both parties,' Veronica offered.

'Vee, believe me, this wasn't static. For one, static doesn't usually make you feel like you've just downed ten espressos in a row, nor do you usually go on to see …' Storm hesitated, not quite wanting to say the next bit out loud.

Vee's eyes widened again. 'See what?' she all but demanded.

'See the aura of the other person light up so brightly they look like they're holding their own private fireworks display,' Storm said before taking a gulp of her brandy-laced coffee.

'Aura? You saw an aura?' Veronica shrieked, her voice lifting a whole octave in excitement.

'Yes,' Storm said, unable to control the excitement in her voice. Then her eyes swam with tears. 'Three years in the spiritual wilderness. Or three years and two months if you really want to get picky.' She sniffed.

Veronica's cherubic smile started to wobble at the edges, her eyes teared up too and she grabbed her handbag and rummaged for a hankie. 'I knew it. I knew it would come back. Oh, my darling girl, I'm so happy for you. Nick would be …' The tears rolled then, and she got up from her seat to give Storm a hug, enveloping her in a cloud of perfume and richly scented lotions. 'Do you think it's coming back? Is that how it works?' Veronica asked hopefully as she dabbed at her eyes and then blew her nose delicately.

'I have no idea, Vee. Please God that it does because right now I feel like someone just dialled up the colour and cranked up the energy generator to mark five, but I'm afraid to hope, if I'm honest. What if it's a one-off? A fluke? What if it's got more to do with this Jack person than me?'

'Look at me,' said Veronica, 'can you see my aura?'

Storm concentrated, scanning her friend's outline for any trace of a glimmer. After a few moments, she shook her head in disappointment. 'A faint glow, perhaps, but nothing compared to what I just saw.'

'Doesn't matter. A faint glow is a start,' Vee said, pointing to a pencil on the kitchen table. 'Now try your magic. Go on, give it a little shove.'

Storm focused on the pencil, but then got up abruptly. 'Nothing. Maybe I imagined it, Vee, maybe in my desperation I—'

'Rubbish,' Vee said. 'Something just happened, I can feel it myself.' Then after a pause, she said, 'Why don't you call Margot? She'll know.'

Storm glanced at the clock, hoping that the time delay would provide an excuse. She didn't want to ask Margot. She'd been so upset when Storm's connection to spirit and magic had been lost, she didn't want to get her hopes up. She shook her head.

'Doreen!' Vee exclaimed. 'She asked you to call her and I bet you haven't yet, have you?' Storm shook her head guiltily. 'Please, darling, for me.'

Storm sighed, knowing that Vee had just played the card she could never refuse, and went to get her mobile from her bag. The phone rang until Doreen's voicemail kicked in.

Storm hesitated, unsure what to say, but then hung up without leaving a message. Vee frowned at her, but before she had time to say anything, the phone rang.

'Hi Doreen, it's—' Storm didn't get chance to finish her sentence. She listened for a few seconds, then, struggling to keep herself together, she cleared her throat and asked, 'Could you please send me the details once the arrangements have been made? I'm so very sorry. Your mum was,' she choked up but added quietly, 'a very special woman.'

Vee reached out to grab Storm's spare hand and held it tightly.

'Doreen had an accident. She must have gone for an early walk. They found her body in the canal a few days ago,' Storm said in disbelief.

'What? But she was only here what, last week? She was so full of life and so lovely. Oh, darling girl, I'm so terribly sorry. Come here.' Veronica got up to wrap her arms around Storm as she sobbed.

CHAPTER 17

When Jack got back to the flat the sun was hanging low and heavy in the sky, bathing everything in a warm, golden light. The crystal sun catchers hanging in the window were throwing dozens of multi-coloured sunspots around the room, like fairies having a party in a rainbow. It was such a beautiful space. He could feel the power of it, the love that practically seeped out of the brickwork at you. This was the home that Lilly deserved; granted, it wasn't their real home, but until they could get back there, it was the second-best place he could imagine for her.

Lilly was fast asleep on the couch, lying on her side, her hands resting under her cheek. The sight of her took his breath away and it was only when his lungs gasped for air that he realised that he must have quite literally stopped breathing. Her auburn hair, falling loosely over her shoulders, looked richer in this light as if the sun itself was calling to it and reminding it to shine. Her skin, always so pale and fragile-looking, had taken on a glow he couldn't ever remember seeing before. There was colour in her cheeks and her lips, pinker today than usual, were gently curled into a smile so sweet his knees almost forgot how to hold him upright. It took all his strength of will not to rush over to her, take her in his arms and tell her everything. To hell with the Remembering; if he told her now, maybe that was all it would take for her to remember everything. Their plan, their life, all of it.

He stood there watching her sleep until he couldn't trust himself to not betray the plan. He put her backpack quietly on the floor by the couch, picked up a blanket from the back of the armchair and placed it as gently as he could over her legs, his attempts to cover her shoulders thwarted by the cat, who hissed him a warning from where he was curled into her chest. Jack narrowed his eyes at him in return and he responded with a long, bored yawn which showed off an impressive set of teeth then snuggled even closer to the still sleeping Lilly. Little shit.

Jack headed for the door – old habits die hard – but hesitated. It was obvious that Storm had seen him, but just like her cat, he'd not allowed it, so technically, it shouldn't have happened. Except that it had. And judging from her expression, he guessed that she had seen his aura too. While that suggested she had abilities of her own, it didn't negate the most fundamental point, which is that without his express permission, she shouldn't have seen him in the first place. When he'd consulted them, the other guides had suggested that he might have made himself visible subconsciously. It was rare they said, but it could happen in times of high stress. Jack thought it highly unlikely but had to entertain the possibility. It was a mistake he'd vowed not to make again – and he hadn't. The encounter with Storm however had brought him right back to square one. With one last look at the sleeping Lilly, he disappeared.

CHAPTER 18

*W*hen Lilly woke the fire had burnt down to a steady amber glow and the last beams of the setting sun had turned everything in the flat golden. Her backpack was on the floor by the couch and there was a blanket over her legs; she guessed that it was as close as Jack could reach without earning himself another swipe from Anchor, who was curled up on her chest, his little head snuggled into the hollow under her chin. She thought briefly about getting up but drifted off again. The next time she woke it was to a soft paw tapping her cheek as the morning sun streamed through the skylights.

Her first morning in her new home and she couldn't ever remember feeling so content, not to mention well-rested, even though she had accidentally spent the night on the couch and not in the lovely big bed. For the first night in months, she hadn't dreamt, hadn't been hauled back to the horrors of a previous life. She could start her morning the way normal people do – not analysing whatever misfortune her brain had dragged up for her to pick over.

The revelation of her borrowed time returned to her, a

knife twist in her gut, and her heart was suddenly heavy with the inevitability of it all. She'd not have a Christmas here, or a birthday. She'd barely have a summer. To have found this place now, only to have to leave it so soon. Perhaps that was part of the plan too, a final place of respite for her last days.

A chirrup from Anchor was followed by another soft paw on her cheek, then he yawned, opening his mouth so widely it all but split his head in two. When he closed it again he was a little cross-eyed. Lilly laughed and tickled his ears, delighting in the instant purring that ensued. She decided right then that she'd not think any more about being a Last or waste even a second more of her time worrying about how it might happen. It wasn't like she could change things and she'd already had her fill of sadness. She was determined to spend whatever time she had left in the here and now.

CHAPTER 19

*L*illy spent her first week in her new home playing house. She spent many a happy hour just sitting, watching the sun as it moved the light around the space. Her favourite spot was the chair by the window in the living room. If she looked up, she could see the clouds chase across the sky through the large skylights. To her left, the rearing horse painting which, no matter how often she saw it, or indeed stared at it, always imbued her with a sense of calm. It was a strange emotion to feel, she thought, for such a powerful image. This was no pony in a quiet field, but a rearing stallion ready to fight as a tempest bore down upon him. Yet it was the sheer power of him, the confidence and certainty he had of his place and purpose in the world – that was what helped her feel calm.

She'd counted seventeen tiny paint splashes on the floor-boards under the skylights in no fewer than eleven colours. Had she placed her desk and drawing board where Nick had once positioned his easel? She wouldn't ask Storm, of course, that would be insensitive, but what felt like a small, silly part of her hoped that she might be able to share something, even something trivial with the man who had created such exquisite art.

She loved listening to the silence here too. The bedsit had never been quiet, being too close to the road and too poorly insulated to stop the lives of others seeping in through the windows and walls. But here she could almost forget that there was a bustling café two floors down. Maybe it would be different in the summer when it would, she hoped, be warm enough to open the windows. She'd even ventured down to Cordelia's a few times to grab a take-out, or as Veronica often called it with a giggle, 'a take-up' lunch or dinner. The food really was amazing and just a couple of flights of stairs away, so it seemed silly not to. Plus it was nice to break up her day with a quick chat with Storm or Veronica as she collected her meal.

The armchair in the window was perfect for reading, although she rarely got to do so alone as Anchor had become something of a fixture. He slept on her bed every night, on her head if she let him, and followed her around constantly, even escorting her to the bathroom and perching on the loo seat while she took a shower. She didn't mind a bit, but what concerned her was what Storm might be thinking. Knowing she couldn't put it off any longer, one evening Lilly gathered her courage and headed downstairs, Anchor at her heel. When he pawed at her leg and looked at her with his big amber eyes, she scooped him up into her arms. She had no idea why she was nervous; Storm had already been so kind to her, but people weren't Lilly's strong point and she knew it.

Lilly's hesitant knock was answered first of all with a scrabble of paws on floorboards followed by a soft woofing from Hope. When Storm opened the door, Hope rushed out to meet her, all feet and ears and very little composure.

'Hi, Lilly, come on in,' Storm said, holding open the door.

'I see you've brought your shadow,' she added, smiling, giving Anchor a chin tickle in Lilly's arms.

'It's actually Anchor I wanted to talk to you about,' Lilly said anxiously.

'Oh, okay, come on in. I've just brewed some coffee,' Storm said brightly.

Once they were settled at the kitchen table, Anchor still on Lilly's lap, she said, 'I'm just really conscious that he's been with me almost twenty-four-seven since I moved in and, well, I didn't want you to think I'd cat-napped him or anything. He is your cat, after all.'

Storm laughed and pointed to Anchor, who had turned and was staring at Lilly as if she'd said something mildly offensive. Lilly laughed too at the look on his face. 'Oh, darling, Anchor is his own man, always has been. So as long as you're happy to put up with him, I'm happy. Honestly. I miss the ginger puffball of course,' she leaned forward speaking directly to him and he stalked over the table to headbutt her affectionately, 'but nobody owns a cat – they deign to share their lives with whomever they choose and he has chosen you, whether you like it or not.'

A huge sense of relief washed over Lilly. While she knew she needed to give Storm the option of reclaiming her feline friend, so much of the joy Lilly was feeling, she realised, was to do with her new-found companion. For his part, Anchor ambled back across the table, settled back on Lilly's lap and yawned, then curled himself up for another nap.

While she'd only intended on staying for five minutes, Lilly was still in Storm's flat an hour and numerous coffees later when Veronica popped in after closing up.

'I should probably get back and leave you to it,' Lilly offered, disappointed but feeling that she should be polite.

'Oh, don't you dare,' Veronica said warmly, 'we've not had

a chance for a proper natter yet, so if you've got time, I'd love to hear about how you're settling in. I see you've been claimed by Anc already. He's a smart cat, that one.'

Lilly beamed in spite of herself. 'Oh yes, he's like a limpet. Follows me everywhere, sleeps on my head – I've not met a cat like him before,' she said.

'Did you not have pets at home?' Veronica asked casually.

Lilly hesitated, then said, 'I grew up on a livestock farm and all of the animals were ...' she faltered, not wanting to ruin the mood, 'let's just say they didn't know a lot of kindness. I learned pretty young not to get attached.'

'I've just the remedy for that,' Veronica said excitedly. 'My sister and her husband run a farm sanctuary just a few miles away. All the animals are there for life. They've got cows, pigs, horses, sheep – you name it. Next time my nephew comes with a delivery, I'll introduce you. He'll take you to meet them all – it's a truly magical place.'

'Really? I'd love that,' Lilly said, then, wanting to change the subject, asked, 'so how did you two meet?'

'That's a story I never get tired of telling,' Storm said. 'When Nick and I moved here and opened the bookshop we were utterly clueless.'

'That's a bit harsh. You just hadn't worked in retail before and you were both so young,' Veronica said in their defence.

Storm smiled at her friend, then turned to Lilly and continued, 'So, we were basically clueless, but we had this dream and we so wanted to make it work. Veronica there was our very first customer. I can't remember what you bought, Vee, but I know you needed a couple of bags to carry it all. And you brought us champagne and flowers to welcome us to the town, which I'll never forget.'

'I had to support the town's newest venture, didn't I?' she said. 'I used to have the little boutique next door, but oh my, selling frocks is seriously boring. I don't know what I was thinking.'

'Anyway, when it became apparent that books alone would not sustain us, Vee, who was by then a really good friend, convinced us to think about adding a café. Nick loved to cook so we went for it. Then she begged for a job,' Storm said, mischievous now.

'I did not beg, Lilly, I merely offered my services to help run the place,' Veronica said, feigning indignation.

Lilly laughed. 'So, did you sell the boutique?'

'Like a shot!' Veronica said. 'Can you believe that will be eleven years ago this year, Stormy?'

Storm shook her head. 'Time certainly flies,' she said, getting up to put the kettle back on and rummage in the fridge.

'Loo break before I can do any more tea,' Veronica said, excusing herself.

Returning to the table Storm said, 'What Vee won't ever tell you, or anyone else for that matter, is what she did for us when Nick became ill very suddenly. One minute he was fine, fit and healthy as ever, and the next we were back and forth to the hospital on a weekly basis, sometimes daily. We couldn't focus on anything else, but Vee just picked up the reins of both shop and café and said, "go do what you need to do". Then when we knew the worst, she just carried on, spinning all the plates, dealing with the staff and the wages and the orders and just everything. She gave us precious time together and then, when there was no us anymore, she gave me the time and the space to grieve. When I was ready to work again, she handed me back a business that was even more successful than the one we'd had.'

Hearing the loo flush and then Veronica's footsteps in the corridor, Storm said loudly, 'So we keep her on because she knows literally everyone in town and if she didn't come here every day she'd fill her McMansion with stray cats.'

'Oh, you're hilarious!' Veronica said, play-batting her friend across the head as she came back to the table. 'And Asim is bloody allergic to pets, remember?'

'How could I forget?' Storm says. 'He has to take twenty pills before he can even set foot in here, poor love.'

'Is that your husband?' Lilly asked.

'Yes. He's a complete sweetheart. We've been married twenty-five years, but he's a total workaholic so I rattle around in our monstrosity of a house on my own most of the time, which is why I hang around over here. Storm thinks it's because I like her company but it's really just an excuse to see the animals and eat free cake.'

The banter between the two women was so easy and so, Lilly thought, full of genuine love and respect. She'd never had a friend apart from Jack. Never a female friend. She and her mother had never been close either. Sandra was a strange woman, weighed down by life and obligations that were always opaque to Lilly. Growing up, Lilly often wondered if she'd really been wanted or whether she was more of a late accident – tolerated rather than longed for. Her mother was perennially in the shadow of her overbearing father and never once stood up for her against his harshness, not in the way Lilly would have defended someone, at least. Neither of them had tried to stop her when she left home the day after her sixteenth birthday. Her father had handed her an envelope with two hundred pounds inside and her mother had hugged her briefly before driving her to the bedsit flat. Lilly hadn't invited her in and Sandra hadn't asked.

It was after midnight when Lilly said her goodbyes, getting a hug from both Storm and Veronica in the process. She didn't get hugs, except from Jack, and the gesture had really moved her. Her mind was whirling with all the local events that they'd invited her to and that was in addition to a proper dinner at Storm's later in the week – apparently the tapas feast from tonight hadn't been sufficient. As she carried Anchor back to her flat, she felt a warmth that she couldn't ever remember feeling before.

When Lilly stepped into the flat, Jack was sitting in the armchair. 'Bit late for a school night isn't it?' he said tartly. Anchor growled quietly from her arms.

Lilly felt her wonderful mood begin to curl at the edges like singed paper, but decided to ignore it; she didn't want anything spoiling her evening. 'I was downstairs with Storm and Veronica. Aw, Jack, they're so lovely. Storm said I can walk Hope whenever I want and—'

'I know. I saw,' he said matter-of-factly.

That got her attention. 'What do you mean, you saw?' she asked carefully as Anchor emitted another low rumble.

'I mean …' He hesitated. 'I just stopped in to check that you were okay, and I saw you were with them.'

'So, you're spying on me now?' Lilly was suddenly furious. 'What the actual fuck is wrong with you, Jack? I thought we had rules. Your rules, if I remember correctly.'

Pushing himself out of the chair, he crossed the room, palms raised in placation. 'Look, Lil, I was just checking that you were okay, alright? I didn't stay long.'

'So that's meant to make it okay? You only spied for what, one minute, ten minutes? An hour?' she shouted, angry at the intrusion but also at herself for not having sensed him.

'My job is keeping you safe,' he hissed. 'You don't know who these people are. They could be anybody, but you're happy to just move in here and cosy up to them like a little lost lamb without knowing anything about their intentions.'

Lilly closed her eyes and took a deep steadying breath, trying hard to control her anger. Anchor, still in her arms, kept time with his slashing tail, his whole body vibrating with a low, resonant growl. With a great deal of effort, her body shaking with suppressed rage, Lilly said through gritted teeth, 'Just get out.' Jack raked his hands through his hair and looked like he was at a loss for what to say or do next. Lilly turned her back on him. When Anchor resumed his cheerful purring, Lilly knew Jack had gone.

CHAPTER 20

*L*illy woke from another deep and thankfully dreamless sleep. Anchor was lying on her chest and the deep rumbling purr kicked in as soon as he noticed her eyelids flicker. Lilly tried not to smile. Any moment now there would be a gentle pat on her nose just to make sure that she was fully aware of his presence – as if she'd have had a hope in hell of ignoring him.

Sleeping in a double bed still felt like a bit of a novelty for her. She was still getting used to being able to roll over without face-planting the wall and the bed was so comfortable that she rarely wanted to get up. It was such a far cry from the bag-of-spanners mattress in the bedsit. Storm had given her a set of bed linen. It was thick white cotton and felt expensive, like the stuff Lilly imagined you'd get in a posh hotel. Because it was now usually covered with a layer of long ginger fluff, she had treated herself to a beautiful throw from the charity shop. It was a bit girlie for her usual tastes, being covered in tiny pink, blue and yellow wildflowers, but she loved it the minute she saw it. Even after getting it cleaned it was less than twenty pounds, which she considered a bargain.

When she eventually got up, Anchor in her arms as usual – she would swear he'd forgotten how to walk – she saw Jack sitting in the living room reading the paper. Anchor's pneumatic purring stopped at once.

'Hateful bloody cat,' Jack snapped, narrowing his eyes and glaring at Anchor. He jumped up. 'I'm sorry, I didn't mean that. I'm being an idiot.'

'Are you apologising to me or Anc?' she asked, raising an eyebrow.

'Both of you,' Jack said, although she could see that it was galling him a little. 'Anchor really is the only cat, only animal in fact I've ever met that doesn't like me. Honestly. You should know,' he adds emphatically. 'So I'm a bit pissed that he's ruined my unblemished approval ratings, that's all.'

It was hard for Lilly to stay mad at Jack. He had really annoyed her last night. He was right in that she didn't know Storm or Veronica very well, but he needed to give her some credit for her instincts and every inch of her just knew that they were lovely, kind people.

'How about I make us some breakfast to say sorry?' Jack offered.

Giving up on the idea of holding on to her anger, she nodded and, as if sensing the truce, Anchor jumped down and settled onto the part of the sofa that Jack had just been sitting on, stretching out in an overblown display of relaxation. If Lilly didn't know any better, she'd say that his choice of seat was deliberate.

'Bloody hell, Lil, you actually have food in your cupboards,' Jack said as he rummaged around the kitchen.

'I know. Get me. I've been trying to recreate some of the food they do downstairs, and I've already had to let my belt out a couple of notches.' The statement instantly made her feel ridiculous, like a little kid bragging about school, but she'd always wanted Jack's approval.

'I'm happy you're happy, Lil,' he said, 'and you're looking great. Healthier as well as happier.' He looked as if he was about to say more but instead just smiled at her.

Lilly sat on the counter while Jack rustled up a tofu scramble with mushrooms and beans. Anchor had taken up watch on the back of the sofa, obviously keen to keep an eye on things, but Lilly decided not to mention it.

After breakfast she suggested taking Hope for a walk and to her surprise Jack agreed. To his obvious relief, Hope couldn't see him until he allowed it, but when he did, she raced over to him, tongue lolling, and greeted him with the same enthusiasm she showed everyone else. He lit up like a little kid and Lilly realised that Anchor's reaction really had hurt his feelings. She decided to try and have a word with her furry friend later – anything was worth a try.

They spent the morning exploring the woods, Hope running wide circles amongst the trees, rarely raising her nose from the ground and demonstrating a seemingly endless supply of energy. They chatted easily, just like usual, about everything and nothing, but when he asked about her nightmares and flashbacks, Lilly felt caught off guard and didn't know why. She felt like a little kid having to tell her parents about doing something wrong at school. She told him the truth – that they seemed to have stopped, and though she couldn't swear to it, he had looked upset by that. He covered it quickly enough, saying something like, 'That's good news,' but she could tell he didn't really mean it. They'd been having such a lovely time, but it had broken the spell.

When they got back to Cordelia's, Jack, keen to show how much Hope liked him, Lilly thought, volunteered to towel down the decidedly muddy spaniel before taking her back up to the flat. As Lilly hung up her coat in the small back porch, she heard Storm on the phone. 'Don't you worry about that – you just concentrate on getting better, okay? We'll hold the fort here. No honestly, Rose. Now, back to bed, okay, no arguments. Take care.' She must have hung up because Lilly heard her mutter, 'Shit,' then, excited, 'hello, my gorgeous girl,' as Hope wriggled free of Jack and the towel and scampered around the corner.

'Everything okay?' Lilly asked, following her.

'Oh, hi, lovely,' Storm said warmly and, looking right at Jack, added in the same tone, 'hello again, Jack.' Her eyes lingered on him for a few seconds as if she'd lost her train of thought, but then she remembered Lilly's question and answered. 'Yes. No. Rose is down with a bug and Jen is due to finish in half an hour but can't do a double shift – she's got her son's birthday party this afternoon. And we've got our own party booking later, but Veronica is away with Asim in Italy and …' Storm trailed off, looking like she was trying to think herself around the problem.

'If it's just waitressing, I can do that,' Lilly said, surprising herself but feeling the need to help Storm easily overcome her natural disinclination to spend a lot of time with other people. She could feel Jack staring at her; if she looked, she wouldn't be surprised if his mouth was hanging open, but she'd said it now.

'Really?' Storm said, looking taken aback. 'No. Don't worry, I don't want to mess up your day, especially if the two of you have plans.'

'Storm,' Lilly said pointedly, 'we don't have anything planned. Let me help, please. I'd like to. I can practise my social skills, which we both know are sorely in need of some polishing.' They all laughed at that, Jack included.

Storm hesitated for a second, then relented. 'Okay, but only if you're absolutely sure. And I'll pay you, naturally,' adding, 'and that's non-negotiable!' when Lilly made to dismiss the offer. 'Thank you so much – you're a lifesaver. It's an eightieth birthday and I didn't want to let them down, you know?'

Lilly smiled and felt an additional rush of purpose in the idea that she'd be helping someone celebrate eighty years on the planet, help make memories for them and the people who loved them; it was a small part to play but it felt important.

'Half an hour then?' Lilly asked, wondering if she looked too excited. She was nervous too and the two emotions were tangled up in her like two puppies play-fighting.

'Perfect,' Storm said, clasping her hands over Lilly's briefly. 'Thank you so, so much.' Jerry called her from the doorway and with a final grin at them both and a head scratch for Hope, she dashed back into the café.

Jack was a picture of practised control when she turned to him. 'Looks like I have a job this afternoon,' she said, smiling, and Hope thumped her tail enthusiastically against the wall as she looked between the two of them.

'That's great, Lil,' Jack said. 'I'll leave you to it – you'll not want witnesses when you pour soup in someone's lap.' She pretended to punch him on the arm, and they laughed. She studied him and wondered, not for the first time, where she stopped and Jack began. He felt as close as any twin. She wrapped her arms around him, squeezing him tightly as if the pressure could push in all the love she felt for him.

'I'm glad we're friends again,' she whispered into his shoulder, 'I missed you.'

He stroked her hair but didn't say anything for a minute. 'I'm glad we are too,' he said quietly.

They stayed like that for a few seconds more, then he pulled away. 'Right, I've got stuff to do so I'll catch you tomorrow at some point – you can tell me how much pay you were left with once Storm deducted the cost of the breakages.' He laughed and she narrowed her eyes at him, pretending to be mad, but also worrying that he might have a point.

She waved him off and headed for the stairs, Hope at her side. 'Come on, sweetie, let's get you settled. Auntie Lil has a job to do this afternoon!' Hope wagged her tail in approval. It was only after Lilly got back to her flat that she realised she'd not asked Jack why Storm had remembered him.

$\mathcal{L}$illy let out a long sigh as Storm turned the key in the café's front door, then leaned against the glass. 'Who knew octogenarians could party so hard?' Storm said, smiling.

Lilly laughed. 'I know! When you said it was an eightieth, I thought it would be tea and scones, not gin and dancing. It was bloody brilliant!'

'Jean is certainly not one for letting life pass her by. And you, you were a complete superstar!' Storm said, pointing at Lilly. 'Talk about a hit with the customers. And you said you were shy?'

'I am shy, honest. But everyone was so nice that it was so easy to chat. I really enjoyed myself. Thank you.'

'It's me that should be thanking you,' Storm said, crossing to the cash register and opening it. 'You dug us out of a hole today, Lil, thank you.'

Lilly held up her hands when Storm held out her day's wages. 'I meant what I said about not needing to be paid, honestly. I wasn't doing anything else and I so enjoyed myself, I really did.'

'You might not need to be paid, but I need to do the paying. Give it to a charity if you want or spend it all on sweets, but I can't ask you again if I don't pay you. Please.'

Lilly took the money reluctantly and thanked her. 'And please do ask me again any time you need a hand. Today was great fun. It was like a whole different world.'

'Judging by today, I dare say I'll get complaints if customers don't see you in here more. What have you got planned for your dinner?'

When Lilly shrugged, Storm said, 'I've made enough chilli to feed the five thousand if you fancy it? And I tried a new lemon cake recipe that I could do with a second opinion on too if you've time?'

As Storm put the dinner on, Lilly played with Anchor, swishing a shoelace for him that he seemed incapable of ignoring. Hope, living up to her name, was stationed in the kitchen where she'd be first in line for any scraps. When Anchor took his leave, stalking off to claim a spot on the sofa, Lilly took a seat at the kitchen table. They chatted easily, about Lilly's illustration work, the state of world politics and the environment, and then Storm recounted the highlights from the latest book club to lighten the mood.

'I did give you dates for the next one, didn't I?' Storm asked.

'You did, yes, along with the other clubs and things,' Lilly said.

Storm laughed. 'Sorry, we got a bit carried away the other night – we probably bombarded you a bit.'

'You didn't at all. It was lovely to be asked. I've never liked the idea of clubs, but it was so nice having company today that I'll definitely give the next one a try,' Lilly said.

'Excellent. Next book is *The Remains of the Day* by Kazuo Ishiguro. I've got two copies if you want to borrow one,'

Storm said. 'Fiction is on the far left of the shelves in the living room.'

Lilly hopped up, glad for an excuse to peruse the shelves. She loved that Storm's flat was stuffed to the gills with books. So much was read online these days, but she still loved the feel of a real book in her hands. You just didn't get that same flutter of anticipation holding a piece of tech.

She located the Ishiguro book and tucked it under her arm as she scanned the shelf, ohing to herself as she found titles that she'd love to read. She didn't want to be rude, even though she could have happily spent the next hour short-listing books she might like to borrow, so was about to tear herself away when the name on a book jacket, entitled, *In Service to Spirit*, caught her eye.

Lilly rushed back to the kitchen with the hardback in her hand. 'Is this you? You're Storm Aubrey?' she asked excitedly. It was a stupid question as Storm's photograph was on the back cover.

Storm paused for a few beats before answering, then nodded.

'You're a medium! And an author!' Lilly clutched the book to her chest like a best friend. 'But you never said anything.'

Turning down the heat on the rice, Storm took a seat at the table. 'I was a medium. Past tense,' she said matter-of-factly.

When Lilly frowned in confusion, she pressed on. 'I thought seeing spirit was normal. But, when I went to school and found out other people couldn't see what I saw, well, I quickly learned to shut up about it. Then I met Margot, a friend of my parents. She was a medium – is still a medium – and a very successful one at that, and she took me under her wing and helped me develop my …' She paused, searching for the word. 'Gift.'

'Do you mean Margot Depworth? The woman from the

big American TV show?' Lilly asked, placing the book on the table.

'That's her, yes. She wasn't famous when I knew her, that all came later, but she's the real deal – she's an incredibly powerful …' Storm looked up, catching herself, 'medium.'

'But you wrote a book,' Lilly said, curious but already wishing she'd not blundered into a topic that was patently a bit of a sore point for Storm.

Storm smiled and reached out to brush her fingers across the cover of the book. 'I did, yes. With Margot's help, I had developed into quite a competent medium myself. I worked all the way through college giving readings and by the time me and Nick bought this place, I had waiting lists months long. I used to do readings in your attic flat. A publisher approached me to write the book, which I did gladly. There are some very genuine, very talented mediums out there, but there are those who don't do it from a place of service, and I saw the book as my way of addressing that – of bringing some sense of honour and service back to the work, which is first and foremost about serving spirit.'

'Was it popular? The book, I mean,' Lilly asked.

'To my amazement, it did really well. I was so lucky. Soon there was a ridiculous amount of money on the table to do a theatre tour and a TV show. When they found out I had been trained by Margot they added zeros. I think they thought they could capitalise on the Margot's mini-me angle.' Storm pushed back her chair and went to check on the rice.

'But you said no?'

'Yep. It was financial suicide at the time. We'd only just opened the bookshop and it wasn't doing well at all, but I just couldn't bring myself to do it. Readings have always been private – they're not a spectator sport. So I politely declined. The readings were still going well and I was teaching and mentoring so I was still able to do the work.'

Lilly sensed that there was a but coming.

Storm took a deep breath. 'Nick, as you know, died a few years ago. He had an extremely rare form of cancer. He was diagnosed on the eighteenth of July and was dead by the fifth of September. They told us pretty early on that there was nothing they could do. It was my faith in spirit that made each day bearable. I thought my gift would help us face the unthinkable. I thought I would be able to walk with him to the last and see him safely into spirit.' Storm's eyes swam with tears and her voice trembled. Lilly, saying nothing, tentatively put her hand on Storm's arm.

When she was able to continue, Storm said, 'But I lost my connection to spirit just before Nick passed. I'd had a terrible nightmare. I don't remember what it was about but it had me screaming at the top of my lungs. When I woke, my connection to spirit just wasn't there anymore. There were other losses too that I won't bore you with, but suffice to say, I was lost.'

Lilly squeezed her arm. 'I can't imagine how horrific that must have been for you,' she said sincerely.

Storm was crying now, fat tears sliding silently down her cheeks. Anchor jumped onto the table and head-butted her. At the same time, Hope pawed her leg and whined. She pressed on. 'Nick slipped away peacefully at home while I dozed in his arms one sunny September afternoon, and I didn't even feel him leave. It was Hope who woke me, wasn't it, sweetie,' she said, rubbing the dog's ears, 'barking and whining and turning in circles. I lost my lifeline just when I needed it the most.'

Lilly had tried so hard to be strong and keep it together, but it was such a sad story that she thought her heart might burst at any moment. Swallowing hard she tried to stay quiet, but without warning a huge hiccupping sob escaped her.

Storm snapped her head up. 'Oh God, I'm so sorry,' she said, getting out of her chair and wrapping her arms around Lilly as they both cried. Unsure who to try and comfort first, Hope resorted to barking anxiously at them. Anchor opted for clowning and rolled on his back, his fat fluffy orange paws batting an invisible shoelace.

After reassuring the animals, Storm dried her eyes on her hankie, then after failing to find a second, handed Lilly some kitchen towel. 'What a pair we are!' she said. '"Born too close to the river", as my grandmother used to say – liable to blub at the drop of a hat.'

'Hardly,' said Lilly. 'That's the saddest thing I've ever heard. And it's never come back?'

Storm shook her head. 'I called, begged and then wailed for my spirit guides, but nothing. I prayed, I meditated, I fasted, I walked every sacred site I knew of and I felt nothing. Absolutely nothing. It was like whatever umbilical cord had connected me to that life had suddenly been cut.' She got up and turned off the rice.

'How did you go on?' Lilly asked quietly, thinking about how she would have felt if she'd lost Jack. Granted, he was more a brother than a husband, but still, it was as close to trying to understand as she could get.

'To be honest, there were occasions when I seriously contemplated not bothering,' Storm replied, coming to sit back down, 'but I had this pair to take care of,' she continued while tickling Anchor under the chin with one hand and rubbing Hope's ears with the other. 'They needed me. My friends needed me, so …' She smiled a faint, sad smile, letting the sentence hang unfinished.

'And your family?' Lilly asked, not wanting to be nosy, but suddenly needing to heap as many things as she could find onto the pile of reasons for Storm to stay in the land of the living.

Storm looked down again. 'My parents are both gone, sadly, same with my grandparents, but I wasn't really close to any of them, which sounds awful but it's just how it was. The rest of the family are too distant to worry about. Some of the less-well-heeled lot crawled out of the woodwork when the book came out hoping for some sort of payout. I don't know what was sadder, their gall or their complete ignorance about the reality of publishing.'

'That must have been so tough,' Lilly said.

Getting up, Storm crossed to the sideboard and pulled out a bottle of red. She held it up in question. When Lilly nodded, she grabbed two glasses and sat back down.

'It was bloody horrendous if I'm honest. There were so many days when I just didn't want to be here, just wanted to lie down on the earth and have it reach up and swallow me. But one day I was out walking Hope and I realised that life is a two-way deal – we get to live it, but it gets to exist through us. So, it wasn't as simple as me saying that I was done with it because I still had a duty to life. I suppose I just realised that I wasn't willing to let it down.' Storm frowned. 'I've not even had a glass of wine yet and I'm talking nonsense.'

Lilly shook her head thoughtfully before saying, 'Absolutely not, that makes perfect sense.' Then she raised her glass and offered up the toast: 'To life,' she said.

CHAPTER 22

*S*hared dinners became a regular thing after Lilly's first shift at Cordelia's. Lilly and Storm ate together at least a few times a week, sometimes finishing off anything left over from the day's trade in the café. Other times they took it in turns to cook, comparing notes and recipes and sharing the best ones with Jerry, who usually managed to take them to a whole new level.

If Asim was away on business, Veronica would join them, as would Jerry if Denise was working late. He had taken to bringing in a selection of random misshapen veg from the market and challenging them to cook-offs.

Veronica flatly refused to join in on the grounds of not wanting to poison anyone, so she took on the role of official taste tester while the other three took it in turns cooking dishes around a theme or a random selection of ingredients. After the first few weeks, Jerry was perhaps predictably top of the leader board, but Lilly was nipping at his heels in second place and seemed to have developed not just a flare for cooking, but a new interest in food altogether.

Storm had never asked him outright, but she had a

sneaking suspicion that there was more to Jerry's veg challenge than met the eye. He was a quiet man, but the knowing smile on his lips every time Lilly waxed lyrical about a new dish or declared herself fuller than an egg told Storm that he had probably shared her concern for Lilly's waif-like appearance. She'd come such a long way in just six weeks, not just physically, although the much-needed weight made her look so much more like a healthy young woman and far less a bedraggled, sickly teen. She had blossomed too in terms of her confidence.

When Jen announced that they were moving out of the area just a few days after Lilly's first shift, she had jumped at the chance of working in the café a few mornings each week and seemed to be loving every minute of it.

Storm was watching Lilly laughing with old Mr Dodds one morning when Veronica put her arm around her friend. 'If anyone could eventually charm the miserable old bugger it was going to be our girl Lil,' she said, chuckling. 'Look at him, never even cracks a smile for me and I've known him thirty years.'

Storm smiled, suddenly feeling more than a bit emotional. 'Our girl,' she said quietly, looking up to stop the tears that were gathering.

'Freya would have been not far off Lilly's age,' Veronica said knowingly as she squeezed her friend around the shoulders. Storm pushed her tongue behind her teeth, an old boarding-school trick, but it was no good.

'You know, darling girl, sometimes the ones we love have a way of finding their way back to us, especially our sleeping angels,' Veronica said, as she led Storm quietly into the kitchen before the dam burst.

CHAPTER 23

'*I*s there any place where one can feel closer to God than in the forest, Ludo?' Henri asked. Ludo, a barrel-chested brindle Staffordshire bull terrier with a stocky leg in each corner, glanced up only long enough to check that the sound of his name wasn't about to herald a biscuit. Smelling and seeing nothing, he returned his full attention to his beloved ball, his tail wagging furiously in anticipation.

'It's a good thing that was a rhetorical question, isn't it?' Henri said, feeling the familiar complaint in his knees as he bent to cup the mud and slobber-soaked ball with the chucker, an action which sent Ludo scampering ten feet down the path, his great head angled heavenward waiting for it to come into view.

If people grew to look like their dogs, Henri had a lot of filling out to do, which, being just a few years off eighty, he thought unlikely at his stage of life. If he had been minded to find his canine equivalent then perhaps a greyhound or saluki might have been more fitting, but Ludo had found them and, physical likenesses aside, the match had been perfect.

That a Staffordshire bull terrier was an unfitting breed for the local vicar was something Henri and Dorothy heard whispered by parishioners on more than one occasion. The day Ludo qualified as a Pets-As-Therapy dog was one in the eye for all his detractors.

Henri's thoughts drifted to his late wife Dorothy and he felt the familiar ache. Time was an incredibly poor healer, in his view. There was still not a day that he didn't feel her absence like a knife in his heart – didn't have to push those memories of the hospice from his mind for those of happier times. A throaty pant followed by a soft woof snapped him back to the present. Ludo stared into his face; his muzzle may be greying but he could still wag like it was an Olympic sport.

'I'm sorry, old boy, have I been neglecting my duties again?'

Ludo's eyes gleamed as his tongue lolled out of the side of his mouth, spit pooling in the corners of his smile. Cupping the ball in the chucker once again, Henri sent it flying down the track and smiled as the brindle barrel raced joyously after it.

When Ludo hung on to the ball instead of dropping it, Henri took his cue and turned for home. On the walk back along the forest path it occurred to him what had been absent from his walk again today. While it was officially spring, he had heard no birdsong, seen not a single creature, come to that, not even a squirrel. He knew in his heart what the news reports were saying was true, but he too had lived in hope, or, he thought now, was it just wilful blindness.

The small terraced cottage was a far cry from the high-ceilinged Vicarage in Pont Nefoedd he and Dorothy had lived in for most of their married life, but Dorothy had loved it on sight and that was always enough for him. Not many couples waited until retirement to choose their first home, but such was life in the Church. It was certainly quaint, he'd give it that, with leaded windows, a front door built for a time when people were at least a foot shorter, and a rambling rose covering the porch that would be a mass of pale pink flowers come the summer. To see the delight on his wife's face every time they rounded the corner was worth every banged head he'd endured before ducking had become second nature.

Ludo wasted no time in settling himself on his end of the sofa and was already snoring by the time Henri joined him with a mug of tea and his laptop. After an hour or so paying bills and replying to emails, one from each of his two sons, he was pleased to see, he rustled up a quick dinner which he ate on a tray on his lap. He managed just five minutes of the news before turning it off at the mains and retiring to bed with a book, Ludo padding sleepily up the stairs ahead of him.

Henri woke with a start. He must have cried aloud because just a heartbeat later Ludo was on the bed, whining and frantically licking his face. Even in the pitch dark, Henri could tell that his long whippy tail was on overdrive – his anxiety wag, Henri called it, the one that was usually reserved for those rare situations when even he was not quite sure what to do for the best.

The perspiration was running down Henri's neck and back. His pillow was damp with it and his pyjamas were ice cold against his skin when he sat up, trying and mostly failing to avoid Ludo's incessant face washing.

The dream was so vivid. He had thought these visitations a thing of the distant past, but here they were again. 'That I might live to see the day,' Henri said out loud without thinking. The emotion of it caught in his chest and he struggled to suppress a sob. It was only then that he realised he was shaking like a leaf too.

Hugging the wagging dog for a moment to steady them both, Henri swung his legs onto the floor. 'Come on, my friend, I think I know what I need to do,' he said, pausing only to change into fresh pyjamas and grab his dressing gown before heading downstairs. It was going to be a long night.

Henri didn't notice the sun rise. With Ludo lying on his back by the dying embers of the open fire and snoring like a truffling pig, Henri wrote without seeing the words. The old notebook, already half filled with to-do lists, had been the closest thing to hand when he'd hurried down to the living room in the early hours, Ludo anxious and close at heel. It was a far cry from the elegant books that Dorothy had bought him all those years ago – the books that went on to serve as the most curious of all of his journals – but it served its purpose well enough.

The well of words that had been pouring from his hand for so many hours dried up suddenly and Henri sat back heavily in his chair, slumping slightly with the effort and with relief. He rubbed his eyes, then blinked in the watery sunlight as if seeing the room for the first time.

He flicked back through the now full notebook and saw that he'd even written on the back cover. The small neat lettering, although recognisable as his hand, was a million miles away from his usual hurried scrawl. He didn't know exactly how long he'd been writing but he guessed it had been hours, a hunch that the aching in his neck and stiffness in his hand corroborated. Just like before though, he had not a clue of what had been flowing from his pen. After making himself a cup of tea, he did what he'd not dared to do all those years ago – he opened the notebook, put on his glasses and began to read.

A while later, his face pale, Henri rested his head in his trembling hands. When he composed himself, he slid his palms down his face and lifted his head to the ceiling. 'Well, you certainly don't do things by halves, do you?' he said gravely.

CHAPTER 24

*M*argot's phone vibrated in her handbag. 'Do you need to get that?' asked Damien, the brash American producer of her highly successful TV show as he glanced up from Le Bernardin's dessert menu. She had waved the waiter away when he had proffered a menu in her direction.

'No,' Margot said, reaching into her bag to silence the phone that was still buzzing, angry as a late summer wasp.

She hated men like Damien. Obnoxious 'executives' who were blind to their own privilege and dumb luck but who seemingly never tired of telling the world that hard work and determination always wins the day. If hard work alone was the key, then most women in developing countries would be millionaires, she thought angrily. Her most recent show ratings had certainly put her in his good books, hence the fancy lunch at one of New York's finest eateries, but if this was meant to be her reward, he'd missed the mark.

When he ordered his second bottle of wine and two desserts, she excused herself and went to the ladies'. After checking that she was alone, she flicked a confusion spell at the door to ensure that she wouldn't be interrupted and dialled. The tightening in her chest that had begun a few hours ago had warned her to expect something and the caller ID confirmed it when a single letter loomed large on the screen. C. That was never good.

'You're in New York,' he said flatly, always keen to demonstrate his reach.

'I live here,' she said without elaboration.

There was a pause on the line before he said, 'We have a problem. What do you know about the Ethereal?'

'I know the meaning of the word obviously, but are we talking about a spirit?' she asked.

Charles snorted. 'Well, well, Margot. It seems you're not the all-seeing eye after all,' he said sarcastically. 'I would have thought that something this fucking material to the plan might have shown up on your radar, but no – I have to hear it from Wang.'

Margot shuddered at the mention of his name. A fellow seer, she'd only met the pint-sized psycho once and even that had been once too often. He reminded her of the golems from old fairy stories, functioning, intelligent but so devoid of any humanity that he might as well have fashioned out of clay.

'What did he say?' she asked coolly, refusing to rise to the bait.

'Oh, just that he had a vision in which a being called the Ethereal could move the whole fucking world into fairyland and basically screw up our entire plan,' he said, his voice rising and conjuring for Margot a near-perfect image of the little spit balls that formed in the corners of his permanently wet fat lips. The salad she'd picked at for lunch turned in her stomach at the thought.

'You mean energetically? As in the great shift?' Margot asked, careful to keep her tone curious but neutral.

'Yes, yes, some bollocks like that. And something to do with a magical book, but we're looking into that. Why is there always a magical fucking book? Look, the point is … if there's a credible threat to the plan we need to find it and get rid of it and as our council seer I expect that to be *your* job.'

Matching the steel in his tone Margot, enunciating every word carefully, said, 'As I have said many times before, the world of spirit doesn't work like that. I don't choose my visions and neither does Wang – visions choose the seer. And check your tone with me, Charles.'

She heard him snort but he didn't retaliate.

'I'll start some research,' Margot said calmly, 'and report back when I have more.'

There was another long silence on the line; he was such a child when put back into his box, and she was about to hang up when he said, 'And the book. Wang got a possible location and I'd like you to check it out because it's something of a coincidence.'

Margot felt the back of her neck prickle in warning. 'In what way?' she asked coolly.

'Wang's vision took him to Pont Nefoedd.' He paused. When she didn't reply, he said, 'Which is where your one-time protégé lives, if I'm not mistaken.'

Margot laughed. 'And you think Storm has a magical tome in her provincial little bookshop?' There really were days when she thought she'd missed her vocation. Then again, when the stakes were this high, acting became second nature. 'That whole area has always been a hotbed of energetic activity, but as I can tell it will put your mind at rest, I'll pay her a visit just to make sure. Urgent business in the UK will at least give me an excuse to get out of this meeting.'

By way of reply Charles said, 'Good. Give Damien my best,' and hung up.

Once Margot's hands had stopped shaking, she called Storm.

CHAPTER 25

$\mathcal{L}$illy loved her shifts at the café. She had been doing three mornings a week since Jen left and they were the highlight of her week. The regulars were so nice, and she had such a giggle with everyone that the time always seemed to fly by.

She knew Jack thought that she was wasting her time waiting tables and getting to know people she'd soon have to leave behind. He hadn't said as much, but she could tell just by his reaction to her many stories. He just didn't understand.

She had tried to include him in the dinners and the book group but had eventually given up. He had said something about 'the rules', but she didn't think that was the reason at all. He must have let Storm see him on purpose because she often asked after him, so Lilly didn't see why he wouldn't take the next step and just join in and let his hair down for once. She missed not seeing him as much, but he was so gloomy when she did that he just brought her down anyway.

She had woken before the alarm. Her shift started at

eight, but she was up, showered, dressed and breakfasted by seven. With an hour to kill, she decided to see what was ready for picking in the garden and grabbed the trug and secateurs from where they lived by the back door. Jerry had wanted thyme for something yesterday; they always needed salad leaves and if there were more sweet peas, she'd pick some for the counter, maybe some for the tables if there were enough. For a small courtyard garden, it packed above its size in terms of produce. It had troughs full of salad leaves, shallots, beetroot and baby carrots and dozens of herbs, most of which she could name, thanks to Storm and Jerry. The old stone walls were all covered with something either edible or fragrant and the garden was already buzzing with bees enjoying the spring flowers when she stepped out into the morning sunshine.

It only took Lilly a few minutes to pick what she needed. The sun was already warm on her face and she felt almost giddy when she leaned in to smell the sweat peas. They didn't have flowers on the farm and yet she seemed to remember the smell – a memory from a past life perhaps, tugging at her sleeve. She closed her eyes in the hope that she'd remember something else.

The creak of hinges which accompanied the opening of the back gate jolted her back to reality and she turned, expecting to see Jerry. Instead, though, she saw a young man, slightly older than her she thought, carrying a cardboard box. He was tall, over six foot, and well built. Not gym toned though, like the young guys who sometimes came into the café with their muscles bulging out of deliberately ripped T-shirts; he looked like he might work outdoors or do rock climbing or surfing or something. He had sandy-coloured hair that looked slightly slept in. It wasn't an unattractive look though, far from it. Lilly felt the blush start somewhere at the base of her neck, which only intensified its climb northwards when she realised that he was staring at her.

'Can I help?' she offered, realising that regardless of how he looked, she probably should be challenging strangers who wandered in unannounced.

He continued to stare for another moment then ran his hand through his hair, which seemed to reanimate him. He stepped forward, hand outstretched in greeting. 'Michael,' he said slightly sheepishly, 'Veronica's nephew. I'm delivering the veg and the cakes. From the farm. My parents' farm. My sister makes the cakes though. I help ice them sometimes. When I'm home at least. From uni I mean. Not that that's what I do, I'm not a professional cake decorator or anything …'

Lilly watched his cheeks redden so jumped in to save him. 'I'm Lilly. I'm new. I rent the attic and waitress a bit,' she said, conscious that she was about to start babbling too.

The gate swung open, startling them both, but Lilly was relieved to see Jerry arrive, pushing his bike. 'Hello, mate,' he said, 'they've got you slaving already, have they?'

'Hey, Jerry,' Michael said, completely animated now as Jerry gave him a one-handed hug and slapped Michael's back affectionately. When Michael stepped back he put his hand on Jerry's shoulder, looked him up and down and, with a tilt of his head asked, 'Have you grown?'

'You're not too big to go over my knee, you know,' Jerry said, waving his hand. 'And for the record, I think I'm bloody shrinking.' They laughed together and Lilly felt a small pang of something like envy. For what, she wasn't quite sure – their easy banter, their history maybe? She knew she was being silly but she couldn't help it.

Noticing her look of bemusement, Jerry filled her in. 'Sorry, Lil, a not-so-private joke and entirely my fault for doing the "my, haven't you grown" thing every time I saw him when he was a kid.' Looking at Michael he says, 'But in my defence you were like a complete midget until the day you began springing up like a bloody weed. Honest Lil, he shot up about two inches in a week once, I swear.' Michael held up his hands and nodded while trying but failing to look serious. The two men laughed again, easy and companionable.

'I'd better get cracking,' Jerry said, 'but see you soon now you're home.'

'Definitely,' Michael said.

'Is there much more to bring in?' Lilly asked, for want of anything better to say.

'A couple more trays of veg and the cakes,' Michael said, 'but I can manage.'

'It's no trouble, I'm early for work and I'd like to help.'

There was a small white van parked in the lane with its hazards blinking. Michael unlocked the back doors and handed her a tray of mushrooms, which, being a lot lighter than she'd expected, she nearly flung in the air. They both laughed and it served to break whatever weirdness had been lingering between them.

'I can handle something a bit heavier and I promise not to try and fling this one down the lane,' she said, gesturing with her head for him to add another tray to the top of the one she was holding, which, to his credit, he did. 'Just don't give me the cakes,' she added with a smile.

They chatted more easily from there, Lilly asking questions about the farm and him waxing lyrical in reply, telling her all about the different heritage varieties of produce they grew and the seemingly endless list of cakes his sister made. Lilly's mouth watered just hearing about them.

When they had unloaded the last of the stock into the kitchen, Michael hovered awkwardly in the doorway. 'Well, suppose I'll see you tomorrow then,' he said to Lilly.

'Yes, definitely,' she said, then kicked herself for sounding quite so enthusiastic. Michael had already said his goodbyes when she realised that she wasn't actually meant to be working tomorrow.

When she turned around, Jerry, grinning, wiggled his eyebrows at her and she blushed scarlet.

CHAPTER 26

Storm edged back the heavy brocade curtains to check the street for what must have been the tenth time in the last half hour. The high street was all but deserted. The rain had returned. Hope, lying on the sofa with her crossed front paws dangling just off the edge, cocked her head as if she was wondering what on earth Storm was doing. She thumped her tail against the cushions when she saw that she'd caught Storm's eye and collapsed onto her side for a belly rub as she passed. Restless, Storm obliged, before continuing to roam around the flat, plumping cushions and wondering if the old mantle clock needed winding again.

She'd not seen Margot since Nick's funeral, although they had clocked up hours, possibly days worth of transatlantic calls in the weeks following it as Storm tried desperately to understand why her connection to spirit had been lost. Margot's call today had come completely out of the blue though; since those first dark days and weeks, the gaps between calls had grown longer and longer.

It had been weeks since Storm's strange encounter with Jack and, to her immense irritation, she'd only seen him once since and that time his aura had been nowhere to be seen. Granted, she'd been pretty harassed at the time, wondering how to cover Rose's shift, but she was starting to wonder whether she might have just imagined the whole electric shock and light show of their first meeting.

In the weeks that followed she felt she'd made the right decision in not asking Margot – no point getting her hopes up, especially since it looked as if it had been a fluke. She had texted Margot to tell her about Doreen, of course, but had received only a short reply expressing her shock and sadness and with the usual 'must speak soon' sign-off that she knew, from experience, rarely materialised into an actual conversation. But now, with Margot about to arrive in person any moment, she felt like fate might be intervening.

As Storm checked the window again her phone pinged with a new message. Old friends it seemed were like buses. Henri was asking if he could pop in early tomorrow. Another dear friend too infrequently seen re-emerging into her life – what were the chances? She texted a quick *'Of course! It will be fabulous to see you'* reply and hit send. She smiled at the thought of seeing Henri and should have felt comforted, but the sense of uneasiness wouldn't leave her.

Margot had originally been a friend of Storm's parents. She hadn't been famous back then, of course, but she was young and glamorous and had always had a remarkable gift when it came to spirit, which was why her parents liked her, Storm supposed. They had had a habit of collecting people – the more unusual the better – and Margot's uncanny ability to see and speak with those who had passed made her one of her parents' more colourful dinner party regulars. Had they had the slightest inclination about her magic too she would have had permanent top billing, but that was a secret that Margot held close.

That her parents had a natural medium and witch already

in their midst in their daughter had passed them by. Some only children become the suns around whom their parents orbit – but Storm's orbited only each other. Saved from the tyranny of work thanks to family money on both sides and, on her father's side, a minor title to boot, her parents had dedicated their lives to their own enjoyment. Their love of parties and adventure was eclipsed only by their enduring infatuation with one another. Bookish and undemanding, Storm was their satellite child, of their world but held apart from it and, as such, often went overlooked. There was no malice in it, just absence.

Margot saw her though. From the first day they met, Storm knew they were the same. Storm was twelve the day Margot first came to the house for lunch with her mother, Clemmie. She had been talking to her late great-grand-mother Viola when the doorbell rang. Margot stood on the doorstep, muffled in a long camel-coloured coat, a thick cream scarf at the neck which brushed the edge of her razor-sharp glossy black bobbed hair. She wore a large pair of sunglasses even though it was a grey winter's day. Standing next to her was a short, stout jowly man with long white hair, dressed in a rumpled morning suit.

'Oh, my word!' Margot had said, pulling the sunglasses off and leaning in slightly to get a better look at the child. 'You can see Claude.' Viola had stepped closer to her. 'No need to worry, Grandma,' Margot had said with a disarming smile, 'it appears that I'm here to help.' It was so Mary Poppins that Storm had been instantly awestruck.

Margot had been true to her word. In the years that followed she had taught Storm how to control and hone her various gifts. She'd answered enough questions to fill an encyclopaedia, dished out reading assignments, taken her to innumerable mystical sites around the country and even put up with the teenage tantrums when being different was the very last thing Storm had wanted to be, gifts or not. When her parents upped and left for an ashram in India one summer when Storm was fifteen, it was Margot who took her in to save her the indignity of having to stay with yet another new live-in nanny. Though she'd had many amazing summers since, that one still stuck out in her memory, maybe because it was the first one she ever remembered enjoying. Margot had just finished writing her first book and was desperately trying to get it published while coping with a backlog of private readings she did from the drawing room of her town house in Chiswick.

Storm was both assistant and apprentice that summer. Organising meetings and readings, copying manuscripts for posting off to publishers and trying, just as poorly as Margot, to feign disinterest when yet another rejection letter flopped like a dead fish onto the doormat. In between readings and bookwork, Storm continued her magic lessons, practising hour after hour on the spells and meditations that Margot set for her. When the clients allowed it, Margot would let Storm sit in on the readings and this was how she honed her gift for mediumship and learned to fully appreciate the power of it. To see people broken by grief practically float out of the room on a current of joy and connection was the best kind of magic.

Storm always knew that Margot would have to leave eventually, but it didn't make the loss any easier when it came a few years later. With her book published and riding high in the bestsellers list, Margot had laughed off Storm's prediction that she'd need to move to the States to continue her work – declaring her undying love for 'Old Blighty' – but they both knew it would happen. You didn't need to be psychic to see that the US was far more ready for a conversation with the afterlife than the Brits were.

Storm tried to savour every moment of their time

together, committing to memory the lessons and instructions, trying to freeze-frame the best of the days and store the memories away on an internal hard drive. She had just turned eighteen, a milestone her parents had managed to forget, but one which Margot had gone to town on celebrating, when, as they were hailing a cab home from the restaurant, the call came from her agent. He was practically hysterical with excitement at the prospect of his client landing a TV show in the US. Margot was on a plane to New York three weeks later for a fact-finding trip, but they both knew she was very unlikely ever to call the UK her home again.

Even though Storm had been waiting for it, the buzz from the intercom made her jump. Hope woofed and hurtled off the couch towards the door, pawing at it in frustration when she found it closed. Seeing Margot's face appear on the intercom screen, Storm pressed the door release button, and said to Hope, 'Guess who's here, sweet pea? It's Auntie Margot!' Hope wagged harder and snorted under the door, trying, Storm supposed, to get a whiff of the visitor as early as possible. Storm opened the front door to the flat and a blur of liver-and-white fur whipped past her legs and down the corridor to meet their guest.

A few seconds later, pre-empted by the creak of the old treads, Margot emerged at the end of the corridor, her dark red lips breaking into a wide smile and displaying the sort of ultra-white teeth only US TV stars seemed to possess. She quickened her step and, in a few paces, had enveloped Storm in a familiar hug. 'Hello, sweetheart,' she said, giving Storm another squeeze before releasing her. Margot smelt of the same blend of verbena perfume she'd always worn and it swept over Storm like a soft blanket, bringing with it so many memories that a lump rose in her throat and she had to pull away from Margot before the emotion of it completely overtook her. She only half registered Hope stalking back past them into the flat, her tail hanging low and not a trace of her trademark bounce remaining.

The first hour slipped away as they chatted in the kitchen while Storm prepared dinner and Margot answered endless questions on the new book, the TV series and life stateside. Margot had always been so passionate about her work, but Storm noticed a distinct lack of enthusiasm about her this evening – a dismissiveness that had never been in her character. Margot had always taught Storm that to work in service of spirit was an honour and a calling and yet today she seemed so flat about it all. Maybe it was the jet lag.

'Enough about me,' Margot exclaimed, draining her water glass and pouring herself another from the jug on the table. 'What's going on with you?'

Storm had been dying to ask her about her strange experiences with Jack, but now that the opportunity was here, she felt the flesh on the back of her neck prickle, followed by a cold wash of warning down her spine. This wasn't the first time she'd experienced such a feeling. Her instincts, until Nick's death anyway, had always been sharp as pins, but this sudden resurgence caught her off guard.

Torn between the desire to tell Margot everything and the heavy sense of caution she felt settling on her shoulders, she chose to stall for time.

'Are you alright?' Margot asked, sounding concerned. 'You've gone quite pale.'

'Just overheating, I think,' Storm said, pointing to the hot pan in front of her. Forcing a smile and hoping Margot hadn't registered her hesitation, she said, 'Cordelia's is doing well despite the state of the world – we've got a fantastic group of locals and goodness knows how many clubs and groups meet here now. Tourism is up, especially the Brits, but then again, overseas holidays aren't as easy as they once were, are they? Lots of people working their way through their bucket lists, which would be terrifying if I actually stopped to think about it.'

Storm had been about to say something else when Margot interjected. 'And what about spirit? Anything changed there?' Her cool grey eyes studied Storm's face intently.

Storm felt silly now. She needed to know what was happening to her and here, sitting right in front of her, was the woman who probably held all the answers. Why on earth was she holding back? She'd been her friend and mentor for close to thirty years – and she'd been more of a mother to her than the woman who'd given birth to her.

She chided herself for being ridiculous but, as she opened her mouth, a loud crash came from the living room which stopped her in her tracks.

She ran to investigate. The large peace lily in its ceramic pot was shattered in the hearth – a full ten feet from where it had been sitting on the desk by the window. Hope, who she had last seen asleep on the sofa, was standing with her front feet on the arm, staring intently at a spot around six feet above the shattered pot. Storm followed her gaze back to the spot above the hearth, only to see a small dot of light no bigger than a penny piece disappear before her eyes. Hope ran along the sofa towards her, whined and pushed her head into her hand, her tail, low and rapid, beating a nervous tattoo on the back of the cushions.

'What the hell happened?' Margot said from the doorway.

Storm didn't intend to lie, nor did she want to, but every sense she had was telling her that now was not the time to share her suspicions. Feeling a pang of guilt for blaming Hope for something she blatantly didn't do, she said, 'Oh, it was nothing, just a waggy tail mishap and a pot plant in the wrong place.' She stroked Hope's ears and kissed the top of her head by way of apology.

Storm had never been a good liar and she doubted that her attempt to pass the incident off as an accident washed with Margot – the arch of her eyebrow told her as much, but she didn't comment further, just scanned the room like a detective looking for clues. Tellingly, she didn't repeat her question.

The rest of the evening passed without incident, although Hope slunk off to her bed in Storm's room as soon as the two women came into the lounge with their coffees. The conversation ebbed and flowed. They reminisced about Doreen, Margot bemoaned the shallowness of the TV industry and the expectations of her agent, then they moved on to discussing the sepsis crisis, the global climate emergency that was long on words and terrifyingly short on action, and the unrest that was escalating around the world.

When Margot said she'd better head off, Storm was, to her shame, slightly relieved. The effort of pretence weighed heavily on her, but so too did her disappointment. This was not the way she'd expected the evening to pan out. They made small talk as they walked down the stairs to the door but, as Margot stepped out into the courtyard, she surprised Storm by pulling her into another hug. In a voice that seemed to be shaking slightly with the effort, Margot said, 'You take great, great care of yourself, my precious girl.' When Storm, still wrapped in the hug, nodded in reply, Margot added, 'Promise me. I need to hear you say it.'

Swallowing the lump in her throat with considerable effort, Storm croaked, 'I promise.'

Margot held on for a second longer, then stepped back. 'We'll see each other soon.' She paused. 'And all will be as it's meant to be. Remember that, okay?' She was clearly aiming for brightness, but her words fell like hammers in Storm's mind.

Not trusting her voice right away, Storm forced a smile. 'Take care too, won't you?' she said once she was able.

With a brisk nod, Margot pulled up the collar of her trench coat, held up an immaculately manicured hand in farewell and strode off down the path to the back gate. Storm bit back a sob as she closed the door against the dark.

CHAPTER 27

*M*argot waited until she was back in her rental car before she made the call.

He picked up on the first ring. 'Well?' he snapped, without bothering to say hello.

'As I suspected,' Margot said with a well-practised sigh. 'She's still utterly oblivious to everything. I think the dog is more sensitive these days,' she said with a little snort of derision. 'Whatever Wang picked up certainly wasn't our little Stormy. Maybe next time he could try to be a little more specific in his visions?' she added icily.

Charles let out an irritated grunt at the other end of the line and Margot, conscious that she was holding her breath, forced herself to breathe naturally in case her voice somehow gave her away. There was a long pause and she bit her tongue to stop herself from filling it.

'Okay,' he said eventually. 'Get back to London and we'll discuss the next steps.' He cut the call before she could reply.

Slipping her phone into the signal-blocking case she kept in the glovebox, Margot let out a long breath and allowed the tears to fall. 'Please forgive me, sweetheart,' she whispered. She rested her head on the steering wheel for a long moment before turning on the ignition and pulling out into the night.

CHAPTER 28

*J*ack stood in the shadows in the back lane and watched as Margot got into her car. From the glow, it was obvious that she was making a call, but he couldn't risk getting close enough to listen in.

He had distrusted Margot on sight. He knew that someone or something was headed their way because every instinct he possessed had been on high alert all day. He had hung around, watching and waiting. He had felt it – the power – from miles away, so by the time Margot arrived he was already in position, his shields at full strength.

He had only had seconds to observe her, but he knew without doubt that she was dangerous. When someone went to that amount of trouble to cloak themselves, they were hiding something. Yes, she had a few glamours going on – he didn't know a witch alive who didn't – but this was different. This was hard-core concealment using powerful magic and he didn't want that coming anywhere near Lilly. His job was to protect her, but he had no idea how his abilities, such that they were, might fare against that sort of power. It felt akin to putting daisies into the barrels of AK-47s.

He still didn't have an answer for why Storm had been able to see and remember him. He had been happy to write it off – everything he'd learned about her since told him that she had a genuinely good heart and would never do anything to hurt Lilly. But this Margot woman had changed things. She had threat written all over her and he couldn't risk Storm telling her anything about them.

He had sat with Hope on the sofa once Storm and Margot had returned to the kitchen after the incident with the pot plant.

'You're a good girl, Hope,' he'd whispered as he'd tickled her silky chocolate brown ears. She had sat tall, leaning into him, her eyes trained in the direction of the kitchen. They could both hear Storm speaking, but when Margot replied, he had felt Hope emit a low rumble of a growl and seen her lip lift to expose a shiny white canine. 'I know, I don't trust her either,' he'd said.

When he had heard the scrape of chairs being pushed back, and after one last tickle for the dog, he had left. No need to leave a spirit light this time – he knew that Storm had already got the message.

Jack had waited in the lane until Margot had driven away before appearing in Lilly's flat.

'Hi!' Lilly said brightly, looking up from her drawing board. She was beaming at him and he felt his stomach flip. She was practically glowing and her aura was seriously off the chart. She was looking more and more like her true self, the one he knew from their life together in the forest, so much so that he had been finding it hard to be around her. He'd been making excuses, but he doubted she'd really noticed his absence.

Even though Jack desperately wanted them to be home in the forest, he loved seeing her so happy. They didn't have long to wait and while this was always the hardest part, he consoled himself with the fact that it would soon be over for good. He didn't know how she would die. They had decided many lifetimes ago that knowing would just get in the way of the mission.

He consoled himself with the knowledge that Lasts usually left quickly and quietly. An undetected heart defect that allowed them to slip away as they slept was a popular choice, as was a sudden brain aneurism. He had been banking on that, he realised. It was that thought that had got him through the worst, but Margot's appearance had changed everything. When he allowed his intuition to speak, he was left with the terrible feeling that Lilly's last passing might end up being worse than any of her nightmares.

'What are you drawing?' he asked, forcing the dark thoughts away and leaning over her shoulder. She moved a sketch of Anchor to try and cover a line drawing of young man with floppy, surfer-type hair. Jack pretended not to see it, but the image already felt seared into his mind.

'Oh, this and that,' she said, not meeting his eye as her neck began to redden.

Jack felt as if he'd been kicked in the gut and for a minute he couldn't trust himself to speak. He walked over to the kitchen and reached for the kettle, wishing that Lilly was the type who kept a well-stocked bar. Having to make do with caffeine instead, he grabbed the cafetière and spooned in the ground coffee that had replaced the instant stuff she used to buy.

'Are you having coffee?' Lilly asked, taking a seat at the breakfast bar.

'Did I need to ask permission now?' he snapped before he could check himself.

Lilly frowned and he kicked himself. He could already tell where this was going – it was already in the air. Then he thought of the drawing and decided that he didn't care if they argued.

'Which wasp flew up your arse?' Lilly asked, glowering at him.

'Pretty turn of phrase, Lil – been hanging out with sailors, have you?' It was a ridiculous thing to say, but he couldn't help it. 'Your new pals been teaching you some cool stuff?'

Lilly laughed at him then, a short, tired little laugh that he totally deserved but it stung all the same. 'Don't be petty, Jack. You've been conspicuous by your absence since I moved here to the point that I'm wondering if seeing me happy actually just makes you miserable.'

'What? That's absolute bullshit, Lil,' he said, but even as the words came out of his mouth, he realised that there was a lot of truth in what she was saying. It was so hard to see her enjoy all this now, when she was going to have to leave it. Yes, she'd been through worse, they both had over their various lifetimes, but those lives were like dreams once they were over, the emotion of them blessedly out of reach until the Remembering. The important one was always the one you were living in the here and now. He wanted her to be happy, but he also wanted her home. Safe forever and away from this shitshow that was careering towards all-out apocalypse. Humanity was about to pay the price for its greed and Jack didn't want either of them to be a part of it ever again.

'Really? Don't lie to yourself, Jack, and while you're at it, don't lie to me either,' she said, her eyes hard and fixed, unblinking on his.

Jack hesitated, which told her everything she needed to know. She swung her legs off the bar stool and stalked back to her drawing board. 'Nice one Jack,' he muttered to himself.

He waited a beat then poured the coffee into one of the

mugs. After taking a deep breath he carried it over to her. As he leaned over to place it on her desk he noticed that she was working on the drawing of the surfer again. He put the mug on the desk, leaned down and kissed her on the top of her head. 'I'm sorry,' he said quietly. Then he disappeared.

CHAPTER 29

*H*enri stopped midway up the hill, not to catch his breath, as a casual onlooker might have thought; he was a fit as a flea thanks to his swimming, walking and Tuesday night yoga class where he was still the token chap. Had his knee allowed him, he would still be running, but he'd had to hang up his trainers five years ago after the last knee operation.

It was his knee that held him up now. He'd been pain-free for months, but it was complaining today of all days. Ludo took advantage of the pause to sniff and then water a nearby postbox before fixing his eyes on his companion and offering a questioning wag. 'I'm fine, old man,' Henri said, scratching the dog behind his ears. 'Just having a rest.'

It felt strange to be back in Pont Nefoedd. It had been their home for such a long time. The boys had gone to school here and he and Dorothy had been so much part of the community. He thought of his late wife and tapped his breast pocket unconsciously, reassuring himself for the umpteenth time that the notebook and letter were still where he'd put them.

With little traffic on the roads and Henri's impatience with himself adding weight to his right foot, the drive had taken just half an hour. Looking for a space to park had taken nearly as long though. With the fuel shortages, people had taken to walking, cycling or lift-sharing wherever they could, but cars needed to live somewhere and this morning it seemed they were all in residence on the high street. He'd eventually found a space at the bottom of the hill by the chemist just big enough for his Smart car. It was still early and besides him and Ludo, the only souls out and about seemed to be delivery people and the usual gathering of optimistic pigeons.

Just ahead of them, a man in a dark blue overall and a white cap was hauling trays of bread rolls out of a small van that was parked on the double yellow lines, hazards flashing to ward off the wardens. His stomach growled as the smell of warm bread met him on the breeze.

Across the road, another man in whites stained pink whistled cheerfully as he hefted the carcass of a gutted pig onto his shoulder into the butchers. Henri recoiled, said a prayer and hurried on up the hill.

The high street was sandwiched between a park at the top, complete with a Victorian bandstand that was still used for plays and concerts in the summer months, and a supermarket at the foot that none of the locals had wanted and few had frequented. It had been one of the first victims of the flooding and hadn't re-opened. From the reports online, Henri doubted anyone was sorry to lose it.

Cordelia's Café was set exactly in the middle of the hill with nine shops to its left and nine to its right. It was an imposing building made from local stone in an era when things were crafted rather than just constructed.

Henri felt the knot of anxiety soften as he looked at it. It was exactly as he remembered. Two huge bay windows flanked a half-glass door, the woodwork was painted in a smart dark grey, and the name of the café was picked out in a rich, elegant cream font on the sign above.

Despite the great expanse of plate glass, he was pleased to see that it had not succumbed to the metal shutters that had sprung up across the fronts of shops in his own village. Cordelia's looked immaculate. Then again, he noticed, so did every other shop on the small high street.

The windows were edged in garlands of paper leaves and flowers. Fat papier-mâché bees, dragonflies and birds hung from the ceiling; a mismatch of old terracotta pots filled with spring flowers lined the low windowsills. There were anemones, hyacinths, tulips and of course daffodils beaming at him from behind the glass. He imagined that the smell would be incredible. Three willow sculpture hares danced amongst the pots. So simple and, as ever, magical.

Henri had barely touched the buzzer when a light blinked into life from the back of the shop, then she was there, keys in hand, walking swiftly to the door to let him in. Ludo, never one to stand on ceremony, was first through the door, wagging and wriggling and plastering the kneeling Storm with adoring kisses. Henri paused, enjoying the reunion of two old and dear friends. She was just as striking as always. The long thick wavy hair the colour of polished teak and the wide, generous mouth which was always so quick to smile and find just the right words to comfort and reassure. Dorothy always said she would have made an amazing vicar had the Church been enlightened enough to recruit a witch.

Storm rose to greet Henri. 'It's been too long, my friend,' she said softly as she swept her arms around him and hugged him tightly.

Anchor strolled in to join the party and wove happily around Ludo, bumping his head into the old dog's neck and jaw, much to his delight. Ludo knew better though than to shower this particular old chum with kisses after his first attempt years before had earned him a bloody nose.

A clatter of claws on floorboards heralded the arrival of Hope, the remnants of her breakfast still in evidence around her muzzle. She skidded into the shop in a flurry of ears and paws. Anchor stalked off, his limelight stolen, but ever the gentleman, Ludo waited for her to right herself before reintroducing himself with a friendly wag and then a round of rear-end sniffing to reacquaint themselves formally.

'Come on, before she has half of the shop over. Kettle's boiled,' Storm said, smiling, sweeping Anchor up into her arms and leading them through the back of the shop and up the stairs to the flat.

An hour later, with the dogs snoring one at each end of the sofa, Storm and Henri sat at the kitchen table and, just like old times, put the world to rights while refilling their mugs from a teapot that gave the impression of being bottomless.

When Storm and Nick had first moved to Pont Nefoedd they had been largely welcomed to the close-knit town. They had, however, drawn the ire of some of the less tolerant members of the community for stocking what they considered to be 'occult' books. That Storm and Nick looked rather bohemian was, Henri supposed, the real reason that some folk gossiped about the 'hippies'; objecting to their youth and good looks would have appeared churlish.

Storm and Nick became good friends with the vicar and his wife, which surely rankled with a few, and the day Storm, at Henri's invitation, spoke about paganism at the interfaith event, Henri found it hard to suppress a chuckle at some of the twisted-lemon mouths in the front row.

Henri never needed to defend his friendship with the young couple – the small band of gossips was never bold enough to challenge either him or Dot – but had he been called to, he would have told anyone who asked that they were probably the most Christian-minded people he had ever had the pleasure to meet. That they chose to live under a different banner meant nothing to him.

Sitting here now, in Storm's elegant yet homely flat, Henri found it hard to believe that Nick had been gone almost three years. He remembered his friend, so young and always so full of fun, bursting with ideas and such a genuine willingness to help anyone who needed it. All that vitality, gone. It had broken his heart.

Storm rose to put the kettle back on, the movement bringing Henri back to the present moment. Although he had rehearsed what he was about to say, he felt suddenly awkward bringing this to his friend's door.

He knew that Storm hadn't lost her faith in the world of spirit, just her place within it, which to Henri felt a hundred times worse. He had been over this in his mind so many times but it was so much harder than he'd imagined.

Taking a deep breath, he offered up a quick prayer and hoped on everything that was holy to him that she would still be willing to help.

CHAPTER 30

'*A*m I going to have to break out the chocolate biscuits to get you to talk about whatever it is?' Storm was leaning against the kitchen counter, smiling at him patiently, her eyebrow arched in amusement. Henri knew he had a habit of occasionally thinking so hard he lost all track of time and he suspected that he'd just been doing one of his best zoning-out acts.

'What? Oh. Yes. Sorry,' Henri said, trying to force his brain back into gear. Taking a deep breath, he added, 'I'm not sure even your home-made biscuits will be enough, my dear. You may decide that brandy is more appropriate when you've heard this, even at this ungodly early hour.'

Taking the fresh pot back to the table she said, 'Well now I'm officially intrigued.' Then her face paled. 'You're okay? I mean, you're not poorly, are you?'

'Heavens no, nothing like that,' he said quickly. 'Fit as a fiddle, apart from this wretched knee of course, but that's by the by.'

The relief was obvious on her face and Henri waited for Storm to refill their mugs before taking another deep breath, sitting tall in his chair and, without further hesitation, launching into his story.

'When I was a young man, I had visions. They started as dreams. Vivid dreams from which I'd wake sick to my stomach, bathed in sweat and trembling. At first, I had no recollection of what they were about save that they unsettled me in a way I could never quite describe. Dot and I were only just married and, bless her soul, I couldn't have been easy to live with back then. But true to form, rather than get ratty with me, she'd get up, bring me fresh pyjamas and a cup of camomile tea. Sleep was usually impossible after that, so we'd sit up together talking until I had calmed down. She never pushed me to speak about it, but I did try – many times.' Henri took a mouthful of his tea before continuing.

'It never really worked, the talking about it, I mean. It was as if my head was full of the information, but I just wasn't able to articulate it. A bit like hearing a ghost story told in a language you don't understand – you can't elucidate on the details but somehow you still manage to get the shivers down your spine.

'This went on for weeks, sometimes up to four or five nights a week until Dot, ever the smartest half of the double act, bought me a journal,' he said, smiling at the memory of her. 'She'd read that sometimes, when trying to access things that the conscious mind finds difficult, one can write almost automatically as if the hand and the subconscious can go to work without having to navigate the complexity of our thinking mind. She hoped it might work on my dreams.'

'She was a wise one,' Storm said softly, a sad smile on her lips.

'And it worked,' Henri continued. 'I'd wake, go down to my study and sit there with the journal and a pen. The first night I tried it, Dot found me asleep on my desk in the morning. I got the shock of my life when I looked at the journal and found that there were twenty-three pages in my own hand.

'After that, the dreams came every night for a little over three weeks. It was as if in writing them down, I'd opened the sluice gates. I'd filled the first journal and three-quarters of a second before they suddenly stopped. Just like that. As quickly as they'd come, they went. I was so relieved to be free of them if I'm truly honest.'

'What did you write about?' Storm asked.

Henri waited a beat before answering. 'You have to understand that I was a young man. I was newly married, and I saw my life in the Church. I loved the Church and when the dreams first started, I confided them to my mentor, Bishop Gregory. I had thought the dreams a test of my faith, or perhaps messages from God, but he had very different ideas. He was a kind man, but very traditional. He had no time for anything that defied rational explanation, which I suppose is the ultimate irony. He told me to destroy the journals and never speak of them to anyone. I suppose he worried about what people would think of me and, by association, him and the Church itself. Had my mental health been called into question it might have well ended my career before it had properly begun. I couldn't bring myself to destroy them, but I vowed never to read what he had called my mad ramblings. So, I asked Dot to hide them away. She did and then we simply got on with our lives again.' Henri paused.

When at last he spoke again, he met Storm's eyes and said, 'Then a couple of weeks ago the dreams started again. And after all these years I found myself scurrying off to my study to find a notebook in the middle of the night.'

Henri reached into his overcoat that was hanging on the back of his chair and pulled out the small red notebook. Flicking past the shopping lists and hastily jotted phone numbers he opened it and, after a moment's hesitation, handed it to Storm. He knew what was written, repeated on every available page of the book, including the back cover without looking. Storm read them aloud, her voice barely above a whisper.

'The Falling is upon us. All the bounty of the Mother lost to man's greed. The sky screams. It too will fall, piece by terrible piece. The seas rise as the Mother in her desperation engulfs her ruinous children, but it is too late. One of the new will decide our fate. To rise - or to fall. All rests with the Ethereal.'

STORM READ the lines again slowly, but before she could speak Henri said, 'If you'll indulge me, my dear, there's another piece to this that I need you to read.'

Reaching back into his coat pocket he retrieved the second item he had come here to share with her. He pulled the letter out of the envelope, enjoying the familiar feel of his wife's linen writing paper under his fingertips and imagined he could still smell her perfume.

'Dorothy wrote this to me from the hospice,' he said, still holding the letter gently, his thumb moving idly over its surface. 'She wrote me letters almost every day, even when I was there sitting right next to her. She said I had a hard enough time remembering what I'd had for lunch so thought she'd leave me some more reliable reminders of our life together.' His voice trembled, and he was glad of the letter's distraction to give him time to regroup.

Henri proffered the letter and Storm took it as if it were made of glass. 'I know it sounds strange, but I've not been able to bring myself to read them all,' he said when he was sure that his voice wouldn't fail him. 'The later ones, the ones she wrote towards the end when she was dosed up with so many drugs, were often, well, nonsensical. There were a few that were lucid, but to tell you the truth, I've not found the strength to relive those last days – not yet.' Glancing up, Henri saw Storm's grey eyes full of tears. She had been there every day too as her dear friend had slipped away from them and Henri knew that she, more than most, understood completely.

'To tell you the truth, I've prevaricated on this for too long. I thought I was losing it, to be honest, tried to push it all out of my mind, but then I had a dream about Dot. I'll spare you the truly weird bits, but clear as day she told me to find her letters.' He spared her the saga of the search which had turned his cottage into something akin to a bomb site. The only thing that mattered now was making sure Storm understood. If she thought he was missing a marble or two then he really was lost. She gave his arm a reassuring squeeze, which encouraged him.

'It took me an age to find them, but when I did, as I suspected, many of them made no sense at all. But then I found this one.' He pointed to the still-folded letter in Storm's hand. 'It was her last letter and it was still sealed,' he said with a sigh. 'I've no idea how the hell I missed it. She wrote it just three days before she passed, so close to two years ago – or to be precise about it, twenty-two months, three weeks and one day.' He gave her a brief, rueful smile.

Storm squeezed his hand again. 'It was something of a difficult time, as I remember,' she said kindly. 'The important thing is that you've found it now.'

Henri wasn't convinced she'd feel the same after reading what his wife had to say.

* * *

MY DARLING HENRI,

One of the surprising things about dying is how much

you suddenly seem to remember about one's life. Things long cast to the sands of time seem to be suddenly so vivid and important. I dreamed last night of your journals. Do you remember, my love? Those awful weeks you endured the nightmares and then the long nights writing like a madman at your desk? It broke my heart to watch you in such distress.

My love, I have a confession and a plea to make to you and as I write I can think of nothing more *urgent* or *important*. I promised you I would never read your journals and it's a promise I almost kept. Please forgive me, my darling, but as I tidied away your journals from your desk one morning, I saw that you had drawn a face so exquisite that I was utterly captivated.

I never intended to break my promise to you but you always joked you could barely draw breath, and having seen your attempts at art over the years, I was minded to agree with you, but then to see this face – this heavenly face from your own hand – I was mesmerised!

I tried to speak to you at the time, but the dreams upset you so much and with the Church and their nonsense, I had to let it go. I put the books away just as you asked me and never looked at them again.

By my reckoning that was fifty-three years ago, or there abouts. Can you believe it? I've barely thought of it since, but then this morning, it came to me, not the face, more's the pity, it's driving me totally bonkers trying to recall it, but what you had called it. Underneath the picture you'd written: 'The First Ethereal'. I remember that clearly because it seemed so strange.

Please don't say it's the drugs. I've had many a trip these past few months thanks to all that happy juice they're giving me and believe me I know the difference. I think, my love, it is spirit reaching out to me – not to take me, not yet anyway, but to tell me something vitally important. And it *is* vitally important – of that I am utterly convinced.

Please, dig out your journals and read them. I know now as I knew then that those dreams came to you for a reason. Perhaps it's my increasing proximity to the hereafter, but I have a grave feeling that the information you were given then is hugely important. I know in every fibre of my being, my love, that you were meant to hold it and keep it safe until the time was right and I sense that *now* is the time.

Now, don't roll your eyes and mutter things about my love of the dramatic; this is altogether different. I also fear that there is very little time left – not just for me, and this is where I *will* be dramatic without apology, but for ... everything – for all creation itself.

Please, do this for me. For our boys. Be strong, my love, and do it *now* – there's so *little time.*

All my love, always,

D xxx

* * *

THE TEARS SPILLED SILENTLY from Storm's eyes and she wiped them away with the sleeve of her cardigan. Henri had anticipated how she'd feel, reading her friend's words from beyond the veil, but there had been no way to prepare her for it. Her eyes darted back to the top of the letter and Henri waited as she read it again, more slowly this time as if she were drinking in not just the meaning, but the essence of her friend too.

Henri waited for a long moment before he spoke again. 'Does it mean anything at all to you? Have you heard about the First Ethereal anywhere before?'

Storm, her eyes still on the letter, shook her head. 'No,' she said, 'nothing ...' She trailed off, but Henri didn't need her to say any more. The loss of Storm's gift had rocked them all. They had once all been so connected by their belief in the spiritual, Storm, Nick, Veronica, him and Dot, sitting up late into the night drinking wine then rocket-fuel coffee and putting this world and the next to rights.

'You didn't bring the journals though?' Storm asked.

Henri shook his head. 'That's where it gets complicated. My darling Dot hid them from me just as I made her promise she would and I cannot for the very life of me find them. I have searched through every inch of the new house and they're just not there.'

Storm nodded, but said nothing; instead she got to her feet and walked to the sideboard to retrieve her phone from a drawer. 'We can put our heads together on the journals in a moment, but first let's get Veronica on the case to see what the library has to say,' she said, the phone already ringing on loudspeaker. Henri felt the tension slip from his shoulders and his heart lift for the first time in days.

CHAPTER 31

*V*eronica's phone rang until her voicemail kicked in. Henri and Storm looked at each other. He looked as deflated as she felt. When Storm's phone burst into song a couple of minutes later they both jumped. She answered quickly and put it on speaker phone.

Veronica was out of breath. 'Sorry to miss you,' she said, puffing slightly. 'I left my phone in the garden room.' Storm smiled to herself, picturing her friend hotfooting it through her truly enormous house trying to remember which of the dozens of rooms she'd left her phone in this time.

'You so need a belt clip for that phone!' Storm chuckled, but hesitated. There was something not quite right in her friend's tone. 'I was wondering if you could help with a bit of research—'

Veronica cut her off sharply. 'That recipe? Yes, of course, but I think you need to come over so I can show you. It's not the type of dish we can discuss on the phone, Storm.' The use of her full name and not one of the innumerable pet names Vee usually used confirmed her suspicion that something was off.

'That sounds like a plan. Thanks, Veronica. Give me half an hour and I'll be with you,' Storm said, trying to keep her tone neutral.

'I'll dig out the book while I wait. Cheery bye,' Veronica said and then promptly hung up.

The look on Henri's face told her that she wasn't imagining it.

'Cheery bye?' he said, frowning. 'Something's definitely not right.'

The dogs, snoozing companionably one each end of the sofa, barely registered their departure.

CHAPTER 32

Five miles out of town, Veronica was heading to her library, which was the one and only reason she was living in a four-thousand-square-foot glass-box new build and not a nice little cottage in the village as would have been her preference.

Veronica had inherited the library from her mother. It was already five generations old by that time and had always been held by the women, although she was planning on breaking that tradition by asking her nephew Michael to become her apprentice. A number of the books had not just been owned but had been written by the women in Veronica's family down the ages – not that anyone would have known, of course, because these weren't the type of books destined, nor indeed safe, for public consumption.

Veronica herself had been collecting and adding to the library for as long as she could remember and there were days when she wondered where the library stopped and she began. The library gave sanctuary to those hunted books that would never be safe elsewhere – the ones whose very existence posed a threat to some people and their world views.

There were books in the collection so old that they were kept in hermetically sealed rooms. It was the one upside Veronica had seen when her husband, Asim, declared his intention to fulfil his lifelong ambition to self-build. In reality that had meant commissioning a fancy architect and an equally fancy contractor to erect the glass monstrosity she was now forced to call home. She had much preferred the old house but had had to give in when a break-in made her realise just how vulnerable the library was in a house so old it was always in need of repair. Then there had been the river. While people were still, to her complete bafflement, willing to pay through the nose for a grand house with a river frontage, it was only a matter of time before it would rise up and deluge the place and on that front she'd been sadly proved correct.

Once the decision had been made, she enjoyed the process of designing the library. It was tucked out of sight in the basement of the house and secured behind doors usually found on bank vaults. Unlike everything else in the house, which was ultra-modern, the inside of the library looked like something out of Hogwarts and it still made Veronica beam with delight every time she stepped inside it. It was her duty to protect the collection and she had gone to extraordinary lengths to ensure that as few people as possible knew of its existence.

A few well-timed disagreements with architects and contractors throughout the process, plus some magical help from Storm back when she still had her magic, meant that the basement had been omitted from the final plans and, even if quizzed, no one involved in the project would remember exactly what they'd been building on the property.

Computers had been invented under her late mother's guardianship and, while she had investigated the opportunity for at least cataloguing the thousands of books, instinct had warned her against the idea. In the years that followed, as Veronica watched the internet bloom from flower to something akin to Japanese knotweed, she was grateful for her mother's wisdom and foresight. If these books got into the wrong hands, if even the names or authors of some of these books got out, it just didn't bear thinking about.

As she hurried down the stairs to the basement, Veronica felt the knot of panic in her stomach ease ever so slightly knowing that her friend was on her way. All she had to do now was make sure that the library hadn't been compromised.

CHAPTER 33

*H*enri and Storm headed out of town on the high road that wound its way around the mountain, climbing to offer stunning views of the verdant green valley below. The spring sunshine was still weak and there was enough of a nip in the air to warrant putting on the heater. Storm chewed her lip anxiously as she drove, her foot heavy on the accelerator. She wondered what she'd say if stopped for speeding. 'Our friend didn't sound herself on the phone, officer.' It was beyond weak but that was the thing about friendship – sometimes you just knew.

The huge wrought-iron gates were all that interrupted the ten-foot-high brick wall that encircled the grand design. Asim had spent a fortune on them, but they were usually left open, a source of much eye-rolling from Veronica and ribbing about what a waste of money they had been. So Storm was surprised to see them closed today and even more surprised when a security guard with a beautiful long-coated German Shepherd marched out from behind them, his face set and his hand holding tightly to the dog's lead. Unsmiling, he gestured for Storm to get out of the car.

Storm approached him cautiously, her sense of unease growing.

'Name please,' he demanded when she was still some ten feet away. He gave an almost imperceptible nod, then fixed his eyes on Henri who was peering out of his rolled-down window.

'I'm going to have to ask you to step out of the car, sir,' the guard said in a tone that brokered no argument. When Henri complied, he asked them both to stand in front of the video camera mounted on the wall. A second later, after cocking his head to listen to whatever had presumably been said into his earpiece, he told them to return to the car and the gates swung open.

Henri and Storm exchanged worried glances but kept their thoughts to themselves. Veronica was standing at the front door as they pulled up, speaking to another security guard. This one had a springer spaniel sitting at his heel and Storm smiled, thinking about how useless Hope would be in any sort of canine profession beyond biscuit tester or perhaps court jester. The guard nodded to them stiffly as he passed them on the steps. Veronica hugged them both in turn and Storm could feel the tension in her friend.

'Henri, it's been too long, my friend, it's so wonderful to see you.' As he started to reply, she held her finger to her lips. 'Not here,' she said, her face pale and anxious. They followed Veronica through the vast hallway and down the corridor to a kitchen larger than Storm's entire flat.

Henri was the first to speak. 'Are you quite okay, my dear?' he asked, resting his hand gently on Veronica's shoulder as she busied herself filling the kettle. He took it from her and deftly guided her to one of the tall chairs at the enormous central island. Veronica was not a flapper. As steady as a rock in any kind of crisis, to see her so jangled was unsettling.

Allowing herself to be steered, Veronica sat down. 'I'm okay,' she said in a voice that told long-term friends she was anything but. 'Just a bit frazzled if I'm honest. But …' She faltered for a second and Henri used the pause to continue filling the kettle and preparing three mugs. Storm sat next to her friend, her hand over Veronica's.

After a few moments, Veronica took another deep breath and began again. 'When you called me, I was hunting for the phone. It rang off just as I got into the garden room but then just as I picked it up it rang again and it was Asim. He's in Hong Kong on business, some big deal they've just landed, it's all very hush-hush, but anyway, he called to say that his team had,' she mimed quote marks in the air, '"detected suspicious activity on the line." I laughed, to be honest, I thought he was joking, but apparently not.' Veronica's usually soft features were all angles and shadows and when she tried a little laugh, it came out flat and unconvincing.

'Take your time, sweetie,' Storm said, rubbing her back.

'Even for a cyber-security boffin, Asim's been paranoid of late. This deal is huge, and he's been concerned that a competitor is trying to find a weakness in the company's system. He's been going on about it for weeks and I've not paid a lot of attention. You know what he's like.' She smiled then, a little of the usual Veronica back when talking about the love of her life.

'Anyway, this morning he calls to say that the security team, the cheery-looking chaps you met outside, and their pals had also found six drone-type devices watching the house, waiting for their chance to get in, no doubt. They can be as small as flies apparently – can you believe that? Good job it's been chilly and I've not had the windows open. They'd also found,' she mimed the quote marks again, '"issues with the house phone lines and my mobile", which basically means that someone has been tapping into my calls and emails and who knows what else. Which is why I was a bit rude when you called me. I'm so sorry, poppet, but I just didn't want you to say something about the library.'

'I knew there was something wrong. You poor love!' Storm said, leaning over to squash her friend into a bear hug.

'I take it we're free to speak now?' Henri asked, his eyes full of concern.

'Yes, we're fine now. They've dealt with them all and they've put some sort of electronic shielding thing around the house so if whoever it is tries to send a drone in again, or lurk outside listening, they'll be blocked and the techies will be notified.'

'So Asim thinks it's a competitor?' Storm asked.

'Well, no, this is where it starts to get really frightening. The security team … they said that the drones that they intercepted were military-grade. Absolutely state of the art and nothing they'd ever seen before, which is saying something – this lot work for Asim and they're at the top of their game in this field. He's adamant that none of his competitors are anywhere near that sort of technology, so now he's worried that whoever it is might know about the library.' Veronica almost wailed out the last sentence and her huge blue eyes swam with tears.

'But it's okay now?' Henri asked, the concern evident in his voice.

Veronica nodded and then managed a little smile. 'Asim usually handles the library security himself. Only he and Georgina at the company have anything to do with the library, but they're both in Hong Kong. He didn't want the security team who turned up today to know, so as well as checking some stuff remotely, he told me where to find a handheld detector so I checked it myself.'

'That's a relief. Just the thought of someone coming after

the library makes my blood run cold,' Storm said with a shudder. 'I'm glad it's okay.'

Veronica let out a sigh. 'Well, there are no bugs or drones down there, but I wouldn't go as far as to say it was okay,' she said, the worry creeping back onto her face. When they turned questioning glances in her direction, she said, 'I could try to explain, but I really think you need to see this for yourself. But before we do though, what did you need me for?'

Ten minutes later, with his story told, Veronica handed Dot's letter and the notebook back to Henri, pushed herself out of the chair and said, 'I think you need to see this right away.'

After leaving their mobiles on the island – all technology was banned from the library – they followed her to the large walk-in larder at the back of the kitchen that concealed both the lift, insurance against any age-related mobility issues that might one day keep Veronica from her charges, and the flight of stairs. To Storm's relief, Veronica opted for the stairs.

CHAPTER 34

'*C*an you not get a bloody move on, man?' Marcus van de Meijer snapped after yanking back the glass partition between him and his driver. 'Did you know that this car has a top speed of one hundred and eighty miles per hour? Take a short cut or something or we'll be late.' He slammed the partition back into place without waiting for a reply. He could have more easily used the intercom button, but it lacked the impact that he wanted. Seeing Kevin, or was it Kalvin, he could never remember, shrink back in his seat reassured him that the message had been felt as well as understood. Damned idiot.

Slumping back into his seat he watched with mounting irritation as the car crawled through the West End of London behind an armoured personnel carrier. He actually quite missed the days when traffic congestion was all you had to deal with. Now the challenge was avoiding the great unwashed who seemed to have nothing better to do than take to the streets to protest or, as was happening with increasingly regularity, stage a full scale riot. While the City was patrolled by private security teams, once you left the square mile road you were at the mercy of the live sat nav feeds to chart a route out of the chaos.

When at last they arrived at the gates of the Hatman estate, after enduring a seemingly endless series of twisting country lanes, he checked his watch. They were ten minutes early, but they might have been ten minutes late had he not put a rocket up the chap's arse.

A butler was waiting on the front steps to meet him. It was ridiculously pretentious in this day and age, Marcus thought, but he couldn't quite bring himself to disapprove entirely. He certainly looked the part – early sixties, neatly trimmed greying hair and a slight stoop to balance the some-what superior air about him.

'Good afternoon, Mr van de Meijer. Mr Charles will see you in the library,' the butler said, turning into the house and setting off down a long wide panelled corridor to the room that Marcus could have found with his eyes shut. Marcus never remembered the butler's name despite frequent visits over the years, so he simply nodded and followed.

Charles was with his PA, a horsey-looking woman in her middle years. 'Marcus, good of you to come,' Charles said, extending his hand and pumping it warmly. 'That's all for now, Carole. Get someone to grab us some drinks, will you, there's a love,' he added without looking at her. Closing the folder in her hand, she headed for the door.

The men took a sofa each facing one another over a low, highly polished coffee table, and made small talk until their drinks had been delivered by a tiny bird of a woman dressed in a pale grey uniform complete with a screamingly white apron. She was probably pushing sixty, Marcus thought, and chuckled to himself. Victoria, Charles's long-suffering third wife, at least had the sense not to put temptation in his way. Every member of staff at the estate, male as well as female, was at least forty years north of where Charles liked them.

When the maid closed the heavy panelled door behind her, Marcus spoke. 'You have news then,' he said, rolling his whisky around his glass.

Charles drained his drink in one hit. Things were worse than Marcus had thought. As he poured himself another, Charles said, 'Looks like we have a little problem.' The way he pronounced 'little' made it clear to Marcus that it was anything but. He said nothing, just raised his eyebrows and waited.

After a sip of his second glass, Charles said, 'Wang called me with a vision. The Ethereal. It's here.'

Marcus froze, his glass halfway between table and mouth. 'But we'd dismissed that as legend years ago. He's wrong. You know he wanted Margot's slot on the council, so he's trying to game us, creepy little sod.'

Charles was shaking his head. 'That's what I thought too, to begin with, but think about it. We rejected Wang, not because he's not a gifted seer, but because he's hard to control. He's a fucking psycho and because of that we have no leverage. He doesn't lie because he sees no point to it. He's got more money than he can spend and he knows we need skills like his. His world is black and white and while the lack of any level of conscience comes in handy for the trickier stuff, there's nothing in it for him at this point. Besides, I've checked with other sources and they confirm what he said.'

'Christ,' was all Marcus could think to say and they sat there in silence, the only sound Charles angrily swirling the ice in his whiskey glass until Marcus asked, 'How did you check?'

'Martin finally tracked down another one of the libraries. Or I should say, part of a library. The keeper had managed to relocate all but a handful of books by the time our people got there. She was no bloody help, despite pretty forceful persuasion, but we got lucky on one of the books and that, combined with the testimony of a few of our other seers, well, let's just say it's enough to be sure,' he said, and all but slammed his crystal tumbler down onto the coffee table. Then, like some predator in a zoo, he got up to pace around the opulent room.

'Any clues on location?' Marcus asked, slumping back into the sofa and feeling the full weight of the setback beginning to sink in. 'Could we lean on the keeper for any more information? I know they're hard-nosed bitches, most of the time, but—'

Charles's snarling grin cut him off. 'I think we'd need Margot's talents for talking to her now,' he said with a snort. Marcus shuddered and swallowed the beginnings of the bile that had risen in his throat. He understood that these things happened in the course of their business, of course he did, but Charles had a habit of looking for all the world as if he took pleasure in it, and that he found hard to stomach.

'What of Margot? Why the hell didn't she pick this up?' Marcus snapped, his anger redirected.

Charles sighed, retaking his seat on the sofa opposite Marcus. 'She seemed genuinely baffled when I spoke to her. Keeping the stories of the Ethereal to only the chair and deputy,' he said, nodding to Marcus, 'was a deliberate and, I see now, a wise decision by our predecessors. She'll scry for it now, of course, or whatever the freaks call it when they go searching for stuff in the tea leaves, but I'm confident that she was unaware. As she's fond of reminding us, the visions pick the seer.'

'And no other leads on a possible location?' Charles asked.

'No, not on the Ethereal anyway. The prophecy talks about a book that's integral to the whole woo-woo bullshit and Wang did pick up an energy trace around that. Turns out though that it's in the same town as Margot's failed protégé,' Charles said, raising an eyebrow.

'Bit of a coincidence, don't you think?' Marcus said, snorting.

'My thoughts exactly. I sent her down there to check and her report tallies with what I got back from other sources. The Storm woman is about as psychic as a brick. So no, I don't think she's the link, but that area has always been a hotspot. I'm having it checked out again now.'

'Assuming that either the Ethereal turns out to be a fairy story after all, or it's a threat we can easily eliminate, where do we stand in terms of the plan?' Marcus asked.

Charles brightened visibly at the mention of his favourite subject and recharged their glasses. 'As you know, the systems collapse is well under way and, according to the eggheads, is gathering pace nicely. We're doing all we can to keep the news of the additional deaths out of official records and away from the news and social media channels, but as you can imagine, even with our considerable reach it's impossible to get to every conscientious local official. So, we're playing distract and undermine – a civil war here, a terrorist attack there, throw in a royal wedding, a few celebrity babies and add a dash of that pantomime we called our political systems, and nobody knows quite where to look next. Stupid fuckers,' he laughed. 'And speaking of stupid fuckers, when stories do surface, we shout fake news.' He raised his glass. 'Cheers to you, the Donald, for that little gem, even if it wasn't your idea.'

'Like shooting fish in a barrel.' Marcus shook his head in disbelief. He'd never quite believed that it would be so easy, but he had been wrong on that particular point – it really was that easy to deflect and distract the masses.

Charles stretched theatrically and sat back, spreading his arms along the back of the chesterfield. 'It's almost no fun any more, it's so easy. They have absolutely no idea of what's coming either, which I suppose is for the best.'

'And what about the schedule?' Marcus asked.

'If the modelling is correct, we'll need to bunker by the end of July, sooner possibly if the shit really starts to hit the fan with the melting. My chaps are worrying their eggy little heads about atmospheric methane absorption or something or other at the moment. They think it might kick off a massive feedback loop and deliver a huge adrenaline kick to the temperatures. That'll be the tipping point for the floods and of course they'll be far bigger than the current estimates, we've seen to that.' He nodded matter-of-factly.

'And where are we on the numbers?' Marcus asked, keeping his gaze steady. This was always the point at which he felt a tad queasy. He supported the plan, of course he did, it was the only way, but there was no denying that the collateral damage was significant.

'We're already well on our way, thanks to the sepsis stuff, but if everything else goes as projected, we're looking at least a billion dead within the first nine months. When you also factor in deaths from fire, extreme heat, famine and civil unrest, which is basically code for the survivors turning Mad Max and offing each other,' he snorted as he laughed, losing his thread momentarily. 'Anyway, at that point disease kicks in in a big way, the usual stuff mainly – cholera, malaria, diarrhoea – and there's a good chance that Ebola will play a bigger part too apparently.' He got up, went to his desk and rifled through some paperwork. 'I've got a graph here somewhere. Anyway, there's also the bacterial stuff – that'll take out a huge swathe. Even those able to get their hands on existing antibiotics will find them next to useless in more than eighty per cent of cases now. I'm assuming you got your delivery of the new broad-spectrum one?'

Marcus nodded. 'Yes, all received and stowed. Hang on. Eighty? So, the forty per cent stat quoted in the reporting of the sepsis crisis is our doing?'

'What?' Charles asked distractedly, still riffling through papers before giving up and retaking his seat. 'Yes, we didn't want too much of a panic around the whole antibiotic thing – the big-ag chaps were getting a kicking in the stock markets. So we massaged the numbers down to something more palatable. Anyway, bugger about that graph – it's here somewhere – but the headline is that we should still be on track to be clear in under a decade, all things considered.' He smiled as if he'd just presented an impressive set of year-end numbers to the board of a PLC. 'Oh, and I should say that's just organic loss. It assumes we don't need to resort to releasing Dennis's nasty little bug.' He shuddered theatrically.

Marcus sucked in a deep breath. 'I was never a fan of that route – way too messy for my liking and no guarantees that it wouldn't still be waiting for us when we emerge. No, this is …' he struggled to find the appropriate word, 'safer.' Then he realised the absurdity of his choice; for ninety-nine per cent of the human population there would never be safety again.

Charles threw back his head and laughed as if the irony had been intended. Marcus smiled then drained his whiskey, but the taste of bile was still there. It was Charles's nonchalance that scared him most. While most of their community reluctantly accepted the sacrifices and difficult choices that were needed to save their species and start afresh, Charles genuinely seemed to be looking forward to the collapse of human civilisation, the deaths of literally billions of men, women and children. Cold bastard.

'Got time to see the bunker? They finished the E.O.G room yesterday – do you like it? I thought *Eye of God* seemed appropriate. We're banned from playing with the drones yet, no need to draw unwanted attention, but you can still get an amazing view of practically anything on the planet with our satellites. I'll get Cook to fix us some lunch and we can test it.' Glancing at his watch he said, 'Doubt the Yanks will be scrapping this early, but it's a permanent bloodbath in Hungary these days. We could snoop in on them, maybe pick up some street-fighting tips, just in case our security chaps mutiny.' He laughed again as he headed for the door, Marcus in his wake.

CHAPTER 35

*H*enri and Storm followed Veronica down the winding wrought-iron staircase, which was dimly but adequately lit from caged lights on the walls and on each tread. Veronica liked it like that, she said; the change in the light level helped her prepare herself for the transition between her two worlds – the always slightly too bright existence as Mrs Burman and this, her real life as the keeper of words and secrets.

When they reached the heavy steel door at the bottom of the stairs, Veronica bent to have her iris scanned, inserted her finger into a reader and then stated her name. She moved aside as Henri and Storm went through the same procedure. A series of metallic clunks preceded a swoosh of artificially cool air around their ankles as the door swung slowly open. They followed Veronica through to a small connecting room as the heavy vault door closed behind them. As they waited for the frosted glass wall in front of them move aside, Veronica turned to face them. 'Just stand still, don't panic, and let them come to you. Okay?' she said, her face earnest and pale. Neither of them had time to respond to their friend's strange instruction because the door was already opening.

Though they had both been here before, the scene before them was so startling that neither of them could do anything but stare. Books were flying through the air in all directions. Some were flapping their pages like angry geese as they screeched passed in a rustle of old paper, others were bullet-like, bound tightly shut and zooming off at speed like birds of prey homing in on a mouse before taking ninety-degree bends to career down the stacks. Storm remembered Veronica telling her that there were close to ten thousand books in the collection now, and it seemed that every single one was at this moment animated with such urgency that not a single volume could hold itself still. There was panic in the air as if a predator had run into a resting flock. Even Storm could feel the energy that crackled and spat in the air around them.

They stood mesmerised for a few seconds then Henri whispered, 'How long have they been doing this?'

'They were like this when I first came down with the detector, so at least a couple of hours, but in all honesty, I don't know. They were quiet as mice last night. I was down here reading until about seven, so whatever spooked them must have happened after that. Maybe that was when the drones appeared.' She shrugged.

'Or maybe there's something in the ether about the Ethereal,' Henri wondered aloud.

At the mention of the name, the books stopped abruptly. They hung, suspended in the air for a few heartbeats, and then one by one, they filed back to their shelves, some waiting politely as others passed them before slotting themselves back into their respective places. The three friends stared in disbelief. The space, which just a few seconds ago had been filled with books, was now empty, save for one battered little volume that hung in the air just a few feet in front of them. Small enough to fit into a palm, it was a truly ancient book with dark, rough-cut edges to its pages and a dilapidated teal cover. Its title and faded gold border, in a filigree design, were worn to a shadow by time and hands. As they stared at it, it floated calmly to Veronica who, as if welcoming a shy puppy, extended her hand. 'Come on, little one,' she whispered softly as it settled itself tentatively on her upturned palm. As she stroked its cover gently, she said softly, 'Can you hold your horses for another five minutes? I think my friends here need to fill me in on some background before you and I have a chat.'

A full twenty minutes later, Henri had told Veronica the story again, but this time filling in all the background – his visions as a young man, the advice of the bishop and the message from Dot in his dream. She asked questions and scribbled notes and a rough timeline on her notepad. The little book, now sitting on the large oak reading table they were sitting around, was growing visibly impatient because at various points in the story it hopped and shuffled towards Veronica. There was a fizz of energy emanating from it that was obvious to them all. It pleased Storm more than she could admit to feel it, although she guessed that the energy was so high here at the moment that anyone with a functioning nervous system would have been able to detect it, but it felt good nonetheless.

'I knew it had to be more than a security breach by a competitor,' Veronica said, dabbing at her eyes with a hankie after reading Dot's letter over once again. 'But this. This is end of days stuff.' She buried her head in her hands for a moment before she spoke again, but her voice was stronger now and focused. 'So, my little friend,' she said smiling at the book, 'tell me all about this Ethereal.'

Like an eager cadet at last able to salute, it wasted no time in flipping itself open to the page the whole library had been so desperate for them to read. Knowing that the reading of such magical texts was the preserve of the keeper, Storm and Henri resisted the urge to huddle around her and, instead, settled into their seats and tried not to count the seconds. The book might have been small, but where magical books were concerned, appearances could be deceptive.

After what felt like an age to Henri and Storm, but in reality was probably no more than ten minutes, Veronica suggested that they make some lunch while she read. Grateful for something to do, they were on their feet in seconds and heading for the stairs.

Back in the kitchen, Henri and Storm busied themselves, chatting as they found plates and raided the fridge. 'Spirit does indeed move in mysterious ways,' Henri said with a tight smile as he piled salad leaves into the colander to wash. 'Oh, Stormy, I'm sorry, that was tactless.'

'No, it wasn't, lovely,' Storm replied as she decanted plump green olives into a bowl. 'I can't expect people not to talk about spirit around me in case I get upset. Hell, if we were going down that path then the list of exclusions would make normal life impossible.' She smiled at him and he smiled in reply. Hesitating for a moment, she said, 'And, look, don't get excited, but something weird happened recently.'

Henri's face broke into a wide expectant smile. 'As in spiritual or magical things?' he asked.

She nodded. 'Spiritual. Look, I don't want to go into detail, not yet, not until I understand things a bit better myself – it might have been a one-off – but something is shifting, I can feel it. I just wish I knew what it was.'

Henri put down the salad spinner and smiled at her. 'Have you spoken to Margot?' he asked.

'Funny you should say that. She dropped in last night. It was all very last minute, she's over on a book tour I think, something like that, but the funniest thing, Henri ... I was so excited to see her, but when she was here ...' Storm fiddled with the crudités she was arranging on a plate. 'I'm being silly, but I couldn't bring myself to speak to her about the thing that happened. I almost caved in, but then a plant pot smashed in the other room and I swear I saw a spirit light disappearing as I rushed in, so there's someone around for sure. After that I was even more confused, so I said nothing. Daft, I know, but ...' Storm hesitated, wondering whether or not to tell Henri all about the encounter with Jack, but she decided against it. They had enough on their plates without getting distracted by what could likely be red herrings.

Henri said nothing for a while, focusing instead on the empty bowl in front of him as if what he wanted to say might be written inside. 'Is there anyone else who might help shed some light?'

Storm shook her head. 'That's another sad coincidence. One of my old magic tutors visited the shop recently.' She felt her heart ache as she remembered the look on the older woman's face when she saw the absence of Storm's magic. 'Doreen. I'd not seen her in years. She was the most amazing witch. I was a star pupil for her back in the day and—' She broke off, not sure how she wanted to finish the sentence.

Henri's smile faltered. 'Was?' he asked.

Storm nodded sadly. 'She knew just by looking at me that my magic was gone. She was so upset, bless her – made me promise to call her. When I did, though, her son told me she'd passed. It must have been just a few days after I saw her.'

'Dear lord,' Henri said, 'what happened?'

'He said she'd fallen by the canal and drowned,' Storm said, her eyes filling at the thought.

Henri put down the bread knife he was using and gave Storm a hug. 'I'm so very sorry to hear that. Poor lady.'

Storm dried her eyes on her sleeve and forced herself back to the present. 'It doesn't sit right with me though. I've been thinking about it ever since I found out and, well, it just doesn't seem like the type of thing that would happen to her. She might have been eighty, but she was a witch and a half in terms of her abilities,' she said.

'It sounds as if she would have been exactly the person to speak to about this Ethereal character and would probably have been able to tell us how we might be connected in some way to this quest,' Henri said.

Storm smiled. 'Don't you go all Frodo Baggins on me, mister. You'll not cast me as the fat hobbit sidekick,' she said, poking him gently in the shoulder with a carrot stick.

They were still laughing and trading lines from the film when Veronica walked into the room looking pale. 'I'm glad you've managed to find something funny in the coming apocalypse,' she said, smiling weakly. 'Stick the kettle on. I think we're going to be here a while.'

CHAPTER 36

*L*illy kept telling herself that it wasn't a date. They were just going to meet the animals at Michael's parents' sanctuary, that was all. She had already swapped shifts with Jen when he asked her, so she was working afternoons today. Probably for the best as the time would go quicker, she supposed.

She had spent the whole day thinking about Michael after that first meeting, so had decided that the only way to put him out of her mind was to see him again. She was out picking herbs the next morning when the back gate opened. Her heart had done a funny little flip thing but had sunk like a stone when she saw that it was Ash from the paper shop. He'd brought the delivery over because he'd been at the farm dropping off old newspapers or something. It was such a nice thing for him to do, but she had been so bitterly disappointed.

Lilly was back in the courtyard the next day and this time it was Michael who pushed open the back gate. She should have known because Anchor had followed her – forgoing the last of his breakfast, something usually unheard of, to hurry after her down the stairs, chirruping excitedly with each step.

When he had seen Michael, Anchor greeted him like an old friend, weaving around his legs until Michael put down the tray of veg and picked him up. Then it had been all head bops and purrs – the cat really was a complete trollop. Lilly would have to have been blind to miss the contrast between that and his reaction to poor Jack.

With the delivery safely in the kitchen with Jerry, they had sat in the sun with a couple of mugs of coffee. They had talked so easily, like they'd known each other for years instead of forty-eight hours. Even with the world collapsing around them, Lilly marvelled at how Michael could still be so full of stories about hope and inspiration. He told her about his time travelling around Europe last summer and the wonderfully kind people he had met, but the real light in his eyes was reserved for his parents' farm sanctuary. When he had asked if she wanted to visit, she had said yes so quickly he'd barely finished the sentence. She guessed that it probably wasn't the way to go about things, to be so blatantly keen, but, she reasoned, it wasn't like she had the luxury of time.

She surveyed the meagre collection of clothes on her bed and decided that she had no idea what to wear. She ruled out the black jeans as she wore them for her for her shifts at the café. That left two pairs of blue jeans, a white sundress, which given that they were meeting farm animals definitely wouldn't work, or her grey linen trousers, which were a bit smarter than jeans but not much. Sitting in the middle of the bed were the teal blue fingerless gloves one of her lovely regulars had given her yesterday.

Old Mrs Lucas, so called Lilly guessed because there must

also be a young Mrs Lucas in the town, had handed her a small parcel wrapped in blue tissue paper and tied with string as Lilly cleared her table.

'You said last week that you get cold hands like me,' she had said, 'so I got some wool from the farm rescue place and made you these. They've no fingers so that you can still use your phone – I know what you youngsters are like.'

Lilly had stood staring at the proffered gift, unable to believe that someone who she had only known for a few weeks could have done something quite so thoughtful, all because of a chat about cold hands. She had cried when she opened them, she couldn't help it, and told Old Mrs Lucas that it was the loveliest gift she'd ever had, which was true.

Looking at them neatly laid out on the bed, Lilly couldn't help but smile at the memory. She tried to ignore the voice in her head that was trying to tell her that she wouldn't be here this winter to wear them.

'If you just wear the mittens, I'm sure the date will go with a swing.' Jack's voice at her shoulder was flat and cold.

Spinning around she said coolly, 'It's not a date,' but even to her own ears it sounded like a lie and that didn't sit well with her. 'He's a friend. And they're fingerless gloves, not mittens.'

'I thought I was your friend,' Jack said petulantly. Lilly gritted her teeth and wondered why he was being so pig-headed about this. She wasn't a kid anymore. She was more than old enough to date and while she had always loved the way he looked out for her, she wasn't in any danger from a trip to a farm sanctuary. Tired of fighting, she decided on the conciliatory route.

She slipped her arms around his chest and hugged him, leaning her head on his turned back. 'You were my first friend and you'll always be my best friend – you know that.

Nobody could ever come close to meaning what you mean to me.' She felt some of the tension leave him and he bent his head to kiss her hand. Then she said, 'You're the brother I never had, Jack.' She was about to add, 'And I love you to the moon and back,' but she was already holding thin air.

CHAPTER 37

*A*s they picked at their lunch – it was funny how a pending apocalypse could ruin an appetite – Veronica shared what the little book had revealed so far.

'I hope that after all these years you know how the books work, but just so we're clear, while we have regular ink on paper books, the most magical ones are, well I suppose you could say they're conscious. They share information that's needed when it's needed and at a level of complexity that the reader, usually me, but not always, can handle. I can sit there some days and the pages will actually update themselves in front of me if I've suddenly grasped something complex and they think I'm ready to know a bit more. It's magical, clearly, but I want to be clear on this because I sense that what our little friend just shared is only a starter for ten. I would have stayed longer, but he snapped himself shut abruptly, so I'm also guessing that what he's told me so far he wants me to share, so here I am.'

Storm and Henri nodded their understanding so Veronica could continue.

'Do you want the long version or the short one?' Veronica asked.

'Short,' Henri and Storm said together.

'Okay. Firstly, what do you know about the ascension?' she asked, looking from one to the other in turn.

'Written about in lots of cultures and faiths around the world – usually in the context of "God",' Storm mimed inverted commas in the air, 'taking his chosen few and leaving non-believers to rot.'

'Much the same,' Henri said, nodding. 'Christians believe in the Rapture but in the new-age version of things, it's more about attaining a new level of vibration. Same principle, I suppose, just without the judgement, fire, brimstone and threat of eternal damnation.'

'A-stars to you both,' Veronica said, attempting a smile. 'From what our little friend revealed, it's all about vibrational frequency. The ascension happens when the Earth's energies rise sufficiently to pull us into the next phase of our evolution, which by all accounts should be the era of peace and love and harmony. We had been moving steadily up the vibrational scale since the dawn of time.'

'Past tense?' queried Henri, raising his eyebrows.

'Well spotted, lovely, yes, past tense.' She sighed heavily. 'The book was vague on the precise date, but for some years now we've been slipping down the scale, meaning that our collective vibration has been falling, not rising, and the speed of that decline is now escalating,' Veronica said, anxiety gnawing at her edges.

'And that's the problem?' Storm asked.

'I think *problem* is putting it lightly. Cataclysm comes closer,' Veronica said, pushing her untouched food around her plate. 'For one, it's completely unnatural. We have always moved forward in terms of vibration, so what's happening now is unprecedented, but if it continues to gather pace, we're looking at the end of all life on the planet.'

'All life?' Henri said. 'That we're driving our own species off a cliff is a given, but everything?'

Veronica nodded. 'All life needs a minimal vibration in order to exist. What we're messing with now is pure physics – or perhaps metaphysics would be more apt a description. Energy is the very fabric of life and we're screwing with it big time. What we're seeing, the ecological and social collapse, they have their roots in the energetic collapse. Make sense?'

'Sort of,' Henri said. 'Maybe if you say a bit about why it's happening?'

'It's complex, as most things are, but the biggest issue is fear pulling down the vibration level. While we should be playing the high notes of love, peace, and joy by now, we're down in the base notes of fear, pain, and hate,' Veronica said.

'But surely we've been in states of global fear before? What about the world wars? Medieval times when everyone was chopping each other's heads off and dying of famine and pestilence?' Storm said.

'That's true, but there are so many more of us now. In 1940 there were around two and a half billion of us. Now there are close to eight billion. We're not just having an impact on the material plane, but on the energetic one too. Fear is a contagion and with over half the world in crisis at the moment, it's no wonder that people are afraid and becoming even more so by the minute.'

'And it won't be just the people either,' Henri said, his expression hardening. 'You can add another sixty billion souls a year to the total – they're the ones we breed to eat and that's without those in the oceans or the wild creatures in fear of their lives through hunting and our encroachment.'

Veronica nodded. 'Absolutely, when you count all souls

and not just the human ones, it's no wonder that everything is so dire.'

'And that's without the fear the Earth is feeling herself,' Storm said.

Veronica nodded and continued. 'The little book was at pains to tell me that these natural disasters we've been hearing about lately – the fires, floods, earthquakes, that terrible tsunamis in Asia – they're all just the tip of the iceberg. The scale of the devastation is far greater than is being reported at the moment.'

'And did it say why this is happening?' Storm asked.

'It did. It's a combination of all Earth's systems failing and also her attempts to fight back by …'

'Getting rid of us?' Henri offered when Veronica lost her words.

Veronica nodded. 'You can't blame her, of course. You don't need arcane magical books to figure out that we're not just destroying ourselves but pretty much all life on the planet and have been for some time now. All organisms, even usually benevolent ones, have their breaking points. But, of course, as the Earth fights back, the fear levels rise and the energy falls further and so it continues …' She broke off, shaking her head, tears pooling her eyes.

'So in ascension terms, it's like being in a hot-air balloon that's just too heavy to lift off,' Storm said as she got up to put her barely touched plate by the sink.

'But we're approaching the point of no return,' Veronica said. 'The point where, metaphorically, the balloon self-destructs.'

'Did the book say how long we had?' Henri ventured, his voice shaking.

Veronica took a deep steadying breath and paused before she answered. Nodding, she said, 'It said we had a week.'

They sat in stunned silence until Storm, her voice shaking, asked, 'And what happens then?'

Veronica took a deep breath before answering, 'I think that'll be part two when I go back down, but my sense is this is where Henri's vision kicks in. The world in flames, seas rising, sky breaking apart with black lightning.'

'Like reality will tear itself apart,' Henri said quietly.

'That's about the size of it, yes,' Veronica said, hiccupping down a sob.

'Could the book be wrong this time?' Henri asked hopefully.

Veronica smiled weakly at him but shook her head ruefully. 'The magical libraries were founded on truth as a universal principle. They don't make mistakes, play games or otherwise deceive. They're incapable of it.'

'Shit. Shit. Shit. Shit!' said Storm, her eyes filling with hot angry tears as she began to pace. 'Shouldn't we tell the authorities? I mean, surely something of this magnitude ...' The words trailed off as she realised the futility of the idea. Margot's first and most important lesson when she was growing up was that she was to conceal her magic at all costs.

The silence descended again. Storm continued to pace, swiping at the tears that were rolling down her cheeks, until she became aware of the tick of the old kitchen clock. She dried her eyes on the sleeve of her cardigan, blew her nose with the handkerchief Veronica held out to her and then said, 'So the library can't be wrong, but that doesn't mean there's no hope. I mean why would it be telling us this if we were already out of time?'

'And that, my lovely, is our tiny silver lining. Nothing in the universe is set in stone, everything is in perpetual motion, so we still have a chance to change things. You're right, the library wouldn't have told us otherwise. I need to go back down, but with what we know now, we have to assume that's why you had your visions, Henri – you must be somehow connected to the Ethereal and if we can find him or her or it, then we have a chance,' Veronica said, trying to muster an encouraging smile.

'Okay, so step one is finding my journals and the picture of this Ethereal, whatever it is,' Henri said, getting to his feet. 'I already have an idea of where they might be.'

'Marvellous. I'll work on answering the question of who, what and hopefully where it is while you're gone.' Veronica pushed back her chair. She paused on her way to the larder just long enough to hug each of her friends in turn.

'I'll call you once I know more,' she said, trying to be brave and determined, but not quite managing to keep the quiver out of her voice.

CHAPTER 38

'*A*re you out of your bloody mind?' Storm's voice was much louder in the confines of the small car than she'd intended, and Henri winced, making her feel instantly guilty.

'I've been through the house with a fine-tooth comb and the Vicarage is the only other place they could possibly be. There was a little cupboard under the eaves in the attic where we used to hide the boys' Christmas presents. If Dot hid them anywhere, it would have been there. And how else are we going to get in?' he asked. 'As you know, hell would freeze before the Reverend Aiden bloody Corwin would help either of us. I've thought about going to the bishop but he'd ask what I was looking for and there's no way I could tell him. Even if I made up some story, he'd tell Corwin, no doubt – he's his golden boy. So this is the only sensible option.'

'Sensible? What's sensible about breaking and entering?' Storm asked incredulously.

'It's hardly breaking in if you've got a key,' Henri replied calmly.

'How do you know it's even the right key? They might have changed the locks,' she said.

'Firstly, I found the key in a box of Dot's things – it was labelled "Vicarage back door" which I think was a hint. Secondly, we suffered for years with a hole in the roof you could see daylight through, so I doubt the routine changing of locks is high on their list of priorities.'

'But what if he changed them himself?' Storm countered, not quite ready to admit that this really was the only plan they had.

'I doubt that very much,' Henri replied, although he wasn't one hundred per cent certain. There was something about his successor that had made his skin crawl from the day he clapped eyes on him, something underneath the Hollywood good looks that, though he hated to admit it, frightened him. It wasn't just the fire and brimstone brand of Christianity that he preached, so far removed from Henri's own style of love and tolerance, it was something much, much, darker, but every time Henri tried to examine it in his mind, it seemed to slither away from him, retreating to dark corners. He wouldn't have been at all surprised if he'd changed the locks himself – his sort usually had something to hide – but there was only one way to find out.

They spent the next few minutes in silence. 'Well, we need the journals,' she said at last. 'But that creep would have us both locked up in a heartbeat if we're caught.'

Henri nodded, knowing that he'd won the debate but taking no pleasure in it. 'There's absolutely no need for you to get involved at all. If I do this alone, I can talk my way out of it – claim senility or something if I'm caught.'

'Like hell you'll go alone,' Storm said, shooting him an indignant look. 'We do it together or not at all.'

Henri had wanted to insist, but he had already been

through all of the options in his mind and he knew that what slim chance they had would be all the slimmer without help.

By the time they got back into town they had a plan. Courtesy of the St Peter's online calendar, they knew that Aiden would be holding his Saturday morning clinic in the neighbouring village the following morning, giving them a window of at least two hours to get in and hopefully out of the Vicarage.

CHAPTER 39

*T*rade was brisk at Cordelia's when Henri and Storm arrived. They'd said little more after the discussion of Henri's plan on the drive back, neither of them quite ready to give voice to the dark thoughts that were occupying them. The hubbub that greeted them as they let themselves in from the courtyard was a welcome reminder of normality. Despite the horrors they'd just been party to, life, it seemed, carried on.

Instead of heading along the corridor that connected the back door, storeroom and kitchen to the stairs, Storm paused in the doorway into the shop. From there she could see the café end; the lunch crowd had been replaced by the after-school brigade as happened most days, but today, to Storm's delight, Lilly was in the thick of it, taking orders and laughing with some of the regulars. She really did light up when she smiled, Storm thought. Her long silky auburn hair was loosely braided down her back and if Storm wasn't mistaken, she was wearing new skinny black jeans and a new T-shirt. Progress indeed, she thought, smiling to herself.

'New waitress?' Henri asked, following her gaze.

'Yes – and my new tenant for the attic flat. Come and say hi.'

At that point, Lilly saw them. She beamed, said something to the customer she'd been chatting to and bounced over to them. Yes, definitely a bounce, Storm thought, and she smiled again, remembering the bedraggled waif she'd first met who was now looking more and more like a confident young woman.

'Lilly, I want you to meet one of my oldest and dearest friends.'

'Less of the old,' Henri said, extending his hand. 'I'm Henri, my dear.'

Lilly took his hand, smiled, and said shyly, 'Lilly Jones. It's lovely to meet you. I've met your dog already I think – he's a sweet boy.'

'You let madam out for me? Thank you. I should have mentioned Ludo,' Storm said, remembering that when she'd texted Lilly earlier to ask her to let Hope out for a toilet break, she'd forgotten to mention their guest.

'It was no bother,' Lilly said. 'They were both snuggled up with Anchor on the sofa when I went in.' She pulled out her phone and showed them a photo of the snoozing trio. 'They were as good as gold going out for a wee – except Anc, of course. He waited for us on the landing then used his indoor facilities.' She giggled.

'Probably didn't want the wind ruffling his fur,' Henri said, and they all laughed.

'He's such a diva, but so loveable,' Lilly said, stroking the image of Anchor on her home screen.

'It sounds as if he's certainly worked his magic on you,' Henri said, smiling.

'Oh, I'm well and truly his new human slave. I have no complaints though – he's a love,' Lilly said. 'I'd better get back to work, but it was so lovely to meet you, Henri.' She smiled and her green eyes danced. Brighter than before, Storm noticed.

'Likewise. And I hope to see you again soon.' Henri smiled.

As she turned to go, Storm called after her, 'It's my turn for dinner this evening if you fancy it? I'm hoping this one,' she pointed to Henri, 'will be staying too.'

Lilly looked hesitant. 'I'd love to, I really would, but I—'

Storm interrupted her, not wanting to embarrass her by making her explain why tonight would not be possible. 'I'm a dunce – you told me you're out tonight already. My bad. Let's catch up tomorrow. Have fun!'

Lilly looked relieved and, with a little wave, headed back to the café.

'Hot date?' Henri asked.

'I hope so. She's been spending a lot of time with Vee's nephew Michael, and let's just say I don't think it's just my home cooking that's brought some colour to her cheeks.'

'She's a beautiful young woman. I bet they're queuing around the block,' Henri said, following Storm as she made her way to the stairs.

'Indeed she is,' Storm said, and felt a swell of pride rise in her chest on Lilly's behalf. 'I'm not sure you would have recognised her just a few months ago though. Come on, I'll tell you all about it over a cuppa.'

CHAPTER 40

*L*illy jumped as the intercom in the attic flat gave one short, hesitant buzz at exactly 7 p.m. Anchor, who had been sleeping peacefully in the middle of Lilly's bed while she tried on various combinations from her meagre wardrobe, opened one eye, stretched then went back to sleep. Lilly was halfway across the lounge when it buzzed again.

She jogged the last few steps and grabbed the handset on the intercom. 'I'll be right down,' she said to the image on the small screen of Michael, his hands stuffed into his pockets, standing at the back door. It was only when she replaced the handset that she wondered if she'd sounded a bit too eager.

When she ran back to the bedroom to grab her jacket, Anchor was sitting on the edge of the bed. She knelt down and he bopped heads with her in a gesture she had come to love. She tickled him under his chin, told him she loved him and that she'd not be home late. He bopped her again, purring loudly and this time she decided he was saying, 'Go, have fun!'

Michael was standing in the middle of the courtyard

when she let herself out. The light was already fading and the courtyard garden was glowing dimly in the gentle light of hundreds of solar fairy lights. They hung in delicate swags from the tops of the old stone walls, meandered through the climbing roses and lined the edges of the path. There was always something magical about the courtyard; even at night it seemed to have an energy all of its own. Seeing Michael here now, illuminated by just the solar lights and the muted glow from behind curtained windows made Lilly catch her breath. He grinned when he saw her; she smiled back and for a minute neither of them spoke. Lilly giggled and then they both went to speak at the same time.

'Ladies first,' Michael said.

'I was just going to say that you look …' Lilly suddenly realised that she couldn't say what she had just been about to say, so replaced *gorgeous* with, 'taller.'

'That'll be the Cuban heels,' Michael said smiling. 'When you're only six foot two, every little helps.' They both laughed at that, the awkwardness already disappearing. 'And I was about to say that you look lovely,' he added, sounding less sure of himself now that he wasn't in his comfort zone of humour.

Lilly beamed, feeling almost light-headed. She was about to say thank you when one of Storm's beautiful terracotta pots crashed to the floor somewhere behind them. 'What the hell?' Michael said, scanning the dim courtyard and looking confused. 'We're not even close to anything.'

Lilly gritted her teeth against the anger that was rising in her belly. Jack knew how much tonight meant to her and she'd be damned if he was going to ruin it for her. So what if he thought making friends was a bad idea in the circumstances. Why couldn't he see that she just needed to be happy? If this was her last life, why couldn't she spend what time she had left being happy? Was that really too much to ask?

'Maybe the pot was unbalanced and a passing rat nudged it,' she said, hoping Jack was still listening and heard her emphasis on the 'rat'. Then she felt bad about being disparaging to rats.

As Michael located the shattered pot and scooped up the now homeless herbs, Lilly made a decision. Not being able to banish him out loud, she made circles with her thumb and forefinger on each hand, interlocked them and then pulled them apart. Now she'd have a whole twenty-four hours of freedom from Jack's ever-watchful eye. She felt a brief wave of something that felt like grief and anger and sorrow all mixed up together but pushed it away forcibly.

Michael was saying something about having to reimburse Storm if it was one of hers, but Lilly, emboldened by her newly taken freedom, took his hand and said, 'Let's go. We can worry about broken pots tomorrow.'

As they drove along the country roads, they chatted easily about their days. Michael, recently graduated from university, was taking some time out to decide whether to study for a masters, get a job or set up on his own. With a degree in plant and agricultural science, he was well placed to take over his family's farm but, he told her, discounted that as the 'easy option'. Lilly already knew that in Michael's mind, anything he felt was not earned was not deserved.

Lilly told him all about the new commission she'd just picked up from a new author who wrote children's books. Getting a new commission was exciting enough, but this author wrote about two naughty cats, Abbey Cat and Mr Potts. Lilly had modelled Mr Potts on Anchor, who'd been more than happy to sit for her, and the client had been delighted with the preliminary sketches.

They reached the farm twenty minutes later, rumbling

over cattle grids as they pulled off the main road, heading up a winding drive that was flanked on both sides by flat open fields. The house was more modern than Lilly had expected, but the farm she had grown up on was the only other she'd ever visited so she didn't have many reference points. That had been old, draughty and dilapidated, but this was more akin to something you'd see on one of those self-build TV shows. The front of the house was nearly all glass and it tapered down on one side, giving it the look of a giant wedge of cheese.

'My mum and dad's grand design,' Michael offered as if reading Lilly's mind. 'It's an eco-house – hardly needs heating, all the energy comes from renewables, most of them on site, plus there are grey water tanks, a sedum roof, a reed bed for waste, private well. Auntie Vee blames my parents for putting ideas into Uncle Asim's head. He saw this and that was it – he had to build one. Except theirs is about ten times the size, of course,' he said shaking his head but smiling.

'It's beautiful,' Lilly said, and meant it. Despite its angles, it looked warm and welcoming and her apprehension started to melt under the weight of her curiosity.

'What do you want to do first?' Michael asked as he parked the car. 'Animals or house?'

Lilly grinned and Michael rolled his eyes and smiled. 'Stupid question.'

*H*enri and Storm had to wait for their cuppa. Ludo and Hope were desperate for a walk when they arrived at the flat so, deciding that fresh air would do them all good, they headed straight back out to the park.

Henri asked if they could take the long route so he could pass the Vicarage that had been his and Dot's home for so many years. It was an imposing house, built from the same blush-coloured bricks used to build many of the older houses of the town, including Cordelia's and much of the high street. The gate from the churchyard snaked through what was now a bowling green of a lawn but had once been Dot's wild-flower meadow, to a solid dark green front door. Bay windows flanked it, two huge dark empty eyes in the fading light.

They paused, each of them lost in memories of happier times. Back then, the Vicarage had been a beacon for the community. Even those without a faith had found themselves gravitating towards the permanently open kitchen door, the kettle that, no matter what time of day or night, always seemed to have just been boiled. Everyone was assured of a warm welcome and a friendly, non-judgemental ear. The house had seemed so alive then, so warm and full of light and love and laughter. It looked very different now and Storm wondered whether houses too could grieve for what they had lost.

Nothing had been quite the same in Pont Nefoedd since Henri and Dot left. While the community had done a good job of pulling together during the difficulties, its heart was no longer the church and the Vicarage, despite the new vicar's attempts to frighten and bully the faithful into his pews.

The park was busy with other dog walkers making the most of the light when they arrived. It wasn't long before Henri was chatting to old parishioners and neighbours who greeted him like the beloved old friend he was. Storm wondered whether Henri had consciously avoided coming into the village, the ghosts of happier times keeping him away. By the time they turned for home, the light was waning and dusk had arrived to relieve the day shift.

When they got back to Cordelia's, letting themselves in through the back gate, Storm was surprised to see Jack sitting alone on the bench in the courtyard. She'd only seen him once since that first day in the car park and she'd all but convinced herself that she'd imagined the whole thing. But here he was, sitting amongst the glow of the still waking fairy lights, his aura lit up like a Christmas tree. Definitely not her imagination then.

'Lovely evening for it,' Henri said, his voice warm and friendly, a man well-practised in putting strangers at their ease.

'It's lovely indeed,' Jack said, casting his eyes upwards to where the first stars were appearing in the dimming sky, then getting up to offer his hand to Henri and introducing himself. It was a simple gesture that Storm found inexplicably moving. There was an intense vulnerability to Jack this evening – she could see it in his energy and he looked younger. The dogs rushed forward to greet him with gleeful wags and Jack surprised her again by kneeling down to fuss them, earning himself a chin to eyebrow lick from Ludo. Jack laughed and rubbed both of Ludo's ears affectionately. 'I know Hope, but who's this handsome chap?' he asked.

'Ah, that's our Ludo,' Henri said with pride.

'The bringer of light,' Jack replied, smiling at the dog. 'We can but hope, boy, can't we?' he said, holding the old dog's big head gently in his hands before giving him a final tickle and getting up.

'Jack is Lilly's friend,' Storm said to Henri by way of explanation.

'Ah, I met Lilly earlier – lovely young lady. Looks like Cordelia's is becoming something of a hotspot for fine young people.' Henri beamed. 'Really super to meet you, Jack. And just so you know, Ludo is very particular in who he kisses so consider yourself highly honoured with his lordship's slobbery seal of approval.' Henri chuckled and patted Jack on the shoulder as they passed.

Storm's heart twisted again as she caught the glint of sudden tears in Jack's eyes. They were gone again in an instant and when he looked up, he said softly, 'Great to meet you, Henri – and Ludo. Night, Storm, see you again.'

'Definitely,' Storm said, trying to catch Jack's eye but failing; his gaze was still fixed on the dogs. 'Maybe we could have a cuppa soon?'

Still not looking at her, Jack said softly, 'That'd be great, Storm. I'll stop by. Thanks.'

Back in the flat, Storm put the kettle on and at last told Henri the story of how Lilly had blossomed from a bedraggled, dog-rescuing waif into the vibrant young woman he had met. She credited Anchor and more recently Michael for much of the transformation, along with good food and the community that was Cordelia's.

'So Jack is just a friend then?' Henri said, raising his bushy eyebrows.

Storm nodded. 'As far as Lilly is concerned, yes, but I get the sense that Jack might feel differently, especially tonight,' she said as she pulled off the lid of the biscuit barrel in search of the ginger thins she'd made earlier in the week.

'Ah. Michael,' Henri said, putting the pieces together. 'Lovely lad, Michael, but poor Jack.' His tone reminded Storm of just how sensitive he always was to the suffering of others. It was what had made him so beloved in the parish.

Storm was about to launch into the story of her first encounter with Jack when Henri got up to peer out of the front window. 'I wonder how much longer Vee will be?' he said, looking down onto the high street.

Storm was glad of the distraction. Seeing one person's aura was big news for her but it felt somehow selfish to focus on herself at a time like this. So what if her connection with spirit might be waking up again? If they didn't find this Ethereal being there would be no point in any of it.

'I'd phone her but if she's in the library she won't have it with her,' she replied, 'and Asim is still away. You are staying, aren't you? Sorry, I told Lilly you were, but then realised I hadn't actually asked you. The guest room is all made up.'

'Yes please. Under the circumstances, I'll be glad of the company, to be honest, my dear.' Henri smiled. 'And you know how much Ludo adores that eiderdown on the spare bed.'

They both laughed, remembering the blissful look on the newly adopted Ludo's face when he'd been found napping in the middle of Storm and Nick's king-sized guest bed. After wandering off to explore, they had discovered him lying on his back, legs akimbo, snoring like a water buffalo. They'd all laughed, but Ludo had cowered in fear. When Nick returned, he'd found Henri, Dot and Storm all sitting on the bed drinking their coffees around Ludo, his tail wagging tentatively as they offered up treats.

'It broke my heart to think he was expecting to be punished just for finding somewhere comfortable to snooze,' Storm said, looking at the old dog snuggled up to Hope on the sofa, his huge head resting on her back. Anchor was lying stretched out on the back of the sofa above them looking sulky, no doubt because Lilly was out this evening.

Henri chuckled. 'He certainly learned a lesson that day. He's not been off the bed since.' He laughed. 'Although to his great credit, he still asks permission if I happen to be in it at the time.'

'Always the gentleman,' Storm said, 'just like his dad.'

The buzz of the intercom made them both jump. On the video monitor she could see Veronica punching in her code. 'She's here,' Storm said and headed out of the door to meet her.

Storm was at the back door by the time Veronica was halfway through the courtyard. Even in the dim light, Storm could see that she looked pale and her eyes were red and puffy. Storm wasted no time in giving her friend a huge hug.

'You okay?' Storm asked before releasing her.

'Yes. No. Not really, hon,' Veronica said sniffing, attempting a smile but just managing to set off a new wave of quiet tears that had her scrabbling for another hankie.

'Come on. I'm about to put dinner on and I have two dogs desperate to cheer you up with their new brand of bounce therapy, and a cat who might even sit on your lap if he gets desperate enough,' Storm said and Veronica smiled in spite of the black cloud that seemed to have settled around her.

CHAPTER 42

*O*nce the dogs had indeed bounced all over her at the door, Veronica joined Henri at the kitchen table while Storm stirred the curry she'd thrown together and put the rice on to boil. Veronica had always loved this flat and the way it managed to be airy and cosy at the same time. It was warm and welcoming but stylish and elegant without any hint of ostentation, and yet she knew for a fact that it was all a happy accident. Storm was not the type to pore over decorating magazines – everything in the room was something she and Nick had loved, and Veronica suspected that was part of the magic of the place. If they loved it or needed it, they brought it home. The effect was a delightful mix of old, new and handmade, but they all seemed to fit. It was a far cry from her monstrosity of a house with so many of its furnishings bought, not by her but by Asim's design consultant; not that she cared – she had far better things to occupy her time. She loved her husband to the ends of the Earth, but sometimes she wondered how two so completely different people had remained so happily married for so long.

While the rice cooked, they passed the time talking about

everything and nothing. By some sort of unspoken agreement, news of what Veronica had discovered was slated for after they'd eaten. The conversation quickly turned to the rapid deterioration of what felt like the whole world. Barely a day went by without some new 'once in a lifetime' fire or flood and it was taking its toll on the very fabric of society the world over.

'It's almost funny,' Storm said, lifting the saucepan lid to check on the rice. 'I remember thinking this morning as I was listening to the radio in bed that I couldn't remember a time when the world felt more frightening. Then all this happened.' She shook her head and pulled bowls out of the cupboard.

'I think we all feel like that,' Veronica replied. 'It's like we've all been carrying on, trying to pretend that everything's okay, but it's not. Even before this Ethereal thing. The flooding, the weather that's off-the-scale weird even for Old Blighty, the food shortages, the antibiotic thing and the violence everywhere. I mean, how many of our big cities are now under curfew? It feels like it's all a huge tinderbox ready to go up.'

'I heard the home secretary interviewed this morning and she was asked about the possibility of troops on the streets,' Henri said gravely. 'She evaded the question like the slippery politician she is, but the reality is that we don't have enough troops still here to do the job. The police are on their knees and most of our armed forces are still in the Middle East helping our …' he mimed quote marks in the air, '"special friends" across the pond. It's terrifying.'

Storm placed the pans on the trivets on the table. 'Come on. We'll not function without fuel, so dig in, my lovelies, and then we'll talk.'

Veronica eyed the food hesitantly. 'I'll do my best with dinner, Stormy, I really will, but ever since Asim called about the surveillance thing I've been feeling physically sick.'

Storm nodded, chewing her first mouthful, then suddenly said, 'Shit. Are we likely to be monitored here?'

Veronica shook her head. 'We're safe here. Asim had his team sweep the place earlier.' Seeing the confusion on Storm's face, she said, 'They don't need to come in with detectors these days, they can send mini-drone things that can just hover outside the windows and take readings or something. I don't understand it fully, but he said they're 98.7 per cent accurate and they didn't find anything here. Just to be on the safe side though,' she fished in her handbag and pulled out a small black box a little larger than a margarine tub, 'pop your mobiles in here.'

Storm went to retrieve hers from the sideboard drawer, while Henri patted his pockets to locate his.

Phones safely stowed away, while they each picked at their dhal and rice, Veronica shared what she'd learned from her afternoon ensconced in her library.

'When I headed back down, our little friend floated over to one of the restricted atmosphere rooms, where there was a seriously old tome waiting for me. Those old chaps are super serious, so I rarely bother them, to be honest. I think the last time I consulted them was when I was training with Mum, which should give you a sense of how long ago it was. But they certainly delivered today,' she said, getting up to find Tupperware to store her barely touched food, then rinsing her plate and cutlery before putting them in the dishwasher.

When she spoke again, her voice had a harder edge. 'I've read so much this afternoon I don't quite know where to start, but what you need to know is that there are forces at work that are actively blocking the ascension process. I need to do more research on that, but the book was very clear –

there are people who have been working against the ascension for donkey's years.'

'But that doesn't make any sense. If the alternative is basically an extinction event for humanity, why would anyone with half a brain get in the way?' Storm snorted.

'Exactly. As I said, more research needed, but the fact that someone is trying to get in the way tells us something about who might be sniffing around the library,' Veronica replied.

'So where does the Ethereal fit into all this?' Henri asked.

'The Ethereal, the book referred to them as "the First Ethereal", incidentally, is the being that decides on the Earth's readiness – or not – for the ascension, or, as some call it, the great shift. Like a scout – helpfully, the book doesn't say whether it's male, female or something else – it's incarnate here on Earth, lives a life, and through the experience of that life and the state of the world's energy at the time, decides whether the shift can take place. If by the time the Ethereal reaches the end of their assigned life the Earth is at a high enough vibration energetically, then bingo, the shift goes ahead and hello new era of peace, love and unicorns for everyone.'

'But if the Earth isn't ready?' Storm asked, already not wanting to know the answer.

'Well, ordinarily the Ethereal would simply live out their life, the Earth would remain as it was and the process would be repeated the next time they incarnated,' Veronica explained.

'But I'm guessing we're no longer in the realms of the ordinary?' Storm said glumly.

Veronica nodded. 'We're basically out of time because at no other point in creation have we posed such a monumental threat to all life, so we're not even on our last warning – this really is the last spin of the wheel for both humanity and everything on the planet.'

The silence weighed around them until Henri cleared his throat and spoke. 'So, the Ethereal is a person?'

'Sort of,' Veronica said carefully.

'But are we to understand that the Ethereal has the ability to begin the ascension? Is that what the library was so desperate to tell us? That he or she can … what, override the process somehow?'

'Exactly. In fact, that was one of the first things the book showed me. I think it was trying to give me hope, bless its cottons,' Veronica said, pulling a handkerchief from her sleeve and blowing her nose as her eyes filled with fresh tears.

'But how?' Storm asked. 'I mean, how can it begin the ascension if the energies are all so low? Didn't you say earlier that we're like a hot-air balloon, too weighed down to take off?'

'I did and we are. But, as Henri said, it can override the process. It's literally the only being capable of doing that and that's because of the frequency of energy it carries.' Veronica cleared her throat to help push away the emotion and came back to join them at the table.

'Which is?' Storm asked.

Veronica's felt a bubble of hope rise in her chest, then she said with a small smile, 'Angelic.'

The word seemed to hang in the air above the three of them.

'Oh, my dear lord.' Henri smiled as he pressed his eyes shut.

'The Ethereal is an angel?' Storm repeated.

Veronica smiled. 'You're half right,' she said. 'They're sort of half human, half angel. Not in the sense of "my mama was a human and my papa had a harp".' They all smiled in spite of the tension. 'More the frequency or soul of an angel in a human body.'

'So no harps and halos? Shame,' Henri said mischievously.

'No harps, no halos as such, but apparently the wings are a real thing – although energetic not feathered. The wings are what the angels, or in this case the Ethereal, would use to bless with.'

'Bless, as in benediction?' Henri asked, his eyebrows bunching into a questioning frown.

Veronica's smile widened as she answered, but the sadness of the afternoon's revelations still weighed on her. 'Sometimes the books give you images and feelings when they think words would take too long, or when they're frustrated and think you're being a bit slow, which, if I'm honest, happens to me a lot. The book did it with the blessing. It was so beautiful – these enormous, amazing wings unfolding and this incredible radiant light in colours I can't even name, washing over everyone and everything it touched, silently blessing them and every other inch of creation it lit upon. It was so beautiful I bawled my eyes out just seeing the vision of it, to tell you the truth. I can't say I've ever felt such pure love.' She blew her nose again and fished in her bag for another clean handkerchief to dab away the fresh tears filling her eyes.

'It showed you the other scenario though too, didn't it?' Storm asked tentatively.

Veronica felt her face contort into a sob and she nodded miserably. Storm was out of her chair and hugging her friend in a second. She held her until the sobs subsided.

'It was only for a split second. Nothing compared to the blessings feeling, but even that split second made me feel like I'd fallen into hell.' Veronica broke off again as she tried to compose herself. 'The alternative is called "the Falling".' She paused when Henri gave a knowing groan before waving at her to continue. 'The Falling happens at the tipping point – the point when system degradation becomes total system collapse. It happens fast and it's … feral is the only word I can think of. Every creature, every man, woman and child turns against each other in a desperate bid to survive, but it's more than that. At that point, it's like the fabric of the world starts to unravel too. Reality itself goes haywire. I only saw a second or so, but it was the most heinous, horrific—' She broke off as a sob escaped her. 'I'll be back in a minute,' she said, heading to the bathroom.

They sat in silence until Veronica returned, flushed and red-nosed, the smudges of mascara wiped from beneath her eyes and a fresh hankie folded in her hand.

'I'm sorry,' she said, retaking her seat. 'It was all a bit much there.'

Storm reached out to squeeze her arm. Turning to Henri she asked, 'Did you see the Falling too?'

Henri nodded his head gravely. 'In my nightmares the Falling was heralded by a great hammerhead cloud and black lightning that would quite literally fracture the sky. It's scribbled in one of my notebooks. The other things, the feral nature of it all – that feels horribly resonant too.'

They were quiet for a minute, until Henri spoke again. 'So, if I might summarise, I think what we're saying is that humanity plus all life on Earth is basically stuffed unless an angel–human hybrid decides we're worth saving and flicks the override switch on a new frequency that will allow us all to ascend to the next level of consciousness.'

'And to muddy the waters even more, there are some people of unknown origin – or indeed number – actively trying to stop this happening,' Storm added.

'That's about the size of it,' Veronica said. 'The Very!' she exclaimed, clasping her hands together. 'My mother used to call them the Very, as in "Very bloody human"! And not in a good way either. I've been trying to remember that all afternoon. Thanks, brain, you got there in the end.'

'So what did it mean by "actively trying to stop the ascension"?' Storm asked, frowning.

'The book said that the Ethereal is in mortal danger from those who want to stop the ascension, which we can confidently take to mean that the Very are going to try and kill it before it can decide.'

'The slaughter of angels,' Henri said quietly, holding his head in his hands. 'That mankind could come to this.'

illy started the tour in the cowshed. Although the weather was mild enough for them to be out in the fields, Michael explained that his parents had given all the animals a choice and at the moment, the cows preferred to be inside.

'They bring themselves in,' Michael said as they stood in the barn watching the herd of about sixteen all hunkered down for the evening, save for one who looked to be standing sentry. 'That's Walter,' Michael said, pointing to a bullock bigger than any Lilly had ever seen in her life. 'He's papa cow – the head of the herd.'

'They're all so big!' Lilly said, amazed and wondering if they were a breed she'd not seen before.

'That's because they're old. Walter there is seventeen and Poppy,' he pointed to a sleepy-looking cow at the back of the barn, 'she's twenty-two now. Sadly, most cows don't even make it past about five, so we get a warped idea of how big they should be.'

At that point Walter started walking over to them. 'Want to come in and say hello properly?' Michael asked. When

Lilly nodded, he climbed over the gate and held out his hand to help her. She took it, even though she didn't need to, enjoying the feel of his hand holding hers.

Walter stopped about eight feet away from where they stood, regarding them. He was even bigger close up – at six foot two Michael was just about eye level with his bovine friend. Lilly wasn't short by any means, but under Walter's watchful gaze, she suddenly felt like a hobbit.

'What do I do?' Lilly asked nervously. She'd been around cows as a child, but it had usually been a miserable experience – feeling their pain, their fear and the intense longings for their stolen calves that had bordered on madness. She'd eventually learned to block it out with Jack's help, but to do that she'd had to keep her distance.

'You know the drill – no sudden movements, no staring et cetera, but otherwise just be yourself. He'll come to you if he wants to, but he probably won't, he's—' Michael didn't get to finish his sentence because Walter moved past him, heading slowly for Lilly. Lilly dropped her eyes and tried not to think of the hundreds of miserable memories she had from her childhood.

Walter stopped just a couple of feet from her. He towered above her and she felt his hot breath tickle her hair. He was truly magnificent, she thought. There was a presence to him, an air of regality almost that was so different to anything Lilly had ever felt on her parents' farm. Unable to stop them, her eyes filled with tears at the memory and, as they did, Walter lowered his enormous head and looked directly into her eyes; she felt her carefully constructed defences fall away. But what Lilly saw there wasn't pain, but love – so much of it that her heart ached. She smiled, then giggled a snotty gurgle among her tears, and Walter did something that made Michael's jaw drop – he stuck out his huge grey tongue and gently licked her forehead. Lilly burst out laughing so he did it once more for good measure. Then he turned slowly and walked back to the herd. One by one they rose to their feet and came over to meet the new, thoroughly vetted arrival.

More than an hour later, Lilly had met every member of the herd and she was positively fizzing from the experience. Michael had introduced them all, telling Lilly how long they'd been at the farm and a little about their personalities. Lilly was grateful that he focused on the here and now. She guessed that many of them had had difficult pasts, but she was grateful to meet them as they were here – fit, strong, loved and so visibly happy.

When the last of the herd had once again settled down for the night and Walter, it seemed, had been relieved of his sentry duty by a chunky little heifer called Gwen, Michael suggested that they head in for a bite to eat. Lilly's stomach growled loudly, making them both laugh. 'I think I have my answer,' Michael said, holding out his hand to help Lilly over the gate.

CHAPTER 44

'*D*id you enjoy that?' Michael asked as they left the barn, already knowing the answer but wanting to hear her say it.

'I don't think enjoy comes anywhere close. That was magical,' she said, grinning from ear to ear. 'They're,' she scrabbled for the right word, 'see, they've left me all tongue-tied and giddy,' she laughed.

Michael was grinning too, and he had an air of a man whose plan had worked out down to the letter, which of course it had. He'd seen others stunned into silence after meeting the animals here. They'd bring their kids to the fundraising open days his parents ran a few times a year and he'd often overhear the parents' jokes about steaks and bacon sandwiches, but then they'd see their kids meet Napoleon and Josephine, their saddleback pigs, or bottle-feed one of the many bobby calves their parents took from local markets, and the smart-arse comments usually dried up.

Once his mother spoke, sharing the stories of each of the animals, simply and without judgement or anger, he'd see the start of the unravelling. The adults would cave in to their kids' request to come and cuddle the turkey, chicken, or lamb. They'd laugh at how the pigs liked to play, how the ewes would nudge you just like the family dog when you stopped tickling them, and somewhere along the line would come the look between visitor and animal that said, 'I see you.' He wasn't fool enough to think that it worked on everyone. He knew that some would leave mentally building their wall of denial higher than ever, but he liked to think that everyone went away with the mortar fundamentally loosened.

'Happy?' he asked, smiling down at Lilly who was bouncing along like her feet had sprouted springs.

She stopped and looked at him straight in the eyes. 'I can't ever remember feeling happier,' she said simply. 'Thank you.' Her eyes danced in the light reflected from the house. What she did next took him completely by surprise – standing on her toes she reached up and kissed him on the cheek.

They froze, grinning like idiots at each other. Michael took a step towards her, Lilly held her breath and then they both jumped as a super bright security light clicked on, spotlighting them in the otherwise deserted yard.

Michael groaned. 'Come on,' he said with a laugh, 'I think someone's anxious to meet you.' He held out his hand. Lilly took it and together they headed into the house.

CHAPTER 45

*T*he door was opened just as they reached it by a tall willowy blonde of about Lilly's age, with poker-straight hair stretching down to her waist.

'I'm Remy, his little sister,' she said brightly, holding out her hand to Lilly.

Lilly barely had time to introduce herself before the skitter of paws on the wooden floor behind them announced the arrival of what turned out to be six of the family's eight house dogs – two collies, a Bernese big as a bear, a Jack Russell with three legs, a white mini schnauzer and a mid-sized mix of indeterminate heritage. Labradors Boson and Claudia would still be curled up in their beds, Michael explained, old age and deafness keeping them from welcome-mat duty. After meeting all the dogs, which kept Lilly on her knees in the hall for at least ten minutes, she followed Remy and Michael into the kitchen.

While it looked like something out of a magazine, it still managed to be homely. One wall, the one that faced onto the garden and woodland behind, was made of bi-fold doors and that space looked to be where most of the family's living time

236

was spent. Three huge well-loved sofas filled the space and judging by the blankets covering the largest, that one was for the dogs. There was also a dizzying array of dog beds in all shapes and sizes. The two Labradors were curled up in adjoining beds in front of the fireplace, even though it wasn't lit, their noses almost touching. Books and magazines were stacked haphazardly on the coffee table, which lent the whole image a loved and lived-in air.

The kitchen itself was very simple but elegant. Pale wooden units stretched across one wall. Next to a sleek-looking range hung battered-looking copper pans, beneath them utensils were stuffed into an old clay jug that was missing a handle. A huge island, flanked on one side by no fewer than eight high stools, sectioned off the space from the living area.

The walls were a plain whitewash, but huge paintings and photographs added splashes of colour everywhere. Michael pointed to the double height wall at the end of the living room which was dedicated entirely to a stencil of a family tree, the branches bearing photographs of every human and animal on the farm with their names neatly lettered underneath. Some had dates added to them commemorating those that had passed, and it brought a lump to Lilly's throat.

She was still studying the wall when she heard a loud whoop from the door. She turned to see a woman she guessed to be in her fifties carrying a little boy of about four. Her thick hair, once probably as dark as a crow's wing, was shot with silver. It hung in a mass of waves around her head, framing a face that was both strong and gentle. Her blue eyes were bright and Lilly could instantly see how Michael had grown into the man he was with this woman's love.

'Lilly!' she said warmly, stopping only to put the now wriggling child on the floor.

'Arthur, what are you doing up?' Remy said, heading

E. L. WILLIAMS

towards him, but he swerved past her to get to Lilly. 'Sorry, Mum.' Arthur stopped in front of Lilly, looked into her eyes and then his gaze travelled up above her head.

'Are you looking at the animals?' Lilly asked, bending down so that they were eye level. Arthur shook his head and continued staring, his little mouth stretched into a silent 'wow', then he reached out and tentatively touched the air around Lilly's head. He pulled his hand back and giggled. Then he did it again.

'What are you doing, monkey?' Michael asked, kneeling down to tickle his nephew.

Arthur turned at the touch and signed. Michael frowned, and asked him to say it again. He did, then started hopping excitedly on the spot and pointing above Lilly's head.

Remy was craning her neck to see what her son was saying. 'Arthur has Downs so he uses sign at the moment while we work on his speech,' she explained to Lilly as Michael, trying a different tactic, now signed back to him. Lilly's heart did a little somersault.

'He says he's looking at the pretty lights,' Michael said, slightly baffled. 'I asked if he meant pretty lady, but he's adamant, it's the lights on the lady.' He shrugged, tickled Arthur again and then scooped him up before slow jogging around the kitchen playing aeroplanes complete with engine noises, much to the little boy's delight.

'That was quite a welcome,' Lyn said warmly, closing the gap between her and Lilly and enfolding her into a hug. Lilly hadn't been expecting it so froze for a moment, before, to her own surprise, hugging her back. It was over in a few seconds, but Lilly felt tearful for reasons she didn't understand.

Whether Lyn saw it or not, Lilly was grateful for what she did next. Turning away she said, 'You've probably not met the old-timers yet. Come and say hello to our canine elders while one of my gorgeous kids pops the dinner on.'

An hour later, dinner eaten, and Arthur back in bed after falling asleep cuddled up next to Lilly on the sofa, they were tucking into Remy's chocolate cake and drinking coffee strong enough to stand a spoon up in.

The conversation had flowed easily and Lilly felt like she'd known these people forever. She'd not been able to meet Michael's dad, Peter, or Remy's partner, Sam, as they were helping a horse welfare charity with a last minute rescue of a herd of abandoned horses up in Shropshire. There would no doubt be some new arrivals come the morning if all went to plan.

It was after midnight when Lilly reluctantly said she'd better be getting home to Anchor. She didn't want to outstay her welcome but she didn't want the evening to end. Watching them all, so easy and comfortable with each other, made her realise what family, real family, looked like. It was a world away from how she'd grown up, but instead of making her sad, it lifted her to know that her world wasn't the reality for everyone.

When she and Michael got up to leave, Remy and Lyn hugged her in turn. It wasn't the light hug of welcome that Lyn had surprised her with when they first met, but a big squashy bear hug.

'Will you come for lunch on Sunday?' Lyn asked, still holding on to Lilly's hands. 'You'll be able to meet the rest of the animals and hopefully whoever Pete and Sam bring back with them tonight. Oh, and Pete and Sam of course,' she said with a laugh and a wave of her hand.

'Will you?' Michael asked, suddenly sounding a little anxious that she might say no. 'You only met the cows tonight. We've got horses, pigs, sheep, goats and—'

'I'd love to. Yes, please,' Lilly said, laughing, cutting him off before he felt the need to name every creature in their care. 'And it will be lovely to meet Pete and Sam and see you all again,' she said, not wanting them to think it was only the animals she was interested in.

'That's settled then,' Lyn said, clapping her hands together. 'And if you want to come over earlier, I'll give you the official tour.' Lilly beamed and the warm glow that had been slowly spreading through her all evening ratcheted up another ten points.

Lilly and Michael chatted for the whole drive back to town. He told her all about Arthur and how, despite his difficulties with speech, he was a bright and clever little lad, brilliant with the animals and the kindest kid he had ever met. He told her how Remy and Sam, sweethearts since sixth form, had set up the catering business to make sure they could work at home and take care of their son.

Lilly knew a little of their story from Veronica, but Michael filled in some of the gaps, telling her stories about the three winters they'd all spent in a caravan on site when he and Remy were just kids – the first while the original farmhouse was being renovated and then the second, and the third after the fire that had condemned the house just weeks before they had been due to move in. Lilly had no idea how devastated they must have been to come so close to their dream only to see it go up in flames, and said as much.

'It was awful at the time, but after the initial shock subsided, we realised that it was only a house. We didn't lose anyone, none of the barns were affected, all the animals were safe, we just lost some possessions and some time. The new house is half the size of the old one because I suppose we all decided after it happened that a big house just wasn't as important any more. Mum and Dad built the rehab barn with what they saved.' It was obvious that Michael not only adored his family, but that he was incredibly proud of them too.

When they got back to Cordelia's, Michael parked the car

and hopped out to open Lilly's door. It was something that Jack would have done, but she snapped the thought off in her mind before it had time to settle. She did not want to think of Jack tonight.

'I'll walk you to the door,' Michael said, putting to rest any concern in Lilly's mind that he might have other hopes. She relaxed a little, took his hand and punched in the code for the back gate. The fairy lights were still glowing brightly now in the fullness of the dark night.

Storm had left the lamp in the window on for her and the soft glow illuminated the small hallway behind the half-glass back door. Lilly fished in her bag for the long-barrelled key but, before she put it in the lock, she turned to Michael and said, 'I had the best night. Your family, both human and animal, is completely amazing.'

'They think you're pretty amazing too,' he said, smiling.

'How do you know?' Lilly asked playfully.

'Oh, I know,' Michael said. 'I could see it in their eyes.'

Lilly stared at him and for the second time that night, surprised herself by reaching up and kissing him. This time though, she kissed him full on the lips and when he kissed her back, pulling her into his arms, she thought she'd explode into a million stars.

CHAPTER 46

*M*argot rose to her feet and turned to address the other members of the High Council. 'To recap what we know so far. The Ethereal is here. He, she, or, I suppose, it, has the power to usher in the great shift in all its glory. The ancient texts tell of an energetic shift of consciousness and energy so monumental that life on Earth will be returned to a kind of paradise. All life will once again recognise itself, meaning that division will weaken to the point where—'

Sir Dennis cut her off. 'Where we all become namby-pamby hippies with flowers in our fucking hair living in communes and hugging bloody hedgehogs.' The others laughed. Margot smiled for appearances' sake, waiting for the laughs and side comments to die down before continuing.

'To a point where love will overtake fear as the organising vibration. While this sounds on the surface to be all unicorns and rainbows, it will have some unfortunate consequences too.'

'The end of the human bloody race for one!' Marcus snorted.

'Quite,' Margot said, only thinly veiling the irritation in her voice at being interrupted for a second time.

'Marcus is quite correct, of course. If the shift were to happen, then evolution as we know it, the biological kind at least, would cease. Humanity in its purest sense would in effect be lost, replaced with what I suppose we'd now describe as hybrids. Part human, part …' Margot faltered, her next word resting heavily on the tip of her tongue. 'Angel,' she said bluntly, noticing the others shifting slightly in their seats. 'And to remind you again, we use this word in its scientific context as the frequency of vibration identified for the highest ends of our detectable spectrum, so don't get all caught up in religious dogma and new-age rubbish.'

'So humanity as we know it – we'd all be wiped out,' Cynthia said with characteristic timing, never one to say something for the sake of it.

'Yes and no. Yes, in that we would no longer be fully human. During the shift, those who embraced it would end up with their DNA shared between the two vibrations – half human and half angelic, but resonating on a much, much higher frequency overall. As you know, our research so far has all pointed to the fact that our so-called "junk DNA" is basically just awaiting its upgrade to the higher frequency. The shift is of course an invitation, a choice. Those humans who refuse the new energy will effectively be like fish out of water in the new frequency so would be reabsorbed into the One.'

'Which is a flowery way of saying *dead*!' Marcus spat out the words, his disgust apparent.

Margot took a deep breath. 'As I've explained countless times before, Marcus, that's an incredibly simplistic way of looking at it.'

Charles interjected to move them on. 'We all know that's a grossly over-simplistic view of the world, Margot, you'll get no argument there,' he said, aiming a pointed look at Marcus, 'but what I want us to focus on now is how we prevent this. As an ancient organisation, our very existence has been the protection, proliferation and evolution of humanity and this is a clear and present threat to our very existence as a species, which we have no choice but to stop.'

Margot continued. 'Charles is correct – life as we have known it would be unrecognisable. The only thing standing between us and this future is the decision of the Ethereal. He or she is the first of such hybrids. The information we have on this being is very sparse indeed. The ancients ensured that only the keepers of the magical libraries and the magical texts themselves were ever entrusted with their knowledge. As we know, finding and accessing that information is ridiculously difficult.'

'What about the animals?' Zak asked, glancing up from his screen. 'I mean, they'll be dead too, won't they? After the shift? What'll we eat?'

Margot gritted her teeth. This was a tactic of his. Staying silent then interrupting to pull the conversation in a random direction. 'Animals are already on a far higher vibrational frequency,' she said curtly. 'Although the jury is very much out on those in industrial settings. Nobody's done any research on that.'

'Margot, pet, let's cut to the chase, shall we?' Dennis was clearly impatient to get on. 'If this Ethereal is here, what are we going to do about it?'

Margot steadied herself, her glamour holding strong as iron as she delivered the line she had been practising in her mind for days. 'Yes, the Ethereal appears to be here. Its signature has now been picked up by various seers. However, the results of my extensive research and visioning reveal that it is highly unlikely that it will deem humanity ready for the shift. We've seen to that in no uncertain terms. To try and find it now, I fear, will just draw unwelcome attention to ourselves and our members at the most delicate of times.'

The room erupted into a chorus of protests. Margot held up her hands, waiting for silence before speaking again.

'The energies are way too low for the Ethereal to risk the shift at this point. We have wars on three continents, levels of famine not seen in generations, rioting on the streets of pretty much every major city in the world, a global sepsis crisis, food and fuel shortages and natural disasters by the lorry-load – do you really think that this being is going to be able to look through all that and see the light of human potential?' She laughed bitterly. 'Even half of that would be enough to de-wing even the most determined of angelic beings.' Margot hoped her sarcasm hadn't pushed the point too far. It was all true, of course. The chances of the shift succeeding were slim to non-existent.

'Margot, thank you for your assessment. We are indebted to you as our seer and our most trusted advisor and we would not be in the position of strength we are now without your wisdom, foresight and indeed, second sight,' Charles said, nodding and smiling that patronising, tight-lipped grimace he reserved for the help. Despite his words, Margot could feel the malice coming off him in waves and she knew she had already lost. They were all afraid of her, she knew that, but people like this always had a habit of killing what they feared.

Continuing, Charles said, 'However, you will forgive me for seeking a second opinion on a matter of such grave and material importance. As it was our old friend in Shanghai who first detected the Ethereal, I of course reached out to Wang for his counsel on the subject. He is of the clear opinion that the only way of dealing with this threat is through the elimination of the Ethereal once and for all.'

Margot's blood turned to ice. She strengthened her glamour, to save it from slip and give these vultures something to hang on to. 'No forgiveness needed. I'm pleased that you did. Wang is a formidable and gifted seer who I admire greatly,' she lied. 'Eliminating the Ethereal was my first instinct too. I didn't recommend it, partly because of the risks I outlined and partly because we don't know enough about the impact it will have on us here on Earth. We have existed for all time with the influence of the angelic. If we sever the link, there's no telling what the consequences might be, but I'm sure Wang would have pointed that out.' It was a complete bluff, but she was out of options.

'I've considered that,' Charles said shortly, 'but Wang's view is that as the Ethereal is not a constant presence here, the risk of some sort of energetic destabilisation is absolutely minuscule. Eliminate it now, discreetly of course, and we save ourselves and our descendants from ever having to jump through these same hoops again.' Charles tipped his head slightly to the right as he finished his speech. It was a movement so slight, and yet with it he had sealed the argument and they both knew it.

Margot nodded sagely, but before she could say any more, Charles had risen and was asking the council to vote. It took precisely ten seconds for them to decide seven to one to hunt down and execute the Ethereal.

CHAPTER 47

*D*inner abandoned through a shared lack of appetite, Storm opened a nice bottle of red wine she had been given for her birthday by a customer. She hadn't thought that she'd be saving it for news of the impending apocalypse but, now that it was here, it seemed as good a time as any. Veronica's revelation that the Very, as she called them, would likely try to kill the Ethereal sat like a spectre amongst them at the kitchen table.

They were silent for long minutes before Storm spoke. 'So as long as these baddies, the Very, don't find the Ethereal, we'll be saved? The ascension will happen, and it'll be hello peace and love, farewell fear and hate?' she asked, trying to sound hopeful but not feeling it.

'I wish it were that simple,' Veronica said. 'The thing is, the Ethereal is here to make a choice, so it's not a done deal by any means. The book said that the Ethereal's job is to decide whether the Earth is ready to ascend. It can only judge on what it experiences, and it has free will to choose.'

'But why on Earth would it choose our destruction?'

Henri asked. 'Surely, given its angelic side, it would have compassion?'

Veronica sucked in a breath and puffed it out. 'That's the thing – the Ethereal doesn't know what it is. I mean, how could it make a free and unbiased choice if it knew what was at stake? In that situation its compassion would just get in the way. And, of course, what we don't know is what impact saying yes to the ascension would have on the rest of the universe if in fact humanity wasn't ready. There will be a reason it's been set up this way. I sense that the angelic bit is deeply subconscious by design.'

'So, we're doomed,' Storm said flatly, getting up to busy her hands with the task of finding jars of nuts and other nibbles. 'I mean, have you seen the state of the world? There's no way we're worth saving. We mess up everything we touch and as a species we've pretty much single-handedly killed the whole world and most people are still too self-absorbed to see it. We are literally dumber than mud, so maybe the Earth would be better off without us.' She sank into her chair, the fight already drained from her.

'We have a week, then, to find the Ethereal and, appealing to its subconscious side, convince it that there are enough good people in the world to warrant saving it,' Henri said, screwing his eyes tightly shut and leaning back in his chair.

Veronica nodded. 'That's about the size of it, or at least that might have been how it worked in the past. I sense that the rules have changed since the Ethereal was last here.'

Storm and Henri exchanged a look. 'Last here?' they said in unison.

'You said it was the first, didn't you?' Henri asked.

'It is the first – in fact the only Ethereal, but that doesn't mean it's new. Again, more research needed, but it's been here before, incarnating into human form, taking the temperature, so to speak, and assessing our readiness over many, many years. Who knows, maybe hundreds, thousands even. The difference now, of course, is that we're on self-destruct, which means it's unlikely to get another chance.'

'So explain the significance of the first bit again?' Storm asked, confused.

'The Ethereal that's here now is the first, but if the ascension happened, then we'd all be elevated to that frequency, so there would quickly be a second, third, fourth ... and so on, until everyone who embraced the new vibration became Ethereal too.'

'Good lord,' said Henri, 'that's a vision worth holding on to.' Then, after a moment's pause, he said, 'The blessing! The blessing is the frequency?'

Veronica beamed at him. 'Exactly. It was hard to put into words because they gave it to me as a vision, but yes, the Ethereal's wings sort of broadcast the new frequency and everyone willing to attune to it ascends in vibrational terms and ...'

'... their energetic vibration rises up to meet the frequency of the first and so it spreads,' Henri said, pulling a handkerchief out of his pocket to dab dry his eyes. 'That's quite the most beautiful thing I can ever imagine.'

Storm said nothing for a moment. Then, 'But if the Ethereal says no, we're basically not worth saving, we'll get the nightmare version – the Falling.'

Veronica nodded.

'What I don't understand is why this group, the Very, would want to usher in the apocalypse? It would be suicide for them too, wouldn't it?' Storm asked.

'It would, yes.' Veronica paused, picking at the hem of her handkerchief. 'I find it hard to even get my head around the possibility, but the only logical motivation I can think of is that the Very actually want the collapse to happen.'

'But why in God's name would they want that?' Henri all but shouted. 'That would be utter damnation.'

'I have no idea.' Veronica shook her head. 'It's all madness, but nothing else makes any sense. I'm wondering whether they're not factoring in the Falling. Not everyone believes in the metaphysical side of things and even those that do sometimes believe only what serves them. You've only got to look at what's happened to our politics and our culture over the last decade to see that. There'll be more in my mother's files. I've got some of her notes with me, so I'll be working through those next.'

They sat there, each of them lost in the horror of it all, until Storm said, 'The Earth is quite literally going to hell and we have an amnesic angel on the loose who can just possibly save us all. All we have to do is find them before the Very do and try our best to convince them that we're worth saving.'

'Simple,' Henri said, letting out a long breath.

'As my lovely mum used to say, "If you don't try, you've already lost." So all we can do is try,' Veronica said, her voice quivering.

'Okay, so first step is finding Henri's journals. And we have a plan for that.' Storm raised an eyebrow at Henri.

Henri recounted the plan to break into the Vicarage as simply as if he were planning a trip to the seaside. 'As you'll recall, we left in something of a rush, but I don't remember clearing the attic. One of the boys must have done it, which is probably why they missed the hidey-hole as we called it. It's just a small cupboard, more of a crawl space really, under the eaves. We used to hide the boys' Christmas presents in there when they were small. It's the only place I can think of.'

Storm's heart sank at the memory of that time. About eighteen months before Henri was due to retire, the bishop had introduced him to his replacement. Had Aiden Corwin been an actor he would have been typecast as the handsome yet evil villain. At well over six foot, he had the broad chest and bulging biceps of a man who clearly spent too much time in the gym. With his clear blue eyes, angled cheekbones and dark wavy hair long enough to qualify him for a boy band, there was no denying that he was extremely easy on the eye. His good looks, however, hid a brand of puritanical belief that by rights should have consigned him to the Dark Ages.

The bishop had asked Henri to take him under his wing and show him the ropes, this being Aiden's first British parish having only recently returned from a few years in America, although nobody seemed to know exactly what he'd spent his time over there doing. Anyone who asked was always met with the same tight smile and, in his lilting mix of southern Irish tinged with notes from the American Deep South, he'd say, 'God's work,' and the conversation would end there.

The phased handover, designed as much to give Henri and Dot time to prepare for retirement as to ease Aiden into the community, had been something of a disaster from the off. Within just days of his arrival, it became clear that Aiden had no need of any help or guidance nor, indeed, any need to humour the incumbent. He was blunt to the point of abject rudeness, which Henri might have forgiven had his brand of Christianity not bordered on the fundamentalist. Horrified that such a man could be unleashed on his parish, Henri raised his concerns with the bishop. The response of the Church was his second slap in the face; they asked him to see out the rest of his time covering a post in a neighbouring village that had been left vacant following the sudden death of his dear friend Alwyn. He had nearly resigned there and then but, in the end, it was the need to support his friend's parishioners that had won the day.

Just four weeks after Aiden's arrival, Henri and Dot were

packed and leaving the village that had been their home for thirty-nine years. One of Aiden's first acts as the new vicar was to dissolve the interfaith network Henri and Storm had been running for more than six years in partnership with the local mosques, synagogues, and temples. He also reorganised the church fundraising committee, ensuring that Storm was relieved of her voluntary position in the process. Even the yoga class was turfed out of the church hall on the grounds that it wasn't a Christian activity. Henri's messages of love and tolerance were swiftly replaced by sermons dedicated to the topic of sin and repentance – it was like falling into a time warp and emerging in the 1800s.

'But you do know Aiden is a complete nutcase, don't you?' Veronica said, bringing Storm back to the present. 'What if he hurt you? He's got a terrible temper. There were rumours that he swung a kick at Ted's little terrier, Milo, once just for weeing on the churchyard wall. He's a repugnant human being.'

Henri nodded. 'Yes, I had heard that – and many more whispers along the same lines, but I don't see that we have another choice. I'm the only one with a plausible excuse to be in the Vicarage and while I sincerely hope not to get caught, if I do, I should hope to have enough goodwill left with the local bobbies to have them believe I'm just getting a little forgetful. You ladies, as pillars of the local community, can bail me out if it comes to it.'

Veronica and Storm exchanged anxious looks. 'I'm less worried about the police than I am about that psycho vicar,' Veronica said, twisting her wedding ring anxiously. 'The police are stretched to breaking point, so I doubt they'd even have the manpower to pick up the phone these days let alone slap you in irons, but him – he's got the devil about him.'

'That's why I'm going to go and keep an eye on things. I'll take my camera as cover. I'll say I'm doing some arty stuff, but I'll also take pictures should I see anything ...' Storm said, 'incriminating.'

'I'm coming too then,' Veronica said.

Storm and Henri shook their heads in unison. 'We talked about that, Vee, and we think it'll look odd if we're both skulking around in the churchyard. Better if you're in the café as usual but on standby in case we really do need you to bail us out.'

Veronica finished the last of her wine. 'I suppose it would look a bit peculiar. I can't say I like it, but it's the only plan we have and given the stakes and the timing, I suppose we have to try something,' she said reluctantly.

'That's settled then,' Henri said, picking up the wine bottle and topping up each of their glasses.

CHAPTER 48

*M*artyn Flynn-Rivers readjusted his backpack. It, like his fawn-coloured walking trousers, boots and short-sleeved checked shirt, was brand new, purchased by his PA for this trip.

It was early. The shops, save for those taking deliveries, were still closed. He paused halfway up the hill and peered down his long nose to consult his map, but he knew exactly where he was going. He pressed on until he reached a little gift shop, its window stuffed with handmade pots, crystals and other assorted 'hippy shit' as he knew Charles would call it.

Using the plate-glass windows as a mirror, he observed the true object of his attention – Cordelia's Café and Book-shop. Slipping the surveillance report from between the folds of the map he read it line by line.

The most recent attempt to search the property had been thwarted by the ham-fisted attempt to surveil the McMansion of Storm's friend Veronica. Had he been consulted before the operation had been given clearance he would have told Charles of Asim Burman's line of work. There was no way a gnat could sneak into that fortress of a property, let alone a drone. He'd got short shrift, of course, when he mentioned it – Charles was not a man who liked his mistakes pointed out to him. Martin hoped that this little field trip, if it proved successful of course, might get him back in his good books.

The drones had managed to sweep the café and bookshop once before similar protective technology had been put in place and they'd had the building under manual surveillance for a week, although that too had been called off. There was something that still niggled at Martin, though, which was the reason he was here.

He began reading at the beginning. It was when he got to the fourth paragraph that he felt his pulse quicken. '... and no trace was found in the retail spaces, storerooms or first-floor flat.' He read it again just to be sure.

Smiling, he turned slowly, his gaze sliding over the shopfront, the first-floor flat and coming to rest on the windows of the attic. To have evaded not just the human surveillance teams but the drones too meant that whatever was in that attic flat was being protected. Charles was going to be very pleased indeed.

CHAPTER 49

*I*n her dream Lilly was back in the forest, lying in the hammock outside the tree house held in the boughs of the Wishing Oak. She was reading a book and, although all the pages were blank, she was engrossed. Anchor was lying on her chest purring softly and every now and then a small blue butterfly would rest on the top of the book. It wasn't unusual for her to dream of the forest or the creatures who lived there, but there was something odd about this dream that she couldn't put her finger on. She was trying to unravel what it all meant as she slowly surfaced from sleep, but then her mobile chimed and snapped her into full wakefulness.

Anchor was indeed sleeping on her chest in reality as well as dreamworld, and the first thing she saw when she opened her eyes was his impressive set of teeth, jaws stretched wide in a yawn. Lifting the duvet so that she could slide out of bed without disturbing him, she fumbled in her bedside drawer for her mobile which, for once, was actually switched on, and smiled when she saw the message on the screen.

'Good morning, beautiful. Hope you slept well and dreamed of happy bovines! I had THE BEST evening ever. M xxx'

She read the message three times, counting the kisses and feeling as light as the butterfly she'd just been dreaming about. She might have read it a fourth time but Anchor decided that her phone was the best place for a chin rub. Taking the hint, she scooped him up and carried him into the kitchen to feed him. Before she could think of how best to reply, the phone chimed again. This time there were two pictures along with the message:

'Dad & Pete got back at 3 a.m. Here are our new girls. Vet pretty gloomy. Both in a bad way. How could anyone leave them like this? xxx'

The first picture was of two terrified-looking horses huddled together in a loose box. Coloured cobs, one piebald, one skewbald, the bones on their flanks like mountain peaks, their backs hollow and their old winter coats still long and matted with mud and debris. One had what looked to be part of a bramble bush matted in her forelock and Lilly winced at the thought of it scratching her eye. When she saw the other picture, she realised that might be the least of their worries.

The second picture was of a poorer quality and must have been taken at a distance. It was of their feet; all eight hooves were curled into what look like the Arabian slippers of total and utter neglect. Lilly didn't know much about horses, but you didn't have to be an expert to realise that they must be in tremendous pain. A sob rocketed up from somewhere in her chest and, all concern about how best to reply forgotten, she dialled Michael's number to find out how they were.

Ten minutes later, she was dashing to the shower to get ready, Michael already on his way to pick her up. It was only as she was heading out of the back door into the courtyard that she realised what was so odd about her forest dream – it was the first time ever that she'd been there without Jack.

The vet was with the horses in the quarantine block when they arrived. Lyn was standing peering over the stable door, chewing her lip, while Pete paced back and forth answering questions as needed.

When the vet emerged from the box at last, the news was a little better than it had been the night before. After a hurried introduction for Pete and Lilly, Michael's parents headed to the house with Claire the vet to discuss the care plan.

'They're a lot calmer this morning,' Michael said quietly, leaning over the door. 'Poor things were seriously stressed when they arrived.'

'They feel calm now,' Lilly said, imagining a gentle wave of pink light sweeping over them. The skewbald mare with the bramble in her forelock whickered and then to Lilly's amazement, slowly made her way to the door. Lilly's own feet started to smart just at the thought of the pain involved in moving with such overgrown hooves.

'They've been given painkillers,' Michael said by way of explanation, his voice a barely audible whisper, 'and the farrier is on his way to meet Claire and make a plan for them.'

The little mare was only just tall enough to pop her head over the door, but she stopped a couple of steps away and whickered again. Lilly tentatively held out her hand and dropped her eyes and, after a moment's pause, the little mare took the last two steps, nuzzling at Lilly's fingers with her lips and accepting the tiniest of tickles on her muzzle. Lilly could tell Michael was smiling even without looking at him.

'I think you might have been adopted there,' Michael said later as they wandered to the car, his arm resting gently across her shoulders. 'Horses have a way of finding their special people, did you know that?'

'I didn't, no. But I'd like to help if I can. I think they're going to be okay, you know,' she said because she truly believed it. Everything in her told her that those two little souls were going to have long and happy lives and then the thought that she wasn't hit her like a freight train. In less than a heartbeat she was crying so uncontrollably that Michael had to guide her the rest of the way to the car.

She didn't intend to tell him. It was against all of the rules, but it all came tumbling out, a great vault of secrets, most of which, even to her own ears, sounded like the ramblings of a lunatic. She told him about Jack and the forest, her parents' farm, Snow, the nightmares, and the Remembering. Then, after only the briefest pause she told him that she was a Last and was going to die soon, how she hadn't been that upset at first, but how she'd changed her mind. How she really, really didn't want to die. As the last words sprinted from her lips she broke down into complete incoherence. Michael just held her as she sobbed.

When she'd exhausted herself, when every secret had been aired in the bright sunshine, she was horrified. She wiggled free of his arm and made to get up and run, unable to bear the thought that he might gently suggest she see a doctor, but he squeezed her hand to keep her next to him.

'You think that I think you're mad. That I can't possibly believe any of this spiritual past-life stuff, right?'

She nodded, because in that moment, it was all that she was capable of doing. Her misery felt so complete that she no longer had any words. It was barely ten a.m. and she'd already ruined the day – not to mention what might have been with Michael.

He looked like he was weighing up options, but then came to a decision. 'Look, I can't tell you why I know that you're telling me the truth, not yet, but please hear me when I say that I don't think you're crazy. Okay? I believe you one hundred per cent. Got that?'

She nodded again and when a wave of fresh tears erupted, he pulled her close and stroked her hair until she calmed down.

'Now this is important, Lil, really important, okay?' he said, his thumbs sweeping the quiet stream of tears from her cheeks. 'If there's one universal truth I know to be absolutely correct, it's that nothing is predetermined. You always have a choice and if you decide that this isn't going to be your last life after all, then the future will be written a new way. That's how the universe works, it has to be that way or there'd be no point. So whatever Jack told you is one path, one reality, but it isn't inevitable. If you choose to live then you'll live.'

The relief she felt was so palpable she felt giddy with it. It wasn't that she'd not had the thought herself – she had been secretly hoping that the fact that the Remembering had stopped was a sign that things had changed – but hearing it from someone else … it felt like a magic spell, or being released from one.

'Why don't we get back to yours. I need to speak to Auntie Vee and then maybe we can take Hope for a woods walk, if Storm's okay with that. We can pretend we're in your forest.'

Her, 'Yes, please,' when it came out, was accompanied by another wave of tears, but this time it felt like her sorrows were at last leaving her.

The wall of noise hit them the minute they walked into the courtyard – happy chatter over a baseline of some upbeat song Lilly couldn't name. The café was even more crowded than usual and there were even people queuing for a table. Her heart sank a little as she made her way over to Vee, who was manning the till.

'Need me to jump in and help?' Lilly asked, hoping that she didn't have 'please say no' written all over her face.

'Thank you, sweetie pie, you're such an angel, but I've got

Millie coming in any time now. If you and my favourite grown-up nephew there could walk Hope and Ludo for me, though, that would be a big help. I told Storm and Henri I'd take them out, but it's gone nuts because of the fete,' Veronica said.

'We can do that,' Lilly said, making a mental note to hug her later when she didn't have her hands full.

'Got time for a chat later, Auntie Vee?' Michael asked.

'Always, my lovely. I finish about six. Grab me in a break – if I get one, that is.'

He gave her a thumbs up and then, over his shoulder said, 'By the way, I'm your only grown-up nephew.' She winked at him.

As they made their way up the stairs, she asked, 'So what happens at a fete exactly?'

'You've never been to a fete?' Michael said, his face a picture of wide-eyed disbelief.

Lilly shook her head.

'We can't be having that!' he said and leaned in to kiss her gently on the lips. 'Let's grab these hounds and have ourselves a day out.'

Fifteen minutes later, after a mad dash to her flat so that she could change into her summer dress, they were heading out again.

CHAPTER 50

The Vicarage was separated from St Teilo's by a waist-high drystone wall. What the locals called the vicar's gate connected it to the churchyard, the narrow path meeting up with the one that led from the main gate at around the halfway mark. The house itself was shielded from the main road by a row of neat Victorian terraced cottages on the aptly named Church Road. So much so that, despite a sign, visitors often missed the turning into the small parking area between the front wall of the Vicarage and the high-walled back gardens of the cottages. Behind and to the west of the Vicarage was open farmland, so unless someone happened to see him from the churchyard or was out working in the fields, the risk of Henri being seen was quite low.

Storm reminded herself of this as they walked up the high street to the main southerly gate of the church. They'd stayed up late going over the plan, but her stomach was still churning with nerves. They'd decided that it would be better for Henri to slip through the vicar's gate than risk taking the path from behind the cottages. They'd discussed the odds and probabilities, their contingency plans and alibis, but no amount of reasoning could settle the butterflies.

Storm eyed Henri as they walked. While he looked like he was out for a leisurely morning stroll, Storm felt like she must already look like a criminal and that if a police car drove past, she'd probably faint on the spot.

'Are you sure there's not another way of doing this?' Storm hissed under her breath, although as they were alone on the street there was no sensible reason for keeping her voice down.

'Quite sure,' Henri replied before stopping to look at her. 'You don't need to be here, you know, my dear, not if you're uncomfortable.'

'Who else is going to keep a lookout?' Storm replied, her voice coming out as a squeak.

'That's my girl,' Henri said brightly, picking up the pace.

As they turned into the churchyard, Storm relaxed slightly. Glancing over the wall to the car park in front of the Vicarage, she noticed that Aiden's car, a huge gas-guzzling old Jaguar, was missing from its usual spot. She let out a breath and felt her muscles relax a fraction.

She ran over the plan again in her head then pulled out her phone and checked for the hundredth time that it was set to vibrate and that Henri's mobile was in her favourites. She was going to ask to check Henri's phone again but decided against it – he was a patient man, but even he had his limits. If anything went wrong she was to call Henri, hang up after two rings, and then she was to 'get out of Dodge' and deny any involvement. This was the part that Storm found the most difficult. The thought of abandoning Henri to the police, or worse, to Aiden Corwin made her sick to her stomach. Henri was however insistent, saying that should he, heaven forbid, be arrested or worse, finding the Ethereal would be up to Storm and Veronica alone and of course he was right.

After a couple of laps of the churchyard to make sure they were alone, Henri headed for the vicar's gate leaving Storm armed with her camera and what she considered to be a pretty flimsy cover story. She counted to ten and turned to watch Henri march purposefully up to the front door of the Vicarage. This had a dual purpose – to double-check that nobody was at home and to give him an excuse to head around the back. In his and Dot's day, most people came in through the kitchen, so to any of the locals who happened to be watching, it wouldn't look too out of place.

Storm watched him ring the bell out of the corner of her eye as she pretended to take photos. She wasn't conscious of holding her breath until a cheery 'Hello Storm!' from behind her caused her to jump and emit a small breathy shriek. Turning, with her heart hammering, she saw Enid Lark smiling up at her. A tiny bird of a woman, who must have been well into her eighties, Enid and her little bichon Humphrey were regulars at Cordelia's.

'I didn't mean to scare you, my dear. Are you okay?' she asked, resting a dainty hand on Storm's forearm, concern written all over her face.

'Yes. Yes, I'm sorry, I was lost in the moment, so to speak. How are you, Enid? How's Humphrey?' Storm managed, registering out of the corner of her eye that Henri must have already made his way to the back door.

'Very well, thank you. Nice to have some sunshine for a change. Humphrey doesn't like the rain, do you, my sweet?' Enid said, smiling down at the little dog, who was today sporting a very fetching pale blue bandana. Humphrey wagged in response and reached up to put his front paws on Storm's knee so she could better tickle his curly head.

'Well, we'll leave you to it,' Enid said kindly. 'Looks like you need a bit of peace and quiet to figure out how to turn that camera on if you're planning on taking any photos.' She chuckled, calling Humphrey before heading off down the path.

Rolling her eyes at her own oversight, Storm turned on the camera just as her phone vibrated in her back pocket. Grabbing it, she read the message from Henri. All it said was, *'I'm in.'*

Storm spent the next twenty minutes wandering through the churchyard taking photographs, stopping every few minutes to check her phone even though she had it on vibrate and had turned the volume up to its loudest; no need for silence this end, after all, she had reasoned. The Vicarage looked quieter than a grave and Storm, for the umpteenth time, told herself to relax. His car wasn't there, and they knew he had an appointment out of town this morning; she was being an idiot, she told herself.

In the distance, near the wall, she saw the white bobbing tail of a rabbit. Smiling, she kneeled down and zoomed the camera in to get a better look at it. It stopped for a moment and scratched its ear as Storm pressed the shutter to capture the moment. Pleased with herself, she hit the view button on the back of the camera to inspect her handiwork.

'Diversified into wildlife photography now, have we?' Aiden's sarcastic drawl stopped her in her tracks and a cold sweat bloomed almost at once on her back. She tried to quell the panic and wrestle down the fear that was coiling in her belly before turning slowly to smile flatly at him. *He's a handsome man*, she thought, *but there is absolutely nothing attractive about him.* Unbidden, she imagined the satisfaction of punching him in his nasty face; the thought was out of character for her, but in the moment it gave her strength.

'Just marvelling at the wonders of creation,' she countered, still smiling benignly.

E. L. WILLIAMS

He snorted at that. 'Hardly your cup of tea, Storm.' He said her name, as always, in the way that one might name something unpleasant.

Keep him talking. Keep him talking, she thought. 'Whatever gave you that idea?' she asked.

'Oh, let me think, maybe it was the fact that you run an occult bookshop peddling soul-corrupting rubbish, a vegan café that is putting our God-fearing farmers out of work, or,' he paused for dramatic effect, 'that you used to make your living conning the bereaved into believing that you spoke to their dead loved ones.' His eyes were pure flint as he stared directly into Storm's. He had stepped closer to her during his little sermon too, she noticed, in an attempt, no doubt, to use his considerable height and bulk to intimidate her.

The bald accusation had Storm's blood boiling, but knowing that he wanted her anger, she smiled at him and said calmly, 'Well it beats telling small children that they'll burn in hell because their parents didn't christen them, or refusing to marry divorcees and gay people because of your choice to hide your bigotry behind the deliberate misreading of an ancient text, I suppose.'

He glared at her, holding the eye contact, a muscle in his jaw pulsing. Storm's initial surge of pride in not allowing herself to be intimidated by this hideous man was quickly eclipsed by the realisation that she was here to keep him talking rather than score points, but she refused to blink.

'I'd love to stick around and educate a heathen, but I have work to do and I'm sure you have a crystal ball to polish somewhere, don't you?' Before Storm could react, he pushed past her, forcing her to step out of his way or be barged, and headed off down the path towards the Vicarage.

The adrenalin draining out of her, panic began to rise as she grabbed her phone. Her hands felt numb and after rejecting her fingerprint three times, she resorted to punching in her security code with fingers that had all the dexterity of parsnips. She succeeded on the second attempt and then typed the shortest text she could think of – *'Run'*. As she hit send, she looked up to see Aiden step inside the Vicarage and slam the door behind him.

CHAPTER 51

The Eternal Forest didn't seem the same without Lilly, Jack thought. It felt empty, which was an odd thing to think as it was so teeming with life. Maybe it was just him that was empty.

Snow the lamb trotted over to where Jack was sitting under the willow and after pausing for an appraising second, pushed his soft head into Jack's neck just below his left ear and rubbed gently. Jack reached up and stroked his fleece and Snow mouthed the skin along his friend's jaw in response, his lips like velvet.

'Thanks, my friend,' Jack said as the lamb stepped back and then looked him straight in the eye. Snow was one of the wisest and kindest souls Jack knew. 'I'm losing her, buddy,' Jack said, and the lamb settled down beside him, his head resting in his lap, listening. 'This … this last life was her idea, but it's all going wrong, Snow. She's banished me. Actually banished. She even used the sign. I mean, we've argued and she's told me to clear off before, but that was different, that was me giving her space, not being banished from her energy field.' Jack was conscious that his voice had risen, but Snow had not stirred.

'Sorry, bud. It's just that—'

At that point, Snow pushed a picture of Michael into Jack's mind and he groaned. 'Fair point. Yes, I'm as jealous as hell, but why wouldn't I be? It's only because she doesn't remember. That's all it is, it has to be.'

The memory of that day surfaced in Jack's mind. Lilly had been lying on the bank of the stream, the sun dappling her face through the trees, adding to her freckles. She'd giggle every now and again as a water sprite tickled her palm in mischief, or a frog used her arm as a bridge. And so it had been for a little while until Jack noticed that she had fallen asleep, her lips curled into a smile, her long auburn hair spread over her shoulder and chest. When Jack closed the book he was reading, she had sat up and said, 'I need one more life.' Just like that. No preamble. No doubt.

He hadn't been able to speak at first, but when at last he found his voice, the only thing he could manage was a strangled, 'Why?' In what felt like the space between two heartbeats, his whole world had fallen apart.

She had rushed over to sit next to him and held his face in her hands, stroking her thumbs across his cheeks. 'Please don't look so scared, my love. There's one more thing I need to do, and this is more urgent and important than anything I have ever done.' She held him with her eyes imploring him to understand. He knew all too well how this worked. He would have given anything at that moment to say no, to demand that she put them first for once, but he knew it was useless and his eyes had filled with tears of defeat.

'Do you know what?' he had asked, already knowing that this wasn't how the universe worked. The call came, you took it. She shook her head, her brow knitted into a frown.

'We could go together?' she had suggested, nodding in the

vain hope that he might follow suit. But Jack had slowly shaken his head as she knew he would. If she was going to do this, he wanted to be able to protect her and he couldn't guarantee that in human form. There was no guarantee that they'd even find each other in time.

'Well, I'll make it a short one then,' she had said earnestly. 'It feels like the minimum for this is twenty, but we can cope with that, right? We've done much, much longer in the past. Then we'll be home forever, I promise. No more missions – ever.'

She had kissed him then and, as they made love that afternoon, he had tried to imagine how he'd spend the next two decades with her looking at him but not remembering who he was to her.

CHAPTER 52

*S*torm stood frozen in the churchyard. Henri was supposed to text her when he was out; the fact that he hadn't meant that he must be still in there – with Aiden.

Her heart thumped loudly in her chest and, with her knees weakened from the rush of adrenalin, she hurried out of the churchyard and through the front gate of the Vicarage garden. She'd already ruled out calling Henri's mobile for fear that it wasn't on silent for some reason. She'd checked it herself, four times in fact, but the 'what ifs' won. Her only option was distraction. She'd hammer on the door and feign delayed indignation at what Aiden had said to her a few moments ago which, if she made enough noise, would hopefully buy Henri enough time to slip out the back.

Before she could turn and make for the gate she heard a polite cough from behind her, which made her jump and emit a high-pitched squeak. If it was Aiden then her tough-girl act was already blown, but when she turned, to her utter delight she saw Henri. He was smiling but his hands were empty.

He shook his head almost imperceptibly, then said cheerfully, 'Fancy a spot of brunch, my dear?'

Threading her arm through his, she said, 'Sod brunch, I need a bloody brandy!'

Storm and Henri headed back along the main road for a few minutes in silence. Her pulse had only just stopped racing and while she was dying to know what happened, it didn't feel right to talk about it here in the open. Crossing the road, they took a left down the high street heading for the Colliers Arms. Storm sent a quick text to Veronica as she walked which said simply, *'All clear, but not there. Back in a bit. xx'*

The Colliers had thankfully escaped the whitewashed-wall syndrome of so many of its contemporaries. It had certainly not changed in the years that Storm had lived in the village and there was something reassuring about that, Storm thought, especially today given the state of her nerves. There were prettier pubs in town but she liked the fact that the place had remained true to itself. The wood of the bar, beams and windows was stained the darkest of brown, a theme continued in the half panelling on the walls. The carpet might be a bit sticky in places and threadbare in others, but there was always a shine to the woodwork and the lingering scent of the beeswax used to polish it. A high picture rail snaked around two-thirds of the pub and displayed enough antique plates to cater for a small army round for dinner. Behind the bar, a long shelf held the tankards and engraved glasses of its many regulars. Her eyes flicked automatically to Nick's, still there, still clean and polished with the rest.

Finding a table at the far end of the pub, Storm slumped onto the faded pink velvet cushion of the settle while Henri went to the bar, returning a few minutes later with a pint of bitter in one hand and a large glass of brandy in the other.

'So, shall I start by telling you off for your bad intel on the meeting venue or for almost giving me a heart attack by not texting me?' Storm asked, before taking a grateful sip of brandy. 'I nearly had a heart attack when he popped up. Nasty little creep.'

'Ah, well, the intel was good, but it seems dear Aiden had a spot of bad luck last night. Pat behind the bar was just telling me a learner driver reversed into his precious Jag yesterday evening. Some very un-vicar-like things were said and then a right scene when the learner's very beefy father turned up to console his sobbing daughter and give said vicar a piece of his mind, which, by all accounts, ended with our clerical friend back-pedalling like crazy to avoid a thrashing.' Henri chuckled wickedly. Storm felt for the poor girl who had accidentally hit his car, but there was something extremely satisfying about the thought of the bullying vicar getting an earful from someone big enough to make him think twice.

'Anyway,' Henri continued. 'Pat saw the car being towed away this morning so I'm assuming that with no transport he decided to cancel. I can't imagine he'd be the sort to hop on the bus.'

'Okay, but the text?' Storm asked, arching her eyebrows into what she hoped was somewhere near reproachful. 'I was having kittens worrying about you being stuck in there with psycho vicar.'

'Ah, that was my fault,' he said. 'I was coming down the back stairs when I heard him slam the front door. I only just made it to the back door before I heard him come stomping down the corridor. I hid in the old coal store under the kitchen window until I heard the downstairs loo flush and took my chance.' He patted her hand. 'I'm sorry for worrying you, dear heart.'

'Oh, you're forgiven, I suppose,' she said, rolling her eyes at him. 'You would have been forgiven in extra quick time though had you found the journals.' She tried to quash her disappointment that the morning's anxiety had been fruitless.

'Indeed,' Henri agreed with a heavy sigh. 'The attic was completely empty and the cubby hole looked like it'd not been touched in years. If Dot had hidden them in the Vicarage, that's where they would have been, I'm sure of it. So either Aiden found them before we did or Dot hid them somewhere else.'

'We can't exactly ask him,' Storm said with a shudder, remembering how their latest encounter in the churchyard had made her flesh creep. 'If he did find them, what would he have done with them?'

'Who can say? He doesn't strike me as the type who would miss a trick. If he had found them I'm sure I would have heard about it, either from him or the bishop.'

'So, all we have to do now is figure out where else Dot might have hidden them,' Storm said.

The silence was almost deafening as they both racked their brains and sipped their drinks. The creak of the pub door and the thump of a familiar-sounding tail on the wooden partition broke Storm's concentration. Lilly, Michael, Hope and Ludo were at the bar, Hope hoovering the carpet in search of any dropped crisps but Ludo already wagging in Henri's direction. Michael and Lilly were laughing together, and Storm couldn't help but smile.

'Young love, eh?' said Henri, his warm eyes crinkling into a smile. 'Is it me or does she almost glow with happiness?'

'Even more than usual,' Storm said, raising her hand in a wave as, catching the scent of her mum, Hope lunged excitedly to the end of her lead then tried to gain a few more inches by standing on her back legs like a rearing horse.

'Is it okay if we join you?' Lilly asked after Hope pulled her to their table like a sled dog, while Ludo sauntered confidently over to his dad, his whip of a tail in hyperdrive. Michael gestured 'Do you want a drink?' from the bar and they both shook their heads.

'Absolutely,' Henri said while rubbing Ludo's ears, much to the old dog's delight.

'Vee asked us to walk them because the café is rammed. Hope that's okay? We packed a travel bowl and water for them in case it gets hotter,' Lilly said. 'We were heading to the fete, but they must have picked up your scent because they were adamant that they were coming in here.' She laughed.

'More than okay,' Storm said as she tickled Hope's chest, the dog's paw resting on her arm. 'They'll have a whale of a time. Thank you.'

'That's very kind of you, my dear. You'll not get a complaint from Ludo here,' Henri said, smiling down at the old dog. Then he said, 'While you're here, you may be able to help us with a puzzle.'

Storm shot him a nervous glance. If this was all true and, in a small part of her mind, Storm was still holding on to the hope that she was stuck in a particularly vivid dream, Lilly was the last person she wanted mixed up in any of it. But Henri just smiled.

'A puzzle?' Michael said from behind Lilly, his words muffled by the packet of crisps he was carrying in his mouth. Putting down his and Lilly's drinks he then retrieved a second packet from where he had it clamped between his side and his elbow. 'I love puzzles.'

Henri explained that he had given his old journals to his wife for safe keeping many years ago, but that in the hurried move and then her illness, they were lost. He added, without explanation, that he knew for certain they'd not been left in the old Vicarage.

'They must be very precious to you,' Lilly said, studying Henri's face, her eyes wide and suddenly full of sadness.

'Oh, they are, my child. Very precious indeed,' Henri said quietly, smiling at her.

'So why did she hide them?' Michael asked.

'It's a long story, but I asked her to keep them safe,' Henri said.

Michael nodded thoughtfully, then said, 'Maybe if you talk us through the timeline it'll help give you some clues?' as he opened both packets of crisps out flat so they could all share them.

'Good idea,' Henri said, wetting his whistle with a mouthful of ale before beginning. 'We lived in the Vicarage for over thirty years. We moved not long before I was due to retire and, thanks to some help from our boys, bought a little cottage. But then my dear wife, Dot,' he said for Lilly's benefit, 'was diagnosed with cancer. When we were told that her prognosis was likely terminal, we took to the road and spent six months travelling around the country in an old motorhome visiting old friends and family and seeing parts of the country that we'd always intended to visit. We put our things in storage for a while, but I've been through every box we had and they're definitely not there.'

Storm saw that Lilly's eyes were misty with tears by the time Henri finished. Michael handed her a handkerchief and squeezed her hand. Storm smiled.

Michael said, 'So I'm assuming if they weren't found in the motorhome, what about friends?'

Henri and Storm looked at each other incredulously. Storm drained what was left of her brandy before getting to her feet, while Henri, abandoning his half-drunk pint, manoeuvred himself out of the bench seat.

'You, young man, may well be a genius!' Storm said, planting a kiss on the top of his head which made Michael blush, Lilly laugh and both dogs wag their tails in happy confusion.

'All in a day's work.' Michael laughed, looking slightly bemused.

'Well done, my boy,' Henri said, 'well done indeed!' He patted him on the back before bending to speak to Ludo. 'You be a good lad like always and keep this pair out of trouble.'

Hope whined as Storm stepped around her. Leaning down to take Hope's head in her hands, she planted a kiss on her silky soft liver-and-white head, then repeated the process with Ludo and earned herself a chin lick. 'Be good babies, you two,' she said, then as a lump rose in her throat, forced her legs to propel her to the door. When she looked back, both dogs were sitting expectantly in front of Lilly who was holding the treat box aloft. *That's my girl*, she thought.

'I can't believe I didn't think of that,' Henri said a few minutes later as he marched along the high street as quickly as his aching knee would allow.

'You can't think of everything,' she said, 'and will you please slow down or you'll set your knee off again.'

Henri slowed then stopped. 'I'm sorry. I'm just annoyed at myself for not thinking of the motorhome before now. But it makes complete sense.'

'I'm assuming you still have it?' Storm said, trying to think of the last time she'd even seen it, which she guessed was probably their bon voyage party.

'I left it at a friend's. We were staying there when Dot was taken ill. He's less than an hour away.'

'And this friend, you trust him?' Storm asked, not liking how quickly she was becoming suspicious.

Without hesitation Henri said, 'I trust Isaac with my life.' He pulled his mobile from his pocket and tapped down his other pockets, no doubt in search of his glasses, and said, 'I should call him right away.'

'Hang on,' Storm said, putting her hand on his arm, 'let's wait and speak to Veronica, then call him from the flat, okay? As she said, we don't know who's being watched or listened to and until we do we should play it safe.' Henri nodded and, with some reluctance, put his mobile back in his pocket before setting off apace back to the café.

CHAPTER 53

*B*ack at Cordelia's, Veronica briefed, security status verified, and call made to Isaac, Henri sat on the bench in the courtyard to wait for Storm. He was enjoying the buzz of the bees in the honeysuckle when he was pleased to see Jack wander in through the back gate. 'Hello again,' he said brightly. 'Beautiful day, isn't it?'

Jack looked up as if seeing the day for the first time. He shrugged. 'Yeah, it looks like,' he said, aiming for nonchalance but falling a long way short.

Henri gestured to the space on the bench next to him. 'Got two minutes to keep an old duffer company?' he asked lightly.

'Sure,' Jack replied, taking the seat and leaning forward to rest his elbows on his knees. 'This is such a pretty garden,' he said, surprising Henri, who hadn't pegged him for a nature lover.

'Isn't it just. Storm has something of a magic touch where it comes to plants. You a gardener, Jack?'

Jack looked a million miles away. 'Once, yes. A long time ago now, but I used to love working with the land ...' He might have said more, Henri thought, if Storm hadn't stepped into the courtyard, a small open-topped box in her hand.

'I'm sure Storm wouldn't turn down the offer of some green-fingered help,' Henri said, getting to his feet. 'Here, let me take those, my dear.' He peered into the box. 'Dear lord, does Jerry expect us to be gone for weeks? This is way beyond a few snacks for the road.'

Storm smiled and made a 'you know Jerry' face.

'Good to see you, Jack. I'll pop these in the car. No rush, Stormy,' Henri said as he headed down the path and out of the back gate.

* * *

STORM TURNED to Jack and said the first thing that came to mind. 'It was you. The flying peace lily.' It came out more as a statement than a question and Jack looked at her, his eyes appraising.

As if coming to a decision, he said, 'You were about to tell Margot about me, and it would have been a mistake.' He paused then asked, 'How did you know it was me?'

'I didn't so much know as feel that it was you,' she said. 'Maybe, when you zapped me the day Lilly moved in, I got a sense of your energy signal or something, but you were the first person who sprang into my mind.'

Jack smiled. 'I was going to say that you zapped me, but I suppose we'll never know, will we?'

Storm laughed, glad to see him look a little brighter, then let out a long breath as she felt the pieces falling into place. 'You're Lilly's spirit guide,' she said, putting her hand to her head, the relief washing over her. 'Of course.'

He turned to look at her and nodded. 'Guilty as charged,' he said, a faint smile on his lips, but his eyes were still full of sadness. 'The thing is, I've no idea how or why you can see me. Not you, or Henri, or even …' he added with a wry laugh that wasn't unkind, 'your bloody cat, who hates me, by the way. I can't explain it.'

'But that makes no sense. We should need your permission and if you're sure you didn't give it, which of course you would be, then why? And why us? Especially me – I lost all connection with the spirit world three years ago.'

'I'm sorry,' Jack said. 'I can't imagine how that must feel.'

Touched by his obvious sincerity, Storm nodded her acknowledgement, swallowing to loosen the tightness in her throat that always materialised when someone offered sympathy or kindness.

'You had magic too?' he asked gently.

Storm nodded. 'I thought, when I was able to see your aura, I thought that it might be returning. That's why I wanted to speak to Margot. She mentored me from the time I was twelve, but even before you intervened, every sense I had was telling me to keep my own counsel.'

'You were right to be wary of Margot. I felt it too. I wish I had answers for you, I really do. All I know is that something is very, very wrong at the moment – and I mean aside from the seriously messed-up state of the world in general. I mean spiritually, energetically, the whole works,' Jack said. 'I'm going to give Lilly some space for a few days while she's busy with other things and use the time to see what I can find out.'

Storm wrestled with the idea of telling him everything, but at that point, Henri poked his head around the gate. Storm waved at him and stood up. 'Henri and I are heading off to see a friend of his who might be able to give us some answers. Let's meet when we get back tonight, okay? There's a lot more that I think we need to talk about.'

Jack nodded. 'Yeah, sure.'

'Are you okay, Jack?' she asked, concerned.

He smiled, a sad but genuine smile then, looking her straight in the eyes, said, 'Thank you. You've helped already just by listening.' He attempted a wry laugh. 'It's not like I get the opportunity often in this line of work.'

'Maybe you guides should get together, unionise, set up a social club and some decent supervision meetings. Maybe a pension scheme while you're at it?' she suggested, hoping to lighten his mood.

He laughed then, a rich, genuine laugh that creased the corners of his eyes. 'I'll bring it up at the next board meeting for sure,' he said. 'Thanks, Storm, honestly. I'm grateful. I'll let you know if I find anything out.'

'I know I don't need to ask, but just look after Lilly. I know things must be … difficult, but—'

'Always,' he said, with a look that almost broke her heart.

She was almost at the back gate when he called her name. 'Storm. If you need me, call for me, okay? I'll find you.'

Before she had time to respond, he vanished in front of her eyes.

CHAPTER 54

*T*he sun was warm on their backs as Lilly and Michael joined the slow procession of families and locals making their way up the hill to the park. It looked almost nothing like the rain-lashed barren place where Lilly had found Hope. She bent down to tickle the dog's ears and as she did, Hope lifted her head to look at Lilly, and wagged her tail. Lilly wondered if she had been thinking the same thing. So much had changed, and she had this sweet little dog to thank for starting it all. She fished two treats out of her bag, gave one to Hope and one to Ludo as she couldn't leave him out.

Once they had paid their entry fee to the man on the gate, they stood away from the crowd to get their bearings and give the dogs a drink. Lilly was so excited – she felt like a little kid. Or how she imagined a normal little kid would feel, not a messed-up empath who spent her childhood hiding from the world. But she didn't want to think about that now. She wanted to drink in what was right in front of her. There had to be more than thirty different stalls; some selling food, others plants, bric-a-brac and books. There was a bouncy castle and a helter-skelter and dancing Morris Men all dressed in black. The air was warm and on the cooling breeze drifted the smell of fresh popcorn and candy floss.

'This is our funny money,' Michael said, holding up a small fabric bag with 'Handmade Soap' printed on the side. 'It's only to be spent on useless raffles, pointless games and general silliness, which, for the avoidance of doubt, includes libations in the beer tent, although I might have to add to it if we're here a while.' He jangled the bag to make the coins tinkle.

Flinging her arms around him, she kissed him and said, 'It's perfect,' because it was.

They spent the next couple of hours wandering around the fete and by the time they stopped for brunch Lilly had played her first ever game of hoopla and won a small pink teddy, which Hope turned her nose up at, but Ludo loved. Thanks to the various raffles, Michael's rucksack contained a bottle of Blue Nun wine, a tin of peach slices in syrup and a box of loose tea, along with the toy duck after Ludo got tired of carrying it. They found that they were both totally useless at the coconut shy, but she did pull a really pretty jasmine scented soya candle out of the lucky-dip tombola that she decided to give to Storm. They lingered for so long at the book stall that both dogs lay down.

Using the last of their funny money, they bought a stick of candy floss, another new experience for Lilly, and walked home slowly, the dogs plodding contentedly at their sides. Michael said, 'Well, I think we can say that as far as the games go, we had a mixed afternoon. I was rubbish at estimating jelly beans in a jar.' He sighed, pretending to be downbeat. 'I'll definitely have to consider another career now that door has closed to me.'

Lilly laughed and joined in. 'Me too. My duck rescue

won't fare well if I can't even catch the ones with little metal hooks in their heads,' she said seriously.

They were still laughing when they arrived back at the flat. 'What shall we do for the rest of the day?' Lilly asked then immediately wondered if she was being too demanding. 'But I mean, if you have plans, that's fine, I've sort of monopolised you enough today already and—'

Michael cut her off with a kiss. 'How about we watch a film or a boxset or something and keep the dogs company?' he suggested, fishing Ludo's new toy out of his backpack. 'They should be tired enough for a nap after all that walking and we could all cwtch up on the sofa.'

Lilly didn't think she could possibly like him any more than she already did, but found herself melting a little more. 'Deal,' she said, planting another kiss on his lips, 'just so long as you're not expecting me to drink that awful wine!'

CHAPTER 55

*H*enri hadn't told Storm much about the man they were about to meet. They had spent most of the journey into the heart of the Welsh countryside listing the people they knew who could conceivably be the Ethereal. After naming half of the town they fell silent.

Storm reflected on what she knew so far about Isaac: he was botanist, grew vegetables for a living, shared a house with his sister and her young son and was a divorced single father to three children. The only other thing Henri had said was that Isaac was one of the men he respected most in the world, which coming from Henri was recommendation enough.

When they turned off the main A-road, skirting the town and heading deeper into the countryside, the satnav froze. Storm soon became disoriented in the warren of twisting lanes. In places the hedges towered either side of them and she prayed they'd not meet a tractor coming the other way on the single-track road.

When Henri pulled up to what looked like a passing point, she craned her neck to see why they were pulling in, but instead, he got out of the car and walked to the end of an old stone wall that edged the next field. 'Just want to let him know we're coming,' he said when he got back into the car – as if that explained anything at all.

Fifty yards further down the lane Henri pulled the car down a dirt road, flanked on either side with ancient chestnut trees. After about a mile they encountered a sturdy five-bar metal gate. Storm was about to ask if they'd gone wrong somewhere when the gate swung open, allowing them on their way.

'That was pretty flash,' she said, 'an automatic gate in the middle of nowhere.'

'Oh, it's not automatic,' Henri replied, 'they'll have seen us or else we'd have still been sitting there.'

Storm opened her mouth to say something, but decided she'd just wait and see. It was at least another mile before the treeline suddenly opened up to reveal a large whitewashed farmhouse sitting at the end of the no through road. It had a symmetry to it of the kind that children usually drew. Storm guessed that there would have to be at least six bedrooms inside, given the footprint, but there was nothing ostentatious about the building. It was, she thought, possibly the most homely-looking place she'd ever seen.

As they stepped out into the heat, three collies ran to greet them, tails wagging, their coats shining in the sunlight. Storm was still fussing the dogs and laughing as they each vied for the visitors' undivided attention, when she realised that the man they were here to see had joined them too.

The sight of him stopped her in her tracks for a beat and made her chest tighten, because at first glance he reminded her of Nick. He had the same tangle of shoulder-length hair, although Isaac's was bleached a few shades lighter by the sun, the same easy stance. The similarities to Nick were superficial the more she looked. While Nick had been tall and lean, a young willow of a man in her memory, Isaac seemed to be hewn from a much broader oak and closer to her age than Henri's, as she'd wrongly assumed.

Isaac and Henri hugged each other like the old friends they were and Storm took the opportunity to study him a little more. He had a presence that was both reassuring and unsettling at the same time. Even more unsettling was the notion that had Isaac tired of growing veg, a modelling career for some outdoor brand wouldn't be out of the question. She could just see him on a horse in the wilderness or hanging off the side of a mountain somewhere. She pushed the image out of her mind and tried to focus.

His hand when he proffered it was large, rough with callouses, attached to a well-muscled forearm toasted a deep golden brown by the sun and covered with hair the colour of spun gold. Touches of grey mingled at random amongst the wiry dark blond stubble on his chin.

His eyes were fanned with laughter lines, but he didn't seem like the laughing type. As soon as the thought formed in her mind she felt a pang of sadness for him – this stranger whom she'd only just met. She imagined him then, head back, laughing with all his heart, but the picture felt like an ancient memory, like a crumbling parchment that contained a world long lost and all but forgotten.

After their brief introduction, they followed him into the house. The entrance hall was panelled in a dark wood but saved from gloominess by the light flooding through a huge roof lantern above the stairs. She felt it then, the faintest whisper of spirit. The sensation sent a wash of welcome coolness down her back and made her skin prickle in recognition. She bit her lip to ground herself, pushed her hope to one side and followed Henri and Isaac into the kitchen.

A mishmash of wooden units lined the walls of the large room. They were all slightly different and looked as if they were being added to as the need arose. She thought of Isaac's calloused hands and wondered if he could turn his hand to woodwork too. An ancient-looking Aga sat languidly in the chimney breast wall and, at the centre of the room, a long battle-scarred table was flanked by two benches. From the smell filling the room, she guessed that there was bread in the oven too.

'I was thinking we'd talk over lunch,' Isaac said. 'What we have to discuss isn't for little ears.'

Henri, seemingly instantly at home, fell into step with his friend as they prepared the food. When she offered to help, Isaac said, 'Thanks, but it's all under control. Take a pew.'

Feeling like a spare part, Storm sat on the corner of the bench and watched as Isaac gathered mismatched plates from a shelf, pulled glass bowls from the fridge and then, donning a pair of old flowered oven gloves, pulled a loaf of bread from the Aga. *And he can bake*, she thought, putting her fingers to her lips to make sure that she hadn't said it out loud.

Henri added three large mugs, one with 'Best Dad' painted on the side in a shaky childish hand, and a huge green teapot to the collection of bowls and plates on the table. Isaac caught her looking carefully at a bowl of mixed rice and said quietly but matter-of-factly, 'It's all plant-based – it's all safe.' He gave her a brief tight smile as if it were an afterthought.

Once they were all settled at the table, Henri wasted no time in recounting an abridged version of the story. 'Which is why I'm hoping that my dear Dot hid the journals in Erma,' he concluded.

'Let's bloody hope so,' Isaac said. 'We knew something was happening, a tipping point coming. The energies are so low that the shepherds have been barely holding it together for months now and we're losing more and more each week.'

The mention of shepherds made Storm snap out of her train of thought. She glanced at the collies, all asleep on the two long sofas in the corner of the kitchen. 'Shepherds as in sheep herders?' she said, speaking the words out loud before she could think better of them.

Isaac arched an eyebrow at her and then Henri and said, 'No. Of course not,' in a tone that, if he was trying to hide his exasperation, failed miserably.

Storm shot Isaac an indignant look. Henri held up his hand to Isaac and turned to look at Storm. 'It's no failing of yours, Stormy. From what you've told me, Margot was something of an experiential tutor – big on practice and not so worried about the theory and history of things, that's all. As I'm sure Isaac will explain shortly, shepherds are light workers.' He waved his open palm at Isaac, giving him the floor with a pointed look.

Storm felt the colour rising in her cheeks. She knew by rights she shouldn't feel as irritated as she did, but she already felt so inexplicably exposed in front of Isaac that this gap in her knowledge just added to her sense of vulnerability.

Collecting herself and organising her features into what she hoped was a picture of cool neutrality, she turned to Isaac and arched her own eyebrow expectantly.

He began in a tone one might use when reading to a small child who demanded the same story every night. 'Shepherds are light workers who guide animal souls to the next world. All souls, including animals, incarnate with a guide, but now that we're torturing billions of them to the point of utter fucking insanity, their energies are so low that most never even see their guides, let alone bond with them. So when their time comes they are alone and terrified and have no idea of where to go. They don't look for the light because we have damned them to the dark – hence the need for shepherds.'

'So shepherds do the work of an animal's own spirit guide?' Storm asked, trying not to think of the horror. When Isaac nodded, she asked, 'So why can the animals see the shepherd but not their own guide?'

A small pull at the corner of Isaac's mouth gave her a small jolt of triumph. 'Good question,' he said, picking up the teapot to fill their mugs. 'It's because shepherds, unlike the spirit guide, carry mainly human energy.' He nodded at Henri.

'So your energy, your frequency is familiar to the animals whereas that of spirit isn't?'

The corner of Isaac's mouth inched into the smallest of smiles and, looking her directly in the eye, he said, 'Exactly.'

Feeling slightly better, she asked, 'So how long have you been doing this work?'

'Around twenty years, but with the required breaks for healing, of course. You can't bear witness to that amount of pain without either losing your mind or your heart and we need every shepherd we can get,' he said, nodding again at Henri.

'Wait a minute. You're a shepherd?' asked Storm, turning to stare at Henri in amazement.

Henri nodded. 'Only since my darling Dot passed. Alas, I can't manage anything like the numbers I'd like to, and I've not managed anything at all since these nightmares began, but I do what I can.'

Isaac stood up, grasped Henri's shoulder under his wide, suntanned hand and gave a squeeze. 'It's more than enough for every soul you save, my friend,' he said as he put the kettle back on to boil.

'How do I not know this?' Storm asked, looking from Henri and back again to Isaac.

Henri just shrugged and seemed to be lost for words, until he said, 'It was sort of hard to bring up, really.'

Storm couldn't argue with that. While they had loved nothing more than talking into the small hours about all things spiritual, the loss of Storm's connection had rewritten the rules.

'So, can you tell me how it works?' she asked, moving the conversation on.

Isaac, leaning against the kitchen counter, explained. 'It used to be done in meditation. In the old days, Soul Shepherds, to give them their full title, would spend a few minutes each day connecting to any local animal in distress in their final moments. But the numbers were low.'

'Because most had a guide,' Storm offered.

Isaac nodded. 'But today, the numbers are so immense and the conditions so horrendous that the levels of fear and suffering have gone through the roof. There are so few of us left now that we're forced to night walk – using our sleeping hours to get to as many souls as we can.' Isaac looked like his eyes were seeing something aside from the floor in front of him and he closed them tightly for a few seconds. Storm wondered if it helped to block out the memory of whatever it was that was haunting him.

Henri picked up the story. 'While there are some advantages of doing this work during sleep – the ability to have some time for other things during waking hours, for instance – the trauma of it all does take its toll, especially on those who do not rest as they should,' he said pointedly, looking at Isaac.

'You're a fine one to talk, my friend. It's a small silver lining, but I'm almost glad to hear that the return of your nightmares has at least kept you in your own bed for a few nights,' he said, attempting to lighten the tone.

When Isaac returned to the table to get the teapot, Storm

could see the fatigue in his eyes and had an answer to the question of why he looked so sad. Despite his physical strength and presence, she understood now at least part of the reason for his pain.

'How many of you are there?' she asked.

'With fifty-six billion souls industrially slaughtered each year, not counting the creatures in the sea, not nearly enough.' Isaac replaced the fresh teapot on the table and sat back down heavily. 'There used to be millions of Fey, that's a sort of catch-all term for light workers, by the way,' he said, offering up the pot to refill their mugs. 'Not all shepherding, you understand, but just existing at the higher end of the human vibrational spectrum and serving as they felt called to. Some as healers or poets, musicians or teachers ... what they do is less important, it's how they do it that keeps – or kept – everything in balance. Any act conducted with great love, basically.'

'Do you remember Nannette, Isaac?' Henri asked and Isaac smiled a warm, genuine smile. 'Nannette was one of the most beautiful souls you could ever meet, Stormy. She worked as a hairdresser until she was nearly eighty and, I swear, in all the years no one ever left that salon feeling anything less than a goddess. Forgive the digression, Isaac, but my point is that the Fey come in many different forms and do light work of all kinds.'

'Are people born this way then?' Storm asked, her mind crowded with questions yet conscious that in taking time to fill her in, they weren't talking about the thing they were here for.

'No. It's a choice,' Isaac said, 'it's a scale of vibration that we humans can choose to raise through love, compassion and service, or lower through fear, hate and violence. We call those at the top of the vibration Fey because of their light. Those at the bottom we call "Very".'

'So that's where Veronica's mother got it from,' Storm said to Henri, 'and here's us thinking she just made it up.'

'It's from the Latin meaning *true*. That's where humanity started in terms of vibration, but we were always meant to move up the scale – that's the whole point of evolution,' Isaac said, glancing at the kitchen clock.

Knowing that her lesson in spiritual matters had cost them valuable time, Storm decided to move them on; she could quiz Henri on more of the detail later.

'Thank you for that, both of you,' she said. 'I missed out on a lot, obviously, but now I know, I can do some more research of my own.' She turned to Henri. 'Okay, let's get back to the Ethereal. Henri, do you have the letter?'

CHAPTER 56

*S*torm excused herself to use the bathroom while Isaac pored over Dot's letter and Henri's night-time writings. As she climbed the wide bright staircase, she sensed a powerful presence around her. Excitement swelled in her chest at the familiar yet long-absent sensation. She held the handrail and closed her eyes, allowing her feet to guide her up the stairs as the intensity of the spirit strengthened. Most definitely female and older than her, she stopped and focused on the energy. While the spirit was reluctant to give any more details, she left Storm with the strong impression of gratitude. When she asked in her mind, *Gratitude for what?* the answer came at lightning speed: *I'm grateful you're here.* Then as quickly as it had arrived, the spirit was gone.

Three long years in the spiritual wilderness and now, out of the blue in the home of a complete stranger, a message. She felt tears prick at her eyes and was conscious of her heart thumping in her chest. Taking a few deep breaths to steady herself and talk herself out of bolting back down the stairs to tell Henri what had just happened, she climbed the last remaining stairs and headed for the bathroom.

As she made her way down the stairs a few minutes later, she could hear the chatter of kids' voices from the kitchen and felt slightly apprehensive. When she stepped into the kitchen she saw that Isaac had a little blond-haired boy of about five on his lap who was holding up a brightly coloured painting. At the other end of the table, Henri was laughing with an older boy she took to be about thirteen, while two pre-teenage girls were talking to a petite woman with close-cropped blonde hair at the sink.

Her entrance caused everyone to pause and look up and she froze momentarily in the doorway. The woman at the sink was the first to react, smiling warmly and drying her hands as she walked towards her. 'Storm. I'm Katharine, Isaac's sister and William's mum,' she said, extending her hand. William, the young lad chatting with Henri, waved and said, 'That's me. Hi, Storm.'

The little lad on Isaac's lap was on his feet in a heartbeat and ran over to her. 'Storm?' he asked, beaming while pushing his bright-blue-rimmed round glasses up. 'Like in the X-Men?' Everyone laughed and Storm relaxed. The magnification of the glasses gave him the look of a small endearing owlet.

'If only,' she replied, taking the little hand that he offered and shaking it as he told her his name was Finn, with two *n*s.

The girls came over next. Hebe introduced herself and her sister Fleur and told Storm that they were aged ten and eight. Irritated by her big sister speaking for her, Fleur then introduced herself again as if Hebe hadn't spoken, told Storm that she liked her hair and asked if they'd be staying for dinner.

'I certainly hope so,' Isaac said, looking directly at Storm, his eyes softer now that he was surrounded by his children.

Before either Storm or Henri could reply, they seemed to get swept up in the after-school conversation. Finn ran over with his picture. 'Wow,' said Storm, looking at some sort of superhero with long dark hair, a cape and lightning shooting out of its hands. 'Who's this then?' she asked.

Finn frowned at her, 'You,' he said as if it should have been patently obvious. 'I did it in school today.'

'He's getting you mixed up with Storm from X-Men,' said Hebe, earning herself a glare from her little brother. 'And she didn't have a cape,'

'No I'm not and she did have a cape,' Finn said scowling.

Fleur took her little brother's side on the argument about the cape and Storm did her best to mediate the debate, before distracting them all with questions about the dogs.

'Right then, angel-pies,' Katharine said after clapping her hands together a few times to cut through the din, 'upstairs to change, then homework please. We'll see you back down here at sixteen thirty sharp.'

Once the children had left the kitchen, the mood changed almost at once.

'I think we have company,' Katharine said matter-of-factly, picking up a large tablet in a rubber case from the table.

Storm had allowed herself to get so caught up with the children that she had almost forgotten why they were here.

'I thought I clocked surveillance at the school, but I wasn't sure,' Katharine said, 'thought it might have been my old colleagues keeping tabs, but there's no doubt now.' She turned the tablet around to show them an aerial shot with the farmhouse at its centre, woods and open fields stretching all around it for miles. It took a second for Storm to realise what was odd about it, but then she saw that there were dozens of small red dots surrounding the farm.

'Hen, you said Vee was being watched too?' Katharine asked calmly.

'Yes, Asim's team picked it up, but that was drones main-ly,' he confirmed.

'So they're after the library?' Isaac asked and Storm shot them each a confused look.

'I doubt we have time to explain, but yes, we all know each other,' Henri said, his tone touching on the embarrassed.

Katharine was speaking again now as she flicked through screens on the tablet. 'From the timeline, it looks as if they followed you here, then when they were sure of where you were, sent in the reinforcements.'

Storm got out of her seat to stand next to Katharine and get a better look at the tablet. The next picture jumped into a full-screen video and Storm relaxed – this was clearly a film that they were discussing because, on the screen, people dressed in black combat fatigues complete with sidearms in their belts and assault rifles held across their chests prowled through woodland. The relief was short-lived as she saw the farmhouse come into view and her little car parked right outside.

Reality dawned with a sickening feeling. 'But, the chil-dren,' she said, her voice catching at the thought of the danger they might have brought to this incredible family. 'We've put you all at risk. We had no idea … we brought this mess to your door and—'

'Storm,' Isaac said softly, then again more firmly until she met his eyes. 'We are not all we seem. There's no time to explain now, but please believe me when I say that we are safe here and that they would have found us with or without you.'

'But all the better with you,' Katharine said, to Storm's ears, impossibly brightly given the reality of armed opera-tives circling their property.

While she wanted to believe them, fear was getting the

better of her and she could hear herself start to babble. 'But at Veronica's,' she said, 'they had listening devices and drones, they could hear her and—'

Katharine cut her off firmly but gently. 'They are listening, but what they'll be hearing is a recording of us all chewing the fat about old times, you and Henri being persuaded to stay for a few days and then Storm, you confiding in me that you think Henri may be losing his faculties.' Henri laughed and Katharine turned to him and said, 'Sorry, dear, but I had to think of something fast once I knew you were coming up.'

'But we've not had any of those conversations,' Storm protested, confused. 'And you knew they'd be coming?'

'No, but it's standard protocol to prepare and—' Katharine stopped, an alert on her watch interrupting her.

Isaac said, 'This has been our fight for a very long time, Storm. You're going to have to trust me when I say that we are well prepared and well protected here, in more ways than one.' His eyes seemed to shine then and Storm caught a glimpse of the man he might have been before – although before what, she wasn't sure.

Storm didn't understand any of it and that scared her. She felt like she'd fallen into a film script, but when she looked at Henri, he seemed to be taking it all in his stride.

'Time to move,' Katharine said, tucking the tablet under her arm and walking towards the door, pausing to pull aside a framed picture of the kids hanging on the wall to reveal a safe. After punching in the code the safe swung open and out of it she retrieved what looked like a large handgun and several packs of something that might have been bullets.

'You have a gun? In a house full of kids?' Storm hadn't intended for her voice to be so shrill or, she kicked herself, so judgemental.

Katharine put her hand on Storm's arm and looked her

directly in the eye. When she spoke her voice was steady and kind. 'Yes, I have guns. This is just one of them. Look, Storm, we don't have much time, but if it makes you feel better, before I retired I was a major in Her Majesty's Armed Forces. I trained in covert operations and, trust me, I do not wield weapons lightly. This would still be in the safe if I didn't think there was a chance that I may have to use it to protect us all, including our kids, from whoever's out there. We need to go. Are we good?'

Storm felt her head nod, but her brain was still playing catch-up. Following their lead, she and Henri followed Katharine and Isaac out into the hall. Stopping at the foot of the stairs, Katharine called up calmly. When Hebe appeared first on the landing she said, 'Hebes, tell the others we're having pancakes, will you?' Hebe froze for a nanosecond then ran off. 'Dogs!' Katharine added and a scuttle of claws on floorboards from the kitchen answered her.

Isaac beckoned Henri and Storm to follow him down to the cellar from a door under the main stairs. As she descended the steps, Storm heard the pounding of little feet above her and marvelled at how quickly kids could move when there were pancakes on offer then, her brain seeming to grind ever more slowly, realised it was likely a code word. The dogs at their heels, they descended, followed quickly by the chatter of the children.

'Who's got Arty?' Katharine asked from the top of the stairs.

'Arty slipped down as soon as Uncle Isaac opened the door,' William replied.

'Arty is Artemis the cat,' Henri said smiling back at Storm. 'She's a lot like Anchor but even more demanding, if you can imagine that,' he added with a chuckle.

Storm nodded but was having trouble keeping up with

any of it. Her head started to pound and she hoped she wasn't about to get a migraine.

'Katharine and Isaac will explain all once we're secured,' Henri said.

Secured, it transpired, meant their arrival at what looked to Storm like a bunker. On the descent, Storm had been reminded of Veronica's library, but this was no new-build state-of-the-art facility; it looked to be from a time when people put their faith in cold iron, concrete and steel.

Isaac was standing at the bottom of the stairs holding open a large iron door that must have been a foot thick. He nodded at Storm as she passed to join Henri waiting in the corridor beyond. A few seconds later, with everyone now gathered, she heard the creak of hinges and the thud of the almighty door swinging into place. The children started to chat excitedly, and Katharine turned to Storm and began to speak. Storm could see her lips moving and somewhere in the distance she could hear the children and the dogs, but it was all so far away. Bright lights swam in her vision. The last thing she remembered was someone close to her shouting, 'Catch her!' and then there was nothing.

CHAPTER 57

*I*saac had caught Storm just as her legs failed her. 'Well, looks like our theory may have some grounding to it,' he said to Henri as he carried her into the nearest bedroom and laid her down.

'Yes, but for her to react so suddenly? Is that normal?' Henri asked, placing the back of his hand on Storm's forehead.

'I doubt we can say that anything about this is normal,' Katharine said, feeling for the pulse in Storm's neck and checking her watch. 'I've certainly never encountered anything like this before, but I don't think she's in any danger – not now she's here, anyway. Her pulse is strong. You two go – we don't have much time. We'll look after her, you know that.'

Henri hesitated but then followed Isaac out of the room at a brisk march.

'There's an access hatch straight into the barn from the next section,' Isaac said, heading down the long whitewashed corridor towards the door that connected the first bunker to the second. Henri had been here many times over the years, but the labyrinth never ceased to both amaze and terrify him. It had been built for a nuclear attack that had thankfully never arrived and now it protected people from a horror of an entirely different kind.

'I searched every inch of the motorhome after you called, so if they're there, they can only be in the safe,' Isaac said as they strode down the long concrete corridor.

'I still can't believe that the old banger came complete with such a high-end safe.' Henri sighed, cursing the irony that something designed to increase security was now putting them at risk.

When they reached the door, as thick and heavy as the one they'd entered through, Isaac paused to pull a gun out of a metal cabinet bolted to the wall next to it.

'Lilly!' Henri exclaimed. 'Dear God in heaven, I've been such a fool. Why on earth did I not think of her before?'

'The Ethereal?' Isaac asked, holding the door and then bolting it again behind them once they were through.

'We've been through everyone we know, but not once did either of us think of her,' Henri said. 'She's a lovely young girl who's recently rented Storm's attic flat.'

'We'll soon find out if it's her face in the journal,' Isaac said, almost jogging now to a metal ladder at the far end of a cavernous room large enough to store a dozen tanks. 'If she's being protected by magic too then the cloaking can't reach you here, which is probably why you've only just thought of her as a candidate. But there's another candidate far closer to home, you know,' he said, raising both eyebrows.

It took him a second, but then Henri said, 'You mean Stormy?' He thought for a moment but shook his head. 'I was out of it during the visions, certainly, but I'm sure I'd have remembered the face if it was Storm I'd drawn. So would Dot, I'm sure.'

'I suppose so,' Isaac said, swinging the rifle over his shoulder, 'but how many years was it before you met her?' He didn't wait for a reply before climbing the ladder, then pausing at the top to check the video feed on his phone.

Henri stood, lost in thought. He and Dot had been in their sixties when Storm and Nick came to Pont Nefoedd and he'd been what, twenty-five, twenty-six maybe when the visions struck. Maybe …

'All clear,' Isaac said, breaking Henri's train of thought. He opened the hatch, climbed through and then leaned back to help Henri. They emerged into the barn behind a wall of haphazardly stacked straw, one bale of which Henri noticed was attached to the top of the hatch for camouflage.

The motorhome was parked nearby and the sight of it hit Henri like a thump to his chest. He and Dot had spent months touring the country in 'Erma' after it became clear that her cancer was not going to allow them the peaceful retirement they'd dreamed of. He swallowed the memories and went straight inside, pulling up the cushions on the bench seat to reveal the safe. He remembered the saleswoman had made such a big deal about it when they bought the thing. State of the art had been mentioned more than once and yet, to his knowledge, they'd never used it. Leaning in, Henri pressed his thumb to the sensor. 'Error' flashed red on the small screen.

'Shit,' Isaac said quietly, not taking his eyes off the screen of his phone, 'we've got company. Two crossing the yard.'

Henri tried again, the left thumb this time. 'Error' flashed again and his heart hammered harder in his chest.

'Two more coming around the back,' Isaac said. 'We need to go, now.'

Henri rubbed his thumb on his trousers and sent up a prayer before trying again. With an electronic chirp and a metallic clunk the door popped open. Reaching inside Henri grabbed the one thing contained within – a bright pink backpack.

'Move!' Isaac hissed.

CHAPTER 58

When Storm regained consciousness, she found that she was lying on a double bed in a small concrete room that looked suspiciously like a jail cell. Fleur was sitting at the end of the bed leaning against the footrest, reading a book. She smiled brightly when she saw Storm rouse. 'She's awake!' she chirped into a walkie-talkie before scuttling up the bed to get closer to Storm. 'Are you okay? Daddy had to catch you before you fell down,' she said brightly, seeming to scan Storm's face for any signs of whatever a nine-year-old might consider lasting damage. 'Then he carried you in here.' Storm squirmed at the thought.

'I'm okay, I think,' Storm said, although she could hear the lack of certainty in her own voice. 'Maybe I just got a bit claustrophobic or something.'

'Hmm,' Fleur said thoughtfully. 'Maybe, but I don't think so.'

Storm was about to ask her to elaborate on the strange comment when Katharine came into the room with the boys in tow. 'Welcome back,' she said. Finn beat her to the bed and hopped excitedly on the mattress, making Storm's head spin afresh.

'Stop it,' Fleur snapped, 'you'll make her sick.'

Finn stopped bouncing and sat down, studying Storm closely just like Fleur had. 'Sorry, Storm,' he said sweetly, 'I'm just happy you're not tied up any more.'

Katharine groaned. 'Right, you three, skedaddle. Go and help Hebe with …' she paused, 'you know what I mean.'

Storm felt a strange pulsing in her belly, a growing heat that made her hands itch like they were covered in insects. She tried to focus on her breathing, but it was coming in shorter and shorter breaths.

William, who was still hovering in the doorway, piped up. 'I can't see how that's fair. I've not said a word!' he scoffed.

Katharine raised her eyebrows at him and he rolled his eyes. 'Come on, you pair, let's go help Hebes,' he said.

'Someone tied me up?' Storm managed, although the words came out staccato and with an effort that made her wonder whether she was about to get a migraine or have a panic attack. Was this a jail cell after all?

Something fizzed and then crackled, making both women cast around for the origin of the noise. Their eyes came to rest at the same time on the source. Storm's hands were pulsing with what looked like small blue sparks. They were travelling up and down the backs of her hands, wrist to fingers, fingers to wrist, like a caged animal pacing in fury. Storm stared at her hands, horrified.

Kneeling by the side of the bed and looking directly into her eyes, Katharine said, 'Nobody here tied you up, Storm. Listen to me carefully – we are your friends and we want only to help you. Do you understand me?'

Storm was trying to listen but she was having trouble focusing on Katharine's words.

'Nod if you understand me. Okay?' Katharine said slowly, still not breaking eye contact.

With an effort Storm tried to nod but felt like at any moment her head might explode. Her breath was barely perceptible and she could feel the panic start to take control of her body. The pain in her head was dizzying and what had at first seemed like a pulsing in her belly now felt like a knot of angry snakes fighting to get out. Her hands felt like they were being attacked by wasps and she could smell something burning in the air as the blue sparks crackled and fizzed the length of her fingers and palms.

'Come on, my love, I need you to breathe *out*,' Katharine said, reaching to put her hand on Storm's shoulder. Storm felt a pain unlike anything she'd experienced emanating from her shoulder and in the same instant, Katharine went flying backwards onto the floor. For a split second Storm realised that the writhing in her belly, the pain in her head and hands had stilled, like a dog the moment before it bites, and then, all at once, it was free.

A blazing light filled the room pouring from every atom of her in colours so bright even Storm had to screw her eyes shut against the glare. She could hear someone screaming, a guttural, almost animalistic roar of rage, grief and pain. It was only when she saw Finn in the doorway shielding his eyes, his mouth open in shock, that she realised that the noise was coming from her.

The light extinguished itself and Storm collapsed back onto the bed.

'Told you,' said Finn loudly. 'Just like the comics.' Storm had time to register his triumphant smile before she passed out for the second time.

When she awoke Katharine was sitting by her bedside. 'Here, drink some water,' she said gently, handing Storm a beaker.

Storm drank gratefully and used the time to try and formulate the questions that were swimming around her mind.

'I know you'll have questions, but I'm assuming you're also pretty freaked out, so I'm just going to tell you what we suspect. Is that okay?' Katharine asked.

Storm nodded, close to tears and unsure of her voice.

Katharine waited a beat and then said, 'Storm, we think that someone bound your magic and deliberately severed your connection to spirit.'

'What?' Storm said, her voice a hoarse whisper.

'I need you to breathe slowly and focus on my face, okay?' Katharine said, cupping her hands around both of Storm's, which were already beginning to fizz again.

There was something so calming, so strong and unshake-able about the other woman that Storm willingly complied. Once her breathing had settled and her hands were quiet again, Katharine continued. 'The bunker, as well as being a handy bomb shelter, is magically sealed. That means that whatever forces might have been working on you up above have no effect down here. We weren't sure, but your pyrotechnics earlier sort of proved our hypothesis.'

'Did I hurt anyone?' Storm asked, panicked by the memory of Katharine flying through the air on a shockwave of light. She remembered the force of it too and felt it now, curled within her, waiting.

Katharine smiled and shook her head. 'No. We're all good. No harm done – although Finn is now so smug he'll have trouble getting his big head through the door.'

Storm tried to smile. 'Who did you mean by we?'

Katharine took a deep breath. 'Henri, Isaac and me. And the girls … we consulted them too.' Storm could feel the fury begin to stir again, but Katharine added quickly, 'Let me explain. Henri has been concerned for some time that your loss of connection was no accident. He put it down to stress and grief to begin with but as time went on and things didn't improve, he spoke to Isaac. Isaac and the girls are witches – it's in the family line although it skipped me for some reason. Anyway, our theory was that you'd been bound and severed, the most hideous thing anyone could ever do to a witch, but you know that already.'

Storm felt her heart flutter at the news that Isaac was like her – she had thought it impossible for him to be any more perfect but she was wrong.

'Who would do this to me?' Storm asked, working to keep her voice level.

'We don't know. We talked about it when Henri and Dot were staying here. We decided that the only way to check was to bring you to the bunker, but then Dot ...' Katharine looked away, took a deep breath before continuing. 'I know Henri tried to speak to you afterwards, but by then you had decided to put that part of your life aside.'

Storm nodded. She'd worked hard to avoid anything spiritual over the last few years, including, she realised now, Henri. She'd changed the subject every time he'd tried to broach it, shot him down, cut him off; she couldn't blame him. She hadn't wanted to listen.

'Where is Henri?' Storm asked.

'He and Isaac have just gone to the barn to search the old camper van,' Katharine said, checking her watch.

'But is that safe?' Storm said, getting to her feet and feeling them wobble under her weight.

'They have another three minutes before I go after them,' Katharine said with a steadying hand on Storm's shoulder.

'What about Finn and William?' Storm asked, conscious that she was skirting the big questions, but also curious about this magical family.

'William shows all of the signs of being a natural shepherd, but he can't do that until he's twenty-five at least.'

Storm's skin prickled and she felt her energy pulled to her right, where out of the corner of her eye she could just make out the outline of what looked like a human shape. Please, not yet, she thought silently, and the spirit retreated.

'You okay?' Katharine asked.

'Spirit, I think ...' She broke off, emotion catching in her throat.

As if reading her mind, Katharine said, 'Take it slowly. We've just opened the sluice gates, so maybe start with a paddle, not a deep dive, okay? Spirit will wait. They're probably just showing up to welcome you home.'

The tears flowed then – great wrenching sobs that Storm feared wouldn't end. Katharine, a stranger to her just a couple of hours ago, held and rocked her in her arms, stroking her hair and encouraging her to let it all out.

When her sobs subsided, Katharine picked up the story. 'Now Finn, he's a natural seer, hence his smugness at your light show earlier. Seers don't usually get the prophetic stuff till they're older, but he's always been able to see the truth about people. So, fair to say that they all have their father's gifts in one way or another.'

'And you?'

Katharine smiled. 'I'm good with technology, but as for magical woo-woo, I'm more a theorist than a practitioner. I worked special projects when I was in the services, primarily to understand what they know about us, the magical community I mean, but I returned to civvy street when William's dad decided his PA was a better option.'

'I'm sorry,' Storm said.

'Thanks, but we're both better off without him,' Katharine replied.

'Jack!' Storm said, palming her forehead. She had no idea

why the thought had struck her at that precise moment, but now that it had she wondered why on earth she'd not thought of him before.

'Who's Jack?' Katharine asked, looking perplexed.

'Jack is Lilly's spirit guide. She rents the attic flat from me upstairs, works in the café now and, well, since we met a few months ago, has become a really good friend. She's such a sweet kid. For some reason or other I can see Jack and remember him without his permission. And the first time we shook hands we both got a huge electric shock.'

Katharine frowned. 'That's not normal for someone else's guide.' Then the penny dropped and her eyes widened. 'And you think he might be the Ethereal?'

'It's a possibility. Why else would I be able to see him when my magic was still bound? Unless some stronger force was somehow enabling it?' Storm speculated.

'He has to be a candidate for sure,' Katharine began, but an alarm on her radio interrupted her just as William, out of breath, appeared in the door.

'Four of them approaching the barn from the east side, another two from the west,' he said with a look that, while attempting bravery, revealed the young lad he was.

Katharine jumped up. 'The girls are working the distractor spell?' He nodded. 'You know what to do if I don't come back.'

Turning to Storm she said, 'I need you to go with the kids. Don't worry, they'll look after you.'

There was no time for Storm to question the logic of four small children looking after her. She followed Katharine down the dimly lit corridors until William beckoned her into a side room. She watched Katharine sprint to an emergency door at the end of the corridor, pausing only briefly to pull an assault rifle from the metal cabinet beside it. Then she was through the door and gone.

CHAPTER 59

*H*enri and Isaac made it into the ladder just as the first creaks of the old barn door told them that time was up. As Isaac lowered the hatch back into place behind them, he allowed himself to expel the breath he'd been holding. Sealing it behind them, he made a mental note to thank Katharine for her obsessive attention to maintenance, a schedule that included the weekly oiling of every hinge, hatch and handle on the property.

'You can thank me now if you like.' Katharine's voice from the bottom of the ladder was soft and low but it sounded impossibly loud in the confines of the bunker. Isaac, still at the top of the ladder, almost jumped out of his skin.

While he knew that the bunker was soundproof, not to mention magically protected, he couldn't bring himself to answer her knowing that, at this very second, people with guns were sweeping the barn above their heads. He gave her his best 'what the hell?' face instead but hugged her when he reached the floor.

None of them said another word until they were back in

the first bunker and the heavy steel door between the chambers sealed.

'That was a bit too close for comfort,' Isaac said as they walked.

'I know, I was watching you on the monitor as I ran,' Katharine said, stowing their rifles back in the cabinet.

'Do you think they know about the bunker?' Isaac asked.

'Hard to say. The girls have been doing a confusion spell and I programmed the cameras to show us driving out of the south gate through the fields, so that might fool them.' Turning to Henri, she asked, 'You okay? That was such a brave thing to do, Henri.'

'Not really, my dear, when you consider what's at stake, but thank you. My heart is still going nineteen to the dozen, mind you,' he said. 'Let's see what we risked life and limb for, shall we? The weight feels right but I don't dare hope.'

Unzipping the rucksack, he peered in, his face expressionless.

'Well?' Isaac asked a little more abruptly than he intended, but aware that his patience had long left him.

Henri smiled and pulled out two black hardback A4 notebooks. 'Were you expecting some leather-bound magical tome with golden bindings and sigils?'

Isaac laughed. 'You know what, my friend, I think I probably was.'

'I think Paperchase was out of stock on the day Dot went shopping,' Henri said, smiling.

'They're nonetheless precious,' Katharine said, looping her arm through Henri's. 'Come on, let's get back to the others before we go through them. We've waited this long – we can manage a few more minutes.'

CHAPTER 60

The room that William had shown Storm into was large and brightly lit. It reminded Storm of a film set, with a kitchen in one corner, a row of six bunk beds in another and a living area placed nearest the door.

An ancient-looking round rug, threadbare in places, occupied the middle of the floor. It was covered in magical symbols and within a circle of what looked like white daisies sat Hebe and Fleur, kneeling on large cushions.

Hebe had a small white kitten in her lap which, on seeing Storm, opened its eyes wide and stretched before snuggling back into the folds of Hebe's jumper. Neither girl stirred from her focus, the only sign of their work the fact that their lips were moving.

A single green pillar candle flickered gently in the middle of the circle. Storm watched them for a few more seconds, transported back to a time when, aged not much older, Margot had begun to teach her all about the craft. A lump rose in her throat at the memory and then the new sensation in her belly stirred. She quietened it and was pleased when it obeyed, then turned her attention to William who was still hovering behind her.

'We're safe in here,' he said, trying to sound as confident as a thirteen-year-old could. 'The girls are just creating some distractions to buy the others some time.'

Storm smiled at him and nodded. As she took in the rest of the room, she saw that the dogs were curled up together on a floor mattress near the bunks and that a second cat, this one a large slightly tubby tabby, was sprawled on what looked like an altar in the living area, although few items had escaped disruption from a flicking tail and idle paws.

Following her gaze, William said, 'That's Artemis. She never was one for respecting tradition. Mum says she likes lying on the altars because she thinks cats should still be worshipped as deities like in ancient Egypt.'

Artemis blinked slowly as if to agree with the sentiment and Storm laughed.

'I'm drawing her portrait,' Finn said loudly from where he was lying sprawled on his belly surrounded by pencils.

'Shhh, Finn. The spell,' William said in a hissed whisper.

A loud hiss from Artemis, standing now on the altar, was followed by the scrabble of dogs as they ran to the door, whining impatiently. Everyone froze and then Henri, Isaac and Katharine were standing in the doorway.

Henri held up the notebooks in triumph and everyone cheered. Storm let out a long breath and hugged her old friend.

'Can we have hot chocolate now?' Finn asked hopefully.

Isaac rolled his eyes and smiled. 'Yes, pal, we can have hot chocolate,' he said, scooping him up like a roll of carpet and then blowing a raspberry on his tummy, which made the little lad go weak with a fit of giggles.

'We'll take charge of the serious business of hot chocolate

while you three get cracking on the books,' Katharine said, ushering the kids towards the kitchen.

Henri, Storm and Isaac moved towards the table, Henri clutching the books to his chest. He hesitated a second before sitting down and Storm, said, 'Henri, shall we give you some time alone with the books? It wouldn't be right for us to be reading over your shoulder.'

Henri's face washed with relief and he relaxed the books down onto the table. He smiled. 'Thank you, dear heart. If I could just have a look first. I'm sure there's nothing in here that wouldn't be for sharing, but it was such a difficult time back then. You understand?'

'We understand perfectly, my friend,' Isaac said, putting his hand on Henri's shoulder.

'I think I know what we're going to find anyway,' Henri said to Storm. 'It struck me as we were walking to the barn – the one new person in our lives that we haven't even considered as the Ethereal.' Henri raised his eyebrows in anticipation.

'Jack!' Storm said.

At exactly the same time Henri said, 'Lilly!'

They frowned at each other, then Storm said incredulously, 'It can't be Lilly.'

Isaac and Henri exchanged a look. 'Why not?' Isaac asked.

'Because …' she started, searching for words that she knew at once she wouldn't find. 'Because,' she started again, 'because it just can't be, okay? Jack maybe, but not Lil. She's just a sweet kid. She's not mixed up in all this, she can't be.' Tears pricked at her eyes as she realised that denial would get them nowhere.

'I know, my dear, that you want her as far away from all this as possible, but wishing won't make it so,' Henri said.

'You said Jack was Lilly's spirit guide,' Isaac said. 'If she is the Ethereal then he's likely not just a guide but a Beacon.'

'Beacon?' Storm asked.

'Beacons are heavyweight spiritual protectors. If she's under the protection of one of those guys, she's as safe as houses.'

'But if it is her, we need to get to her now,' Storm said, feeling sick to her stomach.

'We can't go anywhere while the goon brigade is outside,' Isaac said, 'but if it is her, she has Jack protecting her, which means that we can take an hour to read the journals, confirm that it is her, and then come up with a plan.'

'Can I at least text her to make sure she's okay? Can I even get a signal down here?' Storm asked, scanning around looking for her bag.

'Yes to the signal, we have a relay, but let me check with the chief,' Isaac said, heading over to Katharine who was whisking cocoa powder into oat milk.

When he came back, Storm's backpack in his hand, he said, 'Katharine can bounce the location if you give her your phone, so it'll fit location-wise with the video of us leaving. Our friends outside will trace your phone to somewhere on the M5 instead of here. Just type what you want to say, and she'll do it now.'

Storm typed the message quickly and handed the phone to Katharine who had brought her laptop over to the table. Plugging the phone in, she opened up a new screen and, after working in what looked like a blur of clicks and lines of unintelligible code, handed Storm's phone back to her in under a minute.

'Wow,' was all Storm could think to say, before adding, 'thank you.'

'You're welcome,' Katharine said with a broad smile. 'When she replies, it'll route through to the same location plus a few miles to align with the idea that you're travelling.'

The ping of the phone made them all jump. Storm read out the message.

'Having the best day!!! We went to the fete with L&H. Now watching back to back Harry Potter, dogs snoring, Anc laying on M's head! At yours, hope okay, but L didn't fancy the stairs to mine. Hope you're having fun. Love n hugs L xxx'

Storm smiled. A second and third ping contained pictures. The first was of Ludo and Hope sprawled out on the sofa, the second was of Michael, buried under a mound of ginger fur.

Storm typed a quick reply, telling them that of course she didn't mind and that they should help themselves to food. She hit send with a palpable sense of relief and felt her shoulders drop a couple of inches.

'Okay, so Lilly is safe. Let's give Henri some space, shall we? Do you like plants, Storm?'

'I love them,' Storm said, slightly thrown by the change in subject.

'Great, I'll show you the hydroponics room,' Isaac said, picking up their hot chocolates en route to the door.

CHAPTER 61

The quiet of the corridor felt unsettling and Storm was acutely aware of being alone with Isaac for the first time. When she couldn't bear the silence any longer, she asked the first question that she could think of. 'So, who built the bunker?'

'We don't really know, to be honest. The Family acquired it in 1923 as a centre for teaching, and the bunker was here then, but the house keeps its secrets well.'

'So this is your family home?' Storm asked.

Isaac looked confused for a second. 'No, you know. The Family, capital F. As in the global family of witches?'

Storm looked blank and felt, once again like an idiot for not knowing something.

'That bloody woman has so much to answer for,' Isaac said, his jaw tight.

'Who?'

Isaac stopped in front of a door. 'I'm sorry, Storm,' he said, his tone softer, 'I mean Margot. As your mentor she had a solemn obligation to initiate you properly, to tell you about your heritage and your powers, and a big part of that should have been introducing you to the Family so that you could connect with other teachers and heritages.' He closed his eyes for a long second as if reining in what he really wanted to say. 'I'm just sad and angry that you've not been given the opportunity to be part of a community that could have helped and supported you. But that pales into insignificance compared to …' He stopped again, with what looked to be a considerable effort. 'I'm going to shut up now,' he said, his hand on the handle of a large metal door identical to every other in the bunker.

'Look,' Storm said, 'before we go in, if Margot didn't tell me things or neglected parts of my training, it could only be because she herself didn't know about them.'

What she didn't add was that had it not been for Margot, her younger self might have thrown herself out of the nearest window when her visions and spirit visitors kept her cowering under her duvet at night and running between rooms in search of company in broad daylight as her spectral friends began appearing whenever she happened to be alone.

'Plants,' Isaac said determinedly, pushing down on the door handle and striding into the room.

It was nothing like Storm had expected. While the rest of the bunker had a decidedly pre-war feel to it, this room looked like it would be at home in some high-tech research facility. It was a vast space, with row upon row of floor-to-ceiling white shelving extending in both directions, each shelf filled with plants basking under the pink glow of artificial lights.

'We have over two hundred varieties in here at any one time,' Isaac said, handing her a pair of safety glasses. 'This bay is for herbs and micro-greens. In the next one we have root vegetables, and on the end we have pulses and legumes. It's all grown hydroponically and controlled by a computer so that we can optimise the amount of nutrients, humidity and light spectrum.'

Storm opened her mouth but didn't know what to say. Isaac smiled. 'The witch in me rails against the use of science over nature, weeps a little for the plants denied the feel of the sun's rays, earth around their roots, the splash of rain and the caress of the wind, but the pragmatist in me knows that, as a species, we might have to rely on this one day very soon.' He stroked his hand over a tray of greens as he spoke, and Storm felt a wave of sadness rush over her. Her head swam and her vision blurred, and she grabbed the shelf to steady herself.

Isaac held her other arm at the elbow to keep her upright. 'You okay?' he asked, looking concerned. He was so close Storm could barely breathe. Her stomach did a somersault.

'I'm fine,' she said, taking a reluctant step forward, not wanting to break their proximity. 'It was just the strength of your emotion – it overwhelmed me for a second. Sorry,' she added.

'You're an empath?' he asked, not taking his hand away from her arm, but instead guiding her to what looked like a small laboratory at the back of the room. As well as a long workbench and stacks of equipment Storm could only wonder at, there was a small battered sofa and an armchair. Isaac walked past the chair to sit on the sofa next to Storm.

Storm nodded. 'When emotions are very high they tend to wallop me a bit. I'd sort of forgotten that, having been so …' she searched for the right word, 'disconnected for so long.'

'Ah,' said Isaac, looking down at his mug. 'I can imagine that can get awkward,' he added without looking up.

'To be honest, I've lived without it for so long now that I'm finding it all a bit disorientating. It's hard to know what I'm feeling at the moment.'

She was about to ask him about what she'd felt, when he said, 'So what's Lilly like?'

Storm smiled thinking of her friend. 'She's one of the most beautiful human beings I've ever met. Kind and sweet and, when we first met, I remember thinking not quite of this world, which maybe makes sense now – if it is her, I mean. It was like she was only barely here, hanging on by a thread almost. I just knew instantly that I needed to look after her. How could we have been so stupid not to think that Lilly might be the Ethereal?'

'It's not stupidity. It was magic, and powerful magic at that,' Isaac said. 'So how did you meet her?'

'She found my dog, Hope. She's never in her life run off before and I was out of my mind with worry because there was a terrible storm, but then the doorbell went and there they were standing on the doorstep, one drowned rat of a young girl and one soggy spaniel looking rather pleased with herself.'

'You sure Hope's not a witch?' Isaac asked, laughing.

'I wouldn't rule it out. Lilly had just been given notice on her bedsit and I was about to advertise the attic flat. It's like it was meant to be. If you see her now she's like a different person, so happy, always smiling – she even has a boyfriend.' Storm paused, her eyes far away,

'Looks like you and Lilly found each other just in time then,' Isaac said.

Storm nodded as she felt tears threaten and changed the subject. 'Do you want to talk about why you were so sad?'

'Sad?' Isaac asked, looking up.

'That's what I got most powerfully, yes, everything else was a jumble. Was I wrong?'

'No,' he said, cupping his hands around his mug before taking a sip and recoiling. 'Careful, it's still too hot. I suppose it's the thought that I've brought my kids into the world just in time to witness its annihilation.'

He stared at the mug and Storm was hit by another wave of his sadness that, had she not braced for it, might well have knocked her out. She noticed her mind incant a spell she'd thought lost to her for good. It happened automatically and, when it was done, she felt her energy strengthen.

'You think we've really come to this?' Storm asked.

Isaac nodded slowly, still studying at the mug in his hands. 'They feel it too. The kids I mean, and that is almost unbearable. They should be spending their time playing, enjoying their magic and learning about the wonders of the world, but instead …' He cleared his throat abruptly. After a breath, he said, 'I caught William wandering the other night, on his way to help the shepherds, he said, because he knew how desperate the suffering had become. He's thirteen, for Christ's sake. I daren't tell Katharine – she'd ground him till he was forty. Even Finn wakes screaming in the night. We tell him it's just bad dreams but he's showing all the signs of being a seer.' Isaac shook his head and a wave of something else now, anger and fear and rage, mingled with the sadness.

Storm put her hand on his shoulder and as her hand fizzed and tingled at the touch she hoped it was only her who was feeling it.

Isaac shook his head slowly. 'I've been fighting this for most of my adult life and yet I still can't fathom it. How could people be so selfish to the point of literally sacrificing most of the life on Earth for their own gain? Greed like that – it's the most hideous thing I can think of.'

They sat in silence for a few moments. Isaac was the one to break the silence. 'What was it like?' he asked, 'to lose your magic?'

Storm wasn't expecting the question, but she supposed it

was inevitable. To a witch, losing your magic was like losing a limb, so it was only natural that Isaac would be curious.

'It was like being a child again, having to learn how to read people's facial expressions – apparently I'd been relying on my empathy before. I had to learn how to cook conventionally, because magic had apparently seeped into that too. The same with gardening, art, sewing – I was just suddenly bad at, well, everything. I had to take Hope to training classes because we no longer understood each other. Even my houseplants suffered because I couldn't hear when they needed watering.'

Isaac laughed at that, but then, putting his hand on her shoulder, said, 'I can't imagine anything more cruel.'

They both felt the jolt of the spark this time and heard the accompanying crackle in the air. Storm quickly moved away.

'I'm so sorry,' she said, wiggling her fingers to dispel the pain. 'I could never do this before, this, whatever this new energy thing is.' She got up, wanting to put some more distance between them, for his safety as much as her comfort.

'It may be temporary. When magic is bound it's often concentrated. Magic is who you are so no matter what the spell, you can't just turn it off. Binding just stops you accessing it and channelling it, but it would still be there, growing, pooling if you like. What you're experiencing now could well be all that pent-up energy finally freed,' Isaac said, looking directly into her eyes.

'I wonder how long my battery will last,' Storm said, trying to laugh as she paced in front of the long bench, a sickening reality dawning. 'Or will I be bound again as soon as I leave here without the bunker's protection?'

Isaac stood then. It was such a sudden move that Storm took a step back and bumped into the chair behind her. He reached out and took both of her forearms in his hands. His touch was firm but gentle and she felt her skin fizz lightly beneath his hands. Looking into her eyes he said, 'I promise you – no one is ever going to bind you again. You have my word on that.'

Storm was the first to break the eye contact, but only because she was sure he could hear her heart hammering in her chest. 'Thank you,' was all she could think to say as she moved away.

'So, we'd better get back so the girls can do their thing and Henri can tell us what was in that journal,' Isaac said, picking up their mugs and leading the way back.

CHAPTER 62

When Storm and Isaac got back to the room, they walked straight into a blazing row.

'I am old enough!' William shouted, his voice high pitched and wobbling.

'No, you are not. End of argument, William.' Katharine's eyebrow was raised in an unmissable display of motherly one-upmanship. She walked over to fill them in. 'We hit a bit of an unexpected hitch with the spell. Turns out this isn't your regular binding spell, which, to be fair, we should have anticipated, but we hadn't met you when we first started looking into this,' she explained, turning to Storm. 'Whoever did this needed to be just as powerful as you and they obviously pulled out the big guns for the job.'

'So you're saying it's beyond our capabilities?' Isaac asked. 'Even together? Me and the girls?'

Katharine nodded. 'Afraid so, bro.'

'Which means what?' Storm asked, feeling more confused by the minute.

'It means that only you will be able to permanently break

the spell,' Fleur said, which made Storm jump; she hadn't noticed the girls had joined them.

'But my magic even back in the day was pretty low-key. I've no idea how to go about breaking binding spells and the like. It took me three years just to move a pencil across the desk!' Storm knew she was sounding a little rattled, but with good cause. Despite what she now felt thrumming through her veins, magic required focus and discipline and since she could barely contain her new-found fireworks, she seriously doubted her ability to perform something as specific as an unbinding spell.

'There might be another way,' Hebe said, chewing her bottom lip and frowning. 'If Storm were to travel, she could sever the bonds astrally. As above, so below – and vice versa.' She shrugged then and smiled as if what she was saying was blindingly obvious and simple.

Isaac perked up at that. 'Hebes, you're a genius!' he said, pulling his daughter into a hug and planting a kiss on her head.

'I'm sorry to be a wet blanket, but I don't "travel"—' Storm started to say.

Isaac cut her off by holding up his hands. 'No, you don't, but I do, which means I could take you and talk you through the whole thing. Once you regained control astrally, the binding on the earthly plane would fall away too, permanently.'

Henri walked slowly over to join them. 'And you'd be on hand should things get out of hand,' he said, his expression grim and his gaze now fixed meaningfully on Isaac.

'That goes without saying. You'd just need to trust me, Storm.' He turned towards her.

Storm didn't need time to think about it. Despite barely knowing this man she knew instinctively that she was safe with him. 'I trust you, Isaac. So let's get on with it,' she said before she could think herself out of it.

Once it had been decided, Hebe and Fleur darted off to begin their preparations, roping in the boys to help gather items from the storeroom.

Storm all but pounced on Henri. 'Well?' she asked eagerly. When he looked at her blankly, she raised her eyebrows to prompt him.

'Oh, the journals. Yes, of course, well,' he began, looking down at his feet. When he looked up again, his expression was close to despairing.

'Henri,' she said softly, 'whatever it is, we can fix it.'

Swallowing hard, Henri said, 'The journals aren't mine. They're the right colour, type and style, they even look the right kind of age, but they're completely blank.'

Storm's mind swam. 'But how could that be? You remember them even if you don't remember what you filled them with. And Dot remembered them – she saw the picture.' Her voice was almost pleading now, desperate for a better answer than this.

Henri shook his head sadly. 'I spoke to Vee. She's going to go home early and see what else the library might have to tell us. When I take magic out of it, all I can think is that they've been watching us for a long time and found an appropriate time to just switch them. I'm sorry, Stormy. I didn't want to tell you until you'd sorted this unbinding thing.'

'Those visions still came to you for a reason, which suggests that we're also here for a reason, so let's see this as part of the plan, not the problem, okay?' She hoped her words would reassure him, but she could imagine how he must be feeling, could see it in his colours now. The weight of her own disappointment weighed heavy on her shoulders, along with the fear of what she was about to do.

Isaac joined them then and Henri filled him in quickly on the situation. He let out a long breath and raked his fingers through his hair. 'Not much we can do about that now. Let's focus on getting Storm back to fighting speed and we can regroup from there.' They all nodded, and Isaac began his briefing.

If Storm were to summarise what she was told was about to happen, they'd enter a deep meditation and Isaac would help her out of her body and guide her to the astral plane. They'd do what needed to be done, then get out of Dodge as quickly as they could before anyone else out walking on the astral plane was alerted to their presence.

She'd of course read about astral travel, but even at the height of her training with Margot, she'd resolutely refused to even try it. She loved the Earth and was happiest with her feet well and truly on the ground. The thought of willingly leaving her body made her feel sick. But even more frightening was the thought of going back to her ruined life – her life without spirit and magic. She wouldn't lose it again and if this was what it took, then so be it.

'But we'll be safe up there, right?' Storm asked.

Isaac stared at her for a moment before saying, 'The short answer is no. Anyone visiting the astral plane is vulnerable because, when we incarnate, we leave the majority of our spirit up there for safe keeping. Just a small proportion of our spirit selves lives here on Earth. It's like keeping your savings in two separate bank accounts. When our bodies die here on Earth we just return to spirit, but ...' he hesitated, took a breath and looked her straight in the eye, 'but when we walk—'

'We've got all of our savings in the one bank?' Storm offered, picking up his metaphor.

Isaac nodded. 'Exactly. So, kill us up there and it's game over. That's why shepherds train for so long.'

'Oh,' said Storm, her mouth dry. 'But is that likely? I mean, who would want to hurt us?' she asked hopefully.

'Given that the fate of the Earth is at stake, you've likely been surrogate mum, landlady and employer to the one being who can stop the apocalypse, and someone went to extraordinary lengths to bind your magic years in advance of all of this, I'd say attack is very likely indeed.'

Storm opened her mouth, but being genuinely lost for words, closed it again.

CHAPTER 63

*L*illy couldn't remember a more perfect day. Yesterday had been wonderful and she had loved meeting Michael's family, both two-legged and four, but it was all so new that she had spent much of the day racked with nerves. Today had been different though. It had been so easy, so natural, like they'd known each other forever. She couldn't ever remember feeling this relaxed – or this happy. Michael just had this way of making her feel like the most interesting woman alive.

'Penny for them?' Michael asked, smiling down at her, his arm resting lightly around her shoulders as though they curled up on the sofa like this every afternoon. Anchor was sprawled on the back above Michael and throughout the afternoon had given him a gentle pat on the head when he fancied a cuddle. Lilly had been reminded again of Anchor's reaction to Jack, but she didn't want to think about him at the moment. She wanted nothing spoil the moment.

Michael had the most amazing hazel eyes, and his lashes were way longer and thicker than hers, she noticed. His mouth hitched into a lopsided smile when he saw her studying him and he leaned down to kiss her. They were still kissing five minutes later when a soft woof interrupted them. Hope was standing by the front door, wiggling expectantly.

'Probably time we took them both for a stroll anyway,' Michael said, glancing at the clock on the wall. Ludo might have refused the attic stairs, but he was on his feet the second Lilly reached for his lead. Anchor surveyed the commotion with disinterest then slid onto the spot on the sofa they'd just vacated and promptly went back to sleep.

Deciding that the park would likely still be full of fete-goers, they turned down the hill instead towards the river. The sun was still warm, but the breeze had died away and there was a happy stillness about the air around them that spoke of long summer days, laughter, and the company of good souls. When they reached the river, they unclipped the dogs and Lilly smiled to see them rushing off along the path together. When Ludo caught a sniff of something they both pulled up to investigate what turned out to be a melted ice lolly. Two friends together. Lilly had never thought about dogs having friends before, but why wouldn't they? Michael was holding her hand and, every so often, she caught him looking sideways at her and smiling. 'What?' she asked after the third time.

'Nothing. Just happy,' he said, rubbing his thumb gently over hers as they strolled. 'Did you know that Hope was Ludo's first proper friend?' he asked, and Lilly wondered if he might be a mind reader.

'I was just thinking about how contented they look together,' she said, feeling like another thread had been woven between them.

'Henri found him in a terrible state and for ages he would just ignore other dogs like they didn't exist. Then he met Hope, who was just a pup and even loopier then than she is now, if that's possible, and, well, she sort of wouldn't take no for an answer. She was so sweet with him and eventually got him running around playing like a pup again.' Michael smiled at the swaying rear ends of the dogs as they trotted side by side, tongues lolling out of the sides of their mouths.

'I forget that you've known everyone for such a long time,' Lilly said. 'Was it through Veronica that you knew Henri?'

Michael nodded slowly as if being caught in the threads of memory. 'We lived in town when I was at school, before my parents built the house. I used to be in Cordelia's all the time, either with my mates or later, after we moved, working on a Saturday to save for uni. I used to do summer holidays there too until I had to concede that I needed to study if I wanted my degree.' He laughed.

'You worked at Cordelia's!' Lilly exclaimed excitedly, another thread taking shape. 'Any top tips?'

Michael stopped and stood facing her, still holding her hand, his eyes locked on hers. Lilly felt her stomach do a backflip. 'Just carry on being your wonderful, beautiful, gorgeous self,' he said, and then they kissed again and Lilly decided that she'd never been happier.

With the sun softening in the sky, they made their way back up the hill. Hope was still full of beans; Lilly hadn't yet managed to wear her out no matter how long the walk, but Ludo had slowed a little, so they let him set the pace and sniff as much as he wanted.

When they got to the bakery, the dogs snuffled for crumbs outside of the now closed shop. 'Make sure you get them all, kids,' Lilly said, 'you're like the community clean-up crew.'

'What the?' Michael said, sounding confused. 'That looks like Margot,' he said with a note of disbelief.

Lilly followed his gaze across the street, but she didn't get a chance to ask him who Margot was, because just then she turned to see two men dressed all in black pull Michael backwards off his feet. The dogs reacted in a second. Ludo cowered but Hope transformed, lunging, her face a furious mask of teeth, aimed, Lilly thought incredulously, at her, until she felt strong harsh hands lift her off her feet. She dropped the leads, fearing that the dogs would be flung to the ground too, but instead of falling, she realised that, to her horror, she was being carried. She screamed, wondering why it should have taken her so long to react. She could hear Michael shouting, but as she tried to scream again, someone rammed a cloth into her mouth and pulled something black over her head. The last things she heard as they bundled her into the vehicle were Michael coughing and trying to call her name and then, sickeningly, Hope yelping in pain. She screamed and screamed against the gag and clawed at the hands that were holding her, digging her nails into flesh and thrashing about in the hope that some part of her might connect, but she may as well have been a butterfly fighting at a window.

Lilly felt hard plastic tighten against her joined wrists and the hands released her, but not before they shoved her onto the floor of the van. She tried to slow her breathing, but all she could hear in her mind was Michael coughing and trying to call her name and Hope crying out in pain. It was only then that she realised that Jack might not have been wrong after all.

CHAPTER 64

*P*reparing for the walk began with the mundane. William brought two mugs of hot herbal tea which, to Storm's surprise, was quite pleasant. Then she and Isaac seated themselves side by side in the circle, while the girls, ably assisted by William and Finn, called the quarters, lit candles and made ready the space. They'd not covered this part in the briefing, save for 'the kids will sort out the ritual part', so Storm decided to just go with the flow.

Hebe stepped forward with a length of plaited cotton. She smiled at them and instructed them to hold out their hands then wrapped it around Isaac's right hand and Storm's left, binding them together. It was so similar to the handfasting that Storm and Nick had had for their wedding that she found herself on the verge of tears. Hebe spoke quietly but with an authority way beyond her years. 'I join these two souls for the duration of their walk in the space beyond and, with great love, I call upon the angels and guardians of the light to protect them in their travels.' Securing the ends of the cotton with a complicated knot she stepped back out of the circle and told them to make themselves comfortable.

Storm had barely closed her eyes when she felt a strange tugging on her solar plexus. She was still trying to process the sensation when she felt what seemed to be a change in air pressure. Then, all at once, she was somewhere else entirely.

'You're a natural,' Isaac said from beside her. He looked normal, but not quite as corporeal. There was a faintness to him, certainly, and to her hands as she held them out in front of her, her left still bound at the wrist to Isaac.

What was stranger still was their surroundings, which, had she been pushed to describe them, looked like a water-colourist had just dipped their brush in a glass of water. Colours swirled around them, so bright they should have hurt her eyes except of course that her eyes, along with the rest of her, were back in the bunker.

'Try not to get drawn into the colour,' Isaac said, leading her forward, although she had no idea how he could discern any direction. 'You're this way,' he said.

Storm was still pondering on the strangeness of the phrase when she stopped short. There in front of her was … herself. She might have been looking in a mirror had it not been for the fact that this version of Storm looked to be deeply unconscious and was surrounded by thick black metal chains. Storm couldn't count them, partly because there seemed to be so many of them, but also because they were moving, writhing like suspicious snakes around the astral version of her body.

'We need to move quickly,' Isaac said. 'Remember what we talked about – you need to see in your mind's eye now whatever you know will break the chains. As soon as it appears in your hands, strike one of the chains. That's it. I'll do the rest.'

Storm stepped towards her astral self, steadied herself, and, to her amazement, a sword appeared in her right hand. Isaac nodded approvingly.

She struck the chain without hesitation. The blow bounced off leaving the chains to continue unaffected. She could tell by the look on Isaac's face that this was not what was meant to happen. 'Try again, but this time make absolutely sure that your intention is focused on your freedom.'

Storm didn't waste time by telling him that she'd been absolutely focused the first time. Instead, she redoubled her effort, and struck. The sword bounced off again and this time the chains writhed with what looked to be renewed determination. The scene around them flickered as if the power on an electric light was about to short.

'That's not good,' Isaac groaned. 'We may already have company.'

He tried to pull her away, but her eye was caught by a fine silver thread appearing and disappearing from view under the writhing black chains that seemed to be gathering speed. As she looked closely, she saw that this too was wrapped tightly around her sleeping body but one end of it seemed to be stretching out into the distance – like a fisherman's line, she thought.

Without thinking, she reached out to touch the silver thread. Isaac grabbed for her a fraction too late. She heard him shout, 'No!' but it seemed to be coming from such a long way away.

She was standing in the corner of her parents' summer house. It was where she and Margot went for her magic lessons. And there she was. For the second time that day Storm had the unsettling experience of seeing herself, but this version was only about thirteen years old. She had braces on her teeth and her jeans were flapping slightly around her ankles thanks to yet another growth spurt her parents had failed to notice. It must have been early autumn because the sun was low in the sky, casting a golden light across the garden and the tumble of crisp red leaves that had gathered around the edges of the summer house.

She remembered this day vividly. It was the day she'd learned how to undo locks magically. They were both kneeling on the floor, a selection of old wooden boxes spread out on the old rug in front of them. Margot looked as if she was holding her breath, her eyes screwed shut, her lips pursed. Young Storm, her brow furrowed in concentration and her lips stepping carefully through the words of the spell she had spent days committing to heart, hovered her hand over the nearest box – a small, plain dark chest with a pewter key. She knew it well because since that very day it had been hers, a gift from Margot to commemorate this milestone. As she watched her younger self, she could see the silver thread, so fine it might have been gossamer, was knitted in overlapping loose strands around every inch of her body like some sort of magical cocoon, save for one trailing end that floated on the air. Storm jumped when the key suddenly flipped in the box and its lid, untouched, flipped itself open.

The elation of the moment came flooding back to her and, without thinking, Storm reached forward towards her younger self and once again took hold of the thread. A pulse of energy sent her reeling backwards; everything went black for a second and when she opened her eyes again, she was in what looked like an expensive hotel suite. The TV was tuned into the evening news and the date on the screen caught her eye: 25 August – the day she lost her connection to spirit and all her magic.

The silver thread was still in her hand and she followed it to where it disappeared through a pair of heavy black lacquered doors into an opulent living room. The room was dim, lit only with candles arranged in a circle in the middle of which a cloaked figure sat, chanting and swaying. The silver thread was spooling above their head and then cascading around them just as it had been with Storm in the summer house. The figure was too shadowed to see clearly but there was something familiar about it. Storm drew closer to the circle and then, peering around the figure, saw the focus of its attention. Hovering in front of the chanting figure was the astral version of Storm.

Storm wanted to scream but bit her lip to stay silent. The chanting was reaching a crescendo now and as she watched in abject horror, the figure said, 'So mote it be.' With the words came the black chains. They rose out of the floor and wrapped themselves around the image of Storm. The face of her astral self seemed to cry out as if in terrible pain, but the figure muttered something else, too low for Storm to hear, and the astral version quieted, but with her face now distorted in silent anguish.

The cloaked figure thrust up her hands. 'It is done!' she announced. Something about the hands, a woman's hands, long fingers, short painted nails, thudded into Storm's consciousness. Standing, the figure said quietly, 'Forgive me, darling girl,' and Storm gasped, recognising the voice at once. As if hearing her, the figure whirled towards the door, the hood falling from her head. Facing her, although not seeing her, was Margot.

Storm stood frozen for a second, unable to take in what she was seeing. There had to be some mistake, some other explanation. Margot, the woman who had been both mother and mentor to her since she was a child, could not be the person responsible for binding her – and worse, severing her from spirit. She, more than anyone on this Earth, knew the agony that she had inflicted. And yet.

The knowing hit her in the gut and, as she doubled over, she felt an almighty pull around her solar plexus and was back with Isaac, who seemed out of breath, in the watercolour world of the astral plane. The scene now was dark and inky as the ether whipped and swirled around them.

'Thank God,' Isaac said, taking her face gently in his hands, his eyes full of worry. 'We're going to have company any second and I don't want us to be here when they arrive.'

Storm had no intention of staying any longer than necessary; she too could feel the darkness approaching, but she wasn't about to leave without doing what they had come here to achieve. With a cold fury she called up a weapon. A small white feather appeared in her hand and without hesitation or delay she stepped forward to her astral self and sliced through the black chain. It recoiled, so much more like a snake now, spitting and rising up for an attack before exploding into dust. The scream from the darkness was deafening. Like the keening of a grief-stricken animal, it was accompanied by what sounded like the thunder of hooves on hard ground. The ether around them seemed to vibrate and all the light began to fade as if it were being sucked out of their consciousness.

The eyes of her astral self snapped open and met her own. The pair smiled at each other. As she watched, thousands of delicate silver and golden threads, as intricate as roots on a tree, began to spin themselves from the ghostly version of herself. Shooting out in every direction, knitting and weaving themselves into the fabric of the ether and, Storm knew, everything that lay beyond. Like a lost jigsaw piece sliding into its rightful place, she knew that she was, once again, part of the all.

'Now!' Isaac shouted, and with the same pulling sensation that had marked their arrival, Storm and Isaac were back in the bunker.

CHAPTER 65

They opened their eyes to see a row of anxious faces. Even the animals stood at the edge of the circle, the dogs' tails low and barely twitching, Artemis just a whisker away from the perimeter. Fleur rushed forward to untie them and Storm sat up and put her head in her hands, not yet having the words to articulate what had just happened. Isaac stood up and, pulling a blanket off the sofa, wrapped it around her shoulders. 'It's done,' he said. A collective sigh of relief went around the room.

Henri nodded at Isaac sadly. 'Was it as we suspected?' he asked hesitantly.

Isaac nodded and all eyes turned to Storm, who was staring into space while stroking Artemis, who had, Storm reasoned, decided that she needed comforting.

'So now we need to prepare for the next phase,' Isaac said. 'Kids, thank you – you've outdone yourselves, all of you. Time to take a break.'

To their credit, the kids, although curious to the point of bursting, took themselves off and left Storm in peace. Only Finn lingered a little longer. Storm thought he was going to ask her about the walk, but instead he just said, 'I knew you were magic and magic people are always okay in the end. You'll see.' He surprised her then by wrapping his arms around her neck and giving her a hug. When he pulled away he treated her to his best smile, pushed his glasses back up his nose and went back to his drawing. Storm's heart heaved in her chest with love and regret and gratitude and an almost overwhelming need to protect these amazing kids. She might have lost it right there and then if Katharine hadn't arrived with a tray of coffee and sandwiches.

'You'll be starving any minute now so best fuel up,' she said, placing the tray down on a nearby coffee table. 'I can't speak from experience, but they say that spirit walking gives you the munchies just like pot.'

'It does,' Isaac and Henri said at the same time, then both snorted a laugh at the other as they took up positions on the sofa. Storm eased herself from the floor onto the opposite sofa and took a deep breath.

'It was Margot,' she said to Henri, 'but you already suspected as much, didn't you?' The fury she had felt had gone now, leaving only a deep, bone-crushing sadness in its place.

Henri nodded. 'Not for a long time, no. While I didn't really agree with Margot's approach to spirit, all that showbiz stuff, I didn't see any harm in her. To the contrary, she was always so good to you and Nick. Like a mother to you in many ways.' He shook his head. 'So maybe I just didn't want to see it.'

'What changed?' Storm asked, curious.

'Oh, I remained blind, but Dot had her suspicions towards the end. When you lost your connection, we all thought it was grief, naturally. But when we were preparing for our trip, Dot started going through her diaries. She was a great diarist, as you know, kept a daily diary since the day we were engaged. She said something curious while we were staying here with Isaac and Katharine. You see,' he paused, 'before I tell you, would it be too awful to tell us what happened the day you lost your connection?'

Storm hesitated for a second then said, for what felt like the hundredth time over the years, 'Nick was at home, the nurses were there around the clock by then. I'd been out for a walk with the dog. I checked in on Nick when I got in. He was sleeping, so I went to lie down because I had a raging headache that came out of nowhere, but I hadn't been sleeping well. I had the most terrible nightmare, although I couldn't remember what it was about. When I woke up, it ...' her voice wavered, 'when I woke up my connection was gone – and so was my magic.'

'And what was the date?' Henri asked.

'The twenty-fifth of August.'

Henri nodded. 'I remember the day obviously, but here's the thing – Margot had been with you on the day it happened. Dot wrote about it in her diary because she had been coming over to yours for lunch, but then Margot had arrived unexpectedly early that morning and you'd phoned to rearrange.'

Storm frowned. 'No, I don't remember any of that ...' But even as she spoke the words, images began to dance around the edges of her mind. Margot sitting by Nick's bed. The hospital bed they'd had installed at home. But Margot hadn't seen Nick while he was ill. She'd been away on tour and had only been able to come back for the funeral. But then she remembered Margot holding her hand as they sat together on the sofa while Nick slept, one of the nurses, the young Spanish girl, Rosa, making them both tea. Anchor scratching Margot's hand and making her bleed. Storm walking Margot to the car and then taking Hope out for that walk.

'It makes sense that a spell that powerful would have

needed something of yours as a catalyst, even just a hair,' Henri said carefully. 'And easy enough to throw in a forgetting spell to make sure that everyone she met that day wouldn't remember her being there. But of course she didn't meet Dot that day.'

'But why?' Storm asked, shaking her head in a fresh wave of disbelief.

'That one, only Margot can answer,' Henri said decisively, 'and I know this is hard for you, Stormy, but that particular conversation is going to have to wait until all this is over. Now that you're back to yourself again, we all need to focus on the Ethereal.'

Storm took a deep, steadying breath and straightened her back. 'Yes. Margot will answer to me for what she did, but Lilly needs to be our priority now. How soon can we leave?'

CHAPTER 66

With the kids persuaded to their beds, Katharine and Isaac were able to fully focus on preparations. While their numbers had reduced, the paramilitaries stationed outside had not pulled out entirely.

'Do they know we're down here?' Storm asked, her eyes flicking across the multiple video feeds on Katharine's laptop.

'Hard to say for sure. Even back when I was in the task force they were working on ways to use tech to pick up the residual vibrations left by spells. That said, they've shown no interest in any of the access points, but even that could be a tactic.' She shrugged.

'One thing's for certain – our chances of stopping this from here are zero so we're going to have to take our chance,' Henri said, getting up to join Isaac who was unfolding maps onto the table. Storm joined them.

Isaac pointed to the first map, a warren of lines and cavernous spaces that Storm assumed must be the bunker.

'We'll only be in the tunnel for about a quarter of a mile,'

Isaac said. Storm's heart sank at the word *tunnel*, but then realised what else Isaac had said.

Henri beat her to the question. 'We?' he asked.

'You didn't think I was going to let you out there on your own, did you?' he asked, looking from one to the other. 'We might have called them the goon squad, but whoever they are, and I think it's fair to say now that they're working for the Very, they're not messing around. We have no idea if they plan to capture and interrogate you, or more likely just …' He broke off, his eyes on Storm's. When he continued he said, 'And besides, another witch on the team might come in handy.'

There was silence for a few moments, the weight of it, the reality of what might be waiting for them pressing itself home.

Henri broke the silence. 'Thank you my dear friend,' he said, clasping his hand onto the other man's shoulder. When Isaac looked at Storm, she mouthed 'thank you'. He nodded in acknowledgement.

'Right,' Katharine said, turning their attention back to the maps. 'You'll need to get to the A-road to the south of the farm. The tunnel comes out in the ruin of an old keeper's cottage, then you have a short walk through the trees and then, sorry about this, but a bit of an incline down to the road. It's not ideal, but once you're on the road, you're away. All the other exit points are just too open and too easily monitored from the air. I'll be able to monitor your progress through the tunnel from here and alert Chris when you exit. He'll then be able to time his passing so he doesn't have to wait around.'

'Who's Chris?' Storm asked.

'Another shepherd and, handily, an ex-police officer. He's a good man. He owns the Fat Pumpkin restaurant in town and lives a few miles from here,' Isaac said. 'He's lending us his car.'

'So when do we set off?' Storm asked.

Katharine looked at her watch. 'Why don't you get a few hours' rest and then leave before first light? That way you won't need to pull Lilly out of her bed in the middle of the night to tell her that you've figured it all out.'

'Or Jack,' Storm heard herself say defensively. 'I mean, we don't know. It could be Jack.'

The others nodded but said nothing.

When Katharine handed her a blanket, Storm realised just how tired she was. She succumbed to a yawn and sank gratefully down onto one of the sofas. Her sleep was fathoms deep and dreamless and, after what seemed to be just minutes, but what she discovered was close to four hours later, Katharine was calling her name to rouse her. As she surfaced, she saw that Henri and Isaac had already changed – Isaac into black combat trousers, jacket and boots. Henri was still wearing his brown corduroys but had at least swapped his tweed jacket and loafers for a black jacket and boots.

When Storm sat up, she saw a stack of neatly folded clothes and a pair of sturdy lace-up boots on the coffee table in front of her. When she returned from changing, Katharine, who was standing in front of a table full of tech, handed them each a mobile phone and charger.

'As you know, your phone signals are being bounced at the moment to make it look like you're miles from here. I'm going to need you to keep your own phones switched off once you leave here – if they pick up two signals they'll know what we've done and they'll be back here in force. I've copied your contacts onto these. But if you need to make a call, use the burner phone, not your own. Clear?'

They all nodded and dutifully turned off their phones and slipped them into the protective sleeves Katharine handed to them. Next she handed them each a pair of night-sight goggles.

While Katharine and Henri went to the supply room to find him a better fitting pair of boots, Storm busied herself decanting the contents of her handbag into the backpack she'd be using.

'How are you feeling?' Isaac asked as, to Storm's continuing disquiet, he checked and loaded a handgun and added additional ammunition to his own pack.

Seeing her watching he looked sheepish. 'I don't like the things either, but if it comes to it I need to be able to defend us.'

Storm nodded reluctantly. 'I'm feeling better now that I know that you're coming with us, but I'm worried about Henri. He's fit as a fiddle, but ...' She trailed off.

'A steep incline and his dodgy knee?' Isaac offered.

'Exactly,' Storm said. 'He's so strong in himself that's it's easy to forget he's not far off eighty.'

'I won't let anything happen to either of you – knees included,' Isaac said, holding her eyes. 'And remember, you have your magic back now and I'm sure your repertoire extends beyond fireworks and electric shocks.' He was even more handsome when he smiled. Storm ordered herself to focus. This really wasn't the time to be getting giddy over a man – especially one she'd only just met.

Twenty minutes later, they were following Katharine through the maze of corridors to what would be the start of the tunnels. Storm felt a pang of regret at not being able to say goodbye to the children. She'd only known them a few hours, but they were amazing kids. Maybe when all this was over she could come back and visit. A small voice in her mind piped up to remind her that if they failed there wouldn't be a world left, let alone four sweet kids to visit.

Turning a corner, the short corridor terminated at a steel

door big enough to drive a tank through. Storm breathed a sigh of relief.

Katharine checked her tablet, switching screens a few times before swinging the door's central wheel to open it. It moved silently and surprisingly easily to reveal a brick-lined passageway. LED lights spaced a few feet apart were bolted in cages from the ceiling and curved off into the dark. 'Remember to leave the radio at the other end – just to be sure,' she said, a touch of anxiety breaking through her normally calm exterior. She looked like she wanted to say more, but instead straightened her back and wished them good luck before giving them each the briefest of hugs.

They walked in silence, watching their step on the uneven surface. The temperature had dropped considerably and aside from the noise of their feet, the silence was enveloping. Storm focused on coordinating her breath with her steps to keep her mind moving forward and not wandering back to the knowledge that they were underground. Every twenty or so feet, a small red dot of light reminded them that surveillance cameras were monitoring the tunnel. With so many bends and twists, it was a comfort to know that it would be virtually impossible for anyone to be lurking in wait for them.

'We should be approaching the end in about six minutes,' Isaac said. 'The tunnel slopes a little from just around the next—'

The crackle of his radio, impossibly loud in the silence, cut him off. 'Receiving,' he said, not even breaking pace.

Katharine's voice burst into the space. 'Veronica just called. They've taken Lilly. I repeat, they've taken Lilly.'

Storm was aware of Katharine saying something else after that, Isaac asking a question, maybe it was Henri, but she felt as though she was being sucked down into the earth. She caught herself this time. Like a bird of prey pulling up from a steep dive, she caught the feeling and with it the immense surge of energy that followed. When she refocused they were both staring at her warily.

'What do we know?' she asked, picking up her pace.

The other two marched after her. 'Michael called Veronica in hysterics to say that men in a black van had grabbed Lilly off the street as they were walking back to Cordelia's with the dogs. He only got part of the number plate – seems like they attacked him first in order to take her,' Henri said, puffing slightly at the effort of talking while keeping up the pace.

'Derek from the bakery saw it all happen from the flat above the shop. He called the police and an ambulance for Michael and looked after the dogs, then called Vee and Michael's parents. Vee was in the library though so didn't find out until Michael and his parents headed over to the house. That was just before she called Katharine. She's on her way to pick up Anchor and the dogs – she'll keep them at her place.'

'Do we know what time this all happened?' Storm asked, surprising herself at how calm she sounded despite feeling her heart was thundering in her chest.

'Earlier this evening,' Isaac said, 'meaning that wherever they're taking her, they have quite the head start.'

Storm felt her hands tingle, then she heard the spit and fizz from the firefly sparks emanating from them.

'Storm, you need to stay focused and calm,' Isaac said carefully. She ignored him and ploughed on. Jogging, he caught up with her and, to her mounting fury, stood in her path. Holding his hands up in placation, he said, 'So it looks like the Ethereal is Lilly after all, which means that you're our best chance of not just getting Lilly out of this alive, but …' He floundered.

'Saving the bloody world?' Storm asked, but she could already feel reason wash over the cold fury in her belly.

Isaac stepped forward and kissed her lightly on the lips. It caught her so off guard that her mind went momentarily blank.

When he stepped back a second later, he said, 'Good, looks like you're controlling that temper just fine.' He gave her a cautious smile. 'And just in case we don't get another opportunity ...'

Storm stared at him. She was so stunned she had no idea what to say, so instead she hastily cupped the back of his neck, kissed him back hard on the lips and then continued her march to the end of the tunnel.

They regrouped five minutes later in front of another steel door.

'There's something more you should know,' Henri said to Storm when he caught up. 'Margot was there. Michael saw her getting into a car across the street straight after it happened.'

Storm nodded once and pulled all her focus back to the task in hand. Nothing could be allowed to come between her and what she needed to do to get Lilly home safely.

Isaac stepped forward, his hand on the wheel of the outer door, his face turned to the red dot of the camera on the wall. Putting the radio to his mouth he said, 'Alpha.'

Katharine's voice responded immediately. 'Bravo receiving.'

'Status?' Isaac asked.

'Cameras and sensors show all clear. Pick up on way. Proceed,' came the reply.

CHAPTER 67

*L*illy had been screaming for Jack since it happened. That he hadn't arrived told her that something was very, very wrong. Banished or not, he should be able to hear her in an emergency, it was one of the rules. She couldn't even sense his energy. In fact, she felt nobody's energy but her own. It was a strange sensation and made her realise that even when she had been shielding herself from others, something must still have been getting through. She had never before felt so disconnected. So utterly and unbearably alone. She wondered whether this was what death felt like.

The scene on the high street kept replaying unbidden in her mind. Michael's gut-wrenching, hacking coughs as if someone had ripped all the air out of his lungs. Hope all teeth and fury, then that horrific yelp. It shred Lilly's heart to think that such a gentle dog would risk herself to try and protect her. She felt fresh tears fill her eyes and wondered if she'd ever know what happened to them. If they had been hurt because of her – or worse – she couldn't bear to think of it.

Lilly had no idea how long it had been since they took her. Just after they bound her hands and feet, she had felt the cold steel of a needle slide into her arm.

When she came around, she was here – wherever here was. Her hands were still bound in front of her and her wrists felt raw. Moving them even fractionally hurt like hell. They had untied her feet, not that they could take her far; she seemed to be in some sort of glass cell, the walls cold and smooth. She managed just five tentative steps in each direction, but even walking hurt as the floor was made of a hard wire mesh which made Lilly think of those poor animals bred in fur farms. She was at least able to stand upright. She couldn't touch the ceiling even on her tiptoes.

She slumped to the floor, feeling the hard lines of the metal grid bite into her flesh through the thin cotton sundress.

She had been trying to figure out why she had been taken. She couldn't hope for a case of mistaken identity because they had her photograph taped to the inside of the van. She had seen it just for a second, but it had definitely been her, standing outside Cordelia's waving at someone out of shot. The other options were all terrifying. People traffickers? Although would they be so bold as to grab women off the street? The thought of what might await her if that was their intention made her sick to her core.

Of all her past lives, relived in horror over the last eighteen months, she thought that this must be the cruellest life by far. To have lived these past three months in such joy, to have found friends, a home, a community, a family even, and then someone to maybe fall in love with – only for it to come to this? If this was life, Lilly decided that she was done with it.

CHAPTER 68

*S*torm, Henri and Isaac put on their night sights and shouldered their packs. Isaac swung the rifle from his back in readiness. They emerged into the ruined cottage, which was now little more than a tumble of old stones on two sides. The smell of damp earth was what Storm noticed first. She could smell the life in it and, she realised, some of the life that had recently walked across it as the impression of a fox ghosted into her mind. She sensed the trees, the roosting birds in their branches. There was a badger sett just a few yards to their left and if she wasn't mistaken, the rowan tree just behind them was sickening. Her eyes welled with the sense of the familiar and her heart ached for all the years that she'd been denied this part of herself. There was something else, too, something she couldn't put her finger on. Thinking of Lilly, she pressed on.

Following Isaac's hand signals, they emerged onto what was a surprisingly wide dirt road. Isaac ushered them straight across and down a steep incline. There was no path here, just a thick twist of ash trees, bracken and brambles that tugged at their legs and snagged at their clothes and hands as they grabbed for roots and branches to steady their descent.

They made their way slowly, Isaac first, then Henri and then Storm, each picking, sliding and silently cursing their way down the slope towards the promise of the A-road at its foot. Storm's backpack snagged on a branch and as she paused to unhook it, she noticed again the sensation she'd had when they first emerged into the ruined cottage. This time, however, it was followed by the sense that they were being watched. She looked around, but seeing nothing she hurried on, wanting desperately to just get to the road and away from this place as quickly as possible.

They were just fifty yards from the road when they saw a black sports car slide silently into a lay-by on the opposite side of the road. Henri and Storm froze, but Isaac turned and gave them the okay sign. With renewed energy, they slid down the last of the incline to the ground again. Isaac waved to Chris in the waiting car before he and Henri crossed.

Storm was about to follow them when she felt what she knew instantly to be the muzzle of a gun pressed into the back of her skull, then a large gloved hand slid over her nose and mouth. She froze, panic rising and blotting out her ability to think.

She saw Isaac close the passenger door behind Henri and then her night sights went dark. She felt her hands fizz, but her energy felt caged by her fear. Try as she might, she couldn't connect with the fury she needed in order to fight. Her breath caught in her throat and then too many things that didn't make sense happened seemingly all at once.

She heard a metallic click and in less than a heartbeat knew that the man behind her had decided to kill her. Her hands flared into life at last, but then the hand over her mouth flew away from her face and the man was gone. She heard a muffled shout from above her. She tore off her useless goggles, fumbled to turn on her torch and swung it around to see Isaac aim and then lower his rifle in disbelief. Turning the torch beam to follow his gaze, she saw a man dressed in black fatigues hanging limply thirty feet in the air.

'I thought you said your magic was more of the hedge witch variety?' she said when she reached him.

'That's not me. I thought it was you,' Isaac said, dragging his eyes away from the unconscious hovering figure to look at her.

'It's me actually, chaps,' said a familiar voice from behind them.

'Jack!' Storm exclaimed, spinning around and then throwing her arms around him gratefully. 'He was going to kill me …' Her throat was suddenly tight and her mouth dry as sand.

'I know, I felt the intent too – that's when I stepped in,' Jack said. He took a step back to take a better look at Storm. 'My, my, you're looking … different,' he said with a slight frown that was quickly replaced by a wide and generous smile. 'Less café owner, more uber-powerful witch-goddess. Whatever happened, it bloody suits you. I'm Jack, by the way, pleased to meet you,' he said, offering his hand to Isaac.

'Isaac. Wait, you're Lilly's guide?' he asked, shaking Jack's hand.

'Yep,' Jack said casually, and asked, 'so do you lot get a kick out of being chased by paramilitaries with murderous intent or am I missing something?'

'But I thought you were connected?' Henri asked as he hurried over to them, the confusion and anguish etched into his face.

'Me and Lil?' Jack said. 'We are, except, that is, when I get banished for being, what was it this time? Ah yes, I think the term she used was "a total prick". If she does that I'm effectively banned from her airspace until I'm forgiven. It never lasts long, but she's otherwise occupied at the moment, so ...'

Storm put her hand on Jack's arm.

'Tell me,' Jack said, his face suddenly grave.

'They kidnapped Lilly off the street earlier this evening,' Storm said.

'What? Who? Wait,' Jack said, confusion clouding his face as he looked at each of them in turn as if this was some sort of joke.

Storm squeezed his arm gently. 'Jack, listen to me. The Very have taken Lilly. They know that she's the Ethereal.'

Jack screwed his eyes closed, shook his head as if trying to wake himself from a nightmare. 'Who? That's a myth. Lilly's not the bloody Ethereal,' he said, stepping away from them. 'Trust me, if Lilly was in trouble, she'd have called me, banished or not,' he said confidently. 'There's been a mistake.'

'But what if she couldn't?' Isaac looked at Storm. 'What if the person who bound you is now doing the same with Lilly?'

'That's why Margot was there!' Storm said, fury burning in her gut as bright blue sparks shot from her hands.

The realisation that dawned on Jack's face was heart-breaking. 'You're serious,' he said, 'you're actually fucking serious.'

Storm nodded. 'Look, from what Vee told us, not even the Ethereal realises what or who she is, so please, Jack, this is important. Would you have known? If it is Lilly, as her guide, would you have known?'

His face crumpled as the tears fell and he shook his head. 'No, the story, and I swear I only know of this as a story, but it says that the Ethereal has to make a pure choice. Fuck!' he shouted, kicking at the dirt, 'that's why she wanted to come back. This was the last mission. Oh man, I'm such an idiot.'

'Can you still track her?' Storm asked him, grabbing his shoulders and shaking him slightly to focus him.

He nodded. 'Yes, magic doesn't work on me in the same way as it does you. Lilly might be prevented from calling out to me, but now that I know, I can follow her energy trail.'

'Can you get her back? I have no idea of your powers,' Isaac asked.

'Not on my own,' Jack said despondently. 'A bit of mind control and the old freeze and fly trick when absolutely needed, but that's it really. I'm a guide, not a soldier.'

Chris flashed the headlights twice.

'We need to go,' Isaac said. 'Action man up there will be missed soon and then our cover is completely blown.'

'Okay. Jack, you need to find Lilly and then tell us where she's being held. Can you do that?' Storm said.

Jack seemed to snap out of his trance and said, 'Yes, and I can change his memory too, make him think he fell or something – that'll buy you time.' He pointed to the man in black still suspended in the trees.

'Good. Take this,' Isaac said, handing him his burner phone. 'All of our numbers are programmed – let us know once you've found her. We'll be there as soon as is humanly possible.'

Chris flashed again, more urgently this time, and Storm, Henri and Isaac got into the waiting car.

'Katharine radioed. More operatives are closing in. We need to go now,' Chris said calmly. Isaac only had time to close his door before the car slipped away into the dark.

CHAPTER 69

*I*saac squeezed Storm's hand in the back of the car as they sped along the country roads. Try as she might, the thoughts of what they might do to Lilly, might have already done for all she knew, would not be banished from her mind.

'We'll find her,' Isaac said resolutely, 'and we'll stop them.'

'That we will,' Henri said quietly from the front passenger seat.

They drove in silence for a few minutes until the Fat Pumpkin pub came into view. 'I'm still more than happy to come with you if you need some backup,' Chris said as he swung into the car park.

'Cheers, mate,' Isaac said, leaning forward in his seat, 'but I'd rather know that you were close to the farm to provide some backup should Katharine need it.'

Chris nodded, wished them all good luck and got out of the car.

Isaac jumped into the driving seat and they were back on the road in under a minute.

'I'm going to call Veronica, see if there's any news from the police,' Storm said.

She'd been hoping for a breakthrough but was disappointed. Storm listened as Veronica told her that, aside from a five-minute chat with Michael at the hospital, the police hadn't even been in touch to organise statements.

'If it's any comfort at all,' Vee said with a deep sigh, 'I think you have a little time to play with. The library says that in all likelihood the Very will not ...' she paused, '... they'll not execute the Ethereal immediately. They'll want a full ritual, so that'll mean gathering key players from around the world. I saw Sir Dennis What's-his-name being interviewed live on CNN this morning at some charity fundraiser in San Francisco. It was live and I doubt they'd do much without that old snake. Mum's files were full of his shady deals.'

Storm's phone pinged in her ear at the same time as Henri's vibrated. Snatching it from her ear she opened a text message from Jack. It contained a picture of a large Georgian town house and an address in London.

'Shit,' Storm said. 'Vee, we have to go. They're holding her in a house in London and we're heading west when we need to be going east. If I ping you the details can you see what you can find for us?'

'Of course,' Veronica said, 'but please be careful, darling girl. I wish I was there with you.'

'You're more help where you are, lovely. And you're looking after the fur babies. Listen, Vee, if this doesn't work, if anything happens to me ...'

'Stop,' Vee all but shouted. 'It'll work. If it doesn't, we're all gone. And if that were the case, you know I'd—' A cross between a sob and hiccup caught in Veronica's throat. 'You know I'd never let them suffer, Stormy. I have the vet on speed dial and ... look, go. Send me the address and I'll call you if I find anything. Love you,' she said, then hung up.

CHAPTER 70

*V*eronica wrote down the address from the text message and headed for the library, leaving her mobile on the kitchen's island where Michael was sitting, still picking at the sandwich she'd made him over an hour ago.

Anchor was perched on his lap, doing his best to play the part of therapy cat but getting increasingly annoyed by the amount of fidgeting as Michael simultaneously flicked through the TV channels looking for any reporting of the incident on the news, scrolled through news sites and Twitter on his mobile and tried repeatedly to get hold of the detective supposedly in charge of the case on the landline. He turned the policeman's card over and over again, wondering what the point had been in handing it out if the bloke never picked up. What on earth could be more important than a young girl kidnapped off the street?

'Come and get me if I get any more messages,' Veronica had said, not needing to explain to her nephew that technology wasn't permitted in the library.

Michael had nodded absentmindedly as he continued his

search, but he suddenly jumped up, pausing just in time to lift Anchor from his lap and plop him on his vacated chair. He snatched up Veronica's phone before it had time to auto-lock and opened up the messages, found the one from Storm and forwarded it to himself. Giving the seriously disgruntled cat a quick ear rub to make amends, he scribbled an apology to his aunt, grabbed her car keys and let himself out.

CHAPTER 71

The drive to London was quicker than Storm could ever recall it being in the past. With the fuel shortages and the unrest, the traffic felt like a Sunday afternoon during a World Cup fixture.

'You drive like a pro,' Storm said to Isaac, wanting to break the anxious silence that was sitting in the car like another passenger.

'I was a close-protection officer for twelve years – tactical driving was part of the job.'

'You were a police officer?' Storm asked, trying to square the image of the doting father, farmer and witch with Her Majesty's constabulary.

Her incredulity made him smile at her. 'Hard to believe I was a plod?' he asked. If they could still smile, then surely there was still hope.

'Well, now you mention it, yes. What makes a hereditary witch join the police force?' she asked, before immediately answering her own question. 'Ah, I suppose the same thing that made Katharine join the army.'

'Right in one,' Isaac said. 'Ninety per cent of the time we

were just trying to do the same job as everyone else, but it was always useful to understand how much the authorities knew about the magical community.'

'So you were basically spies,' Storm said, teasing.

Isaac laughed. 'I suppose we were.'

'You were never tempted to use your magic in your work?' Storm asked.

'Tempted, yes, but I never did. The risk of exposure was just too great. All the governments around the world have some magical people on their books, but most are there through coercion, not choice. Some sell out, of course, that's human nature, but others are just threatened and black-mailed into it. Had they found out about me, had there been just a hint of peculiarity about my abilities, then everyone I loved would have been at risk.'

Storm was silent for a long time, resting her head against the window and watching the fields whizz pass. An occasional flash from a speed camera interrupted her flow of thought, not that many people would be worrying about brown envelopes in the post.

Her thoughts drifted to Margot. How much had it taken to buy her? Was it the book deal? The wildly successful TV show? Or maybe the Manhattan apartment and the weekend place in the Hamptons? The sting of the betrayal slid like a blade between her ribs again.

'Sorry to interrupt.' Jack's voice was suddenly impossibly loud from the back seat.

'Sweet Jesus!' Henri exclaimed with a start. To his credit, despite muttering his own colourful curse, Isaac kept the car completely steady.

'I thought I'd guide you in. There have been more riots and some of the main routes are blocked. Satnav probably won't have picked them up because of the lack of traffic.'

'Good thinking,' Isaac said, 'thanks.'

'Any news on Lilly?' Storm asked.

'I tracked her energy trail to the house, as you know. They're keeping her in the basement. Remember this is the Holland Park type of basement, before you start picturing dank walls and a place to store old golf clubs. It's more like a ballroom, which makes me think they're going full-on ritual,' he said, his voice full of loathing.

'Vee said something similar,' Storm said quietly. 'Is she safe?'

'For now,' Jack said. 'I was only able to materialise inside the ballroom for a few seconds before the guards reappeared. They have her in some sort of small glass cell. It's blacked out but I can feel that she's in there, although I can't even reach her mind to speak to her, which suggests a powerful cloaking spell.' Jack's voice was thick with fear and frustration.

'Why a glass box?' Isaac asked, his eyes flicking to the rear-view mirror and finding Jack's.

Jack hesitated and when at last he did speak it was as if every syllable had to be forced out of his mouth. 'The box is suspended above what look like gas jets and beneath ...' He faltered, cleared his throat with a forceful cough and said, 'It looks like a giant cooker hood. There's a shiny new chrome pipe vent on the back of the house.'

'Bastards,' Isaac growled from the driver's seat, his jaw set in a tight and furious line.

Storm swung round as far as her seatbelt would allow her and looked at Jack. It felt like his words were still finding their places in the sentence, like wedding guests looking for their name cards. When at last the penny dropped, she lurched forward and dry-retched into the footwell. Isaac placed his hand on her back and rubbed until at last her sobs had subsided.

When Storm sat back in her seat, Henri said, his voice

shaking, 'We'll get her back, don't you fear. They'll not get away with this so long as there's a breath left in my body.'

Storm nodded and sucked in a breath. 'And here I was thinking the burning days were consigned to history,' she said falteringly, still struggling to put what they were discussing into a reality that involved Lilly, her Lilly, being murdered. Her hands fizzed and her fingers twitched impatiently, but she pulled her energy back like one might rein back an eager horse. While part of her wanted to let loose her fury there and then, she knew that their only hope of saving Lilly was for her to try to remain calm and in control.

She realised then that it was saving Lilly that drove her, whereas by rights, it should have been the fate of the world. There was a chance of course that they could save Lilly and as the Ethereal, she'd decide that humanity wasn't ready to ascend. The world might still end, thought Storm, but at least Lilly would be with people who loved her when it did. She was dimly aware that it wasn't her most rational moment, but love did that to you.

When Storm tuned back into the conversation, Jack was talking them through the layout of the house and garden.

'Our trump card is surely the element of surprise,' Henri said. 'As long as they're still tracking our phones they'll hopefully not be on their guard.'

'Well, yes and no. Won't they get suspicious if we don't try and rescue her?' Jack asked.

'They will, but thanks to Katharine's wizardry they won't be expecting us for hours.'

Jack just nodded in response and said nothing more until Isaac pulled off the motorway. 'Left at the lights,' he said.

Isaac pressed the accelerator and swung the car around the bend, ignoring the fact that the light had just turned red. It earned them an angry blast from a lorry, the only other vehicle in sight, but whose driver had clearly decided that, pending apocalypse aside, rules were still rules. Storm was strangely comforted by that for reasons she didn't have time to dwell on.

'It's hard to believe that this is London,' Storm said, staring in dismay out of the window. In the weak light of dawn, the city looked exhausted. The streets were deserted, but the evidence of unrest was everywhere. She counted twenty-three burnt-out cars in just a few minutes. Shop windows were either boarded or, for those who'd left it too late, sporting man-sized holes in the plate glass. Uncollected refuse bags laid torn and gaping on street corners, their contents blown and scavenged as far as the eye could see. Isaac steered the car around a commercial-sized bin that lay blackened and melted in the middle of the road. Everyone had seen the TV reports, but TV was one thing – seeing it close up was entirely different.

As they drew closer to Holland Park, Storm noticed that some of the elegant town houses sported shiny new steel shutters. Others had clearly been the target of the protestors' fury with punched-out windows, graffiti and, most terrifying, some that had been gutted by fire. Storm shuddered and prayed that there had been no one at home when the mob attacked.

They drove on in silence for a few minutes until Storm turned in her seat and asked, 'Jack, does the Ethereal affect the people around her?'

Jack shrugged and Henri said, 'You're wondering why people haven't been trying to kill each other on the streets of Pont Nefoedd?'

Storm nodded.

'This is a guess, but I'd say that the presence of the Ethereal provides a glimpse of a post-shift world where the lower energies of fear and hate can't exist – if that's the energy the Ethereal radiates, then it would be the reason you've not been subjected to all of this,' he said, gesturing to the ruined street beyond.

'But how does that work? Lilly still feels fear, we've talked about it often enough,' Storm countered.

'I don't think we're talking about a conscious thing here, but an energetic one,' Henri cut in. 'The human part of the Ethereal can still feel everything that humans feel – pain, regret, longing, fear – but their angelic part is beyond all that, it knows it's eternal, and it's that part that's doing the radiating. Is that right, Jack?'

Jack shrugged, saying, 'It's plausible,' and turned his attention again to the scenes outside the window.

Storm turned back in her seat. It made sense, of course it did, but something was troubling her. Something was sitting on the dark edge of her consciousness. A truth not yet willing to step into the light.

'Park up here,' Jack instructed Isaac. 'We'll walk the rest of the way.'

Parking in this part of London had ceased to become a problem since the troubles began. Those who were able to had been leaving the city for weeks – a steady stream of school-run Range Rovers headed to country homes or airports as people looked for safety that was increasingly hard to come by.

'It doesn't look like we have much time,' Henri said, his voice shaking as he stepped out of the car. 'I think the Falling has started. Lord help us all.'

Following his gaze, they looked up; blooming in the sky in the distance was a gigantic black cloud. It might have been a regular hammerhead storm cloud had the lightning emanating from it been anything other than red. It forked silently, leaving livid brick-red scars in the pale dawn sky. As they watched it approach, their eyes were drawn to falling dark objects.

Storm squinted, trying to make sense of it. 'What are they?' she asked, pointing.

Jack's voice was thick with emotion when he answered. After clearing his throat, he said, 'Birds. The birds are falling from the sky.'

CHAPTER 72

*I*n the library Veronica rubbed her eyes. She rarely slept well when Asim was away, but her insomnia was supercharged now. She'd been spending as much time in the library as possible, trying to learn as much as she could about the shift, the Ethereal and the Very.

The trouble was, it wasn't just a matter of looking up the right book. In a magical library, you had to be grateful for what you were given and some of the books could be a little snooty, to say the least. Finding information required her to be equal parts researcher, negotiator and diplomat, but her temper, stoked by her tiredness and fear, finally snapped when one old tome refused categorically to allow itself to be lifted from the shelf.

'I don't have time for this, you old fool!' she snarled, stepping back from the shelf and pulling at her hair. The stacks, obviously affronted, seemed to fidget around her like an old hen fussing her feathers above her nest.

'I'm not my mother, okay? I'm not the calibre of keeper she was, maybe I never will be, but I'll never get the chance to try unless you lot bloody *help me*.' Resisting the urge to scream, she turned to walk back to the desk, feeling hot, angry tear prick at her eyes. She'd barely taken two steps when the obstinate old book overtook her. It floated silently, then hovered a foot above the desk before allowing gravity to take it. It landed with a loud thud, but opened itself to the correct page and was still.

Veronica swallowed the lump in her throat and when she said, 'Thank you,' it came out as a whisper. She sniffed, dabbed at her eyes and nose with her hankie and sat down to read.

Twenty minutes later she gave a little shriek of delight. 'Oh, thank you,' she said, feeling the gratitude in every cell of her being. She resisted the temptation to lean down and plant a kiss on the ancient pages in front of her. The old book fluttered its pages slightly in acknowledgement – or perhaps in an attempt to ward off the kiss.

She read a few more paragraphs, scribbling down notes as she went. Then she stopped and asked aloud, 'Can it really be that simple?'

The book ruffled its pages again, but this time with an air of irritation. A line drawing of a clock materialised in the corner of the page, its second hand moving unnaturally fast around its face.

'I hear you, my friend, tick-tock, time's a-wasting. Well, let's find out, shall we?'

Veronica stood up, cleared her throat and said, 'I call the *Book of Telling*.' She'd barely finished the last word when a thin grey volume floated towards her. In its wake followed a small battered brown briefcase. The book hovered about four feet away from her, then, once the briefcase had opened itself, it floated into a perfectly sized hollow in the black velvet interior. The fabric moved around the book, securing it in place, the lid of the case snapped shut and the clasps clicked themselves into the lock position.

'Well then, question answered. Thank you, friends,' Veronica said. She got up, grabbed her notebook and the case and hurried out of the door. Her heart was hammering. Removing a book from the library was almost unheard of. It was the first rule of being a keeper, something drummed into apprentices from the time they were tiny. The books were protected in the libraries, hidden from those who would use them for their own ends. Removing even one made the whole library extremely vulnerable.

When they'd had to move the library here, keepers had come from all over the world to assist with the relocation, bringing with them witches of incredible power to shield and protect it. It had been years in the planning and the execution had been run like a military operation, but now here she was, leaving the sanctity of the library with possibly the most precious book in the world with nothing but a battered old briefcase to protect it. She felt queasy just thinking about it.

She called out to her nephew as she came back into the kitchen. 'You're never going to believe this, Michael,' she said, scanning the room for him. Anchor was sitting on the breakfast bar and meowed loudly at her. She saw the note and swore under her breath. Not that she minded Michael borrowing her car, but as his was still at Cordelia's, it meant she was grounded.

She called Asim. 'Darling, I don't have time to explain, but …' she hesitated, 'can you get me a helicopter?' She closed her eyes, blocking out his questions. 'Asim, my darling man, this is as bad as it gets. Just make it happen, please. For me, right now.' She smiled at the sound of his voice, drinking it in and trying desperately not to think of a scenario in which she wouldn't get to grow old with the love of her life.

'Thank you, my love. Oh, and please feed Anchor and the dogs when you get home. Remember to take your antihistamine, won't you. I love you, my darling,' she said, her voice catching. She waited long enough to hear him say that he loved her too and then she hung up and dialled Storm's number.

Half an hour later, Asim's driver was pulling up to the house just as the helicopter became audible in the distance. Asim was out of the car almost before it stopped. He ran to where Veronica was waiting on the front steps and wrapped his arms around her. 'What's going on?' he demanded, his face full of concern.

'You must have broken every speed record going,' she said, smiling at him. God, she'd missed him so much. 'Look, I don't have time to explain, my love, but it's ...' She faltered, finding every adjective that popped into her mind ridiculously inadequate.

The helicopter was loud now and a rush of air overhead told them that they were heading for the landing area on the vast back lawn.

'Before you say it, you can't come with me.' She held up her hand to silence him. 'I'm going to meet Storm and Henri in my capacity as keeper.' She held up the briefcase and Asim's eyes widened, understanding immediately the significance of a book in transit.

Forcing down the urge to cry, she continued, 'If anything happens to me, you need to look after the library and the animals – Storm's two and Henri's old boy, Ludo. If everything goes south, open this and follow the instructions.' She pushed a sealed envelope into his hands.

Asim looked horror-struck. 'Vee, what in God's name is going on?' he said, his own eyes now misting and fear etching deep lines into his face.

'I'll tell you everything when I get back, but remember, you have to protect the library no matter what. You can't let

them get their hands on it. You know the emergency proto-
cols. Promise me.'

He nodded then kissed her on the lips but too soon she
was pulling away and then she was gone, choking back tears
as she hurried to where the helicopter waited.

CHAPTER 73

Storm felt like they were walking in circles. Jack had told them they were just a few streets away from the house, but as they trailed behind him, her patience was growing thin.

'How much further, Jack?' she asked more sharply than she'd intended. The knowledge of what the Very were planning on doing to Lilly felt like battery acid in her veins.

'It's just around the next corner,' Jack said, not breaking his stride. He got there before them and as he peered around the corner, Storm saw him curse and shake his head. When they reached him, he said, 'It appears that we have a little helper.'

When they looked for themselves, they saw Michael, looking impossibly young and out of place, climbing out of Veronica's Tesla, which was parked directly opposite the house from the picture.

'Oh, bugger it,' Storm said, 'what on earth does he think he's playing at?'

'Same as us, I suspect,' said Henri kindly and Storm found she had no argument. Bless him. She pulled out her phone, hoping that the mobile number he used for organising the veg deliveries was also the one he was now peering at. She hit call and held her breath. A heartbeat later she saw him almost jump out of his skin then nearly drop the phone in his rush to answer it.

The conversation instructing him to get in the car and go straight home was as productive as she feared it might be. Instead they agreed that he'd park the car a few streets away and then take the back streets on foot to join them.

The addition of a second non-magical person weighed heavily on Storm's shoulders. Granted, Isaac was armed, but she guessed that the guards at the house would be too. Jack's levitation trick back in the woods had been a lifesaver, but she had no idea if he could do it en masse. And that left her – the newly unbound witch with tasers for hands that she had no idea how to control. She was just about managing to keep herself grounded, but when her own life had been threatened, she'd frozen in fear. What if she froze again? When she thought of it like that, she felt like they were doomed.

'What if we're too late?' Michael asked anxiously when he reached them, slightly out of breath after his sprint from the car.

'If she was already dead I'd have felt it,' Jack said, doing nothing to hide his slightly proprietorial air and staring directly at Michael, his handsome face a mask of deep dislike.

To his credit, Michael just nodded and asked, 'Is there a way you can check, Jack? You know, teleport in again and have a look?'

Storm saw Jack bristle, probably processing the fact that Lilly must have confided in Michael about who he was. After a moment's pause, Jack rolled his eyes theatrically. 'Sure, if I wanted to tip off everyone in the room with her by now that we're coming,' he said with a dismissive snort.

'I should have stopped them,' Michael said, raking his long fingers through his hair.

'No argument there, pal,' Jack snapped.

'Are we really going to do this now?' Storm's tone cut them both down before either could say another word. 'Michael,' she said, looking him straight in the eye, 'there was nothing more you could have done. They were armed, they were highly trained, and one young man, no matter how brave, wasn't going to stop them from taking her.' She saw the pain in his eyes and the threat of tears and her heart ached for him so she added quickly, 'But now is not the time for self-pity, guilt or any other useless emotion.'

Jack huffed, which had her rounding on him in an instant. 'Nor is it time for any point-scoring,' she said coolly. Jack clenched his jaw but said nothing more. Michael nodded and she hoped she'd helped to lift the burden of guilt just a little. Henri gave Storm a nod of approval.

'Besides, they'll be waiting for that Sir What's-his-face chap to come in from the States before ...' Isaac bit off the end of the sentence.

Michael nodded, only slightly reassured. 'Uncle Asim's team is checking the airport security for him apparently.'

'Then can I suggest we find somewhere less conspicuous than a street corner to go over the plan?' Isaac said, scanning the windows of the neighbouring houses. 'We're sticking out like sore thumbs here. There's a garden in the square down there – it'll give us some cover at least.'

Jack marched on ahead, Henri followed and Michael trailed forlornly behind them. Isaac held back to speak to Storm. 'I think our element of surprise may have been compromised,' he said.

'You read my mind,' she said. 'Even if they didn't spot him lurking outside the house, which they're bound to have, they'll probably be tracking his phone, won't they?'

'All we can hope is that they've weighed it up and decided that a non-magical loved-up kid won't have the bottle to take them on. Although if they think about it, they'll start wondering how he found her.' Isaac shook his head. 'Poor lad. But poor Jack too.'

Isaac's compassion touched her. When he looked at her, she leaned up, rested her hand on his cheek and kissed him gently on the lips, then walked on to join the others.

The communal garden, so typical of this part of London, was ringed by a low wall on top of which stood a sturdy wrought-iron fence painted shiny black and topped with gold-painted filigree. It looked elegant, but those ends were no doubt sharp enough to deter undesirables from scaling the perimeter of this hallowed piece of verdant real estate.

Storm imagined the residents who may use the space. She hoped that they did. Maybe they sat out here to read in the summer or brought their children to play on the grass, had little gatherings with the neighbours, maybe? Whatever they might have done, she wasn't sure what would become of it now. The gate and around a third of the fence had been reduced to a tangle of iron. A sign declaring 'Access to keyholders only', a fat tyre track across its face, lay in a furrow of lawn, chewed up by whichever heavy vehicle had destroyed the perimeter.

Henri had only just sat down on the bench when Storm's phone rang. As she listened, she felt her stomach twist into a knot.

'Thanks, Asim,' was all she managed before ringing off. 'He landed early. The facial recognition didn't pick him up at the airport. Asim thinks they have new blockers or filters or something, but, long story short, facial recognition picked up his driver at the terminal an hour ago and then the ANPR cameras tracked his car here.' It came out as one long, gabbling stream and she sucked in a breath at the end of it.

'But that'll mean he's already in there,' Isaac said. 'It's only thirty minutes from Heathrow if they drive like we did. Shit.' Turning to the others he said, 'Right, here we go. Henri and Michael, you go back and get the car and wait for us at the top of the street. When we come out, we'll need to be away as fast as we can.'

Without a word, Henri and Michael left the garden at a walk so brisk it was nearly a jog, peeling off to the right and the back street that would take them to the car. Storm, Isaac and Jack headed directly back to the main road. They'd hardly gone twenty feet when they heard a whistle from behind them and saw Michael and Henri hurrying after them.

'Trouble,' Michael said when they caught up. 'Gang of thugs lurking halfway down the street, complete with baseball bats. They didn't see us, thank God, but there's no way I want to mess with them.'

Not seeing another option, they made their way together onto the main street. The houses were all almost identical: four storeys, double-fronted and connected to street level by a line of stone steps leading up to a canopied entrance. The one they wanted stood out, not just because of its almost impossibly black front door, but by the absence of either security shutters or any damage.

A perfectly manicured hedge ran across the front of the property, to the left of it, the path that back in the day would have led to the servants' entrance around the back of the house.

'Time to move,' Henri said, pointing down the street. 'Looks like they've been partying hard all night.'

Approaching in the distance they saw a double-decker bus swerving all over the road, its top deck in flames. They heard the roar of voices next. Behind the flaming bus was a mob of more than a hundred people carrying whatever weapons they could find. Some were wearing scarves pulled up over their noses in an attempt to hide their faces, but most had long since stopped worrying about the long arm of the law.

'We need to move now,' Isaac said, and the others followed him as he crossed the road and pressed his back to the hedge in front of the house. Isaac gestured to the side gate, but before they could move they heard the front door open. Storm peered through a gap in the hedge and saw two men in black army fatigues come out of the front door, their attention, thankfully, on the approaching mob.

'Stay really close to me and say nothing,' Jack hissed at them urgently. They crowded around him; Storm reached instinctively for Isaac's hand. The bus was less than twenty feet away from them. There was no way that they could go unnoticed by the approaching mob.

As the bus drew level with them, it swerved to the opposite side of the road where amongst the line of burnt-out cars, one ancient but untouched Mercedes was parked. The bus smashed into the side of the car, caving in the back-passenger door and shunting it half onto the pavement. A young woman standing on the back platform of the old bus hurled a brick through the passenger window to the appreciative whoop of the crowd behind. She bowed theatrically, then picked up another brick in readiness for the next target. A man broke cover from the crowd and hurled a petrol bomb through the broken window. The mob shrieked in delight as the first flames started consuming the upholstery, sending thick black smoke spiralling into the air.

The mob was less than five feet away now and Storm was sickened to see that there were women and even children amongst them. The brick-hurling young woman on the back of the bus gave a blast on an air horn and pointed animatedly to a house across the road that only had steel shutters on the ground floor. A loud roar went up from the crowd and then a hail shower of petrol bombs was released towards the upper windows.

They were well-practised and, while a few missed their mark, at least two sailed through the glass to light up the room beyond in an explosion of fire. Pleased with their handiwork, the mob paused to cheer, then erupted again as they spotted an overweight middle-aged man dressed in shorts, vest and socks, trying to escape from a first-floor window. Storm instinctively made to move, but Isaac held her back. Like hounds on a scent, the mob whooped and surged forward, swarming down the sides of the house to try and block his escape route. A cry of 'catch the pig' sent the mob into a frenzy and Storm gasped in horror. Isaac squeezed her hand and when she looked at him, furious tears clouding her vision, he put his finger to her lips then motioned upwards. The security guards had walked halfway down the steps to get a better look. The man's voice when he spoke was loud and way too close for comfort. 'He's a goner then,' he said without a trace of sympathy.

Storm reluctantly turned her head away. She knew that they couldn't save the man from the mob, but her soul felt cleaved with the knowledge of it.

'Are you sure this hocus-pocus shit means they can't see us?' the other guard asked. 'I'm all for the survival of the fittest and all that shit, but I ain't taking that lot on – they're seriously off their nut.'

'We're safe as houses in here, mate. Don't ask me how it works, but you could stand a foot in front of one of them and they wouldn't see nothing. I'll put a brew on. It'll be ages yet.' As they walked away, he said, 'And remember, if you see any of the targets, shoot first, right?' He laughed and they heard the front door slam.

Just after it did they heard the remaining guard mutter, 'Wanker.'

Jack inclined his head to the open gate at the side of the house and beckoned for them to follow him. They were in full view of the front door and Storm was convinced that the security guard would any minute turn and shoot, but to her amazement, they reached the garden without incident.

'I had no idea that would work,' Jack said when they were safely in the garden.

'I'm assuming you just cloaked us?' asked Isaac. 'I'm impressed. I thought that was something you could only do for your charge.'

'So did I,' said Jack, 'but we were out of options otherwise.'

'Maybe it's the shift,' Isaac offered. 'It certainly doesn't seem like normal rules apply any more.'

'And what the guard said – how come we could see the house but the mob couldn't?' Henri asked.

'Not sure, but I'm guessing that the spell cloaks it from all but those who are looking for it specifically. They'll want witnesses to this so they wouldn't be able to hide it completely or their esteemed guests wouldn't be able to find it.' Jack shrugged. 'It's my best guess anyway.'

When they got to the back door, Storm reached for it, her heart sinking to find it locked. 'Aren't you going to unlock it?' Jack asked as if it were the simplest thing in the world to open a locked door without the convenience of a key. She frowned at him and was about to snap off a retort when he said, 'They're going to kill Lilly, Storm,' as if she could have somehow forgotten.

She remembered the day in the summer house all those years ago, the row of locked boxes, Margot's delight as one by one she had opened them. As she closed her hand around the brass handle for a second time, Storm felt the key on the other side of the door turn and, as it did, she felt the action mirrored in herself. It was a curious sense of something being released. She had no time to dwell on it as a surge of energy like none she had ever experienced raced up her spine and she staggered from the shock of it. Four sets of hands seemed all at once to be reaching for her and she held up a hand to reassure her companions that she wasn't about to faint – far from it, in fact. For the first time she could ever remember, Storm felt completely herself.

CHAPTER 74

Storm glanced quickly behind her, only to see a row of astonishment faces staring back at her. She opened the back door and stepped into a large boot room. The glow emanating from under the interior door to their left suggested that the main event was happening in the next room.

'Storm,' Isaac hissed, grabbing her arm, 'you can't just go charging in there – they'll kill you,' he said, 'and that's not going to help Lilly.'

Their whispered conversation was interrupted by a round of applause and then a man's voice. From the applause, Storm estimated that there were no more than eighty people in the room, which she guessed occupied the entire ground floor of the house. Ballrooms or party rooms had been all the rage even in her parents' day and her time playing runner for Margot on her mediumship tours had given her a good ear for the size of a crowd, even from the wings.

'Thank you, Cynthia, for that warm welcome and introduction,' said the voice from behind the door. 'We stand

together here today, friends, on the edge of history itself.'
The voice was strong, confident, and polished and Storm
sensed that whoever he was, he was a man who wasn't just
used to public speaking, but one who relished it.

'We have battled for centuries against those who speak of
the great shift and the next evolution of humanity as if there
is something wrong with our species. As if we were apes in
the trees and not the rightful lords and masters of this world.
They would have a world of homogeny, where all differenti-
ation between people is stripped away. Where a leader of
nations or the CEO of one of our great corporations would
be nothing more than a beggar in the street. A world where
lineage and hard work count for nothing. Where the bounty
of this great world is squandered on the lazy, the dim-witted
and the undeserving. Where riches are bestowed on those
who place a greater value on bugs and beasts than their
fellow man.'

Applause filled the room and a few shouted, 'Hear, hear.'

He continued, 'As an order, we, and those who have gone
before us, have worked tirelessly through the ages to prevent
this nightmare ever becoming a reality. It has been a constant
battle to maintain the status quo, but today we will bring to
an end our great struggle. Today, we will forever remove the
threat from our door, because after centuries of searching, I
can announce that we have found the First Ethereal.'

From the gasps that preceded the shouts and whistles,
Storm could only assume that Lilly had somehow been
revealed. Using the cacophony to mask any noise, Storm slid
the old barrel key from the lock and peered through the
keyhole.

The man delivering the sermon was pacing back and
forth so it was a few seconds before he moved far enough
around the space to give Storm a clear view. When at last she
caught sight of Lilly, it was all she could do not to scream.

Surrounded by tall white pillar candles and still dressed in her long white sundress, Lilly was standing in a small glass box, her hands bound in front of her and a black gag tied tightly around her mouth. Her long auburn hair was plastered in places to the sweat on her young, terrified face. Storm's heart lurched and were it not for Isaac's hand on her shoulder she would have burst through the door there and then to carry her away.

When the crowd eventually quietened, the man's voice continued. 'Now, I am not a man who enjoys violence. But neither am I a man who's scared to do what needs to be done for the sake of my family, my country and my church.' The assembled crowd mumbled their agreement. Storm could feel the wave of fury emanating from Henri at that, so strong that it dented her efforts to block out all emotions but her own.

'She may look like an innocent, but believe me, my friends, this is the most dangerous beast on the planet. This thing, this abomination is not human,' he thundered, pointing savagely at Lilly, who was crying and shaking her head in protest. 'It is not one of us. It is here in this form to act as judge and jury on our species. To judge *you* and find wanting! This one pathetic creature is all that stands between us and oblivion and, believe me, she has chosen for you,' he paused for dramatic effect, 'oblivion!' he roared, reaching his well-practised crescendo as a cry not far from feral rose to echo around the vast room. While they might have been clad in sharp expensive suits and tailored dresses, this crowd was just as terrifying as the mob from the street, perhaps even more so.

Storm saw Lilly shake her head vehemently, try to speak, to plead her case perhaps. 'Oh, it lies,' he said, 'be sure of that, my friends. It will say anything to save itself and complete its mission. But if this shift happens, make no mistake, our world will fall. I have no idea why the universe would organise itself in a way that puts the future of humanity in the hands of something that isn't even human, but I do know that we can take back control. We can make that choice for ourselves and I don't know about you, but I choose life!'

Once the rapturous applause had died down, to Storm's amazement and disgust, the voice invited them all to pray together. She knew then that their time was up.

CHAPTER 75

*B*efore Storm could reach for the door handle, several things happened in quick succession. Isaac and Jack flew backwards out into the garden and the back door slammed shut behind them. Michael and Henri too defied the laws of gravity as an invisible force hurled them into the cloakroom. Storm had just enough time to see them struggle to their feet before the door slammed closed and the key twisted itself in the lock.

'Why do you never bloody listen?' said a woman's voice from behind her. Storm had expected Margot to be there, of course, but she had hoped … what? The woman who had bound her powers, ruined her life and kidnapped her friend might cut them a break?

Storm turned around slowly to face her.

'I tried everything in my power to protect you,' Margot said quietly. Her face was a study of composure but it didn't match her weary tone. A glamour, of course, Storm realised. How silly of her not to have noticed before.

There was so much Storm wanted to say, but in that instant, nothing would come, so Margot barrelled on. 'Please don't do this, Stormy. It's too late – don't you see? They're monsters, but they are only monstrous because they're right. We have damned this beautiful planet, but we can't change that now. The only way out is to start again, to evolve into better versions of humanity. There isn't another way. We have to let humanity fall so that we can rise again. My bunker is all ready, I even have provision for Anchor and Hope.'

Finding her voice at last, Storm laughed bitterly. 'What the hell happened to you? You're talking about the annihilation of what, ninety-nine per cent of humanity – and they're not going to go peacefully in their beds, for fuck's sake! The Ethereal is our way out of this mess – why are you not embracing that? Why in God's name would you choose death and destruction over peace and love and ascension?'

'Because I believe in humanity, child! We may be flawed, but they're right to want to protect our ...' she scrabbled for the right word, 'purity. Our integrity as a species. If the ascension happens we will no longer be human. We'll be hybridised with the angelic and then everybody could do what we do.'

Storm shook her head in disbelief. 'You'd honestly let billions perish over some sick need to feel special?'

'This isn't about me!' Margot snapped. 'It's never, ever been about me.'

Storm didn't recognise the woman standing in front of her now. 'You used to be so full of love and kindness,' she said. 'You showed me the magic in the world and in myself, but ...' She faltered before asking the one question she needed answered. 'Why did you do it, Margot? Why bind my magic? How could you sever me from spirit? Why?' The last word came out as a whisper.

Margot dropped her eyes then, and Storm saw a remnant of the woman she had known and loved. 'Because I love you,'

Margot said, 'and because they would have taken you. It was kinder this way.'

'Kinder?' The word flew from Storm's mouth as a growl. 'You think it was kind to rob me of my connection to spirit when my husband was dying? When he begged me to ask his mother if she'd be there waiting for him when he passed? You think it was kinder for me to live all this time without hearing from him? To think that something I had done had caused spirit and magic to abandon me? Was it kinder to take from me the only things that gave me comfort in this awful world?' Storm shook with fury.

As Storm reached for the door handle, the pulse that hit her in the back did little more than slightly wind her. Margot was a witch of incredible power who, had she really wanted to hurt her, could have done so easily. Storm whirled around and, without thinking, aimed a retaliatory pulse in Margot's direction to slow her down. The energy rebounded off the shield that Margot had projected in front of her. Storm tried again, but Margot was too quick for her. Grabbing Storm's hands, she said, 'There's no time to explain. See for yourself.'

Storm had the sickening sensation of moving; her head spun and she blinked hard to clear her vision. When she opened her eyes she was standing in what looked like the dressing room of a theatre. A young Margot sat at the mirror applying her trademark red lipstick and smiling as if practising her poses for a camera. The knock at the door made her jump, but before she could even get up, a young, unsmiling woman in a navy skirt suit walked into the room.

'Can I help you?' Margot said, irritated. 'I'm pretty sure that door was locked.'

Without preamble, the young woman said, 'My employers enjoyed your show this evening, Ms Depworth. They have instructed me to ask for your assistance with a small matter of national security.'

It took Margot a full five seconds to laugh and, when she did, Storm felt her heart sing. It had been such a long time since she'd heard Margot laugh like that and yet they had once laughed all the time, hadn't they?

Composing herself, Margot turned back to the mirror and said, 'Tell Bob that he's hilarious but I still won't have dinner with him.'

The smile in her voice died when the woman pushed a photograph onto the dressing table in front of her, knocking over the cosmetics in the process. Storm peered at the image of herself, aged around twelve, sitting outside the summer house, her face a picture of complete wonder as in front of her, three books hovered in the air. Margot, standing behind her, had her hands clasped together, her head tipped back in what Storm remembered to be a whoop of delight at her pupil's achievement. The woman slid another photograph on top on the first. Then another.

'She was such a talented little witch even then, wasn't she. And now she's off to university and striking out on her own in the big bad world. It would be such a shame if we had to commandeer her services for the public good.'

The sight of such fear in Margot's eyes when she turned around to face her blackmailer twisted like a knife in Storm's gut. 'What do you need me to do?' Margot asked quietly.

With a lurch in her chest, Storm found herself standing behind Margot. She was seated opposite Sir Dennis Taylor in an expensive-looking restaurant where they were the only diners. He was red-cheeked and laughing, his plate of food half demolished, while Margot sat stony-faced, her food untouched.

'That's a good one, M,' he said, dabbing at the spittle at the side of his mouth. When he put the napkin down, all traces of humour had vanished. 'This isn't a fucking golf club, lady.

You don't just resign your bloody membership,' he spat, pointing a fat finger at her.

'I am well aware of that. I'm not here to negotiate, Dennis. I'm done,' Margot said coolly.

He regarded her for a few moments while he ran his tongue over his front teeth searching out fragments of meat. 'Some might find your decision a little … ungrateful,' he said. 'Who you are today is all down to the gifts we've bestowed upon you. Your fame, your fortune, all your little books and programmes on the telly.'

Margot clenched her jaw, took a deep breath and pushed back her chair. Throwing her napkin on the plate of uneaten food, she said, 'Do your worst. Take it all. I can't be a part of this any more. I'll take my chances with the rest of humanity.'

'This is a war, Margot. A battle for survival – and people die in battles. That's just the way of the world. You need to get some balls and remember what's at stake here.' He leaned back in his chair and tipped his chin up to fix her with a hard stare.

Margot hesitated for just a second then shook her head. 'I won't be part of this,' she said, then turned on her heel and walked away.

Storm braced herself, expecting the memory to end with Margot's departure. 'Why am I seeing this?' she demanded, casting around. 'How can this be your memory, Margot, when you weren't even there?'

'I had to know,' Margot's voice was clear in Storm's mind. 'I scried for it and then I travelled back to watch what had happened – to be sure. I had to be sure, Storm.'

Sir Dennis watched Margot leave, his tongue back to searching out pieces of his meal from between his teeth. Appearing to come to a decision, he retrieved his phone from his jacket pocket and dialled. 'It's me. It looks like our seer needs a lesson.' He paused while the other person spoke then said, 'Tempting. I'd like to see the bitch suffer a bit, but no, we need her. There's no one else of her power. I've got a better idea. That kid she was tutoring is all grown up now, isn't she?' He paused again, listening. 'Storm, that's her. Stupid bloody name, but no, don't go after her direct, she's still on our watch list in case we need to commandeer her in the future.'

Storm could almost feel what he was about to say next and she wanted to scream, to reach out and grab the phone, clamp her hands over his wretched fat mouth and stop the words that she knew were coming.

'Go for the husband. Nick isn't it? Something slow though so the cheeky cow gets a reminder of what we can do. The new untraceable, perhaps – it's time it got tested in the field,' he said, a satisfied smile creeping across his ruddy face. Listening again, he replied, 'Oh, she'll listen alright, and if she doesn't, take the girl into the facility. We'll see how long Margot can hold on to her high bloody ideals once her precious little protégé is living like a lab rat.' He snorted, then as an afterthought added, 'Wait. Give it a few months until the husband snuffs it and then take the kid in anyway. I don't buy Margot's line about her being low potential. Just call it a grief-induced suicide or something. Nobody's going to come looking for her.' He ended the call, smiled and then ordered dessert.

Storm felt the now familiar pull on her chest and, back in the basement she bent double, both hands clamped over her mouth to muffle the sobs that were threatening to overtake her. When she looked up, Margot's glamour was gone and she saw her friend's face, lined and crumpled in grief. Shaking her head, Margot said, 'I'm so sorry, my darling girl. Had I known they'd go after Nick …' She shook her head. 'They would have taken you and when they found out …' Tears welled in her eyes and she bit her lip, cutting off whatever she was going to say next. 'This way I can at least keep you safe. Don't you see? I know you're fond of this girl Lilly, but it's too late, everyone is going to die anyway and at least her death will be quick. This is how I can make it up to you, don't you see? This way I can keep you safe.' Her tone was pleading, but her eyes were those of someone on the very edge of their sanity.

From the other side of the door, Storm heard the crowd say together, 'Amen,' and then the voice struck up again. 'So now we end this once and for all. We remove this Sword of Damocles that's been hanging over our species from time immemorial. Today is the day that we take back our future!' The room filled once again with excited applause and Storm grabbed for the handle of the door.

Out of time, and unsure whether what she was intending would even work, Storm grabbed Margot's arm and pushed her own memories into her old friend; Lilly the half-drowned waif returning her lost dog. Lilly's face as they sat in the café after hours with Veronica, eating cake and laughing. The light Storm saw in her eyes when she saw Michael; when she cradled Anchor like a baby in her arms; Lilly laughing with customers; dancing with Jean at her birthday party. Still holding her arm, Storm pushed harder, flooding Margot with every ounce of love she felt for the girl who might as well have been her own flesh and blood.

When Margot opened her eyes the madness was gone. In its place, Storm saw the woman she knew and loved so much. With tears sliding silently down her face, Margot took a deep breath and said, 'Let's go save your girl.'

Storm reached for the door, but Margot got there first. 'Stay behind me and shield yourself,' she said, reaching back and squeezing Storm's hand for the briefest of seconds. Storm felt rather than heard, 'I love you,' as if the molecules in her being were all resonating with the same message.

Margot pulled open the door and before Storm could even think about how to conjure a shield, she found herself on the floor with Isaac lying over her. It was hard to tell who was the more surprised. 'I didn't know you could do that,' she spluttered.

'Neither did I until just now,' he said, looking dazed.

The reason for the action became sickeningly clear when the crack of automatic gunfire sounded over their heads and one of the guards burst into view, gun held in both hands.

Isaac rolled away from Storm, pulled out his handgun and shot the guard. Horrified, she threw an energy pulse at the door to close and bar it. Struggling to her feet, she turned. Margot lay a few feet from them, the blood from the wounds that had torn through her neck and chest pooling silently around her. Storm screamed, no longer caring who heard her, and rushed to Margot, her knees slipping on the warm blood. Her hands shook as she reached to stroke her friend's face. 'N-no,' she stammered, the word sounding feeble and ridiculous in her mouth. Tears blinded her and in that second she wanted so much to lie down and join her friend, to admit defeat and see an end to it all. But as she heard more gunfire ricochet off the shielded door, she thought of Lilly, so, choking down her tears, she leaned down, kissed her friend on the forehead and said, 'I love you and I forgive you.' Then, with a power born of grief and love for all that was precious in the world, she rose to her feet.

She felt a force in the pit of her belly that eclipsed anything she had ever felt before. Lilly was suddenly all she could think about. It was as if she herself had ceased to exist and in her place was this creature, this pure, beautiful creature whose only wish was for peace and gentleness, and here were these men set to destroy her for their own ends and damn the whole world with them.

'You can't go in there alone,' Isaac said, standing in her

way, but Storm just smiled, kissed him briefly on the lips and stepped around him. Pushing and holding him out of the line of fire with an energy pulse, she stepped forward and with a force that came as naturally as breathing, sent out a wall of cold fury that had the door flying off its hinges and the guards behind it reeling into the air.

As she surveyed the scene, she saw Lilly scream against her gag as the flames licked just inches away from the bottom of her thin white cotton sundress.

People ran in all directions like ants scurrying from a disturbed nest. The congregation had dressed well for the occasion, Storm noticed, with most looking like they were attending a wedding instead of an execution. She even spotted one woman in a tiara. The first wave of guards hit by Storm's pulse lay unmoving, but more streamed in from the back of the room where people fought one another like savages to try and escape to the stairs.

As the flames rose, Jack appeared in the box next to Lilly, pulled the gag from her mouth and, coughing against the smoke, cut the ties to free her hands. Storm aimed a careful pulse at the glass box which shattered outwards, sending shards of glass flying around the basement and straight into the new wave of guards who had been rushing in to apprehend her.

With relief she saw Lilly and Jack clamber from what remained of the platform then Isaac, at the door, ushering them out.

'Storm!' Isaac shouted, exasperated, as he tried to run towards her, but he was still held by her invisible field. She stood where she was in the centre of the room and smiled at him as a brief thought of what might have been flashed through her mind. Then she sent out a firm but gentle pulse, infused with all the love she had in the world, and pushed her friends out of the door and into the garden.

More guards stormed into the basement. 'Shoot the bloody witch!' screamed a man in trendy glasses standing at the foot of the basement stairs, obviously intending to make good his escape while his staff did his dirty work. He had sounded so much more confident a few minutes ago inviting his friends to pray before he burned a young woman alive.

'I don't think so,' Storm said as she lifted him off his feet, swung him in the air and held him there. She wanted him to have a front-row seat. Then she bolted every exit with a thought and turned towards the guards, hands at her sides, palms up in welcome as their useless bullets fell around her.

She remembered being a child, how scared she had been of letting go of the rope swing over the river. Margot's voice in her head, just as it had all those years ago, 'Let go, darling,' so she did.

The light was so bright. It poured from her every cell, from the very centre to the very edges of her being and it felt so pure, she knew that nothing else had ever existed before it. It felt like coming home. The circle complete. She smiled knowing that this was the end, her end at least, and she was glad.

CHAPTER 76

*L*illy didn't remember it all until the moment the flames started. It had been coming back to her slowly from the moment she stopped screaming. The snatches of past lives relived in such vivid detail that she felt in those moments as if she had slipped through time itself. She remembered moments of such exquisite love and tenderness that her heart ached with the sheer joy of it all. The birth of her first child; the smell of her head as she held her safely delivered into her arms; her first kiss; seeing her grandchildren play on the lawn; collecting her doctorate; riding through a forest, the wind in her hair and her long skirts flying behind her; diving in the ocean and swimming with tropical fish; dancing in the rain; flying her first plane; watching the sunrise – on and on they went, feeding her soul and swelling her heart.

When the flames flared up through the wire floor and she realised what they meant to do to her, she remembered. She remembered it all. She finally remembered who she was.

CHAPTER 77

*T*he force of the pulse pushed Isaac, Jack and Lilly to the very edge of the garden where the others were standing, each of them wearing a horrified look of anguish. Like a strong wave at their backs, it was unyielding and deliberate, only dissipating when they were all safely together. Lilly made to run back to the house but hit an invisible barrier after less than ten feet which bounced her gently backwards. When she made to try a second time, Jack grabbed her hand.

'Johan, please, I need to help her,' she pleaded, trying to pull her arm away. It was only when she saw his face crumple as he sank to the floor sobbing, that she realised what she had said. She wrapped her arms around him as he cried, rocking slowly back and forth. 'My turn to comfort you, at last,' she said as she planted a kiss on the top of his head and stroked his back.

Lilly had no idea how he'd found the strength to do this, to live with his memories of all of their lives so vivid and bright in his heart while she had lived for the last two decades as if she had just been born.

'You remember?' he asked once he had regained his voice. 'How much?'

She looked into his eyes and held his face softly in her cupped hands. 'Everything,' she said. Then she kissed him lightly on the lips and watched as a fresh flood of tears ran down his beautiful face.

'I'm sorry, Lil, I didn't know. I swear to you I didn't know what you were. If I had,' he began, his voice thick with anguish.

Lilly was about to reply, but just then the invisible barrier around them fizzed with tiny threads of vibrant blue light and, with a sickening, muffled boom, the house exploded. Masonry, wood and remnants of what was once fine furniture hit the barrier and bounced off like flies bumping into a windowpane. They all ducked reflexively; someone screamed. Then the dust was falling, settling on the edges of their protective dome like some macabre reverse snow globe.

Seconds later everyone was hammering on the barrier, screaming Storm's name, their pain ripping through Lilly like razor wire until she regained control and pushed their emotions aside to focus on her own. Quieting her mind, Lilly focused on Storm. Searching for her in her mind, she heaved out a huge sigh of relief when she sensed her friend's heart beating strongly and felt Storm's new-found power charging through her veins.

Turning to the others, Lilly shouted, 'She's alive. I can feel it. She's alive!' Letting down her own shields, Lilly, for the first time in her life, allowed the feelings of others to flood through her, revelling in the shared joy and elation with her friends as they took it in turns to hug one another, most of them crying with relief. After a few minutes, and with a final fizzle, the dome vanished, showering them with a thick cloud of dust as they all raced towards the wreckage.

a fter the light, all Storm knew was the comfort of darkness. In the darkness she was held, cradled, warm and content as a newborn kitten. She thought she heard Nick call her name, heard him laughing ... oh, how she loved to hear him laugh. He sounded so close, like he was just in the next room. She could hear him telling that awful joke about – what was the joke about? It was too faint to hear now, like he was walking away. It was his favourite lame joke, for God's sake, what was it? She had to remember. As she racked her brain for the answer, the darkness retreated, his voice faded and she felt herself surfacing, like a free diver coming up for air. No! She tried again to sink back into it. She had to remember the joke. What was the bloody joke? She saw him now; he was smiling, waving at her, his hair falling in his eyes slightly. He pushed it back like he always did, then he said, 'Remember,' before turning away. *No!* She screamed the word with everything she had but no sound came out.

Light was pouring into her eyes and she flung her arm across her eyes, trying to block it out in the hope that it would help take her back to where she had been just seconds ago. Sensations crowded in. Cool fingers checking the pulse in her neck, brushing the dust from her face, someone holding her hand, calling her name. It was all too much input; the darkness shrank until it was just a spot and all at once she was back in the world, coughing out the mortar dust from her lungs.

When the coughing had stopped, the scene that met her eyes was one of utter devastation. The house she had been standing in just minutes earlier was now no more than a very large pile of rubble. There was a fire burning in what might have been the living room, maybe the kitchen, and various burst pipes were spraying feeble jets of water into the air. A thick layer of chalky white dust covered every available surface, stripping away colour and replacing it with a milky monotone grey.

'Lilly,' she said, her voice hoarse. Scrambling to her feet, Storm pushed away the hands that tried in vain to encourage her to stay still. She didn't feel broken but even if she was, she'd have to deal with that later. Wheeling around almost blindly, she shouted, 'Lilly!' then bent double to cough again as her throat burned and her chest tried to expel the dust.

Isaac put a hand to her cheek. 'She's fine,' he said, the relief in his voice obvious. Storm straightened up to see Lilly running towards her. When she reached Storm she flung her arms around her neck and held on tightly.

'I thought for a second I'd lost you,' Lilly said in staccato sobs.

Storm stroked her hair. 'And me you, little one,' she said, 'but you're safe now. We're all safe.'

Lilly pulled back to look at Storm. Grey eyes the colour of a dove's wing met green eyes that were the colour of the Eternal Forest.

'Oh my,' Lilly said, laughing, 'of course,' then Storm

laughed and then they were both laughing and crying, much to the bemusement of the others.

The whir of a low helicopter interrupted them. 'That'll be Veronica with the book,' Isaac said, eyeing the sky and its red lightning. The black hammerhead cloud seemed to be growing by the second. 'We're not out of the woods quite yet, I'm afraid. There's still the matter of the Ethereal's choice. According to Veronica, the library was clear that the ascension can't happen until the Ethereal makes their decision official. And the decision needs to be given formally to a witness.'

'Which happens to be a very old book,' Henri put in.

'Then the sooner we get this done the better,' Jack said.

'I wouldn't count my chickens just yet, dear boy. Remember, the Ethereal's choice is an unconscious one,' Henri said.

Noticing that Michael had wandered away from the group, Storm squeezed Lilly's hand and gestured in his direction. 'We still have a few minutes,' she said.

Lilly's shoulders slumped, but she nodded sadly and went to join him.

CHAPTER 79

'ey,' Lilly said when she was still a dozen or so feet from Michael. He turned quickly and Lilly's heart twisted when she saw his expression. Picking her way over the rubble, she hurried towards him and found herself quickly enfolded in a hug. It had been less than twenty-four hours and yet everything felt different. He felt like a stranger again, not the man she'd spent yesterday afternoon snuggled up to on the sofa. The man whose lips seemed to fit hers so perfectly. He felt it too, she could tell. He leaned his chin on the top of her head, stroked her hair and rocked ever so slightly to and fro.

Michael was the first to speak. 'I can't pretend to understand exactly what's going on here. To tell you the truth, I'm half expecting to wake up any time soon and find out that some arsehole spiked my drink in the pub. Look, what I'm trying to say is that I know this changes everything – for us, I mean.'

Lilly studied the floor, unable to speak, but because she knew he was waiting for an answer, she nodded. He let out a long breath and squeezed her gently before releasing her and taking a step back. 'Just promise me that you'll wait until all this is over one way or another,' he said, gesturing to the devastation all around them. 'We had something special for a minute there, Lil. I'm just asking that you give me something to hope for, just for a little while.'

She nodded, felt tears prick at her eyes and said, 'I promise.'

CHAPTER 80

*J*ack watched Lilly and Michael but felt nothing but sorry for the other man now. He knew all too well the pain of watching someone you loved with someone else and there was no doubt that Michael already loved her; it was written all over him.

Jack looked up. Despite it still being morning, the light seemed to be fading rather than strengthening. The black cloud seemed to be expanding relentlessly in all directions, eclipsing the sun and dragging the temperature downwards as the wind picked up and sent the dust eddying around them.

Henri came to stand at Jack's side. 'Is this what you meant by the Falling?' Jack asked quietly, his eyes on the cloud.

'The cloud forms when the balance of energies tips in the wrong direction. Once the low energies outweigh the higher ones, the feedback loops kick. It's like a runaway train now,' Henri said.

'Can we stop it?' Jack asked.

'The only thing that will stop it now will be the ascension.

The viability of our world as we know it is over,' Henri said gravely.

'It would have been nice for the universe to have given me the right handbook on this one from the start,' Jack said, huffing out a breath as he kicked up the dust at his feet.

'Maybe there was a reason for that,' Henri offered, putting his hand on the younger man's shoulder. 'We know now that the decision of the Ethereal has to be pure. If you'd known, how could you have ensured that you didn't bias things in some way?'

Jack nodded, contemplating. 'I suppose I got part of it right – whichever way this pans out, Lil is living her last human life.'

*V*eronica clutched the handles of the battered old briefcase as the pilot circled, looking for a safe place to land. She had called Isaac en route to explain the process, such that it was, but the noise of the chopper combined with a poor signal had made the communication patchy.

When they landed in the garden of a neighbouring house, Veronica sent up a prayer to anyone or anything who might be listening. She wasn't a believer in the traditional sense, but, she reasoned, they really did need all the help they could get.

As she opened the door, she was relieved to see Michael running towards her with a young man she assumed had to be Jack. Michael greeted his aunt with a hug and hurriedly introduced Jack. With a worried grin Michael said, 'Sorry about the car.'

'Oh sod the car,' Veronica said. 'Come on, let's get on with it.'

The house, or what remained of it, was only a few

E. L. WILLIAMS

minutes away, but Veronica was out of breath and cursing her lack of fitness by the time she arrived.

Seeing Lilly and Storm sitting together, Lilly's head resting on her friend's shoulder, made Veronica forget all about her screaming lungs.

When she reached them, she flung an arm around them both and pulled them into a tight group hug. Gulping back tears and releasing them, she said, 'Right, I'll bawl my eyes out later, but we've got work to do – and quickly. Come on,' she said to everyone as she reached into the briefcase, 'the book came with very scant instructions, so parts of this I'm making up as I go along, but join hands – form a circle. Quickly.'

Everyone did as they were asked and Veronica put the briefcase on the ground. Opening it, she pulled back the velvet cloth and retrieved the small ancient grey book. It was barely bigger than her palm and no thicker than her finger.

'We gather today in the presence of the Witness so that it can record the decision of the First Ethereal,' Veronica said, her usually calm, soothing voice wobbling around the edges. Turning to Lilly, she held out the book to her and said, 'Let your decision be pure and true.'

The first shot missed its mark, hitting what was left of the wall behind them, but more followed in rapid succession. Isaac shouted, 'Down,' and Veronica just had time to see someone slam Lilly to the ground, before she caught her own foot on a lump of masonry, stumbled and fell to the ground. She saw the little book fly out of her hands, but when she tried to cry out, she realised that all of the air had been knocked out of her lungs.

Before she could see where the book had landed, she heard a metallic clatter followed just a fraction of a second later by a dense cloud of orange smoke which swiftly engulfed them all. More shots rang out accompanied by the sound of heavy footsteps, too close for comfort.

Veronica coughed, the dust and smoke all but choking her, but all she could think about was the book. She was the Keeper, the book was her responsibility and hers alone. She dragged herself forward across the rubble, ignoring the bite of the debris as it cut into her hands and arms. Through the smoke, she caught sight of the book. Hauling herself forward she reached out her arm only to see another hand inching out of the smoke towards the fallen book. 'No!' she shouted.

Two more shots rang out, lower in tone and closer. Isaac shouted, 'Clear!'

Veronica watched in horror as the hand slammed decisively onto the cover. It illuminated at once, filling the sky with brilliant blue light and then crumbled before her eyes to join the dust that surrounded it. The wind picked up at once, carrying the smoke away and all traces of the little grey book.

Isaac jogged over to help Veronica up, his gun still in his hand. 'You're bleeding,' he said, looking at her hands.

'Yes,' Veronica said, looking at her hands as if they weren't her own. 'Just scratches though, I'm fine. Did you ... ?' She glanced at the gun, then noticed the body of the would-be assassin crumpled where he had fallen.

Isaac nodded. 'No choice I'm afraid.'

The others congregated around Veronica. Henri was the first to speak. 'Was that it?' he asked, looking at the hammer-head cloud still hanging above them. 'Is it done?' The lightning had stopped but the beetle-black scars in the sky remained.

Veronica nodded, scanning the ground just to be sure. 'The book said that once it had the Ethereal's decision, it would sign in light and return home, which I'm assuming means the library. But ...' She hesitated, feeling sick to her stomach. 'But what if I missed something? Surely if it had worked that would be gone by now, wouldn't it?' she said anxiously, pointing at the cloud.

They all turned expectantly to Lilly, but she was looking at Storm, a huge grin spreading across her face and her green eyes dancing with joy. Storm was standing just a few paces away from them, her head tilted skyward. As they followed her gaze, they saw that the black scars in the air were scuttling back to the body of the cloud, which began shrinking before their eyes.

Veronica was the first to notice. At first glance, it looked like just a softening of her outline. What was once a defined edge became less so. Veronica blinked, but it made no difference. The pen line turned to pastel and then to watercolour right before her eyes. Then suddenly and without fanfare they appeared, emerging from Storm's back like new shoots bursting out of the earth – great wings of white light so vast and so pure that the whole world was blessed within seconds.

A silence settled over the Earth. It lasted for the briefest of moments – the pause between the inhalation and exhalation – the gap between the notes that turns sound into music. And in that pause, the world shifted, and the Ethereal age began.

The End

ACKNOWLEDGMENTS

This book would never have made it from short story to fully-fledged novel without the encouragement of my husband Stuart. Darling, thank you for spending so many dog walks listening to my ramblings, but most of all, thank you for always encouraging me to follow my dreams.

To my editor Lesley Jones for her patient guidance and support, Katherine Stephen for her eagle-eyed proofing skills, Richard Butler for my website and Andrew Nickson for designing a cover I love so much I cried!

Heartfelt thanks to my beta-readers: Katie Brunskill; Jo Kinnaird; Judith Oak; Lynn Driver; Sarah Smithies and the ever-inspiring Write Honourable Ladies: Ruth Swain; Theresa McAdden; Daphne Oates; Dianne Butler; Anne Coffey; Louisa Somerville and our lovely teacher Becci Fearnley.

Special thanks to Wenda Shehata, founder of Hugglets Wood Farm Animal Sanctuary for her advice on farming terms, practices and animal behaviour – and to the resident animals who proved to be such an inspiration.

Although I threatened to cut them out of the acknowledgements page for excessive barking and, in the case of the cats, frequent keyboard invasion, a huge thank you to my amazing fur babies; Bailey, Annie, Vizzy and the late Camden for always making me smile and ensuring that I am never at my desk long enough to risk a DVT.

Last, but by no means least, my enduring love and thanks to my amazing mum Joy for making sure that I grew up surrounded by books and steadfastly believing in the power of love and magic to save the world. I so dearly hope that there are libraries in the Eternal Forest.

ABOUT THE AUTHOR

E L Williams grew up in the Welsh Valleys in a tiny house full of books and stories of magic. She's passionate about animals, nature and all things spiritual and frequently combines all three in her writing.

As a sustainability specialist by profession, her work is influenced by her desire to protect and cherish the natural world. The First Ethereal is her first novel.

Emma lives in Berkshire with her husband, two elderly dogs and a geriatric black cat. When she's not working, writing or pandering to the needs of her furry charges, she's usually to be found gardening or coddling her dozens of house plants.

Thank you for reading The First Ethereal. If you enjoyed it, please consider leaving a review and recommending it to a friend.

KEEP IN TOUCH

For news of the sequel, please head over to the website and add your email to the mailing list. No spam I promise, just a monthly update, plus occasional giveaways and interviews with inspiring people.

You can also find me online, usually blathering about books, dogs and writing fiction. I love a natter, so please stop by and say hello.

Website: www.elwilliamsauthor.com
Email: hello@elwilliamsauthor.com
Facebook: @ELWilliamsAuthor
Instagram: @el_williamsyoung